ry,
.reet,

The Harlot's Press

HELEN PIKE

Published in 2011 by Short Books

Short Books
3A Exmouth House
Pine Street
EC1R 0JH

10 9 8 7 6 5 4 3 2 1

A CIP catalogue record for this book
is available from the British Library.

ISBN 978-1-907595-13-4

Printed in Great Britain by Clays, Suffolk

To my parents

Part One

1

HAVE YOU EVER SEEN the new King's bare backside? If you have, it was most likely on a cartoon – unless you are one of the Ladies of the Quality and have been honoured to witness the royal nether parts in the flesh. If Mr Cruikshank and other artists like him have it right, there are quite a number of Royal Mistresses in your ranks – more than there are female printers in London, in fact, which makes me and my inky hands a sight rarer than you and your raised silk skirts. His mistresses all have my condolences, for the King's girth is now said to be mighty on account of his taste for brandy and beef for breakfast.

For those of us who know him only through the cartoonist's eye, King George IV is a balloon, or else a rutting stag with cuckold's horns: all white hair, red face and blue frockcoat, the black lines which ink him in scarcely capable of containing his vastness. Perhaps you own one of these images. More likely, you have seen a poor reproduction in some cheap newspaper; the *Twopenny Trash* perhaps, before the Government tried to tax it out of existence; or on a card or handbill from a street-seller. If the street-seller was a girl who seemed mute and, from the solemn look she gave you, could have been anything between twelve and a hundred years old, then she might have been my sister. Look carefully at the handbill – if *Isaiah Douglas, Friday-street, London EC* appears on the back, it might have been printed by me.

Isaiah Douglas was my stepfather, and a hellfire preacher who had set up his own chapel. Too turbulent for Methodism, he saw signs of the Second Coming in every aspect of this city. His preaching occupied more of his energies than his printing or his family, which meant that I spent much of my life working our two presses by myself. Our shop was on a quiet street which runs parallel with Cheapside. We picked up some of that thoroughfare's passing trade, in the way ditches bear crops from seeds which the sower scattered wide of the furrow. For all its nearness, Friday-street is a different world from Cheapside: so dark that it is scarcely more than an alley, Friday-street at noon resembles Cheapside at dusk, but without the prospect of the illuminated displays in the shop windows which make the Cheapside cobbles glow.

Our neighbour was a shoemaker who kept a cow in his attic. He carried her up there when she was a calf, but soon she was so heavy that he feared his floorboards would give under the weight of her. Still, she produced some milk, and our neighbour said that eventually he would ask my Uncle John the butcher to slaughter her where she stood and throw the meat back down the trapdoor. Many nights I woke to the sound of her shitting, and in the summer it was a wonder the air was not green with her – though while our nostrils were full of cow dung, at least we were not breathing in some of the worse stenches of the city.

In early January 1820, just before the story I shall tell begins, my nose was too full of acid and ink to notice anything else, for we had never been busier. There had not been a good season for the country in the five years since the wars against Napoleon had ended, and this distress was a bounty on political unrest. The images we sold were a chiaroscuro of crimes against the people: desperate men transported for smashing the machines which had destroyed their liveli-hoods; women and children trampled by Hussars for protest-ing peacefully; men driven to drink and women to vice by poverty and despair. And now the cartoonists and squib-mongers such as ourselves had an unlikely heroine: Caroline of Brunswick, the estranged wife of the new King, who had signalled her wish to return to England to claim her rights. But George said he would rather divorce her than see her crowned as Queen beside him and a royal divorce was a legal process which threatened to clog up Parliament like cess in the Fleet. As it was, Caroline was being paid enough to feed a hundred thousand journeymen each year to stay on the Continent with her alleged lovers, but this did not prevent the cartoonists from suggesting that her becoming Queen would ensure pies, ale and prosperity for all. Likewise, for men like Isaiah, the King's desire to keep Caroline from the throne became a symbol of all that was wrong with the nation.

And so the wronged Queen of England became the People's Caroline, as Radicals and revolutionaries of all com-plexions congregated under the ample tent of her skirts. If Caroline refused to stay abroad, the King wanted a divorce – but his Conservative advisers feared the consequences, arguing that the debate in Parliament which this required would only increase the demands for political change. For if the Lords could pass a Bill permitting the King to put away his adulterous wife of nearly thirty years, why could it not agree to a ten-hour working day for honest men, the repeal of laws which would execute a man for the theft of six shil-lings, and the vote for men who owned property and had made the country rich through the sweat of their brow?

In the summer of 1820, the House of Lords debated if the Queen had lifted her skirts for sundry Gentlemen. (It was rumoured that she had done a lot more than bare her bosom for at least two of the Lords who were sitting in judgement on her, but this was excluded from the proceedings, as was any mention of treason, though it is treasonable to be unfaithful to the heir to the throne.) This so-called Delicate Investigation centred around evenings spent on a tented deck with a certain Italian Count Bergami. Or at least, so said the servants; for a few weeks in the summer of 1820 it looked as though the Italians who had changed the royal sheets held the keys to the Kingdom.

As for the would-be Queen, Caroline was like London: brash and showy, all glamour above and something reeking unpleasantly below. It is said that the King insisted that she bathed her privates before he would touch her, and that he only did so once, on their wedding night back in 1795. They had a daughter nine months later, and their love for Princess Charlotte was the only thing they ever had in common. She died three years ago, and some say that Caroline travelled Europe and Africa all the more restlessly as a result, while others insist that the loss made her more determined to return to London, which in early June 1820 she did.

I spent many hundreds of hours inking in the Queen's skirts. We were the envy of many of our rivals for having two presses, which meant that we could do fine copperplate work on one and produce cheap handbills on the other; last summer the market for both was as accommodating as the Queen herself was alleged to be. And in a strange way, just as the domestic and the political were united in her ample figure, so these two arenas collided in our modest shop.

I have done nothing admirable during my seventeen years, and am certain I will go to Hell if I die tomorrow, but I was good at my work. All the same, it is unlikely that you ever bought one of my prints, for we did not have as many customers as the grander establishments such as Tagg's on Cheapside. Perhaps the reek of cowshit discouraged passing trade, though very few fortunes would be transacted in this city if men allowed their noses to rule their sensibilities, for the Stink of London is as powerful as the Sin of Sodom. If you did come to our shop, the chances are that you would not have met my eye, for most of our customers did not like the idea of a young girl being soiled by the handling of such images. Some requested to be served by Isaiah, and as they handed over their shillings, they remonstrated with him for allowing me into the shop at all. I wonder how many of our customers realised that most of the printing and all of the careful inking-in of the King's nether parts had been done by me.

Not that I am complaining. I could tell you that I loved my work, but it was more than that: looking back on it, our old press was my truest friend, and the feel of the tympan on my thighs as I closed the lid was the most honest comfort I knew.

Myself, I have seen the Queen once and the King twice – which was more than the Queen had in the three years since they buried their only child. The first time I saw the King was in January of this year: I was on Jermyn-street, and so taken with a cheesemaker's window on the other side from St James's Church that I stepped into the road. A stinging crack on my left side, and I was hurled back onto the pavement; a coachman had forced me out of the way with his whip. As the coachman swore that stupider whores were roasting chestnuts in Hell, the sun caught the gold of the King's livery on the carriage door. A florid face topped with a white wig appeared from behind a red velvet curtain to see what the commotion was. With none of the cartoonists' strong black lines, the royal face and neck seemed to spill onto its shoulders. The King regarded me with watery blue eyes which had seen at once too much of the world and too little. I now understand this look; I might only be seventeen, but my eyes have something of it too.

And what was a mere printer doing sweeping up her silk skirts on Jermyn-street? you might ask. Well, if you know anything about our city, I'm sure you can guess. The strange thing is, although I invented some lies to explain to my stepfather where I had been for the six months he was imprisoned, and would rather impale myself on the iron railings which surround St Paul's churchyard than tell him this story, the desire to recount the events of those six months is gaining on me by the minute. At times like this I almost understand the Catholics, for their sacrament of Confession strikes me as a wonderful cure: if I could just tell my story once, not leaving out the worst parts, in fact dwelling on them in the name of absolution, then perhaps I would stop going over and over them in my mind, inventing more and more ways of dressing up my shame in fancy images. The second time I saw the King comes at the end of that story, and will take as much explaining as the day I saw the Queen. I am resigned to having to recount both, if my story is to make any sense.

My brother Tom used to say that it was not good for a poor girl to spend so much time inking in the private parts of the rich. Watching me painting the skirts of Mrs FitzHerbert – the King's great love – a violet more vivid than anything we ever saw in our small shop, Tom said that my long apprenticeship at my stepfather's press would make a scarlet woman of me, for I would come to view life as little more than a series of rackety scenes to be coloured as brightly as possible. I laughed and told him that my mind was leaden with the weight of all the Scripture-reading I had done, and my soul was as drab as my pinafore, but he shook his head and said that unless he was mistaken, I would end up with caricatures for brains.

And Tom was not mistaken, as it turned out. He only ever made one mistake that I know of, and he hanged for it.

2

THE DAY BEFORE TOM'S execution was the longest of my life, and it was made all the longer for it being late June and a Sunday. His crime was to encourage a sorry congregation of men in a rising against the Government. The rising did not occur, but the prospect of it was enough to hang him. There was a chance that he would be pardoned, but we would not know until shortly before he mounted the scaffold. The news would come to Tom in his cell at Newgate, but every time someone walked past the shop I couldn't help glancing up. To see the way I was carrying on, you'd have thought that every tradesman was a messenger from the Home Secretary himself.

Customers would have been a welcome distraction, though the shop was closed, of course, it being a Sunday. Even if we had been open, I would not have had much to sell them on account of Isaiah's recent imprisonment for Blasphemy, of which more soon enough.

I had come down at four-thirty, when the cow's snuffling and stomping had woken me, to find Isaiah wrapping bread in a cloth. This meant he was going out walking in Moorfields, as he often did when faced with difficulty.

He had nailed a notice to the door: the usual Sunday meeting was postponed until the following evening in the expectation of Tom's return. It was left to me to print the sermon he planned to distribute at the end of that meeting. Based on the text from Samuel, it promised deliverance from our enemies. He had spent all the previous afternoon pacing up and down the chapel while he had crafted it. The language was high-flown even by Isaiah's standards, as if he hoped to bamboozle the Lord Himself into sparing Tom.

'What of the power of prayer?' I had asked him, as he stowed his bread in his pocket. 'Surely today of all days, you should be praying for Tom's rescue from the Lion's Den?'

'You sound like your mother, may the Lord rest her soul,' he said.

'I hope the Lord is resting her, for she had no rest here,' I replied.

'You are still distraught, so I will forgive you your sharpness. But I can pray for Tom just as well under an open sky.' He glanced upwards, in the way he always did when my mother was alive, for she had spent her last months confined to the room above our heads. You cannot bear to be here now that she is not, I thought. Even imprisonment would not have seemed such a punishment, with her recently dead. He was the only printer in the City with perpetual green stains on his britches from his walks in Moorfields, and brown ones from the time he spent in coffee houses, but no inky ones. I would have liked to go walking with him, but I felt I could not ask, after his reproach. And I had work to do.

Soon after eleven, so five hours after Isaiah's departure, my sister Meg was standing in the middle of the shop, stepping from one foot to the other. This was her latest fancy, that she must be at the very centre of any room, and as far away from any objects as possible. Through all her twelve years, she had never been a child for coddling, and since our mother died she had gone to elaborate lengths to avoid

touching anyone, or even brushing against wood, walls –
anything that might connect her with the world. In the morning, she'd leap up from the floor as if her damp blanket had
stung her awake. She was watching the door in the belief that
if she was like the good servant who kept her lamp trimmed
for the master's return, then I would not die like our mother
did, Tom would come back soon, Isaiah would not go to
prison again, and therefore she would never again be sent to
live with our aunt and uncle. If I tried to tell her that we
would not leave her, she rolled herself up like a hedgehog.

It being just after midsummer, the long day stretched
ahead of me like an unpunctuated sentence. I prayed all that
day that my brother would be saved from the noose, but I
needed to keep my hands busy. Meg was not going to tell
Isaiah that I had broken Our Lord's Commandment to keep
the Sabbath while he abandoned his flock, and I knew that
this was the least of what the Lord must forgive me, if I am
ever to sit at His right hand. I blew the dust off one of our
old copperplates and took down a tray to mix some ink.

'We will need new plates, now that Queen Caroline has
just returned to Hammersmith,' I said to Meg. She did not
move, still less answer, and I did not expect her to. The
Queen's house was a garden cottage near the Thames, a few
miles outside town. At first, the frenzy surrounding the
possible return of the sluttish Caroline had been a
disappointment to God-fearing men like Tom and Isaiah;
another example of how men were distracted from the
true ills of the regime by salacious gossip. But it had not
been long before they had seen her as a herald of political
change, and one of Biblical proportions. Caroline encouraged her unlikely ragtag of supporters, promising to
champion working men's rights. She gambled that fear of a
revolution, as well might happen should these radical
supporters of hers be disappointed, could persuade her

husband to install her on the throne.

So a happy pairing between Radical and would-be Queen was cemented, and in these god-botherers' minds, Hammersmith became the Garden of Eden, Westminster and the City Sodom and Gomorrah, and the two political parties, the Whigs and the Tories, identical in their wickedness. In truth, there was not that much between them, except that the Tories tended to favour the King and the Whigs were more wary of his power – particularly since the new King and his father had kept them out of office for close on forty years. As Tom had been fond of pointing out, for all we had a Parliament, we might as well have had a despot for a King, for no one could sniff at governing without his nod, and what sham elections we had involved few voters and changed nothing. But the prospect of a royal divorce pointed a cannon at these political skittles.

Until that Sunday, I would not have believed it was possible to miss my brother as much as I did. 'There is only one man in London who does not want Caroline, and that is the King!' Tom used to say. Listening to Tom was like seeing one of the ribbons of speech unfurl on a cartoon of Mr Cruikshank's, and men had gathered in fields and taverns to hear him. None of his speeches carried any more weight than the ink it took to print them, but on the evidence of a spy employed by the Magistrates he had been arrested for seditious libel and incitement to murder, which in layman's terms meant spreading lies about the Government in order to destroy it. The Magistrates wanted to make An Example of him: he became an indefinite article, as if he had already ceased to exist the moment he was sentenced. And Isaiah had been released in time to see his rebellious stepson die.

But looking at Meg, it was possible to imagine it was any ordinary Sunday. If it had been the previous summer, then Tom would have been out, for he could scarcely bear to be in the same house as Isaiah. I would have been working, and tending to my mother while she lay dying. I believe that much of the story that follows was my attempt to escape the empty space she left in this house.

~~~~~~~

My head was bowed over the mixing tray when a customer rattled the door. I ought not to have served him on a Sunday, but then I ought not to have been mixing ink, for that was also work. When added to the dungheap of things I ought not to have done in the months prior to that Sunday, selling a print for a shilling did not seem so sinful. Isaiah was fond of saying that Hell was at the end of a primrose path, though I could find no reference to primroses in the Bible. If such a path exists, I had surely slid down it on my backside long before that morning, and a little printer's grease was not going to make much difference.

'Good morning, Miss,' the customer said, waiting at the door for Meg to move.

'Come away, Meg,' I said. The shop was small, and she was blocking the route to what few prints we had. I looked around for a counting job to give her, for it was the only thing that would persuade her from her post.

'You are our first customer today,' she said to the gentleman. 'I am counting.' There is a flatness to Meg's voice as if she is dumb, but she hears perfectly well. The Lord only knows what she understands.

'That is all you ever do,' I said. 'Now let the gentleman pass.' It looked as though she might refuse to move, but she stepped aside, and our customer was in.

The gentleman approached but did not remove his hat. This was a familiar scene: I had learned from my mother how to serve a gentleman politely without seeming too interested in his face. His coat was of fine quality – a light wool that would not sit too heavily on a day like this – and quite new, to judge by the evenness of the seams and the shape of the pockets. I decided that this was his first visit to a shop such as ours, and shame – or else fear of the Government spies who kept an eye on our transactions – kept his eyes averted. When it came to satirical prints, the line between what was legal and what was not seemed to be redrawn and extended more often than the King's waistline.

'Good morning, Sir,' I said, flustered because we did not have any new lithographs from our finer quality press, prints which are then coloured by hand; it was just our luck that such a man would call now. 'You would perhaps like to see something from the window, Sir?'

'Not exactly, Miss,' he said. 'I am wondering if your stepfather can procure *Convents of Marseilles* for me.' No souvenir for the pious traveller this, but a set of prints so debased that even my eyes widened: the artist imagined the first encounters between sailors fresh off slaving ships, their minds full of the debauched practices which only the French can conjure, and nuns who turn out to be even more ingenious in this respect than the men who invade their houses.

But the most shocking thing was that I recognised the gentleman's voice. It was this, I realised, which had been familiar to me when he arrived, not his unease as a prospective customer. What had brought to my door the life I had hoped to leave behind, in the figure of Mr Edwards?

As he wandered over to the window and made a show of peering at the prints there, I pondered this. He would be well occupied elsewhere, for he had made it his business to prevent Caroline from securing the crown. He was a friend of the Tories, and how I knew this – and him – is the substance of the first part of this story. Had he not appeared in our shop that Sunday, I might never have had to tell it, but there he was, and so here am I.

He seemed uninterested in me, and for a moment I allowed myself to imagine that his visit was pure chance after all, and it was possible that Mr Edwards would not recognise me in a plain dress and printer's apron. In fact, I reassured myself, this would be the last place he would expect to see me – he would most likely assume that I was still living like a caged canary in St James's Square, for news of my departure would be beneath his notice, eclipsed by my companion Hetty's marriage to Sir Robin Everley and the shock of the death of Sir David, Sir Robin's cousin.

He turned round, his foot catching Meg as he did so; she curled up and made a keening sound until I shushed her.

'Mistress Nell,' he said, 'I have a proposition for you.'

He saw my alarm, and smiled. 'Fear not, it is a proposition far less physically onerous, shall we say, than the ones you undertook until recently. Though potentially far more taxing, I fear. It is however beautifully simple: assist me in some small but important matters, or take the noose, as an accessory to murder.'

Click, click click, went Meg's buttons: bone on bone.

'Murder?' I said. 'Who has been murdered?'

Mr Edwards looked at me, his face momentarily losing its frown of calculating amusement. 'Why, I almost believe that you have no idea what I am talking about.'

'I promise you that I do not, Sir,' I said, and I was not lying.

He stowed the package of writing ink he had settled for in one of his empty pockets, handing me a few coins and a calling card.

'You will assist me, or you will swing,' he said. He took his leave, turning as he reached the door. 'Most likely you do not trust me,' he said in a low voice. 'For you do not understand that our cause is the same. Indeed, I did not understand that, the first night we met. You might help me, and I might see you hang anyway; how can you tell? You are caught, Mistress Nell, on a pair of horns. Not the cuckold's horns of our new King, but the horns of a dilemma.'

I watched him turn left, leaving our bell jangling behind him. As soon as his coat-tail disappeared, I wanted him to return: whatever Mr Edwards' business was with me, I had to know it.

My fear propelled me out of the shop, with only a passing thought for what Meg would do in the meantime. I threw on my old shawl as I went. I was halfway down Cheapside before I realised that there were more facets to the foolishness of pursuing Mr Edwards than in the paste diamond necklace I was wearing the last time he laid eyes on me. He was unlikely to reveal his purposes to me – after all, such convenient developments only occur in the novels my friend Hetty used to read during the long evenings of waiting for the clatter of returning carriage wheels on St James's Square.

⁂

At St Paul's churchyard, Mr Edwards slowed, then descended the steps to the crypt. He meant for me to follow him, I was sure.

I had not reached the first tomb nor had my eyes adjusted to the gloom before I heard a familiar voice at my ear.

'Miss Wingfield! For the second time this morning! What a happy coincidence. But these days you are no longer wearing silk, I see – nor lace, I imagine – which is a pity.'

In fact, it was not a pity, but I was not about to tell him how I preferred simple cotton to the catch of lace on my softest parts. These days I am lucky to have a pair of clean bloomers. Like most of the women of London, I am forever worrying about how frequently to wash them: too often, and they will fall apart; not often enough, and I will smell like a fishmonger's slab. But one thing I know for sure: this is preferable to the itch of fancy undergarments. I think Mr Edwards read something of this in my face, and I looked away: I wanted him to know that I was no longer someone who would sit for hours with a group of girls, fiddling with our curls and pretending to be interested in needlework, while we waited on the arrival of a gentleman's carriage and with him whatever desires the wine, that evening's theatre or his idle imagination had stirred in him. Hetty, who had entered that house the same day as me and was my true and constant friend, became so bored some evenings that she used to prick herself with her needle to check that she was still alive. I used to warn her that she would poison herself, but nothing stopped her summoning the red drops and staring at them.

'What do you want with me, Sir?' I said, feeling the blood pumping in my neck.

Mr Edwards snorted and nodded to himself, fixing me with a languid stare from under his hooded eyelids. His was a dissolute face, but I knew him to be a man of singularly few passions. He did not drink, paid little attention to the pleasures of the table, showed no carnal interest in men, women or children – and neither did he share the passions of other men (and here I think of Isaiah and Tom) who avoided such things: namely religion and radical politics. All this despite the company he kept – and I suppose it was this that made him so useful to his employers.

'There will be a coronation here soon,' Mr Edwards said. 'Will you come to watch it? Perhaps you will wear your finery for that? You would gain a great many admirers. Or are you saving your satin for the New Jerusalem? If you are, I hope you have invested in some mothballs, for it looks to be a long time in coming.'

'I am not what you think,' I said, watching the crowd of people paying their respects at Lord Nelson's tomb.

'Ah, I understand,' he said. 'You are not a radical, though your brother is condemned as one. He was eloquent in a naive way – yes, I went to hear him; your stepfather is a far more compelling figure, is he not? And you are not a whore, even though you left 14 St James's Square in a silk dress only a week ago. You remind me of Caroline, our would-be Queen, who insists she is not an adulteress, even though she has shared her bed with half the minor nobles and menservants of Europe. Does your stepfather know of your talents? I wonder,' he said.

'I have no talents, Sir – and Isaiah is a good man,' I said. Two women watched us, one kneading her fur muff in disdain. She would have seen a well-dressed man whispering to a more plainly attired girl, and must have assumed that he was soliciting. When I was a harlot in my blue satin dress, no one looked at me like this – at least, not until I opened my mouth, and sometimes not even then, for a lifetime spent in the back of a chapel gives a girl quite a vocabulary to set her up in life, if nothing else. 'And I paid for my dress, twice over, again I promise you that. I owed Mother Cooper nothing, but I still left her money.' It was Hetty's money I gave her, but Hetty had bought me my freedom just as Isaiah's father had bought his mother's. I'd hidden the dress in the chapel, of all places, at the back of a cupboard which only I used because it housed my broom and the printing inks. I knew I ought to get rid of it, but I could not think how to, without drawing attention to where I had been.

Mr Edwards steered me away from the disapproving women, back up the steps and towards a costermonger. Two pyramids of oranges flanked handbills of the new poem by Mr Shelley about an Egyptian king whose name I cannot recall.

'Isaiah Douglas, a good man? I would not be so sure about that, Miss Nell,' he said. 'You must not have read any accounts of how the slave races disport themselves when they are alone in their lodgings, away from the white man's gaze. Indeed I hope you have not seen them, for you and your imbecile sister would sleep considerably less easily in your beds, and your mother would turn in her grave.'

'Isaiah is not a monster, and my sister is not an imbecile,' I said. 'And if you will excuse me, she awaits me.'

'Ah! You do keep excusing yourself, Nell. How you dote on that prating God-botherer of a stepfather! And you are the dutiful sister, are you not? How you move me: the good-hearted whore! So much so, in fact, that I will not report your whereabouts to the Magistrates. Provided, of course, that you co-operate with me. We could find enough evidence against you to have you transported away from your sister and guardian for considerably longer than six months.'

Here Mr Edwards had gathered all my worst fears in a skein which he might as well have tightened round my throat, for all I could breathe. 'I left that house, Sir, with nothing,' I said, rehearsing the words I had gone over in my head each dawn in the week since I'd left. 'I was careful to leave more than enough money for my clothing, board and food – no one, least of all Mother Cooper, could accuse me of theft.' My cheeks were hot and my mouth was parched with fear, for I knew very well that this was how most girls were trapped into the trade I had escaped. We spent our nights in satin and lace, our arses plonked on damask sofas, our beds all cherry wood and goose down, so that our fannies might be poked by the richest pricks in the land – and we were continually in debt to Mother Cooper, who ran the house.

'Theft, pshaw!' he said, with a flick of his hand. 'A mere trifle. No, no, my dear Nell: if anyone wanted, they could have you up for murder, could they not?'

'What?' I exclaimed. 'Sir, of all the hours I have spent worrying that I would be transported on some trumped-up charge, I never imagined that anyone would accuse me of something as terrible as this!'

'Save me your protestations. I know you are no murderess, though you were the – how shall we put it? – *constant consort* of a man who was murdered in his bed.'

He waited for this remark to take its effect.

'Sir David?' Merely uttering his name again conjured the horror of his death. The footsteps around me, which had seemed so discreet and distant a few moments before, now became too loud and close.

'So,' he continued, counting on his bony white fingers, 'in spite of the company you keep, you are neither radical, nor accomplice to murder, nor whore. I might as well respond that I am not in the new King's employ, and am employed by King Nebuchadnezzar instead. It seems we have yet to become properly acquainted.'

'B–but there was no murder,' I stammered.

Mr Edwards watched me. 'All this really had never occurred to you, had it? You trusted your friend Hetty, just as Sir David kept company with his cousin.' Mr Edwards studied my face, and something of the terror he read there must have registered with him. 'But fear not: they are unlikely to come looking for you,' he went on. 'Unless, of course, you are brought to their attention. But believe me, Nell, the wonder of our situation is that I will only be helping you. All is as it was when you resided at 14 St James's Square: although our roles are very different, once again our interests coincide.'

He led me back up the steps and gave an orange-seller tuppence, which bought me a bulging bag of fruit.

'I know you will find this impossible to believe, still less understand. No doubt you and your stepfather would like to ensure that Tom will not die for nothing?'

'Tom will live, and you are not worthy to speak his name!' I said.

'What!' Mr Edwards snorted. 'You are not about to make a false god of your brother, are you? That is blasphemy, Nell: ask your stepfather, for he knows all about that, even if he knows nothing about you.'

I knew better than to plead for secrecy: whatever Mr Edwards wanted, I would agree to it, for my stepfather must never learn of where I had been – he would surely cast me out if he did.

Mr Edwards put on his hat and turned to me with the slightest of bows. 'But mark this: if you help me whenever I call on you, you can rest assured that your beloved Isaiah will know nothing about where you have been these last months, for I'll wager you haven't told him.' He watched me as I studied the cobbles. 'I thought not. And if he finds you have been lying about where you were, how much harder will it be for him to believe that you had no involvement in the murder of Sir David Fairfax.'

I shook my head, as if there was not room for all his words in it. 'David – Sir David,' I said, unable to think of anything except the memory of him as he lay dead on Hetty's bed, his face caught forever in something like pain or surprise. He was the only good man in that house, and the only man I'd ever known of whom I hadn't been at all afraid. It took most of the time I knew him, but he taught me to forget fear. Then he died.

'One day you will forgive me for speaking to you so,' Mr Edwards said, his voice taking on a different tone. 'You think you have escaped the life you led, but you are in considerable danger. And so is Isaiah. He must cease his preaching, or I cannot vouch for his safety. And as for you – our paths will cross again soon, you can be sure of that.' He walked towards Ludgate-hill, leaving me with a bag of oranges, and more worry and fear than I had felt since my mother died.

Until that moment, I viewed us ordinary Londoners and the Quality as if we were divided by great continents, as if the Strand was an ocean that separated my life here off Cheapside from my six months in St James's. In those six months I never happened across a soul who knew me, and I had hoped the same would apply once I returned to Friday-street. Even lying awake in the small hours, my stepfather's and Meg's snores competing to keep me awake, I did not imagine that my life in 14 St James's Square would catch up with me as quickly as this. I dreaded being hunted down as a whore and a thief, but I had never dreamed I would be called an accessory to murder.

I sheltered against one of the cathedral's buttresses and peeled an orange. For all my fears, the flavour made my mouth weep with pleasure, and I got into a rhythm of peeling, separating the segments and popping the flesh into my mouth. As I watched him go, I reflected on all that had happened since my mother died and tried to make sense of what Mr Edwards had just told me.

3

W<small>HEN</small> I <small>LEFT MY</small> scarlet days behind, I had fancied that my time at 14 St James's Square could be packed away in a trunk and transported like a criminal – until Mr Edwards' visit, when its lid flew open.

If I were to make my confession in the way the Catholics do, my story would begin like this: I arrived at St James's Square believing that it was a place of refuge for the destitute, and my only terror was that the proprietress would discover that I had an uncle with whom I could lodge, and that I was not as alone in the world as I felt and had claimed. My mother had been dead less than three days when I arrived there. The night she died I had spent by her side, at which point our landlady had insisted that the shop closed until Isaiah was released from prison six months hence. Six months with no source of income and no roof to shelter us might as well have been a millennium, so the second night I spent under my uncle's roof. A third night I could not endure, on account of my uncle; what he did to me is predictable enough, so more of his sorry story will wait until later. I slipped out of my uncle's premises convinced I was utterly alone in the world, and decided that I would trust divine providence to guide me towards a righteous path.

I made for Covent Garden. I knew that the costermongers

there would discard their rotting wares at the end of each day, but I had no idea of the swarms with whom I would have to compete for these dubious treasures. Their hunger made them as nimble as they were desperate, and I found myself a conspicuous sight in my black shawl – it might have been threadbare, but it had no holes, and this marked me out as affluent. I had passed through these arcades only a few times in my life, my stepfather judging Covent Garden (rightly) as a rotting fruit of a place: the outside pleasing to the eye at a glance, but festering and putrid within. On those earlier visits I must have displaced the poor from my sight as I stepped over them, and indeed I found that dozens of people fell over me as I crouched on a kerb. I watched those who had a few pennies devour their pasties and prayed that they would toss aside their crusts. Eventually one dropped to the ground as if under the weight of my stare, and I fell on it with only a perfunctory smoothing away of filth; I had not eaten at all that day. It was my first experience of real hunger since my family had arrived in London – but how swift was my descent! As they stepped onto the kerb, ladies hitched up their velvet skirts, as if they were lifting curtains on a life I could never see. The necessity of survival distracted from the loss of my mother, but as it is in the darkness where the Thames and the Fleet join, so it is difficult to tell where the one ended and the other began.

My story is, I now know, one familiar enough to a certain type of literature. The crust I had eaten was small, and soon I was trying to cadge some stale bread from a flower-seller. He was about to toss it to a flock of avid pigeons, and so he was content to give it to me – or he was, until a middle-aged woman who had been watching me from across the piazza marched in and insisted that such behaviour threatened the moral fabric of the city. Ha! If I'd only known at that moment what kind of house she kept! As it was, the man told her he saw no reason why feeding pretty girls was worse than feeding birds, and perhaps it was his interest in me that confirmed her in her idea of employing me. When she asked where my mother was, I could only shake my head. Though not kindly, her gaze showed an interest in my mother's death which I mistook for goodness.

She told me she ran a house which provided rest for girls such as me, and I would be welcome to lodge with her for a week. 'Only a week, mind,' she said, as if anticipating my expressions of wonder at her generosity, 'and if you like it, you can join me in my work.' She did not say what would happen if I did not. As for the work, I assumed that I would be sent out on charitable expeditions akin to the one which had brought her to me, or given sewing, or else asked to help in the kitchens to feed other poor girls. As we quit Covent Garden and skirted around Leicester-square, I wondered if she would have need of a printer; how delighted she would be, when she discovered what a singular talent I had! I now see that grief and desperation had given me tripe for brains, but at the time I felt only gratitude. If I noticed the gaudiness of her costume, it was only to think of how my mother, who had always wanted to sell buttons and ribbons, would have applauded this philanthropic woman's colourful taste.

And rest I did, though not for a week. Two nights I had, in a mews house so close to St James's Palace that I could smell the royal kitchens. But I was not driven mad with longing, for I was fed chicken legs and beef tea, porridge and oranges, and allowed to sleep all the hours I could. The taste of those oranges Mr Edwards bought for me almost re-kindled the simple joy I had felt at being cared for and well fed. In that bed, I found that years of tiredness leached from my limbs, and a cough which I'd had for months rattled its way out of my chest.

I was surprised that my room did not have a book of

Scripture or some other religious text tucked away, but this absence was sweetened by the arrival of a cake or, if the clock had struck six, a glass of sherry. I wondered at the bounty of such a place; certainly Isaiah had never hinted that the money we gave to houses for the destitute might permit others to live in such opulence. I prayed whenever I woke, and convinced myself that it was perfectly possible to live in a house without a bible since I could recite so many verses by heart.

When I woke the third morning, I was struck with some force by the realisation that the price of all this seeming kindness would be hefty, but I was deterred from fleeing by a sense that I might be wrong about this, and it would be sinful to leave without thanking my benefactress and taking her particulars, so that I might repay her in future. Looking back on it, I think Tom was right about me: all those years of inking in suggestive prints had softened my mind to the enormity of what I was about to embark on, and made part of me long to live my life in the kind of colour that I had spent so many thousands of hours mixing.

In any case, the smallness of the windows rendered flight impossible, and the door was always locked. I am ashamed to say that the finest breakfast I had yet eaten then arrived, beating the previous day's feast only because my coffee was even thicker with indulgent cream. (Though not as thick as my clotted brain. I was snared, I was being fatted: why did I not perceive this more clearly? I doubt Isaiah has ever truly understood how men will roll on their backs submissively once their stomachs have stopped growling, but I now do.) The maid who brought me my food saw me looking at her keys, and said that the door was secured to protect me from some of the other waifs and strays who had been rescued. 'We wouldn't want you to do anything more than sleep easy in your bed, would we?' I think she said. How she must have been laughing at me.

There was no lunch that day. Instead, my benefactress arrived, though her air was considerably less beneficent than it had been when we had first met. She left me to dress, then I was taken to 14 St James's Square by an old woman whose protestations of deafness in the face of my questions did not strike me as convincing. After all, she had heard me ask her name, which was Martha. There I found two other girls, one a heavy blonde with smooth pink skin; the other a tiny girl with delicate features. Mother Cooper, a hulk in maroon silk skirts, met us in the kitchen. She explained that she was the proprietress of the house and we were to call her Mother. 'I do not insist on *Mother Abbess*, as many women in my position do,' she said, pausing a moment as if in expectation of sighs of gratitude, 'but you are to look on me as the closest you have to a mother, and hence my title.' I thought of my own mother, lying in earth which would be even colder than this kitchen. For all the cake and sherry she had given me, I could never call this hard-faced baggage *Mother*.

'You've entered here,' she continued, 'and will proceed to the dressing rooms. If what I see there is not suitable, you will be offered a position in the kitchen. Should you prefer death in the gutter, you may leave through the door you entered by. If you stay and work upstairs, you will have no need of that door again – it will be the front door and the main staircase for you.' She paused again, as if she was offering us unlimited use of Jacob's Ladder. The kitchen door was bolted, and I understood that she did not mean to offer us our freedom. Still we said nothing, and she adopted the petulant scowl that became her habitual demeanour. 'And I might as well mention this now – I've only room upstairs for two of you.'

A bell jingled from the front of the house, and Mother Cooper left us standing there. We listened to her leather

slippers slapping on the floor. Despite myself, I wanted to see what it would be made of: parquet or marble?

'We'll be needing the back door plenty, no matter what she says,' the blonde girl said to me with a laugh much less innocent than her eyes, which were round and lilac and managed to look deep and empty at the same time. 'I'm Hetty,' she said.

'Nell,' I said. I had no idea what she was talking about.

'Ann,' said the tiny girl. She came to just below my chest, and I envied her that slightness. She had no need for a corset, for a man could circle her waist with his hands.

'She'll save Mother Cooper a fortune on tailors' bills,' Hetty said. 'She'll stay.'

I later learned that women were abandoning corsetry, so Ann's slender body was newly fashionable. And there was Hetty herself: her bosom, lips and cheeks so overripe that men would jostle to pluck her. Which left me, taller than most men and far too lean, for all the chicken I had recently scoffed.

I imagined myself as Mother Cooper would: too tall and awkward to afford the luxury of self-pity or to risk looking down in the mouth. Now Hetty, she had one of those faces which looked pretty even when she pouted, and I was soon to discover that she often did. It seemed most likely that I would be offered a job below stairs. I looked round the kitchen, and felt a great surge of longing for our shop on Friday-street. But I might as well long to join my mother in heaven, I told myself, as wish to return there. So would I rather sleep in the slums of Seven Dials than bake fancies down in this kitchen? I watched a girl of no more than twelve who was rolling pastry. Were the dough not flattening, I'd have sworn she was a ghost. All over London, children were being worked into an early grave to bake sweet morsels for the men who had thrown Isaiah into prison for preaching that an angel spoke out of Balaam's Ass. Was this to be my fate?

Mother Cooper had locked the door behind her. Jesus said that the truth sets you free, but he never set foot in a London townhouse. Standing in that dark kitchen, I saw no prospect of escape, for all Mother Cooper's insistence that we could leave. I thought that even scullery work would tide me over, though I was determined not to go into permanent service.

Slap slap slap of slippers in the hallway. 'Very well,' said Mother Cooper, 'let us see how you take to silks.'

Silks! How that word worked a spell on me. All the hours I had spent inking them, longing for the roughness of the paper to come to life under my brushes and pens, for I had heard it said that silk is a fabric spun from living things, and has the life of a brilliant second skin when worn. I longed for the kind of truth that enslaves, and so, God forgive me, I headed upstairs. *Vanity of vanities*, I heard the preacher Isaiah saying in my ear. *And what of it?* I said back. My days of being infested with lice were over, but stale worsted, rough linen and cheap cotton were the only materials that had ever met my skin. I thought of my mother, and how much less she would have suffered if she'd had soft clothes when she got so uncomfortable that even her skin ached. I considered how appalled she would be if she could see me here, breathing the same air as the other inhabitants of this house, but I sent the thought scurrying away with a flea in its ear – the kind of creature I hoped never to see the likes of again. I put Satan behind me and satin before me.

How easily she fell! you might be thinking. *What a fool she must be!* You might also be wondering if you should toss this book aside before some of my lewdness stains you, in the way that the ink from all those prints marked my hands. I could have prefaced my tale with all the misfortunes that had led me to this sorry place, but I have a bigger story to tell, one which Tom would have judged to be far more important than my puny attempts to excuse myself.

And I also know that your frowns will be nothing compared to St Peter's when the Apocalypse comes, which it soon will.

We followed Mother Cooper up a narrow stone staircase that brought us to the servants' passage on the first floor, which was indeed parqueted. As we walked towards the next staircase, I heard footsteps on the front stairs, and caught sight of a lady in pale green silk, her blonde hair fastened with diamond pins. She was escorted by a gentleman with black shoes, white breeches and hefty calves. They shared a joke, and the lady said, 'Oh, Charles, you are *too much!*' Whereupon he murmured something in her ear and she rewarded him with a laugh which sounded both scandalised and delighted. I marvelled at how she had captured this man's attention. As I soon learned, a head full of the Old Testament did not make me a diverting prospect for a soirée at St James's Square.

'Good afternoon, Lord Charles,' said Mother Cooper, sounding like nonchalance itself, but this only made her pride that such a man was to be found on her stairs the more obvious. I wondered if I would ever have the courage to call Lord anybody Charles, James or William. I wondered if the Williams of the Quality abbreviated themselves, like Isaiah's friend Will Davidson, and again I remembered the key in the lock downstairs and wondered that I had not run. I suppose I still could have done, but I didn't.

Hetty pulled my arm. 'Listen to what Mother Cooper asks me. Do not be afraid. Try to do what I do, and we will come out of this together,' she said.

I nodded, fearing I would weep in the face of her kindness.

4

HETTY, ANN AND I entered a room lined on its far side with mahogany wardrobes. A gilt mirror which looked taller even than me was standing in front of the fireplace. The windows were covered with cream gauzy curtains, and opposite them was a phalanx of lacquered screens. We were each directed behind a screen, and hanging behind mine was a dress of periwinkle satin. Its skirts were so full I pressed myself against the wall to avoid soiling it with the merest touch.

Next to it was a corset. The waist was so tiny that I was convinced there had been a terrible mistake, and some elf was supposed to be there in my place.

'Normally you would help dress each other,' said Mother Cooper, 'but today I will assist you, on account of your ignorance of these matters. Pray remove your garments and await me.'

I had my pinafore and underskirts off in a moment, but Mother Cooper began with the screen furthest from me, so I had plenty of time to feel the draught which ran in from under the door. My flesh went grey and goosepimply, and I rubbed it. *A tall turkey*, I thought: *that's all she'll see when she gets to me*, though I was astonished to see that the days I had spent eating and resting had left me with something which almost passed for a cleavage if hoisted aggressively.

Hetty emerged first, and I peered through the gap in the screen to see her. An apparition of grey silk she was, more like something out of the next world than this one. The colour was wonderful on her, making her skin golden and giving her a gravity that only accentuated her youth. She gasped and giggled in front of the mirror, and even Mother Cooper seemed to soften at her twirls and sighs.

Then Hetty lifted her skirts high, flashing silk knickers and stockings, laughing and winking at us in the mirror. So much for her otherworldliness.

'You will need to attend to your deportment,' said Mother Cooper. 'And a girl of your proportions will be heavy on undergarments,' she said, shaking her head and pinching Hetty's breast where it bulged a little under her arm. From these remarks, it was obvious that Hetty had secured herself one of the two places which Mother Cooper had offered.

It was equally clear from Mother Cooper's exclamations that Ann had not even removed her dress. Ann was whispering something to her, and I stepped into the corset while I listened. I took a deep breath and tried to pull, but my arms were not long enough to make the threads taut behind me. I began to perspire, and worried that this would damage the dress, which made me sweat all the more. Ann said something about being on her rag again, and soon Mother Cooper said, '*How* often?' in a screech of disgust. I could hear poor Ann crying as Mother Cooper said, 'No, your curse arriving every three weeks will never do. You are constitutionally unsuited to this kind of life.'

Which left me. Sorry though I was for Ann, I made a hurried effort to lace myself, but I stopped when I had the idea that I was trussing myself up like a rump of beef and destroying the corset into the bargain.

'You're keen to get the corset on, are you? Breathe in,'

Mother Cooper said. I took a great gasp, and Mother Cooper laced me. Her breath was wheezy and sharp with gin. I kept my eyes open as the dress went over my head, for it was like watching a summer sky slip over me. My mother used to let out my grey high-necked pinafore when I had grown so much I could no longer reach over the press for straining against it, so it was quite a thing to be pulled in so tightly that my new breasts looked like clouds floating out of the front of my dress.

Were it not for my rising anxiety about how I was to breathe, I would have been ecstatic at that moment. My head ought to have been full of verses warning of the dangers of vanity, but it was not.

Mother Cooper led me to the mirror. I counted it a miracle that I managed the walk. My waist felt half its natural size; Mother Cooper had carved curves into me where normally there were boyish lines. My hair seemed to fall prettily on my shoulders, and I understood that I had been ennobled by this dress, that fine clothes might be as important as fine birth for a person's standing in the world. (I now say that this is foolish vanity, but much has happened since that day.)

Mother Cooper stepped back and sighed. 'You are a gangle of a thing,' she said. 'And there are streaks of grey in your hair already.'

My hands fluttered through my hair, though I was sure she was right, for my mother had also begun to go grey when she had been in her teens.

Mother Cooper walked round me. 'And to cap it all, there is a wilful turn to your head that the other girls will not like.'

Hetty halted her prancing. 'Forgive me, Mother Cooper,' she said, 'but I think the bearing you describe will be an advantage in dealing with the gentlemen.'

Mother Cooper narrowed her eyes. 'She will need some tutoring, and she had better keep her God-bothering gob shut in the parlour.'

'She will,' said Hetty.

I opened my mouth to speak, but Hetty shook her head. Mother Cooper saw this. 'Very well,' she sighed. 'You have vouched for her, so she can stay.'

Smiling shyly at Hetty, who was pirouetting behind me in the hope of catching another glimpse of herself in the mirror, I believed that for the first time in my life, I would have a friend.

I had scarcely breathed since the corset went on, and slowly I permitted myself a few snatches of air. I worried that if I breathed remotely normally, my stays would snap, my corset would flap free and the periwinkle silk would be ripped like a sail in a gale. It was only later, when we had begun our long evenings of waiting for our gentlemen to come, that I learned how to sip a glass of sherry and not to panic at the constriction.

In the weeks that followed, Hetty said she often wondered how many of the corseted ladies who shopped on Regent-street were on the edge of fainting, or else orgasm. She would often keep hers on all night, and when she came to me in the morning to help her take it off, there were red weals at her hips and across her chest where the bones had dug in and chafed. She wore her corset low, just under her nipples, but soon these were usually purplish red and swollen. She would stroke these marks affectionately, as if they were bites left by a boisterous kitten. She was always keen to recount her adventures, as keen for me to applaud her inventiveness in pleasuring her oafish patron as a novice pianist would be in seeking praise from her governess. I told her little of my experiences, for a range of reasons. But I am getting ahead of myself.

'There will be a medical examination, of course,' Mother Cooper said to the two of us; Ann was still behind the screen, only her boots and the odd snivel in evidence. 'To verify your maidenhood.'

Hetty raised her hand to her mouth like a poor actress would on receipt of shocking news.

Mother Cooper narrowed her eyes. 'Fear not, virginity can be infinitely renewed, especially in one as young as you.'

She saw the look on my face: what place was this, which could alter nature?

'It's a matter of careful stitching, that is all,' she pronounced. 'For which there is of course a small charge.' This last comment was aimed in Hetty's direction, and she denied that she would be in need of such a service with eyes widened in horror that Mother Cooper could have thought such a thing.

'And I also will not be in need of that *service*,' I added, with as much dignity as a newly-apprenticed whore could muster.

'Well, the *services* of a hairdresser's irons will be needed to tame *that*,' she rejoined, in a tone which convinced me that this would also be costly. My hair needs the discipline of its own weight, or else it sticks out like some terrible halo. I'd never had my hair cut in my life, and I assumed it would be only slightly less painful than having a tooth removed. I gripped my hair anxiously at my neck, wondering if she would spare me any of her gin for the occasion.

It might seem strange that so many girls stayed to be fleeced by Mother Cooper. But on entry to the house, the bargain looked a sound one: Mother Cooper did after all provide fine lodgings, clothes the like of which poor girls would only otherwise glimpse getting out of carriages, and introductions to the kind of men who would have run us over in those carriages without troubling to stop given half the chance.

'As novices, you will each be assigned a sister,' said Mother Cooper. 'Seeing as there's the two of you, that's taken care of. You will lodge together while you are not at work.'

Hetty caught my eye and giggled with delight. I smiled back, reflecting that this was what I had always missed so keenly in Meg.

'And as for you,' Mother Cooper addressed the snivelling screen, 'I will take you downstairs. Let's see if there's space for you in the kitchen, while these girls *carefully* remove these dresses.'

As soon as we were alone, Hetty skipped for joy, until she almost rent her dress when she caught her toe in the hem.

'Look out,' I said. 'You'll tear the veil of the temple from seam to seam.'

She looked at me. 'Are you really a God-botherer? You don't look like one.'

'That's because I don't have a beard,' I said. Only later did I tell her about Isaiah and Tom: I did not want her to know that my stepfather was in prison and I had abandoned my sister while my brother consorted with his turbulent friends. It did not occur to me to wonder how Mother Cooper knew me for a godly girl; I thought she had seen some essential goodness in me.

Hetty laughed. 'But there is a cleverness about you. You should be careful.'

I diverted myself from this remark by wondering how Ann would manage scullery work, when Mother Cooper had judged her too weak to loll about the livelong day in fine clothes. This thought shows you how little I understood of what was in store for me at 14 St James's Square.

One thing I did understand, that first day: I would not

survive without a friend, and though the luck of Job when his patience was being tried most sorely had brought me to Mother Cooper's door, I was fortunate to have found Hetty.

5

ONCE MOTHER COOPER HAD accepted us, Hetty entertained the fancy that we would waltz upstairs, don the gown of our choice and become women of the town faster than you can say French pox. Seeing Hetty's enthusiasm, Mother Cooper informed us that we were not able to meet the Gentlemen she had in mind for us until we had undergone the medical examination she had mentioned.

'You girls are lucky,' she told us. 'You will not have to pay for Dr Lutter out of your own pockets.'

'We are most grateful to you for this kindness, Mother Cooper,' said Hetty, her eyes shining like Mary Magdalene's might have done when Our Lord rescued her from stoning.

'*Kindness*!' said Mother Cooper, as if Hetty had just insulted her. 'Do not expect any kindness here. The Gentlemen who have expressed an interest in you wish you to be verified, that is all.'

The Gentlemen who have expressed an interest in us? Had I been plucked from the street like a Christmas turkey? Before I could ask, Mother Cooper disabused me of such a vanity.

'The Gentlemen in the plural are interested in this one' – here she pointed at Hetty as if she was about to prise open her jaws to show me the quality of her teeth – 'but they are willing to consider you as they accept that only one of them can have her first.' She laughed, delighted at the cleverness of her observation, revealing a rack of teeth whose blackness seemed to be oozing from under their gold caps.

'So if you have been with a man,' she gazed at us sternly, 'you must inform me now.'

I had not, but I had no idea how she would be able to tell. Mother Cooper was waiting for an answer. I imagined her flinging me back on the street with a wooden board proclaiming HARLOT chained round my neck. The thought of leaving this place strengthened me a little, and I met her gaze. 'I have not,' I said.

'I have not, *Mother*,' she said. 'We will need to teach you some manners. But that will wait: I ask because it will cost more to mend you, and that will certainly not be coming out of the Gentlemen's pockets, will it?' Clearly she was a woman who saw the humour of our situation.

She asked if we had ever ridden on a horse, for this might have 'disturbed us in our innermost parts'. I told her that I had walked all the way from Preston to London and would have been glad of any disturbance a horse would have offered. Any hope I had that she might have laughed at this was dispelled by the look she bestowed on me, which was as black as her grate of teeth. 'I do not need any clever hussies under my roof,' she said. 'That is the one thing I cannot abide in a girl. I would sooner pass off a poxy girl as clean before I would countenance cleverness in my boudoirs. The Gentlemen do not pay for it; they do not welcome it, and *neither do I*.' This latter point she underscored by taking hold of my wrist and pressing it tight between the two bones, a manoeuvre which was remarkable for the simplicity of its execution and the agony it induced. As it turned out, the only Gentleman I entertained welcomed a little chatter, even some small wit. Sir David Fairfax was a good man, and rich too, and I often told him that I could not understand why he came to me, when he would find love more easily than a beggar finds pennies in the gutter. He would shake his head sadly, and once or twice he said that most girls were not like me, but again I am getting ahead of myself, for I will recount much more of my time with him presently.

'Will we meet the Gentlemen tonight?' Hetty said, with an avidity which reminded me of Meg when she was counting out coins.

'I doubt Dr Lutter will be able to call today though I will try to summon him. But there is no need to worry,' she said, with a dusting of kindness in her voice. 'I will give you a room in the attic as an advance on your wages.'

She saw our surprise. 'No one lodges here for charity,' Mother Cooper said, folding her arms under her velvet bosom. She was like the divan she had consigned to the kitchen for the servants to sleep on: saggy and tired, even her phrases worn out with overuse.

'What happens if we do not meet a Gentleman?' Hetty asked.

'Then you must pay for your lodging, you silly girl,' she replied, 'and if you cannot, then after a fortnight, you will be out. Now I have Ann, I have no need of any further hands in the kitchen.' Then she puckered her lips as if we were new-borns she was about to coo over. 'But don't fret, I wouldn't have chosen you if I didn't think you'd pay handsomely.'

Hetty smiled and wrinkled her nose at me. I smiled in return, glad of her attempt to reassure me, but all I could think was: and if we do meet a Gentleman, what happens then? The thought of two weeks in an attic was a world less terrifying than what I might be required to do in one of the fine rooms we had glimpsed on our way to try on our dress-es. I remembered Isaiah practising one of his sermons; how he'd said the road to damnation was upholstered and brocaded and edged with piped satin. And how he'd looked over at my mother as he'd said it; she'd never mentioned her dream of owning a haberdasher's in front of him again. And who knew? Perhaps Isaiah was right about Providence but wrong about how it worked – perhaps it had brought me here, and I was being called in to look beyond the sinfulness of the place and find goodness in it. I truly believed this, and was calmed by the idea that the life I would have there would be fundamentally different from Hetty's. And in many ways, I was right.

I did not curl up and weep, in part because my terror of seeing a doctor had such a powerful effect on me that I could hardly think about anything else.

We were led up to a room which was practically filled by an iron bedstead. The roof sloped so steeply that the person sleeping against the wall had to take great care not to rise too swiftly, or else suffer a serious blow to the head. Hetty offered to take this side the first night as she was so much smaller than me, but when she also mentioned that she suffered violent dreams, I feared she would clobber herself into idiocy, so naturally I said I would take it.

But the bed was not the first thing we noticed about the room, for it's size was dwarfed by the power of the cold which had gathered there. We sat on the edge of the bed. We watched our breath come in clouds as we listened to the clatter of carriage wheels and people talking below us. Their words were indistinguishable, as though coming from the bottom of a frozen well.

'How long will we be here, do you think?' Hetty asked, darting out and checking the corridor, then sitting down again. She saw me looking at her. 'I thought I heard some-one,' she said.

'You did,' I replied, 'but they are outside.' We listened to the world passing below us.

'We will die, if we do not huddle together,' she whispered, shuffling close to me and linking her arm with mine. Her thigh felt soft and plump, her warmth as alien to me and my bony kin as a small animal's might have been.

'What do you think the doctor will do to us?' she asked, after a few minutes had passed and our shivering had subsided.

I had no idea, but I did not want to alarm her, so I thought quickly: 'Er,' I said, exhaling into the cold, 'he will want to know that we are not diseased, so he will have to inspect us.'

'But how?' she persisted, her face a perfect wide-eyed blank.

I felt myself tighten at the very idea of it, for she was asking the question that I was most keen to avoid. Still, I thought: it will be good for me to face this, for her sake.

'Most likely he will prod us with a stick like Elisha in the First Book of Kings,' I suggested, remembering suddenly some ploughing I had seen on the journey down from Lancashire to London. We had almost lost my mother then, until a farmer had carried her to a barn and given her cow-warm milk. The moment I tasted it, I knew she'd get well – it was like drinking in life itself. Each evening, I'd helped the farmer drive the cows home to my mother's barn, and we would have more of the milk we'd collected that afternoon. He'd encouraged my mother to stay longer than she needed to, and I wished we had stayed with him.

'A stick?' Hetty repeated, with the same blank expression. Then she laughed, and it was as if a different girl altogether was emerging from inside her. 'A stick!' she crowed, poking me in the ribs so hard that I leapt up and hit my head hard on the roof. My vision went yellow and pink while her laughter seemed the louder for the shock of the pain. She had been gulling me, and had known all along what the doctor planned to do to us.

And so I began to cry. Though it might be a prideful indulgence for me to say so, when the River Jordan burst its banks there would not have been as much water as there was that afternoon. For I had not cried even when my mother died.

Hetty was a portrait of the Blessed Virgin in her sorrow. She fluttered her hand over my shoulder. 'I should not tease you so. I know what will happen to us, for my father was a physician who specialised in such matters.'

I stopped sobbing enough to speak. 'You said he *was* a doctor?' I ventured, not wanting to say anything involving the word 'death' for fear I should start crying again. Isaiah's small congregation had had a collection for a qualified physician to visit my mother. He had arrived, the soul of importance with his creaking leather bag. After two minutes he had pronounced my mother beyond hope, pocketed the proceeds of the collection and wheezed back down the ladder, telling Isaiah that it was fortunate that he, the doctor, had not taken a tumble, for he would have had no hesitation in charging him for the treatment of his broken leg if he had.

'Yes, my father *was* a doctor. And now he is a bankrupt: it is a booming profession. He is out in the Hulks, for there are so many other debtors now that there is no room for him in the Fleet.' The Hulks were the great floating ships which accommodated the overflow from the other London gaols, of which the Fleet was the main debtors' prison. It was one of the crueller ironies of the city that men who owed money were denied the opportunity to repay it. Hetty's father would be there a long time, most likely. Unless one of his relatives could stump up the cash to release him, of course.

'What happened?' I asked, for Hetty was giving me the expectant look employed by all storytellers who require some token of interest before they will deliver the next instalment.

'He took out a mortgage on a mews house near Wimpole-street. You might know them – one of the new dwellings they have been building. All seemed well: the bank arranged a mortgage, and my father's business was flourishing. What he did not know was that the bank and the speculator were in business together – in league, I should say – and once my father had moved in, the bank started to raise the interest on the loan. Soon, my father was in serious difficulty. So he tried to increase his practice. He had built up a clientele of ladies in the district, but they were not keen to see him except in the mornings, or possibly between the hours of four and six, as any other appointment interfered grievously with their At Homes and Dinners.' Hetty shook her head. 'Most of them were not truly ill, of course: nothing ailed them that could not be treated with a dose of beef tea or some cod liver oil, though my father became adept at prescribing the aforementioned in complicated sachets – like the bank and the speculator but on a much smaller scale, he too had an arrangement with an apothecary which was to their mutual profit. And those who were ill usually sought to conceal this from their husbands, so again, they were loath to have the doctor in the house except in mid-morning, when even the most idle of this city's bankers could be relied on to have gone into the office before returning for lunch.'

'That does sound very difficult,' I agreed, trying to imagine what it would be like to have a father who went out to work each day in pressed clothes. I knew all too well how his leather medical bag would smell, but this took me back to the weeks before I lost my mother, and so I hauled my thoughts back to the present.

'But this is not the end of it. For he became weary, and his patients became restive. My father was not as attentive towards them as he once was, they complained. He was distracted, impatient even, and looked in need of a physician himself. So fewer and fewer of them recommended him to their friends over tea. At least, so he thought. In truth, his banker had let it be known that the good doctor who was so solicitous to their wives in their absence was having financial difficulties. At the time the rumours began this was not true, though soon enough it was.'

'A self-fulfilling prophecy,' I offered.

'Yes,' said Hetty, looking at me with a new admiration.

In truth I was giving her tale only half an ear, having seen where it led as soon as Hetty mentioned the connection between the bank and the speculator. Such allegiances were the stock of Isaiah's sermons; to him the entire edifice of the Kingdom was a web of corruption the scale of which now extended far beyond the bounds of Christendom. My thoughts were stretched between Hetty's story and what I would tell Isaiah of my absence when I saw him again. I decided I would tell him that I had set out for a farm where we had rested on our journey to London, but like Joseph on his way to Bethlehem, I had got lost, and had not been able to locate the exact place. When I had understood that the barn represented a sort of Canaan to me, (see how desperately I was concocting from the Old and New Testaments!), I had accepted work at the first farm that would take me. I realised that if I were to have a hope of convincing Isaiah, I should have to go out beyond Moorfields one Sunday to remind myself of the countryside. It did not occur to me that unlike even a parlour maid, I would not have the leisure of an entire day to myself once a month. It did not occur to me either that I would not be at liberty simply to leave this house and return to my printing once Isaiah had been released.

'And so –' said Hetty portentously, sensing perhaps that my attention was waning, 'he has an acquaintance with women's bodies. There were even some who said –', and here she coloured, though more with pride than with shame, 'that some of his ladies paid him well for his special services.'

And so you have followed his example, you looby, I thought, out of a bizarre admiration for him blended with desperation. If she did well here, he could quit the Hulks. I wished that Isaiah was in prison for something as simple, and I understood why Hetty was willing to sacrifice so much for her father, for I would have done the same for Isaiah.

'And your father performed these examinations, then?' I said, trying to stop my teeth chattering.

'Oh yes,' she said, putting her arms round me. 'It became quite the fashion, you know, presenting a certificate of purity to one's future husband, as signed by my father.'

'But – how could he tell?'

She sighed, as if I had just asked a question as obvious as 'Where is the heart located?' and raised her eyes to heaven as if remembering a recitation. 'There is a covering of skin which is ruptured on the first encounter. Or as often as not, long before the first time, by some violent activity such as horse riding.' Mother Cooper's earlier question about physical activity now made more sense to me. 'And my father became skilled in resealing the vessel, as he put it. It is a simple matter of a stitch or two.'

I tried to put out of my mind the vision of a man with pipe tobacco on his breath advancing towards my privates with a needle and thread.

Hetty leaned sideways, her breath hot on my cheek. 'He did this for me, two weeks since, just before he knew he was going to be carted off to prison again. That is the time he reckoned I would need to heal.'

'Your father knows you are here?'

'Oh yes,' she said, as if she had gone off to run an errand at the bakery. 'But he said I should not simply make myself into a wage slave; I should try to find a husband, if I could. He knows how much I hate dull bank clerks and fumbling quacks, and these were the only respectable men I ever met. Here we shall encounter an altogether better class of man.'

Unable to comprehend a father who would countenance such a thing, I turned my mind to the mechanics of what she had told me. 'But what of your monthly – visit?' I fumbled for the correct term, the one which would not provoke more harsh laughter.

'I wondered that, at first,' she said, her voice rounder with kindness now. 'But he said the blood flows from a different source. That's a nice way of thinking of it, wouldn't you say? I like the idea of my private parts as a river, meandering this way and that.'

This sounded more to me like the description of a balloon than a river, but I nodded in agreement. 'So he will rummage about inside us?' I said.

'Yes, he will, and you'd better get used to it, for he won't be the last, and the others will go much further. *Much further.*' Her expression changed; I soon learned that her thoughts were like stones that disturbed the stillness of her face, and I dared not ask any more.

Mother Cooper called for us, and we scuttled barefoot down the corridor. The marble stairs were so cold we skittered over them as if they were hot coals. I thought over Hetty's story. I stopped for a moment, imagining what Isaiah would say if he could see me, barefoot in Sodom with a girl whose father had given her his blessing to sell herself.

As it turned out, Dr Lutter had already arrived; it became a familiar trick of Mother Cooper's, to make something which had already happened or was about to happen sound fantastically improbable and far off. The doctor was altogether an anonymous man, the kind I was likely to have passed dozens of times a day on Cheapside. If I had given him any thought at all, I would have assumed that he was nothing more sinister than one of the dull clerks

Hetty was so keen to avoid.

Hetty had lain down on a table with her feet flat on it and her knees up, and began such a liturgy of questions about what was required of her that I would have judged her an innocent half-wit, had I not heard her description of her father's business.

Mother Cooper cut her short: 'Anyone would think you had no idea what it was for,' she said, interrupting the doctor's explanation of where he had to insert the strange instrument he was holding, which looked like a cross between a blunt knife and a lorgnette.

'Would you like me to warm it for you, child?' he enquired, holding the circular instrument in front of his face as if he was preparing to blow on it.

'Ooh, no, sir,' said Hetty, 'I should prefer it cold, I should not like to be any trouble.'

Remembering what she had said of her father, I was convinced that I was about to fall into a fit of nervous giggling. The thought that it would go worse for me if I laughed calmed me, for I doubted that anyone would take me for the ninny that Hetty was playing so well.

The device disappeared inside her, and I watched out of the corner of my eye as Hetty flinched and reared up from the bed. The doctor nodded to Mother Cooper, who signalled her satisfaction with a grunt. She placed her hand under Hetty's arched back, saying, 'Mind you do this the next time you feel something hard thrust inside you, and you will do well. Pull yourself in, so' – and here she clenched her fist and waved it over at me – 'and you will do even better. That is the way to keep a client, yes indeed.'

For as long as she spoke, the doctor had his back to her, busying himself with wiping his instrument, and I was convinced that he found her observations as unpleasant as I did.

Mother Cooper stepped towards me. 'Hoist your legs, and I will hold them,' she said. I had not imagined that she would have a part to play in this beyond waiting to hear the doctor's opinion of the quality of us, her new livestock. The prospect of her touching me was worse than that of being examined by the doctor.

I lifted my knees, parting them a little, my back straining with the effort of keeping them up. I knew it would be easier if I lifted them higher, but I worried that too much enthusiasm would make a Mary Magdalene of me. At that moment I realised that I had no idea what I looked like down there; what if the doctor found some fault with me that no man would ever look on without revulsion? As if she had divined my anxiety, Mother Cooper moved to the bottom of the bed and peered between my legs.

The doctor must have seen that I was afraid, for he said, 'There is nothing here for you to fear, of that I am sure,' and he inserted his instrument, which held me drum-taut while he looked and poked. I gripped the sides of the bed so hard that the Red Sea's parting waves could not have swept me away, imagining that my insides were like the cave of Adullam. In this way I took my mind off the doctor's pokings. They were not painful exactly, but I felt I was being stabbed all the same.

'Only a few cobwebs,' said Mother Cooper, hawking when her laughter unsettled her phlegm. The doctor removed his instrument and returned me to my darkness. I glanced up at the ceiling to where there were in fact a number of cobwebs; this was not a room used for entertaining, and so was not deemed to be worthy of cleaning. The doctor said nothing, but he placed his hand momentarily on my calf. I wondered what crooked path had brought this quiet man to Mother Cooper's door.

'Thank you, Doctor,' said Mother Cooper, as he left while

still closing his bag. He paused at the door, looking as though he was about to say something, but then he was gone.

'Now,' she ordered, clapping her hands together, 'we must get down to business. The only question that remains is how soon you can begin to earn your keep.'

6

MOTHER COOPER GAVE US a choice: either we could wait to be measured for bespoke dresses, an operation that would require a minimum of two days' delay; or we could hire one of the dresses we had tried on that afternoon and join the other girls in the salon that evening. Despite Mother Cooper's prompting, neither of us wanted to be launched into the salon so soon: I was hatching a powerful dread of the consequences of the life into which I had stumbled, while Hetty turned up her nose at the idea of a borrowed dress. Then Hetty discovered that we would have to spend a further two or three nights locked in our attic room if we were not admitted to the salon – and we would be charged rent for the privilege. Needless to say, the rent of our room for those three nights was slightly more extortionate than the sum that would be deducted for the use of our dresses, illustrating two of the principles according to which Mother Cooper ran her establishment: that we must be encouraged to work by all means possible; and that we should be given the impression at all times that we were fortunate to be there, should be grateful, and should therefore accept with docility that we would find ourselves out of pocket at the end of each quarter.

'I will have no truck with these ingrate deliberations,'

Mother Cooper said, as she bundled us both to our garret, hurrying us with a few painful prods in our lower backs. 'If you wish to fester in sloth, then so be it, but I will not provide a bounty on indolence.'

'We could leave this place,' I whispered, once we had listened to Mother Cooper's heavy tread descending the stairs. We had not encountered another soul in this part of the house. When Hetty did not reply, I said, 'We could walk to Moorfields, take a cart into the countryside, and find a farmer I used to know.' Here I halted, for if Hetty were to entrust herself to my care, it was wrong of me to say that I knew where this place was, when all I knew was that it was somewhere between London and Preston. And this realisation made me feel all the more desperate.

Hetty took advantage of my hesitation. 'Please do not make me leave,' she said. 'Unlike you, I have some experience of these places, though it is only based on what my father has told me. And really, the life need not be so bad. The guests are Gentlemen after all, and this place is so grand that it imposes elevated behaviour on them, in the way that cathedrals impose decorum and silence on the rabble.'

'It is not the building which imposes fear of the Lord,' I said, unable to contain myself at the absurdity of Hetty's comparison, 'it is the Lord Himself. And while we are on the topic, my stepfather has also told me of these places, and no amount of gentlemanliness could redeem us from them.'

Hetty's eyes darkened and narrowed, as they did when she became interested in a subject. 'What is your stepfather's profession?' she asked.

'He is a printer by trade,' I said. 'But by calling he is a preacher. And though his listeners' arses be only perched on planks in a lowly loft, they manifest enough reverence to make a cathedral of it.'

Hetty nodded. 'He is a Radical, then.'

I was surprised that she knew the term, and it cheered me that she might not have soft curds for brains after all.

Before I could go on, Hetty's eyed widened again and filled with tears. 'Oh Nell, I know that we have been here together for only a few hours, but I cannot bear to stay without you, and I must stay, really I must!'

'Why must you stay?' I enquired, as she launched herself at me.

'My father,' she said, whispering loudly as she warmed my chest with her tears. She smelled of what I later learned was rose-water and also of stale sweat.

'Will he be ruined, if you do not stay here?' I could imagine it all: how he was careful to tell her stories of the genteel life that the ladies led in places such as this, how immodesty could be mended with a stitch or two, all interspersed with hand-wringing and even tears about the parlous state of their finances. He would not have needed to suggest that she come here: one as simple as Hetty would have congratulated herself on having made this sorry patchwork out of the pieces he scattered in front of her.

I held her closer, wondering why she did not say more about her mother, until I realised that I had not said a word of mine, and soon I was crying too.

She pulled away from me. 'You are a kind soul, Nell,' she said. 'A feeling soul. So will you stay?'

I nodded, and with this she leapt for the door as if she were a child who had been allowed into the nursery to open its Christmas presents. She turned and held out her hand for us to go and find Mother Cooper together.

Nurseries come to mind here because we were to discover one on our way to find Mother Cooper. We had descended one flight and turned right down the corridor, past the rooms directly below our garret, hoping for some clue as to Mother Cooper's whereabouts.

'We should go straight down to the kitchen,' I suggested. 'This is where she is most likely to be, and it will go worse for us if we are caught roaming round the house.' In fact, I was just as concerned about what we might see as I was at the prospect of being seen, but I did not say this.

'There will be some stairs at the end of this corridor,' Hetty said. 'All these houses are the same. And Mother Cooper will be all the happier for our having come the back way.'

The doors were all closed and it was curiously quiet; I later learned that the girls on this staircase tended to have fewer afternoon visitors, and so spent this time resting or attending to themselves; even now the thought of an afternoon nap on a silk eiderdown seems a luxury it is impossible to imagine that I ever enjoyed. I used to think of this when I ran my hand over a new batch of vellum destined for our better prints, for vellum's smooth life-warmth manages to be cool at the same time, just as silk does; and I was glad that printing is an honest pleasure, even if the plates were not entirely salubrious.

Only one door was ajar, the one at the end of the corridor, near the narrow wooden staircase which Hetty had predicted would lead to the kitchen. (A house of this size was as unfamiliar to me as the Israelites' route from Egypt, but thanks to her father, Hetty had seen more of the world.) A movement made me step back, until I realised that it was a wooden horse rocking slightly in the draught from the open window. It was a mighty thing, as tall as the horses I had seen on a carousel in London Fields. With its nostrils flared, it would most likely terrify any child who came near it. I was wondering where the nurse was who would lift the poor creature on when a girl appeared and gave the horse another push; it was she and not the chill air that had caused its movement.

'Hello,' I said. 'Do you live here?'

'Oh yes,' she said. Her voice was slow and oddly flat, but her brown eyes flashed the blank knowingness that I had already identified in Hetty; this was no children's playground.

'I would invite you in for tea,' she said in a tone that suggested she would be more likely to place a dish of Earl Grey in front of the horse, 'but Mother Cooper would not allow it.'

While she issued her non-invitation, I took in some of the accoutrements on the wall behind her: a species of climbing-frame with ropes attached, and a collection of perhaps three dozen crops, racquets, bats and canes, many with leather attached and a few with ribbon or silk.

'Would you like to borrow something?' she asked, because I could not help staring. 'For I doubt Mother Cooper will want you in here. You are too big.' The familiar slow, flat yet precise tone; this is what becomes of simpletons like Meg when they do not have family to take care of them.

And then it came to me: *I am living in one of my prints. I am in a Hell of my own creation, an infernal tableau of scenes which I have helped Isaiah publish.* I gripped the banister hard, surprised at the cold metal of a stud under the smooth railing, and stared down the centre of the staircase, watching its rings descend two more flights. 'No, but we are looking for Mother Cooper,' said I, 'and I will be sure not to mention that I have seen you,' I added, turning for the stairs.

'I am Mabel,' she called after us. 'I am fifteen, and I have no monthly curse. And I can't hardly hear you when you turn away from me, for I need to read your lips.'

Hetty remained near the main staircase. 'She is clearly simple,' she said dismissively, as soon as we had continued our descent. Hetty sighed. 'Though I'll wager that men pay dearly for the privilege of ordering their pleasures from a woman in a child's form. And with no curse, she can work every night, too. She must be Mother Cooper's darling.'

I skimmed my hand over the banister all the way, so convinced was I that I would fall. 'She is deaf, Hetty. And if you had seen what was in that room, you would not be so envious,' I countered.

'That equipment will not all be destined for use on her,' Hetty retorted. 'Or at least, so I imagine,' she said, with less authority in her tone.

'That poor child – but imagine too those that inflict such things upon her. To be a torturer is worse for the spirit,' I said, though I was silenced by the sight of Mother Cooper's head. As she came into view, I noticed that her hair was thinning on top and that white was visible beneath the strange red she had dyed it. Most likely she was once in this trade herself: it was impossible to imagine any man wanting to be alone with her, though she was I suppose no larger than the Queen Caroline of the cartoons, and Caroline had beaus aplenty. Foreign and younger than her most of them looked, too. Or at least, that was the way the artists had etched them.

'So,' Mother Cooper said, 'what have you decided?' There was a plump satisfaction in her tone which told us that she already knew what we would say.

Hetty and I looked at each other. 'We will work,' Hetty said.

Mother Cooper, narrowed her eyes as she looked at me, before returning to Hetty. 'You are a gentleman's daughter, are you not?'

Hetty dipped her head and blinked, the sweep of her eyelashes as demure as a curtseying debutante's skirt. 'I am.'

'Then you will entertain Sir David Fairfax, a wealthy man who has asked for an intelligent woman.'

Hetty bowed to Mother Cooper.

'And Nell, Sir Robin Everley is a man whose tastes will not, I wager, be met by this establishment for long, unless you can redeem us. You will suit him well enough, as long as you don't preach at him or fall to your knees only to pray.'

My stomach turned to whey at the thought of the wall of implements we had just witnessed. And I wondered why on earth she was entertaining the idea that I might be able to persuade a man to stay who was about to take his custom elsewhere.

❦

Now it had been decided that we would be 'presented' that night, Mother Cooper became agitated again. 'What are you staring at?' she demanded, the fairer bristles on her chin catching the light as she turned to me. 'You had better not look so half-witted this evening, when you will have a very important guest to entertain. I have warned him that I have not had the time to school you in the art of fine conversation.' It was impossible to imagine Mother Cooper's talk ranging beyond which shops in Smithfield sold the best sausages, but of course I did not say this, and instead tried to look downcast at having missed out on this element of my education.

'But we do not have time for this now,' she continued, giving me a stab in the small of the back which sent tears to my eyes. 'You should be upstairs, preparing yourselves for when Sir Robin arrives.'

Mother Cooper opened doors wide enough for a carriage to pass through, and snapped 'Come on!' to Hetty. It was clear that I was to wait, and that Mother Cooper would communicate with me only if it was absolutely necessary – she had decided that I was Hetty's appendage. I glimpsed a double bed twice the width of a printing press, and wondered if I would ever feel the honest stain of ink on my fingers again, but the pang was dulled by the prospect of Hetty and I having an entire room just for ourselves. The room I shared with Meg was about the size of the fireplace, or so I reckoned in the time it took Mother Cooper to hold my sleeve. 'You are elsewhere,' she said.

In the moments before Mother Cooper reappeared, opening and closing the doors behind her like some grotesque factotum, I felt more alone than I ever had before, more even than on the day we had buried my mother. And although Meg is strange, and many was the time I had scolded her for trailing behind me, I saw that she had brought me the comfort of a shadow.

You are elsewhere. That was what Mother Cooper had said. Perhaps she had no intention of wasting a night of Sir Anybody's time with me, and planned instead to sell me down some gin-alley north of Seven Dials, a place Isaiah called Seven Devils. Some say that even its street plans are not to be trusted, since the surveyors did not linger over their mappings of its myriad courtyards, so afraid were they of the residents of the teeming tenements. And it was unlikely that most of those residents would ever have cause to point out the surveyors' mistakes: it was profitable for them to exist, for a bewildered traveller was one who would glad give a boy a penny for guidance, and was an easy mark for a criminal.

No – I must take my leave of Mother Cooper now, I decided: before she could argue that I owed her anything, and while Hetty was too entranced with her new chamber to notice my slipping away. Mother Cooper would find her another companion soon enough, one who was as willing to become a fallen girl as she was.

'I hope you are not going to stare at Sir Robin Fairfax as if the bottom's fallen out of your face,' Mother Cooper said, at the same time as I blurted 'I thank you for your kindness, Mother Cooper, but I must –'

'Nonsense, girl,' she said, taking my hand and squeezing it. Her palms were cold, and drier than I expected given the sheen on her nose which even hefty dabs of powder could not stanch. 'You will do well here, and I will see that no harm will come to you.'

Am I to live here after all? I thought, looking down the hall. Light garlanded it, unlike the darker upstairs corridor, and the carpets glowed the purest red and blue I had ever seen. *You have never been further from being cast into the pit of St Giles; how can you disappear from here, from all this warmth and light?* And my desire to see Meg abated then because physical comfort and a dash of maternal kindness had been bestowed on me.

Mother Cooper led me into the room next to Hetty's. It had the same voluptuous bed and a slightly threadbare blue patterned carpet which gave the room a settled, gentle air. I would have been content to sleep on the carpet, but as it was, it was all I could do not to leap onto the bed.

'You will be able to help each other with your costumes, I don't doubt,' remarked Mother Cooper, gesturing towards the dress I had tried on earlier, with its bone carapace in front of it. 'Just a light corset,' she said, patting her stomach ruefully. 'You have no need of serious upholstery, and in any case, tight stays are a bugger to undo. There's not many gentlemen who will want to take the trouble. And Hetty, you must attend to Nell's hair, or the straggling frizz that passes for it. And you will need to help each other dress, all the same.'

And we did.

'I am going to leave here a Lady,' Hetty said, as we knotted each other into our corsets. My fingers were more clumsy, but their tips were hardened from my work at the press. Hetty was more nimble, but her trussing-up of me was punctuated with many 'ows' and much sucking of digits. We were wearing the dresses we had tried on only a few hours before, and Hetty was even more excited now that she had escaped Mother Cooper's gaze; her jiggling about and turning to the mirror combined with the effort of working out how to tie her stays made me quite seasick – at that time I had never sailed, but felt I knew enough of it from Isaiah's descriptions.

Hetty's golden toe kicked mine. Her feet did not look incarcerated in her shoes, which I took as a sign of how ready she was to assume the role that was being thrust upon us, and how ill-fitting I was in every way by comparison.

'Listen to me,' she said, taking hold of my arm as she always did when she wished to reinforce her point. 'I am not going to make a parade of my past, not for you, not for anyone. I am going to wear a silk dress and gavotte my way into a fortune, and no man will take me with tears making cart-tracks down my face. So do not make yourself my conscience, Nell Wingfield, or else I will –' And then she stopped and threw her arms round me. 'I cannot threaten you with anything,' she sighed, all the tautness gone from her voice, 'for I will need you far more than you need me, that I know already. So I will be kind to you, because I will never be strong enough to be alone. Silence shouts in my ears, you know. I hope there will be music here!'

'You are pinching me, Hetty,' I cried.

She ran to the dressing table – I got used to her conversation flitting about like this, but at first I found it jarring.

'Rouge!' she continued. 'Come and look.' The carpet was thick and warm under my feet (for I had slipped off my shoes at the first opportunity); I felt as if I was running across the back of some great supine beast.

Hetty smeared something cold and momentarily heavy

onto my cheeks. My childish colour had returned, and at the same time as I had gained my mother's dramatic cheekbones. I was at once older and younger.

'You are beautiful,' observed Hetty, in the matter-of-fact way I used to describe the quality of an etched plate. 'Or at least, you will be. You have one of those faces that men will linger over and admire from afar, like Mrs Perdita Robinson.' Mrs Robinson had been an actress on Drury-lane when she became George's mistress. That had been forty years ago, when the King was still just a prince, and his conquests made women the toast of the town and not one of a scandalous retinue.

'No, I am not,' I said. 'Beauty is terrifying, like gazing on the burning bush, and I am just an inky-handed printer. The only thing that burns about me is the colour of my hair, and that is already fading.'

'Don't be a fool,' said Hetty. It is in places like these that printers' daughters snare princes. Why else would we be here?'

I was about to tell her that I had come here because I thought I would be doing charitable work in return for my board, but I could see how ridiculous this would sound. 'I look like my mother,' I said instead, and the angular face I saw in the mirror made me understand why the men Isaiah drew to him had always treated my mother with a certain deference. They had been jovial with her sister Agnes, even making so free as to pat her ample backside on their way out of chapel. There had been nothing ample about my mother – apart from her hair and her spirit – and these had made men more careful with her rather than less.

'Talking to you is queer,' said Hetty. 'It's like listening to the Bible set in London: you make Our Lord seem so close, I wouldn't be surprised if he was one of Mother Cooper's gentlemen.' She smiled, her eyes widening in expectation of my response to this blasphemy. I asked her about her mother instead.

'She left us, when I was a baby,' she said. 'My father made many efforts to find her, but she had simply disappeared. So we do not talk about her.'

I soon learned that her mother's departure was a cell door in her heart that had clanged shut some time ago, and her father had not been willing to prise it open. He was, I decided, a strange father indeed: Isaiah was not my kin, but he had at least given me a proper trade, even if it was not an entirely respectable one.

In the few minutes that followed, neither of us spoke, and the sounds we made while pulling on and fastening our new clothes were like small animals scurrying about.

'That colour is so fine on you,' she said, glancing at my dress for a moment while gazing at herself in the mirror and marvelling at how the folds of the silk caught the light. 'Look!' she said. 'Is this not like the sea?'

'A stormy sea, perhaps. Have you ever seen one?' I asked, hauling myself into the currents on which she wished to steer the conversation, and casting off the idea that she would be a friend with whom I would share my memories of my mother. I was right about this: she never did ask me, but given that she had no mother of her own, I did not hold it against her that she had no desire to hear about mine. Soon I was grateful to her, for I saw the wisdom of forgetting and inhabiting the present instead.

'No,' she replied, 'but not having seen the sea is an advantage, because I can imagine it without worrying about what it is really like!'

I was about to tell her that I hadn't either, and all I knew of it came from Isaiah's stories of his years in the navy, but her head was too full of shot silk for her to listen to a story about a man she had never met.

7

THOUGH I HAD BEEN brought up in the company of radicals, democrats and Republicans, I found myself shamefully aflutter at the prospect of entertaining a gentleman. As we entered the drawing room at eight that evening, I was also powerfully afraid. While the sundry bewigged and coiffed 'ladies' of the salon introduced themselves, many wearing so much powder that there was no way of judging if they were thirteen or a hundred, it was impossible for me to pay them much heed. My imagination veered between Sir David Fairfax as a Goliath among men with Solomon's head on him; and Sir David Fairfax as the many-headed monster I saw once in a doom painting in a Roman Catholic Church.

I could not take in the characters who were twirling about the salon, apart from one woman who stopped in front of me and took my wrist with a grip so cold and hard it made me think of Isaiah in his handcuffs. The fine cracks in her powder made her face look like a dried-up riverbed. She told me she was called Suky, and that she had been a resident for ten years. Though her hair was plaited girlishly, her eyes looked centuries old. Ten years in this place! I could not imagine it.

She steered me towards a clutch of bottles on a tray woven of fine raffia and silver. 'This tray is one of Mother Cooper's favourites,' she said, her voice low in my ear as she handed me a glass. 'She tells the gentlemen that it sums up this establishment: sophisticated, like all this silver weaving, but natural too.' She laughed sharply, and her breath was harshly fragrant, as if she had dipped her tongue in perfume, but there was the stale scent of gin underneath it, which reminded me of Mother Cooper, and it was this that decided me – I did not trust Suky.

I refused the glass, remembering all Isaiah's stories of men who survived their years on board ship with a slug of rum as a crutch, only to find that they were hobbled without it once they returned to dry land. One day I would leave this strange world, and I did not want to have a thirst for gin to tie me to it.

When I told Suky my name, she complimented me on choosing such a fine one. 'Like Nell Gywnne,' she remarked, nodding and clearly revising the level of regard in which she held me, 'a name which is perhaps more historical now than it is ruthless in its ambition, but which will flatter Tories who frequent this place all the same.' It was all I could do not to laugh, for she rolled her eyes back in her head while she recited this in a way that convinced me it was something one of her Gentlemen had said to her.

'It is my real name.'

'What is real?' she said, gesturing towards a grey cat curled up in front of the fire. 'That cat answers to perhaps a dozen different names. The girl who named him left, and no one could remember what she had called him. And we could not agree on a name, so we have all chosen a different one for him! Why, he has more names than he has lives!'

My sorrow for the cat must have registered on my face. 'Why did the girl leave?' I asked.

'Oh, she married. Or she might have died.' Suky thought for a moment. 'Most likely died. No one ever leaves here!'

'I will,' I said. I was about to explain to her that this was like a cave to me, a time in the wilderness, when the light cascading from the chandelier behind Suky's head reminded me of how absurd this would sound.

Suky saw a man who was bulging out of a naval uniform and turned away without another word. I looked for Hetty. She was standing with a girl in a long frilly pink skirt who had a waist so tiny it was impossible to believe that she had any vitals inside her. She was standing with her leg turned straight out like one of Tom's set squares, and she raised her other foot on a point and twirled about. Hetty was determined to copy her, except it was her arm that she was holding out, and her glass at the end of it, with the result that she slopped some amber-coloured drink onto the pale fronds of a green carpet. So set was she on being the belle of this ball that she had not troubled to wait until the gentlemen had arrived before she began her campaign, and already I could see that the other girls were distracted from a dispute about whether or not the wearing of wigs was attractive into forming an army of disapproval of Hetty. She would not fare well with Mother Cooper if she continued to exhibit herself like this, and this made me all the more fearful, for I had already come to see Hetty as my protector.

So intent was she on learning to pirouette that she failed to notice the arrival of our Gentlemen. I could pretend that we had to wait all evening for them, playing cards and attempting to prevent Hetty from becoming even more tipsy. In truth, the Gentlemen were curious to see the new girls Mother Cooper had procured for them, and so they were early. The clock had only recently struck nine when Sir David Fairfax and Sir Robin Everley were announced.

The other girls shifted into two groups: those with wigs and those without. I thought those with natural, dressed hair were by far the more attractive, but of course I did not volunteer this; I found the other women as terrifying as I would an exotic beast loose on Piccadilly. There were nine women not counting us. (I say women, but their ages were impossible to judge.) Five of them, Suky included, circled round the two gentlemen, with so much fluttering of their fans, thrusting out of their trussed-up chests and general cooing that Sir Robin could be heard making playful comparisons to the pigeons of the new Trafalgar Square. Such was the general clamour that I wondered if there had been some mistake, and the Gentlemen were not destined for us at all. I knew I would never be able to twitter and preen like the other girls, and if that were required of me, I would be back on the streets soon enough. Part of me was relieved at the prospect of escape, but part of me feared it – where would I go? What life could I make for Meg and myself which did not involve service or sewing, neither of which would earn us more than a farthing before we were sacked?

'You will not find these new girls as diseased as those pigeons, Sir Robin,' said Mother Cooper, who came in at that moment.

In fact the only specimen of diseased aspect was Sir Robin himself. He was of middling height, with a taut paunch and a thinning blond pate. He stooped, and this along with the narrow cast of his eyes gave him an insinuating air. His companion, Sir David Fairfax, was well over six feet, so tall that he too had developed a stoop, as if he was forever ducking through a low door. He also had a habit of wrapping his arms around his frock-coat, which gave him the appearance of bracing himself against a gale. I felt an affinity with his awkwardness, with the result that I was more fearful of my own fate than I was of Hetty's. Until that night, the only human I had ever been alone with in the dark was Meg, and what I saw of Sir Robin did not bode well.

Sir David had closed his eyes at Mother Cooper's remark

then looked at me, and for a moment I was convinced that he had as many misgivings about being in this salon as I did – certainly he looked as out of place as I felt – until I recalled that he could remedy his unease by leaving, that his money had bought him a room in this house just as it had provided him with a lavish roof over his curiously square head. I looked away, and watched Sir Robin, noting that something hard glinted in his eyes that even merriment could not mask.

Hetty had her back to me; Sir Robin had already made his way over to her which did not bode well for tonight's pairing, and her face shone so intensely as she gazed up at him that you would think that his ruddy visage was a beacon. 'Ah, but the size of the roobies in India,' he was saying, as I backed out of the drawing room, closing the door behind me. I realised there was a third man with them, and he had noticed me leave, partly because he had little else to occupy him. He did not seem inclined to talk to the 'ladies', and he did not did not take anything to drink.

The air was cooler in the corridor, and my skin prickled at this, and with the elation I felt with every step I took towards the back stairs, towards my old clothes – no, not my *old* clothes, I chided myself: they were simply my clothes, and I longed for their dingy fustian more intensely than I had fancied the silks only a few hours earlier. I might have been tempted, but after all even the Lord Himself had allowed the devil to show Him what might be His if He renounced himself and joined Lucifer. It is true that there is no mention in the Bible of whether the Lord suffered Himself to be arrayed in fine clothes before He climbed the mountain, but then He was not a young woman living in London. And as Isaiah often said, who is to know what Jesus Himself would have done if He had lived in 1820? Isaiah thought He would have been a journeyman carpenter from Essex or the West Country who would have sat on the steps of the Royal Exchange and made fun of the Mercers and Stock Brokers.

As I reached the next landing, I gazed at Mabel's door, but no light shone out from under it. One thing was clear, I decided: Jesus would have thought that London was no haven for the slow-witted. What sort of life would Meg have had, if she had not her family to protect her from a fate like Mabel's?

The cold on the top floor had not receded, but all the same I began to be anxious that if I did not get out of my dress soon, I would risk leaving sweat stains on it, and I did not doubt that Mother Cooper would pursue me with a pack of Sir Robin's hunting hounds if my departure cost her anything more than a farthing of embarrassment. I opened the door, to find an empty room. I was sure that Mother Cooper had told us that our dresses would be stored up there, but I could not be certain of the room, so I went into the corridor and tried the next handle: locked. I scurried along, knocking now before I tried to open the doors, and found them all shut fast. I returned to the one open door, and recognised two imprints on the bed, where Hetty and I had sat and talked. I looked behind the door, and could have fainted with relief when I saw the wardrobe. On discovering it was empty, I still refused to panic – it was most likely that that they resided downstairs, in our new quarters. It was silly of me not to have thought of that first.

I hurried down, taking the marble stairs this time. If anyone asked what I was doing, I resolved I would say that I was looking for the privy and had got lost. I hesitated outside my new bedroom door, convinced I had heard someone moving about inside. When the silence yielded nothing more than the straining of silk as I breathed, I turned the handle, but the door was locked. I rested my forehead on the smooth paint. I could not even run away in my petticoats, for everything

I owned I had taken off, and it would not have surprised me if my corset were worth more than my dress, with all the hours it must have taken to sew the bones and hooks into it. The voices from downstairs became louder: the salon door had opened. A scuffy pat-pat-pat-pat of leather soled-slippers approached. The steps were light and I could not hear any puffing, so it was not Mother Cooper. I decided that it was best to stay where I was, and then I knew I would have to return to the salon. If I was arrested as a common thief in a harlot's dress, I was no use to anyone, and I would never be able to look at Isaiah for the shame of it.

'Nell!' Hetty appeared at the top of the landing. 'You must come back! You are missed.' She glanced behind her. 'Mother Cooper is looking for you.' Her smile flagged a little and she held out her hand, as if to say *I am purposely not asking what you are doing, because I need you to stay here with me*; and this reminded me of how much I wished Meg would do that, and I am ashamed to say that my resolve to return to Meg faltered: I had probably been right to leave in the first place, I told myself, and Meg would not regret my departure. Here in Hetty was someone who needed me in the way my sister never could.

As we returned to the parlour door, Mother Cooper appeared. 'Hetty, go in, child,' she said. 'Sir David will take supper with you in your room.'

'*Child!*' Hetty mouthed to me over Mother Cooper's shoulder, pushing her chest out a little, and there was in fact something so childlike in her preening that I considered asking Mother Cooper how she could call Hetty *child* and send her to a man of perhaps forty.

As I stepped over the threshold, I saw Sir Robin, sprawled in an armchair, examining his boots, turning his left foot this way and that so that their sheen caught the light. He looked as though his feet were encased in dark brown glass. Isaiah had told me that military men spend hours polishing them just so, in order that the blood might run straight off them without leaving a stain.

Mother Cooper grabbed my wrist. It was a struggle for her to whisper in my ear, so she pulled me down to her. Her breath was still heavy with alcohol, but now it was mixed with a complicated sweet heaviness which I later discovered was marzipan. Whether I would have liked the sickliness of almond paste had I not first encountered it on Mother Cooper's breath, I will never know, but now I cannot bear its associations with her.

'You did not find your dress, I take it?' she said, her voice slick with angry amusement.

'I –.' I managed not to say 'How did you know that?' and did not have the stomach for the lie of 'I got lost,' though I now needed the privy and so would have been able to make a pretence of having looked for it without sounding too dishonest.

She poked me hard in the back. 'Too holy to invent a lie, are you, preacher's foundling?'

At this I faced her, my cheeks feeling taut while my stomach turned to cold cabbage.

She smiled, seeing that she had worried me. 'You wonder how I know this about you. Make no mistake, you are not important enough to me to warrant sending out my spies. No, Mistress Nell: one of the gentlemen here recognised you. At least, he thought he did, and your coming over all semolina-like at the mention of it will confirm his suspicions.'

'Was it Sir Robin?' I asked.

'There are more men in the universe than those two,' she said.

To listen to her earlier that day, I would not have thought there were, though of course I did not say this. I now noticed that four more gentlemen of eerily similar appearance had arrived in the salon. I later learned that they were the Duke of Portrose and his three sons; all had the same prominent sandy eyebrows and sloping shoulders. They were making more conversation with each other than they were with the inmates of the house, for inmates was from this moment how I viewed us, and as such, I felt a strange fellowship with Isaiah, and thanked God that my brother and sister remained free.

'You have the look of the bolter about you,' she said. 'But remember, if you leave here before I bid you, I will have you before the magistrates for theft, and any one of these fine gentlemen will witness your presence here.'

I doubted whether any of them would like to advertise their patronage of this place, and Mother Cooper must have seen the question passing across my face. 'Make no mistake,' she continued, 'you will not get away with petty larceny: I will make sure your crime will be greater than the theft of five shillings. And if you are not transported, you will feel a rope round your neck which will be a sight less comfortable than that one over there.' She pointed at the thick cream curtain tie. 'Either way, you will never see hide nor hair of your God-bothering half-cocked family again. Now get over there and entertain Sir Robin. I have some business to transact with Mr Edwards. He has brought us some new servants. Italians, by all accounts, but decent workers all the same.' She pointed to the gentleman who had arrived with Sir Robin and Sir David. I had not remarked him much at first, but now I saw how he assessed all who were present, like one of the spies who sat in taverns and noted all that was said. Such a man had helped to convict Isaiah of Blasphemy.

Mother Cooper poked me hard in the side. 'And remember, you are bound for Hell now anyway, so you might as well put on a fine show for Sir Robin before you go.'

My feet slithered on the carpet as Mother Cooper pushed

me away from her. Suky sniggered and said something to a white-faced girl in a dress the colour of squashed blackberries.

Sir Robin continued to examine his boots. As I approached, he rubbed the side of his right foot hard on the carpet. I half expected to see a smear of blood, but all he had left was a faint ridge in the pile.

'We will remain here this evening,' he commanded, without looking up. There was a shinier, darker patch on the top of his head where his wig would have sat earlier in the day, and the sight of this made me less afraid of him. 'One of my horses fell on its way here. It reared up at the sight of some skittering child, and the other horse in the pair tried to move sideways to avoid it, and somehow slipped its harness and fell. Or so the coachman told me. All I saw was one of the pair trampled by the other. And do you know what I thought?'

He looked at me. His eyes were a yellowish green, the colour of white wine. 'I have no idea,' I replied. It occurred to me that I ought to have said Sir, but he did not seem to notice. We had received very little guidance in these matters from Mother Cooper, and I wondered if this was deliberate, in order that we might make mistakes for which we would be fined or in some other manner punished. I felt a coldness pass through me again, and I understood that until I had spent a night in my uncle's house, my life had been remarkably free of physical fear. I had dreaded my mother's death, my family's starvation and Isaiah's imprisonment, but this danger which set a cringing in my heart was something different again.

'I thought,' he said, 'that it was the gentler of the two horses which had been killed, the more innocent one; it had not reared up, but it was the one which was trampled by the other. And I wondered why it was always thus.' Standing up as he said this, he was a shade shorter than me, even in his heels. I took a step backwards. 'For it is always thus, is it not? Upon my word, I fancied that I could see this question forming itself in the horse's eyes as it gazed up at me from the cobbles.'

'Forgive me, but I hope you are wrong, Sir.' I thought of Meg as I said this.

He narrowed his eyes and looked at me more closely. 'Mother Cooper claimed that your friend Hetty was the more spirited one, but I wonder if she is right.'

I stared at the rope which held the curtains fast. 'What spirit I might have had is recently departed, Sir'.

'You are new here, are you not? He smoked, and scraped his boots together as if sharpening a knife. I wondered if I should sit down, but he seemed to enjoy my discomfort in standing before him.

'I am. A week ago, I was as free as one of the sparrows on the Square.'

He sat back in his chair and clasped his hands behind his head. 'But *unlike* the sparrows, you would not have been free to hop about in those private gardens, surely? And are you now, do you think? Does Mother Cooper issue you all with a key? Or would the other residents object to our dear hostess making a Vauxhall Gardens of St James's Square?'

Hetty appeared beside me, with Sir David not far behind. She seemed at home, and he seemed content to be led about. 'Ooh, Sir Robin, what a wonderful idea!' she cooed. 'We could all go to Vauxhall, a catter' – at this Sir David puckered momentarily with laughter – 'and promenade and eat jellies. Let us not wait for the Gardens to come to the Square. Let us go to the Gardens!'

'A catter!' exclaimed Sir David. 'Hetty, it is *à quatre*. Truly, I now cannot banish the image of us promenading down the southerly bank of the Thames in the company of a man carrying a writhing bag of kittens!'

I smiled, though not too broadly, for I could see that Hetty had no appetite to be teased, and I had no idea what *à quatre* meant until Sir David explained it to me a few days later.

'And if a catter does turn up, I'll see to it that he drowns the blasted kittens!' said Sir Robin. 'I'll pay to watch him wring their blasted necks! We could start with that grey thing over there!' His laugh was too high and too loud, and Sir David studied the carpet for the duration of it.

I glanced at Hetty, wondering what she made of this man whose manners must be far worse than her father's, but she was hee-hee-ing almost as much as him.

'Enough of this,' said Sir Robin, his mood changing in an instant. 'We will retire.'

Panicked, I looked to Hetty, for I had been much happier at the prospect of staying in the parlour, as Sir Robin had suggested. But Hetty was trying to engage Sir David in chatter while he shifted from foot to foot.

I peered at the clock on the mantelpiece, struggling to make out the time for the forest of silvery fronds which surrounded the clock face. *All she would have to do is say I stole that, and I would hang,* I thought. It was ten o'clock already – how could so much time have passed? And we had not done anything yet; our night was only beginning. On a normal day, I would be finishing work, or else listening to a sermon, or else asleep. Unlike the printers of cheap political tracts and illegal newspapers, I was seldom at my press all night. I stifled a yawn and wondered how on earth I was to stay awake. I thought again of what Jesus tells us of the faithful servants who were waiting for their master to return, and wished He had recorded what the servants did to keep themselves alert. My mother often said this: the Bible was a good general outline, and all it needed was a woman to come along and add a few instructions.

'Mistress Nell!' Sir Robin kicked my slipper with the toe of his boot.

'Must we retrieve you from whatever far-off plain you are walking o'er?' said Sir David, with a gentleness which reminded me of Tom when he rescued a trembling thrush from the chapel's eaves. I was sorry to leave Sir David, and fearful of what Sir Robin would require of me.

'Might we retire too, Sir David? Hetty enquired, with the innocence of a child who had been promised some treat.

'Of course,' said Sir David with a small bow. Hetty gave a pretty little bob the like of which I could never master – I would surely have collapsed into a gangle of legs if I'd tried. I became aware of someone watching me: it was the Gentleman who had seen me leave the room. He was perched on a window seat, half obscured by the green and gold curtain. He had a glass in his hand, and he raised it to me before smirking into it and taking a sip. I understood that it was he who had told Mother Cooper of my departure upstairs.

Docility, docility, I said to myself, over and over, as Sir Robin led the way back to my room. I tried to erase the image of that poor trodden-down horse that had slipped from its harness, whinnying in terror and pain as its master watched it die.

8

MY NIGHT WITH SIR Robin was not at all as I had imagined it would be.

The following morning he left me at eight, half an hour before Sir David quit Hetty's room, and I tucked myself into the window seat to wait for her. As I watched a man with a limp shouldering a sack of potatoes on his withered side, I reflected that things had taken a turn for the worse. The houses around the square were grand, though their newish perfection made them look as though they had been set there by an unimaginative child who had been distracted by some other game before she had the chance to colour them in.

I gazed at the wide bed behind me, and longed to lie down, but dared not. I felt tired, and I also had the strange discomfort I'd had during my first night at my Aunt Agnes's, of living in alien surroundings. And although it was perhaps as obvious as the hairs on Mother Cooper's upper lip, only then did it dawn on me that I had fled the onslaught of one man – my Uncle John – only to volunteer myself for the attentions of another. Perhaps my uncle had been right after all, when he had held my hair, pressed my face to the pantry door and told me that soon he would take payment in kind for my time under his roof, and I would enjoy settling my debt to him. He had seen the wantonness in me which had set me on the path to Mother Cooper's door.

My head teemed with a plague of such images. What little I had learned of Sir Robin's taste would have made for a fine tableau: Sir Robin unbuttoning his breeches while he bade me pleasure myself with his empty wine bottle. The absurd grotesquery of this caught me somewhere between laughter and tears, and I escaped both by fancying myself an observer of the scene. This made me all the more apt to fumble. I had never thought to pleasure myself in all my short life, for all I had imagined what it would be like to have a man's hands on me. But my hands had been for work, and my bed, such as it was, for sleeping on. Unsatisfied with my efforts, he twirled it about himself, inflicting such pain on me that I feared he would split me in half or else the bottle would shatter inside me.

Then Sir Robin had dozed by the fire for a couple of hours, but I had not dared crawl onto the bed for fear that he might rouse himself to join me. I had seen enough cartoons of the Prince Regent knobbing his mistresses to know what might await me, but there was none of that. As I watched Sir Robin drool on his velvet jacket, I was ashamed to own that had he been Sir David, I might have viewed being alone with him with less dread. As it was, I spent the time nodding off in a winged armchair and then jolting awake, worrying that Sir Robin would stir and expect me to perform in some other bizarre manner, or else fretting about what Tom would be up to, or else about when and how I would be able to send money to Meg. It would go straight into my uncle's pocket, but this might insure her against the worst of his foulness.

He had woken at dawn, as sour of temper as he was of breath, and suggested that I ought to have taken him in my mouth. He fell asleep again immediately while I swept out the cinders as silently as I could. I could not sit still for fear and revulsion, but I lived in a powerful horror of his waking again.

⚜

But once he was gone, I fastened my attentions to another matter: what we would have for breakfast. We had been given little supper the previous evening, and I did not see how I was going to manage to be a sweet and patient listener if I was not fed more often. In the shop or especially working the press, I always had something to occupy my hands, and I missed it. Sir Robin had noticed the grey smudges on my index fingers, and I had shown him the ink stains with some pride. He had forced my fingers downwards with some comment about grubby hands roving in grubby places. He had been most interested in enquiring whether the work we undertook was legal or not, and I had assured him that it was. He did not ask me the name of my shop, nor anything about Isaiah, which I took as a good sign: Isaiah always said that the authorities would make the soberest of texts dance a jig before them if it would put a man in prison, and I did not want to be brewing any more trouble for him. Sir Robin had been keen for me to describe scenes from the most explicit prints we had sold, and seemed more taken with the idea that I might enjoy the depravity of my work than any pleasure he might summon in himself. He insisted that he would punish me for my wantonness, but he could not muster the energy to rise from his chair.

I listened to my stomach grumbling and studied my hands, seeing the faint ink in the fine lines as evidence that less than a fortnight ago, I had been just a girl with an ailing mother who worked with her stepfather in his shop.

⚜

Hetty emerged, in a prettily half-buttoned pale blue dress

which made her look like one of the milk maids on the cups in front of us. She had a look of triumphant coyness, and I knew that she was longing for me to ask her about her night.

'Do you think Mother Cooper will give us an advance on our wages?' I said.

As she took a slice of toast, I saw that whatever had occurred with Sir David had pleased her, and hearing of this would only make my night with Sir Robin seem the more worrying. 'I have been thinking the very same thing: we are going to need far more dresses if we are to keep our gentlemen interested.' She stroked the soft cotton of her house dress as if it was a baby's cheek.

'Aye, you will need a clean one every day, if you are going to smear honey on it like that,' I pointed out.

Hetty withdrew her fingers. 'Thank you, Nell. I was just thinking that it is not simply our dress we will have to change.'

'I am mystified,' I said.

'Do not take this amiss but I was just thinking that if we could combine ourselves, we would be perfect.'

'Would we?' I thought that only God was perfect, but doubting that mentioning this would add to the proceedings.

'Yes, the blend of your vocabulary and care with speech, together with my, um, diction and, um – no matter. And then there would be your height wedded to my figure, and we would be, well, perfect.' She stuffed a piece of toast in her mouth.

So she wished herself less doll-like and less pillowy in the head, but otherwise was pleased with herself: I did not have it in me to object that she so clearly viewed herself as the better half of the bargain, chiefly because I agreed with her. I recalled Mother Cooper's addressing her as *child*, and I saw the wisdom in that too. In the land of the insane, the mad themselves are the wise, and are thus the best guides.

Hetty took a sip of tea and held her teacup aloft. 'I have decided to learn a new word from you each day, and deploy it in conversation each evening. This might edify Sir David.'

'I doubt very much I know any words which he has not heard a thousand times over,' I laughed. 'After all, the Bible is the length of my education.'

She buttered a third slice of toast. 'I wonder if we are allowed more, when this has gone?' she remarked, examining the rack. There had been eight slices, and I had had only two, so three remained. I wondered who had toasted them for us, and hoped it wasn't Ann. I ought to have envied her a life of more honest toil in the kitchen, for does not the Book of Exodus speak of the whore who envies the virtuous woman? I shifted a little in my upholstered seat at the thought.

'I will only have one more so you can count on two after that. Then we do not have to risk the consequences of ringing that bell. Nor make a stroke more work for poor Ann, or whoever else is in the kitchen,' I said.

Hetty took another slice and set about buttering it, her head bent over the task. 'Do you think this was made by Ann?'

'I don't know, but she brought it up,' I replied.

Hetty leapt towards the bell-pull. 'Then let us order more! She was such a sulky, plain lummox, and another ring of the bell will be sure to incense her.'

I darted up and placed myself between Hetty and the chord. 'Don't you dare!' I cried. 'That would be a wicked thing to do!'

For a moment I could not tell if Hetty was about to giggle, burst into tears or strike me. 'I own that it is unkind of me,' she said carefully, 'but I do not see that it is wicked. That is a harsh word to use, Nell, but I will certainly not suggest such a thing again if it riles you so.'

She looked so serious in her contrition that I felt remorseful. I knew that it was not Hetty herself who had excited me, but my own sinfulness at living in this house and eating food prepared by an unknown hand. 'I am sorry,' I murmured sitting down. 'I should not be so intemperate.'

She set about munching again. 'I do not think I am expressing myself very well,' she said once the slice was dispatched, putting her head to one side.

I hoped that she would soon forget this affectation, for it made her look like an overgrown cockatoo. Hetty's glee in making Ann toil had made her momentarily ugly in my eyes, and it would take longer to dispel this impression than it did to spoon more sugar in my tea.

'Perhaps I should cultivate poor expression for Sir David, and be like the woman he saw on the stage who mispronounced all her words, or rather picked the wrong word thinking it was the right one, so she would say "he is the very pineapple of perfection" instead of the "very pinnacle."' She waited for me to laugh, but such a conceit seemed rather infantile to me. I did not want to say so, so soon after my "wickedness" remark, for it seemed vital to me that we were friends. For all her silliness, nothing was to shake my liking for Hetty.

'If it amuses him, then why not?' I ventured. I waited for her to enquire about my experiences with Sir Robin, for there was much I wished to ask her, but I did not want to be the first to speak of what had happened.

'Do you think that Sir David is all that he seems?' She said this with a shy smile.

'I do not know what you mean,' I answered, spooning more sugar into my tea. I wondered if we were supposed to empty the sugar bowl, and hoped that this would not be deducted from our wages. If it were, it would serve me right: Isaiah used to speak of the amount of distilled slave sweat that went into the production of every grain of sugar. I put my cup down, then reflected that even if I left it, it would only be poured away, so I downed it hastily and felt glad when its heat scalded my mouth and throat.

Hetty passed me a glass of water. 'You must learn to sip,' she said quietly. 'This is what I was trying to say to you: we should not ape the ladies, I do not think, for the men are weary enough of their hoity-toity ways to have to come here; but we must not repel them by behaving like Irish navvies either.'

I almost asked what she knew of the drinking habits of workmen, but I did not think that this was the time for me to hold a mirror to her ignorance – she would only think I was nettled at her criticism of me.

'It is, I think, particularly important, on account of who Sir Robin is – or at least, his connections.'

'I do not follow,' I said. 'We know little of these gentlemen, or at least, we rely on what they tell us.' I thought of Sir Robin, reliving scenes from his schooldays while I made strenuous efforts to stay awake. Until the day before, I had stayed up beyond midnight only when my mother was ill; the night before I had marvelled at the cost of lighting a room so that Sir Robin might sprawl and talk.

'His sister is one of the King's former mistresses,' she said. 'Did he not speak to you of it?'

Sir Robin had mentioned this, but I been so terrified that my mind had fastened on the quality of the candles: beeswax ones which smelled sweet and, unlike the ones my uncle made with beef tallow, did not smoke and threaten to go out.

'He is very interested in politics,' I told her.

In fact, Sir Robin had at first seemed keen to befriend

me. He asked me about my family, and when I told him – reluctantly – about Isaiah and Tom, he listened more intently and soon professed himself a friend of the radical cause.

'Let such men as your father,' – I did not dare correct him – 'and brother foment revolution,' he said, drinking steadily. 'Let them see how flimsy the edifice is, how a few well-aimed blasts of the radical trumpet might shake the foundations of – what is it your brother calls it? – Old Corruption?'

I had nodded. Hetty had warned me that he would take me in some clumsy way, and would be paying fifty guineas for being the first to have me. Girls younger than me sold themselves for a few pennies in this city every hour; I marvelled at how much more I was worth, once I was covered with silk. I wondered what would happen if he ripped the dress.

'Let us encourage the Radicals,' he had continued. 'Not the lily-livered ones who want the vote, but the hellfire damnation preachers who inspire men to destroy us.' (By 'us' I took him to mean his family and other members of the Establishment, for it soon became clear that he was no friend to Isaiah and Tom's cause.)

'And when we have flushed them from their rabbit-holes,' he said – and here his voice grew louder and more high-pitched – 'when we have shown the King the monstrous canker that his wife is encouraging in his breast, then we can cut it out. We will smite our enemies and send Caroline back to the bestial foreigners who harbour her.'

This was not a novel philosophy, for *agents provocateurs* were encouraging plots in this way all over the kingdom, but listening to Sir Robin filled me with a new fear. I had imagined that men as wealthy as he did not notice the likes of Tom and Isaiah, and I had naively assumed that they might even feel some sympathy for their lot if they did. That such hatred was mingled with an interview about my physical appetites made me all the more afraid of him.

I seemed to fail every test. I could not describe my school pinafore to him, since I had never been to school. Isaiah had never beaten me. I had never fallen in with a crowd of ruffians and allowed them to 'educate' me. My breasts were too small, I was too lanky and bony. I could have told him about my uncle's advances, but even I could see that they would need considerable embellishment, if I was to satisfy Sir Robin. I remembered some of the scenes I had printed, but I was so fearful that I would describe a scandal involving someone he knew that I dared not draw from even that experience. He was content only when he listened to my accounts of Tom and Isaiah, and asked how his orations compared. Favourably, I told him, but in truth how different his monologue was from a sermon! For Isaiah's giving of himself was a way of illuminating what lies beyond us, while all Sir Robin wanted was to shine a torch down the murky tunnels within his own mind. I reflected that he was paying Mother Cooper heftily for this, and I wondered if he would not do better at a tavern, where a round of drinks would buy him a keener audience. Until he became angry, he was a hesitant speaker who never called a spade a spade when it *might be more usefully – ahem – referred to as a long-handed shovel, as it were.* He would leave pauses, and I was mostly unsure whether to fill them with laughter, a smile, commiseration or a nod of rapt attention. He did not mention having a wife, and I pitied the woman he would eventually marry, for I saw no instincts of companionship in him.

At length he fell asleep, and I stared into the embers, waiting for morning.

'You are not paying me a farthing of attention,' Hetty complained, snapping her fingers in front of my nose. She was right; the night had left me dull-headed.

The door opened and Mother Cooper wheezed in with

Martha and Ann in her wake. I hoped Mother Cooper would not see the empty sugar bowl, and noticed as I stood up that this breakfast had given me a great deal of frantic energy. If only I could have eaten like this at Friday-street! I could have printed a Babel of books and had enough strength to build a great tower into the bargain.

'Your men did not breakfast, I see,' Mother Cooper said. 'If they continue to make such an early departure, you can come down to the kitchen for a piece of bread, and save Ann the trouble of carting your food up here. Unless, of course, you plan to pay for extra service out of your wages.'

'No, Mother Cooper, I do not,' I said. 'I would not want to give Ann the trouble.'

I glanced at Hetty, wishing her to acknowledge by some small sign that I was right not to have let her summon Ann, but she was running her finger along the edge of the table and avoiding my eye. I guessed that from now onwards she would be at pains to persuade Sir David to stay with her in time for her linen-bedecked tray to appear.

I smiled at Ann, only to receive a face like a squeezed lime in return. 'I am capable of the work,' she said, with a look at Mother Cooper which said that the portly matron's judgement of Ann's ability to wear the flesh off her bones with hard graft was still in the balance.

'What I meant,' I said, 'is that I would like to avoid every farthing of unnecessary expense, and in fact, Mother Cooper, I would be most grateful if we could perhaps learn more precisely the terms of our employ here.' *Even servants know their wages and their notice period*, I thought: what would Tom think of my having volunteered for a situation with no figures attached? If the Lord had blessed me with my brother's head for sums, I might have been more alert to this before I followed Mother Cooper here; Tom was forever complaining that none of us, my stepfather included, had the faintest idea of what money could buy. In his view, it was all very well for Isaiah to abhor riches, but if Isaiah had put as much energy into business as he had into blowing hot air into the rafters of his chapel, he would have made a hefty enough fortune to buy a revolution and have some money left over to see us comfortably to the Apocalypse. Tom had promised me that once he was a man, none of us would be poor, and our children would never endure the kind of England that our mother had brought us into.

'Breakfast is over.' Mother Cooper's comment was aimed at me, as if my need for sustenance were particularly blame-worthy. 'And there is to be a change tonight. Sir David wants you this evening,' she continued, with a nod in my direction. 'But don't flatter yourself; it will be Sir Robin who has changed his mind, and he will have Hetty. How he has per-suaded Sir David to give you up, I have no idea,' she said, eyeing the soft lines of Hetty's cotton dress. She shook her head sorrowfully. 'I had thought they might linger. Some of our Gentlemen have been coming here for twenty years or more, sometimes visiting the same girl. I do not think that will happen here, even if you manage to keep your mouth shut and your legs open. And now I have the Italians, there will be even less room for you in the kitchen.'

'Ignore her,' Hetty said, as soon as Mother Cooper's foot-steps had receded down the hall. 'If she were so disappointed in you, you would have been deposited on the front steps before breakfast.' She looked at me, her mouth a tight line. 'Of course, I am the disappointment.' She sighed, and her face took on the mix of childishness and extreme old age which I often see on street urchins. 'Sir David was very brief last night, and very gentle. He said he did not want to rob me of my innocence, when of course it was he who was being robbed. I almost felt a pang of conscience at the fifty guineas he was paying. I was all sweet and coy, but perhaps

I misjudged his desires. Perhaps he thinks you will be more fun.'

'I do not think so,' I said. I remembered my sense of his unease, and wondered again why on earth Sir David had come here at all, if he had no desire to make sport with a beauty like Hetty.

9

AND SO SIR DAVID came to my bed, and though it is profane to say so, I counted it a miracle he did not want to leave it, and soon he spent as many nights as he could in my company. For all that I was a printer and he a landowner and politician, he often said that we might have been shelled from the same pod, so attuned were we.

My life over the subsequent four months could be portrayed in a series of tableaux, for these were what I imagined in the many hours Sir David and I spent together. The most commonplace scene would involve me sitting by the fire, listening to him as he smoked and talked. To the casual observer, this would be the epitome of marital respectability. A more careful inspection would reveal that one of my breasts was bare, and that there was a rumpled bed behind us. Also Sir David's posture would be a little too open-legged, and his attire too carelessly arranged. A bright-coloured cravat on the floor might advertise this to the viewer.

Sir David never tired of hearing about my work. In a partial exercise of the truth, I told him that we specialised in the moralising prints that Mr Hogarth has made so popular, scenes of London life with Biblical quotations: so 'The Industrious 'Prentice', an insufferable prig with a cheap wig and a blossoming paunch, was graced with St Matthew's

'Well Done, thou Good and Faithful Servant'. Sitting me on his knee, kissing my nipples and rubbing them with his stubbled chin until I cried out with pleasure, he would tease me about *The Harlot's Progress* and enquire why, unlike Mr Hogarth's heroines, I did not have a fondness for gin and seemed loath to display some of the more flamboyant excesses of my trade.

But mostly he talked to me. Truly, he did: above all else, he and I were friends, though I would not have dared say this at the time. Not a fortnight had passed before he confided that he had come to St James's Square to fulfil an obligation he had made to his aunt, Sir Robin's mother. 'I own that it is an unconventional settlement of a filial duty,' he said, 'and look at the joy I have found!' Here he held up one of my curls and stretched it out, watching the candlelight play on it, 'But in all honesty, I came here for Robin. I know how this sounds: this is a palace of selfish whims, but I came along because my cousin has certain tastes which he feels can only be met in a place such as this.'

I thought of Mabel, and wondered if Mother Cooper would set up a school room on the same model as her playroom – this would suit Sir Robin perfectly. I did not point out what might seem obvious to anyone else: that Sir David's insistence that he came purely for his cousin rang hollow in the light of his enthusiastic nights with me, but it did not occur to me to say this, perhaps because I myself was accustomed to performing such sleights of mind. I was on a highway to Hell, and I had never been happier.

'My cousin is an ungovernable man,' Sir David continued. 'No, that is untrue. He might become ungovernable, if he is not' – here his hands fluttered a little – 'governed.' He was usually so eloquent, but at that moment words eluded him. 'And on her deathbed, I promised Robin's mother, my aunt, who brought me up following the shipwreck which took my parents, that I would protect him from himself and find what she called *suitable outlets* for him. She knew what he was like, you see. I remember her emerging from a conversation with Robin's housemaster. This would have been after his expulsion from his final school, a grim place in Northumberland that Robin considered worse than a gaol, for at least there was no Latin grammar in the clink. The report of whatever Robin had been doing to the younger boys aged her.'

'Is Hetty safe?' I asked, looking at the door which connected our rooms, though Hetty was not there. Sir Robin had requested a second room, and now this desire for additional privacy made me anxious for her.

'Ye-es,' he replied. 'She is paid well for what she does – I know, because I pay her.'

'*You* pay Hetty?' I said.

'Yes. My parents' death left me very well provided for. It had been my father's ambition to own a plantation, and had the ship on which he had drowned come in, he would have had funds aplenty to fulfil that wish. But my parents died at sea, and the insurers paid handsomely for the vessel's contents. So I inherited my father's fortune, and more. But appalled at the loss, my Uncle – Sir Robin's father – kept all his investments on dry land, and his person with them. He died in his bed in 1809, but had been ruined by property speculators long before then. Robin therefore depends entirely on me for his, shall we say, livelihood.'

We were kindred spirits, Sir David and his Nell, so he said: we both had lost a parent and found in each other someone who would set us on a fairer path than our own fathers had done. If his father had lived, Sir David would most likely have become a slave owner. I told him tales of Isaiah's father, and he shuddered at them.

'Isaiah's father was old when he was born. Every evening,

they would sit down together at supper, and his father would gaze at his mother. And most nights, he would say to her, "Charity, if there is a heaven, we will dine together like this every night, and wake up together as we did the day we got Isaiah."'

Sir David shifted me on his knee, for most often we sat on a chaise longue together. He did not like to loll about in bed, and said he would prefer to be at least half dressed, in case he was summoned away, which he seldom was. I used to tease him that affairs of state had no bearing on this, and he simply liked the business of dressing and undressing and of taking me in my clothes. All of this he admitted was true, but still: with a royal divorce in the offing, one knew not the day or the hour. I countered that he employed men like Mr Edwards to stomp about the place with his breeches on at all times, which he also owned to be correct, but had I not noticed how much business was transacted on these very corridors? And he had no intention of appearing in front of anyone but me *sans* his trousers, a position of which I surely approved? Given the covetous glances that Suky and her ilk gave him on the rare occasions he took sherry in the drawing room, I could only agree.

And many evenings he did go off to speak to his cousin or Mr Edwards, or he would be called away on business which he would not discuss, and I would be left with Hetty or the women of the drawing room. Sometimes I would go in search of Martha, or sit in the passage just outside the kitchen stroking the grey cat, for I preferred their company to the pinched faces and brittle conversation of the netherworld above stairs.

'I was moved when Isaiah told me this story,' I continued, 'partly because he so seldom talked about his life in Jamaica in anything other than parables.'

Sir David pinched me jealously. Like Tom, he was of the

opinion that I set too much store by Isaiah's good opinion.

'I told Isaiah that his mother was fortunate, and I would like to love someone as much as his father evidently had loved his wife. I was wondering if anyone would ever view my arms as their heaven when Isaiah said "My father's wife was called Constance." And then I saw it: Charity, his mother, was a slave, and would never have dined with them at table. Isaiah said that his father would hold the candelabra to Charity's face as he spoke. He peered at her because he wanted to be sure that his cruelty had found its mark. Some nights, Isaiah's mother was so exhausted by the end of dinner that she would list about while she carried the plates, and he would shout at her not to drop them, which of course made her jump. What was it Isaiah said? "Though he was no longer the master of his wits, the cesspool of my father's will continued to fester."'

Sir David shook his head. 'I wonder which is worse, not knowing your father, or knowing your father and seeing the monster in him... And so Isaiah was sent away to sea?'

'Yes, at fourteen. But by the time he had reached twelve, his father was afraid of him.'

'Why?' Sir David asked.

'He feared him on account of the hatred he saw in Isaiah's eyes; but it was impossible to imagine Isaiah as anything less than the master of his passions, even as a small boy.'

And as I recounted this tale to Sir David, I realised that Isaiah's restraint of character was something which was self-taught; before he became Daniel, he had to overcome the lion in himself.

❧

As my position felt more secure, I became increasingly worried about Ann. She appeared even paler and wraithlike next to the Italian women Mr Edwards had brought, and I confided to Sir David my concerns for her.

'You are a kind girl!' he smiled. 'You see your fate as attached to hers, though it is nothing more than coincidence that she is under the same roof as you. You might as well feel responsible for every other poor soul in London while you are about it.'

'I do,' I said, for I agreed with Isaiah that it was the duty of every Christian to make love of our neighbour the core of our politics.

'You do not need to worry,' he assured me. 'The Italians are not here to evict Ann. You will probably have noticed that they do precious little work.'

I had – or rather, Hetty had remarked on it. For a couple of days she had been concerned that these dark-eyed women had caught Sir Robin's fancy, and had complained to Mother Cooper that the house was being stuffed with idle women. (And one startling handsome if diminutive man, who had been employed as a kind of butler. He stood at the door like a pigmy statue, and the other girls in the drawing room insisted that soon all the ladies would want a pair of them to adorn their hallways and perform whatever additional services they might require when their portly husbands were away doing whatever it was that wealthy men did.)

Sir David continued, 'They are here to reassure the King that if the time comes, we have the evidence to secure him his divorce. These foreigners will attest to what Caroline was up to with her Count Bergami, if they need to. And if we do not want them to speak, then equally we will pay for their silence. For I am keen to avoid a divorce at all costs, and keep Caroline away with threats and money in equal measure. But what better place for these Italians to reside than at 14 St James's Square, where secrets can be hidden and conversations be had behind thick damask?'

'But the Queen has stayed away,' I said.

'She has, though she is in France, and still threatens to sail. We have let it be known that these servants are here; if she chooses to return, she is aware that the King will fight her claim, and that we are massing his forces.'

'But will it not discredit you that they are living here?' I asked.

'We will find them other lodgings soon,' he said. 'Do not worry.'

And then Sir David would tell me that he was massing his force against me, or some other silly pun – how absurd such endearments sound, even to me – and we would retire for another hour, Queen Caroline and her Italian quite forgotten.

If this had been honest work, I would now be inking in scenes within scenes, perhaps in clouds around our heads, or better as a species of frame. For Sir David asked me to entertain him with stories each night, and every one I told confirmed him in his belief that for all our differences, in essence we were similar creatures. Perhaps because his parents had been shipwrecked, he loved stories of journeys. I recounted my own, from Preston to London, though I found it far less exotic than my tales of Isaiah. And so my life became as much a voyage through my past as though my senses.

I told Sir David that I often wondered what it would have been like if we had never left Lancashire, but my mother had insisted that she'd left because she couldn't face another summer in the mill: she thought her lungs might drown in cotton dust. Sir David said that Parliament had just passed Acts making conditions in mills better for women and children. I found it impossible to believe that mill-owners would legislate to the detriment of their profit, but I did not say so. Instead, I told him of my earliest memories: of my mother leaving my father, and of tying threads under the enormous machines, the loom flying back and forth over my head, my mother resting her foot on my neck to ensure that I would not get caught in the loom. She lost her job for arguing with a foreman who wanted to separate me from her on the grounds that her protection of me made her less productive. What the foreman did not know was that I was tall for my age, and not the seven she'd claimed. I was not quite four. She decided that she would not waste her time finding another mill job, for she was sure that she would be on the owners' black list and would not find a welcome in any mill, even if she had wanted one. And so we had set off for London, to the only place she could think of where there were so many rich men that they could not all know each other, and even if they did, they would have better things to do than make sure that Sofia Wingfield never worked again.

In return, Sir David told me of events at Westminster. Caroline was at Calais, and looked set to stay there: *Huzza!* There would be no divorce proceedings. Sir David and his friends celebrated, for their stock had never been higher. This news coincided with the departure of the Italians from Mother Cooper's house. Then Caroline, encouraged by expressions of support in Parliament and outside, arrived at Dover, and was feted wherever she went: the King blamed his friends, who had promised him that fifty thousand a year would keep his consort at bay, and there was talk of his dismissing the Prime Minister and appointing a new government. All this I grasped swiftly, and it amused him that I knew the characters only by how they appeared on squibs. He took to describing them as I did, and said that it was becoming impossible for him to see them in any other way, even when he was talking to them.

At first Sir David brought prints produced by my erstwhile competitors in the hope of amusing me, but he stopped doing so because I alternated between dismissing the workmanship with scorn, and becoming morose when he brought something which I thought well executed.

It was a species of torture to be away from the press at such a time, and Sir David saw how my fingertips itched to be inky again. He offered to buy me paints, brushes, copper-plates and knives for etching; anything that would occupy me and make real the images I had rendered in his head. He found my desire for industry strange: the woman on whose account he had a personal interest in the Queen's affairs, his cousin Evelina, was almost entirely idle. The most work she had ever done, Sir David thought, was atop the King, and any influence she had won as a result was now on the wane, it having been almost ten years since the King had wanted her. I soon understood that to those of us on the outside, Politics was a matter of sheep and wolves, and with our noses pressed up against it, we saw how viciously men like Sir Robin were prepared to defend their plenty against the many. This was the root of Sir David's anxiety about his cousin and indeed the King. To Sir David, only peaceful means would save the kingdom, and violence would only beget violence.

10

In the next scene I might print of my life, this wanton idyll shows signs of strain. More angular poses and greener tints would draw the viewer's attention to the pettish tilt of my head, and a skilful engraver would capture Sir David's exasperated entreaties.

It was June 6th, and the Queen had just come to London in a triumphant procession from Dover. Sir David had come at four, because he wanted to share some daylight hours with me. It would fortify him, he said, before a tedious dinner at which much politics would be talked. It looked more likely by the day that the King would institute divorce proceedings, if he was not to be forced to recognise Caroline as his Queen. Sir David's cousin, Sir Robin's sister Evelina, was braced for the scandal, though I could not see that it would make much difference to her standing, since her husband had known of her liaison before they had married, and her position as a former royal mistress was anything but unique.

'He blanches at the thought of his wife being a subject of your press, Nell,' Sir David said. 'It used to be that there was a divide between the lives of us few and you many, but men like your stepfather and brother are doing all they can to make what was once private most glaringly public.'

'My brother? You have seen Tom?'

'Seen him? No. But I have seen his work, and my cousin has taken quite an interest in him and your stepfather. I must say, my cousin's enthusiasm for the popular cause is not winning us many friends. The stakes are very high in the game he wishes to play to secure our position.'

At that moment I did not have a care for Sir Robin's plans, and asked again for news of Tom.

'My associate Mr Edwards knows of him. Wingfield is an unusual name, so naturally he made the connection. You remember Mr Edwards? The one who brought the Italians here?'

'Of course,' I said. I had not missed Mother Cooper's loud comments about filthy Italians and ignorant Dagoes. Hetty found out from one of the other girls that Mother Cooper had hit on the idea of recruiting the Italians and running a Mediterreanan-style bordello, but Mr Edwards had insisted that this might compromise their integrity as witnesses. Furious, Mother Cooper had refused to house any more Italians, and Mr Edwards had found them lodgings elsewhere.

It was on his travels, Sir David said, that he had happened across my brother. I pleaded with Sir David to warn Tom through his associate, but Sir David was honest enough to say that he could make no promises, Mr Edwards not being the kind of man to make such interventions. This exchange merely underlined the precariousness of my position, and it was this, with all its sharp facets that was the root of the difficulty between him and me.

At around seven that June evening, he asked me to stand by the window, so that he might admire the sunlight in my hair. He grasped my shoulders and moved me from side to side. 'You are as stiff as a corpse, Nell,' he said, smiling.

I shuddered.

He let me go. 'I just wanted to gaze on you fondly, that is

all,' he said. 'Many girls would like that.'

'Why do you not go to them then?' I retorted. I was surprised at my prickliness.

He sat on a low gilt chair which looked like a piece of dolls-house furniture beneath him. 'You do not care for me,' he said, quietly. The chair sighed at the weight of his frame. 'Before you say anything you might regret, you might let wait a while before passing judgement. You might become used to me.'

'*My* judgement, Sir?' I halted the pursuit of this point, for I had always been at pains to efface the transaction that underpinned our time together. Still, it was ridiculous to imply that I might simply reject him, as if I were a fine lady and he a mere suitor.

'And will you always call me "Sir?" he exclaimed. 'You are not a servant, Nell. Heaven knows, I can speak more freely of politics to you than I can to most of my friends, including men who are in Parliament. You took much in during those long hours at the press. If you had been a man, and properly educated, who knows what you would have become.'

'You sound like my mother,' I snapped, determined that I should not spoil the afternoon by crying, for I had been so glad that he had come early. And that was the difficulty: I was already becoming very fond of him, and my soul had leapt like the deer in the psalms at the sound of his clomping footsteps on the parquet. For reasons I could not grasp, the conversation was making me behave like a petulant child.

'You want me to reassure you in the very way that I am doing, but your terror at the precarious circumstances of our intimacy also prompts you to propel me away from you,' he said. 'It is natural: if I am to wound you, you would rather it were now, when the pain might be less. You cannot bear the suspense of it. The only other way of ending the agony of uncertainty is marriage, which is why it was invented.'

'It was not invented,' I countered. 'It is a gift from God.'

He smiled. 'Did God not invent things? You prefer *created*. But this horse-trading of words does not smooth the frown from your lovely face, does it? But truly, Nell, I would have been dreading a long summer in stinking London, confined to barracks by the King's soiled bedlinen when I would usually have gone abroad or to my estate, but I own that there is nowhere else in the world that I would rather be.'

This was no footling thing to say, for he had seen much of it, far more even than Isaiah had. I paced up and down, as I would in the chapel when I wished to be alone to think. Sir David did not stop me, and nor did he stare at me, and so I was able to speak. 'I did not mean to be petulant, Sir,' I said. 'And you are right that I enjoy your company.' Here I flushed, for I might have said *conversation*, but that would not have nudged at the half of it. The first night he took me, he was so careful he made me feel as light as a waif. As the weeks had passed, my desire for him summoned such a strength in me that I began to worry that I might hurt him. He insisted that even if I attempted to pull him limb from limb, he would enjoy the sensation of it, and only beseech me for more. For all my pious comments about God's gift of marriage, I had had scarcely a thought for Him: I was too busy making a shrine of what was between my legs.

I looked at Sir David. The slight down-turn of his smile told me that he had an idea of what I was thinking. I had to keep to my point, or we would be in bed again.

'Sir David –,' I said.

He shook his head. 'I repeat: are you ever going to call me simply David? Surely we are beyond titles, or shall I call you Mistress Nell?' He thought about this. 'Perhaps I will. It rather suits you. But I am interrupting you.'

'All I wanted to say was, you have no need to be here. There are all sorts of ladies who would entertain you, and there would be no need to line Mother Cooper's pockets in the process. You could marry, Sir, and have no need of – all this *shame*.' My cheek twitched with the effort of not crying.

He sighed. 'I think it is best if we do not dwell on this subject. Of course you are right. I should marry. One day, and perhaps not too far away, I will. But you should not assume that I...' He rubbed his thighs, and I remembered the hardness of them under his breeches, how the wiry long hairs on them felt soft by comparison. I shook my head to chase such thoughts away. I was turning into the narrator of one of Hetty's ridiculous novels, with my fixation on hard this and soft the other.

'Why did you choose Hetty that first evening?' I had vowed that I would never quiz him about the events of that night, but as my fondness for him grew, so had this canker of jealousy. 'Any man would want her over me. So tell me, why did you give her up?'

He sighed and waved his hand, as if my questions were the foul London air which had come in with the change in the weather. 'I have told you: I had no real desire to be here. Robin wished to change; he said you were too spirited in the wrong ways – he had you down for a straight-laced God-botherer, but then my cousin's lack of judgement is no secret. And I do not know what Hetty has told you, but he was right in this respect: if he is to be believed, she does seem to enjoy him, or at least, she has not run away, or indeed killed herself, as I feared some girls of gentler dispositions might. But do not worry – he will not hurt her. Well, he will not *harm* her. She strikes me as a robust girl, if not a particularly sensible one. He has been on a quest to find a woman who enjoys the same pleasures as him, and as I have said, he is convinced that in your friend Hetty, he has found her. Time will tell. He tells me she is envious of the regard in which I hold you, a regard which you stubbornly refuse to see, but I could never summon such feelings for her. She and Robin are too... suited.'

'But you are here to keep an eye on him,' I said, wishing I did not sound so testy, knowing that I was proving his point about my stubbornness.

He sighed. 'That was my original purpose in coming here. My cousin had confessed that his desires were overwhelming him, and I thought it best to find an outlet for them, as I had promised his mama. Mother Cooper is well known in our set.'

'And now you have a different purpose?' I said.

'It is... convenient for me to meet people here.'

'What? Other women?' I said, noticing that the gold whorls in the fabric of my armchair looked like serpents suddenly.

He laughed. 'No, Nell. Even if I had the time for other girls, I do not think I could summon the energy. You know that I also transact business here. I talk to you more than to any other creature on earth, but even you must accept that there is value in my accosting acquaintances on these corridors, where we are less likely to be overheard.'

The connecting door crashed against the wall, punching a slight hole in the wallpaper with the violence of its opening, and Sir Robin appeared.

'There will be excitement soon, David,' Sir Robin announced, his face flushed with triumph and booze.

'You Radicals will have your day,' he said to me, 'and do you know what that day will be?'

'Robin,' said Sir David, 'this was never a good idea, and never less so than now.'

'What difference does it make what I say to her?' he demanded.

'Then why say anything at all, if it matters nought?' said Sir David.

'The Apocalypse! That's what the day will be!' he shouted. 'The Apocalypse, I tell you.'

He was clearly taken with this word and all the spittle it entailed in its delivery.

Sir David shook his head. 'I repeat, Robin: that would be a mistake. These days the tide turns more swiftly that it does in the Thames, and such schemes that you have been hatching are as likely to sweep you away as they are the men you profess to detest. Your sister was never a good judge of political matters, and frankly, neither are you. And I know that Edwards agrees with me, insofar as he agrees with anyone, though he will funnel my money where you instruct him. It might be better for all of us if you found yourself in rather more straitened circumstances.'

I was surprised to see how angry Sir David was with his cousin, who seemed no more blustering and foolish than he always was, and I wondered what nonsense Sir Robin had been distilling in his cups. I could not imagine that Sir Robin could ever befriend Isaiah or his kind this side of Judgement Day, but that he was causing his cousin some considerable embarrassment and anxiety was abundantly clear.

'What?' said Sir Robin. 'You would cut me off?'

Sir David hesitated, and I imagined him torn between the promise he had made his aunt and the folly he was evidently witnessing. I doubted he had it in him to act so high-handedly, but he did not get the chance to reply, for Sir Robin cursed him and departed, this time slamming the other door, which led to the hall and the stairs.

Sir David got up, his knees cracking as he did so. 'I am sorry, but in the circumstances I have no desire to continue our conversation. Let us not get foolish about all this, for we are getting on well, and I will neither hurt nor harm you.'

I knew he was wrong about this, for whether he wanted more or less from me, I was convinced that he would hurt me; it was only a question of how, how much, and when.

11

ALTHOUGH I WAS WITNESSING the unwiped arse of the affairs of state with my very own eyes, politics seemed to be going on somewhere else entirely. Oddly enough, I had felt far more connected with the world of Old Corruption when I was inking it in than when I was living in its very corridors.

Until late May, my life with Hetty also continued in the patterns established during our first week. After breakfast, Hetty would read the type of novels which Isaiah would have called Sensationalist Satanism, with plots which were even less probable than this one, or else stare into space. On occasion, she became frantically talkative, asking me endless questions about my mother, Isaiah and Tom, to the extent that I teased her that she was developing a crush on my brother.

The morning after Sir Robin's quarrel with his cousin, I asked Hetty if she had heard Sir Robin speak of my brother recently. His excitement about 'the Radicals having their day', as he had put it, had made me a little uneasy.

'Tom?' she said, looking blank and wide-eyed.

'I have only the one brother,' I sighed, feeling weary with her.

'I don't think so,' she replied, returning to her book.

'Hetty,' I said in a voice I hoped would grasp her

attention. 'You might consider talking to Sir Robin.'

She looked up, with a cross, pinched look on her face.

'I do talk to him,' she remarked coldly.

I knew how to capture her attention fully. 'If he does not desist from ranting about radical politics, and his plans for using the likes of Isaiah and my brother,' I continued, 'Sir David will cut him off.'

Hetty looked around the room in terror, as if all the luxuries she enjoyed were about to evaporate. 'Why would he do that?'

'Sir David is very agitated about Sir Robin's political dealings. He feels he is behaving rashly, and that his actions could have extremely dangerous consequences. Sir Robin should be more careful if he wants to remain in Sir David's favour. And I only thought he might listen to you.'

'Well, it seems that you and Sir David have no problems discussing anything and everything. And mind this: Sir Robin does not listen to anyone,' said Hetty. As she slammed the door behind her, her novel slid from the chaise longue to the floor, making the grey cat dig her claws into me.

❧

Mornings were a strange time for me to be lounging about, and often my hands would stroke the grey cat or else smooth my napkin or my dress in the way they would have flattened a piece of paper over the platen. Never a morning passed when I did not count the hours I could have spent working at the press. There are those who claim that a life of idleness is their ultimate aspiration, but I would not take it if I were offered it. If I had been Eve in paradise I would have gone about pruning the trees and tending the animals rather than wandering about trying the fruit that any passing snake might have offered me. Although, as I sat nibbling my roll on a damask chaise longue and swilling my coffee, it was difficult to see how good I would have been at resisting temptation.

❧

June grew riper with each sunrise, and Sir David and I had no further conversations about the nature of our relations, in part because he was careful not to call again in the afternoons. He claimed that it was affairs at court which kept him occupied, but I fretted that it was my gracelessness, and I longed all the more for some work to distract me from myself. I diverted my energy by spending even more time walking around the garden in the middle of the square. The oak trees were becoming quite established, and the flowers were a welcome relief from the houses, whose white stone was now soot-stained and looked as though Satan himself had wiped his murky fingers down it. I had first developed this habit in March, and Martha, the crotchety woman whom we had met on the first day, was ordered to watch me and ensure that I did not 'do anything foolish'. I did not point out that the only foolish thing I had ever done in my life was to trust Mother Cooper. Unlike an ordinary chaperone, Martha was employed not to protect our honour, but Mother Cooper's investment in us. She'd retired from the trade a good ten years before we arrived at 14 St James's Square, though the men who'd called out after her as she scuttled behind us swore she looked better now than she had for the last of her clients. For a crookback Martha moved with startling speed and a roving malevolence that cleared the path in front of her; if we had any ideas about entertaining clients privately or absconding in our fine clothes, she would witness it, she had assured us in those early days.

At first Martha made a parade of resenting the time she had to spend in the gardens, time she could have spent baking or preparing suppers, but she would deliver these speeches from a sunny bench with her legs stretched out expansively, and sometimes with even the hint of a smile on her face. I soon realised that Martha was a good woman, and even suspected that she wished to atone for my having been brought to the house by stealthy acts of kindness. (It was, she confessed one afternoon, she who had baked the cakes I had been plied with during those first days of rest.) Within a few days of being my chaperone, she took off her boots and socks and exposed pinkish-grey feet and gnarled brown nails. They made me think of hen's feet, rootling about in the grass. Once, when Mother Cooper imposed a fine on me for soiling a piece of linen I had never seen before, Martha defended me. Martha was whacked across the shoulders for her insubordination, but I never received a docket for the cleaning.

One warm afternoon just before Easter, Martha told me that she had lived in Brighton for a time, keeping the society of Gentlemen who appreciated escorts on evenings at the new Pavilion, the favourite folly of the Prince George who is now our King. Though she had never seen Caroline, she had supped with many who had. The curious thing was that through the descriptions of her, Caroline had struck Martha as a grander version of herself: fond of bright colours, of necking liquor and giving of herself liberally. She had been slighter of build in her younger years, though by thirty she had given up any pretence of reining in the excesses of her pleasures, and even her many admirers could not keep the weight off her with their attentions. I got the impression that Martha was taken with the idea of her, and she opined that if more women of the Quality were like Caroline, the likes of Mother Copper would be put out of business. I nodded my agreement, though I was not convinced.

Martha was also an unlikely ally in keeping an eye on Hetty. She had taken an instant and profound shine to her, and provided her with beef tea and extra wine when she was looking particularly bruised under the eyes – which it saddened me to see that she often did. Looking back on it, it had been as early as our third week in residence that she had shown signs of flagging. Hetty would make an attempt at gaiety, often borrowing observations from the silly books she spent her afternoons reading. I knew this because I too read some of them, when I felt too sinful even to touch the beautiful leather bible which Sir David had bought for me.

Back in early March, she had refused to let me help her dress, preferring Martha or even Ann to lace her corsets for her. And the corsets became easier and easier to pull tight, so much so that she had to have a smaller one ordered. When I remarked on this, she said that she had become more expert at breathing in. 'You have sucked yourself back into your ten-year-old self,' I said. She looked fearful and triumphant, so this must have been what Sir Robin required of her. In the meantime, I had taken to walking round the gardens more vigorously, in order to stave off the roundness I felt developing everywhere Sir David most liked to touch. 'You are growing because you please me,' he said, 'like a plant which thrives under my ministrations,' but I did not want to risk another punitive dressmaking session with Mother Cooper, and so stayed more or less the size I had been the first night he spent with me.

12

On June 9th, everything changed. Hetty burst in and plonked herself on a chair in front of me. 'Guess what?' she said. I had no idea, and could not get over my astonishment: most mornings she listed about before lowering herself into her chair and staring at breakfast as though she was hopelessly outnumbered by a massed army of toast.

'I have no idea,' I replied. 'But it must be good, for it has wrought a powerful transformation in you.'

'I am to be married,' she announced.

'To whom?' I knew the moment I said it how stupid this was, but I did not want to believe that she could have consented to spend the rest of her days with Sir Robin.

'To the Scarlet Pimpernel, silly.']Her irritation evaporated as quickly as it had appeared. 'I am to be Lady Everley! I am a heroine in one of our novels! The comely doctor's daughter who rescues her ruined father and herself by becoming a fallen woman, only to rise in society and dazzle her contemporaries! I have stooped to conquer, Nell. Who was it who said that? Is it in your Bible? Or was it one of the Romans?'

'I have no idea. My knowledge of the Romans consists only of what St Paul wrote to them. And of what they did to Our Lord.'

'Why must you spoil everything with your religious solemnity?' she said, cross again. 'Robin is right: your people deserve to be executed, and sedition is merely an excuse – the real capital crime is boring us all to death!'

'Does he say that?' I said.

She clapped her hand to her mouth; truly she was in theatrical mode, a strange one for a prospective bride, I thought – but I had no experience of such matters. 'Ah! Nell! I am so sorry.' She embraced me extravagantly, and I felt her brittle arms and ribs. Her heart almost seemed too strong for her chest. 'He said it only in jest, to impress me and anyone else who will listen. You know what he is like.'

I feared that I did, but this was certainly not the moment to say so. 'I hope that you will be very happy together. Marriage is a great blessing,' I said. 'When will it be? You must eat something, and then go and pack.'

Her face took on something of its old haunted pallor. 'Oh, no. We are not leaving yet.'

We? I thought. *He leaves all the time. It is you who needs to escape from this life, and what fiancé would keep his bride-to-be in a brothel, however well aired its sheets were?*

'We are going to marry soon,' she said. 'As soon as we can.'

'Are you expecting?' I asked, though she'd been moaning to Martha about monthly pains not a week previously.

She shook her head. 'It will be a private affair, and you are not to tell Sir David about it.'

The thought of keeping a secret from him filled my stomach with stones. What ease still existed between us would be blighted by such a significant omission, and I was angry with Hetty for buoying up her good fortune at my expense.

'When you leave, Sir David will have no reason to come here anymore,' I said. I sat, my hands leaden in my lap, imagining a life here without either Hetty or Sir David. I resolved that I would rather be on the streets with Meg selling matches, or even in service in a big house like this, except a respectable one, than stay here alone and entertain new clients. What if another man like Sir Robin came along? I reminded myself that I must be careful not to say this, now Hetty was to marry him and seemed happy about it. But why had she looked so miserable until now? Often she had remarked sulkily that for all my fear of eternal damnation, I seemed to be thriving here, while she was the one who could not settle to the life.

Hetty leaned forward and clasped my hand. She was wearing a new scent, something more pungent and clinging than her usual florals. (Sir David had chosen an orange water for me, because oranges grew in the Holy Land.) 'I have thought about this,' she said. 'I will not leave you here, and I will not see you beg on the streets. I will give you money, enough to satisfy Mother Cooper and get you through those first weeks and even months. You should go back to your family, as you always said you would, once Isaiah is freed. If Sir David does not give you anything, that is, which I'm sure he will,' she added hurriedly, and I saw the gap between her fortunes and mine widening like the parting waters of the Red Sea.

I nodded. For all her flights of fancy, she did not even try to conjure the idea that Sir David might marry me, and I thought her correct in this opinion. My mind was drawn back to the printing press, and to memories of how Isaiah would stroke his chin as he contemplated his sermons, and I told myself that if I could only escape this life without hanging for a false charge of theft or worse, I would return to Friday-street and forget this strange world. 14 St James's Square would become like one of the islands Isaiah sailed past on his journey to England: fantastic and all-consuming in its colour and variety when they were close to it, but once it had receded from view, it would be possible to believe that it had never existed.

I did not tell Sir David about Hetty's engagement, though part of me wondered whether she had confided in me in the hope that I would. She wore a hefty ruby on her left hand, but she kept it on her middle finger. If Sir David ever saw it, he never remarked on it. I thought it an ugly ring, like a great drop of blood. A cluster of tiny diamonds would have suited her so much better, but rubies were Sir Robin's favourites. Of course, I did nothing but coo over it with her when called on, which was often, though every time I looked at it I heard Isaiah quoting the Book of Proverbs: a virtuous woman is priced above rubies.

I also did not ask about her future with Sir Robin again, nor her plans for departure. I worried that Sir Robin was gulling her, though I could not see what he would gain from this. The prospect of marriage had animated her, but she was still prone to her old lassitude. It was as if she had to put her mind to remembering how happy she was, and if she did not, she became exhausted and despondent. At least, this was how I saw it. I knew better than to share my thesis with her, since she would most likely accuse me of envy.

And was I guilty of it? Did I secretly wish that Sir David would propose to me? I often asked myself this, but I simply could not imagine it – any of it, from his asking the question itself, to the life afterwards. He and I had scarcely left the house: he took me to dinner on a few occasions, always booking a snug in one of the restaurants on Jermyn-street, but this held little delight for him, since he was forever dining out. So we tended to potter about in my room and in a parlour downstairs, and we were happy enough.

In mid-June, this also changed. Sir David arrived, pale and more hunched than usual. Instead of his usual smile and kiss, he greeted my enquiries about his health with a sideways look. He appraised me, as if there was something ugly about me which he had just seen, and he was angry with himself for not having spotted it sooner.

'You should not stand so, Sir,' I said.

'My back, aye, I know,' he replied. 'My doctor has told me, often before selling me a powerful remedy.' He shook his head. 'Everybody wishes to sell me something,' he said, with uncharacteristic vehemence.

'I do not,' I said. 'I merely meant that you will make the pain worse. And you are making your jacket shiny where you are chafing it with your fingers.' He did not care for clothes, so I hoped that this would make him smile.

'Show me,' he murmured softly, 'show me where.' He lifted his arms and nodded at me while I reached for the cloth, relieved that our normal intimacy was returning. The cloth was cream and as soft as vellum, but with a heaviness which marked it out from the fabric I had seen on women's dresses. He clasped my hand to his side.

'There!' he said, 'now I can accuse you of mauling me and leaving your filthy paw-marks on my pristine coat, and Mother Cooper will allow me to punish you, then have you in hock to me for ever, while recompensing me with little more than the cost of a good cleaning. For that is how things are here, is it not?' He looked surprised at himself, and sat down, his chestnut boots creaking as he stretched them out and studied them. He looked up quickly, as if he was trying to catch me at something. 'Your face is the perfect picture of terror,' he said.

'I do not know what is wrong,' I said.

'For one so sharp, you claim not to know much, these days. There will be a Bill of Pains and Penalties heard in the Lords, and therefore our family star plummets. Because Caroline has returned to England, the King now wants a divorce. Any man of conscience in the Lords cannot grant one without hearing some evidence, and so the terms of engagement are: garner as much to slur Caroline as possible, while excluding the King's retinue of women from the deliberations. It is impossible, as any decent man in this country knows, but the King insists we attempt it, and we will fail. The King will look more feckless than ever before as his dirty laundry is aired in public, thus fanning the flames of the people's unrest. Moreover, the Whigs have one of their most brilliant lawyers defending the Queen, and the new King is, I fear, about to pay dearly for his father's exclusion of that party from government. And the result of a successful divorce? Status, access, the preferments which come with our royal favour – all lost, most likely. Worse, my cousin has advertised himself as a supporter of radical politics, and his enemies will not see that he has done this for the very purpose of destroying the revolutionaries he seeks to encourage. He is playing a dangerous game. They will argue that he has lost his wits, and it will be difficult to refute them. His sister cannot save us, for she was hundreds of royal conquests ago and is almost as unhinged as her brother into the bargain.'

'But what of the Italians?' I asked. 'I thought the very reason they were here was to show the King you had evidence to use against Caroline if you needed it?'

'Well, the rules of the game have changed once more, which makes our position with the King even more precarious. And my only hope now is that if we can buy the Italians' silence, we might yet prevent a divorce – for without evidence, there will be no grounds for the King to divorce Caroline. And then we can only hope that she will go back to Europe and leave us in peace,' explained Sir David. 'But my fear is that we are not the only men with bulging pockets in this city, and there may well be other witnesses that can be brought forward. Who knows what will crawl out from under which stones?'

'Have you spoken to the King?' I said. 'Surely he will see that your advice was sound at the time you gave, it, but now circumstances have changed, and –'

'Nell, Nell, Nell. Very few people ever speak to the King, and the last man to do so is the most powerful man in the realm. You know how the world is – surely your stepfather's chapel is as full of petty jealousies as the royal court?'

I thought of Isaiah's friend Will Davidson and of my Uncle John, and could only agree: they accepted Isaiah's leadership, but I had often wondered how wholeheartedly, particularly when Tom had chosen to be apprenticed to Will and not to Isaiah.

Hetty knocked and came through. She looked a little nervously at Sir David, who raised his eyebrows at her and bowed. She was not wearing her ring, for once. 'Sir Robin wishes to know if you will accompany us to Vauxhall Gardens tonight. I for one would like to go, and Nell has scarcely left the Square in five months.'

I hated the very prospect of Vauxhall, for it was well known to be full of Gents and their harlots, their faces painted with considerably less skill than I would have applied to them on the page. The evening would only hold up a mirror to the ugliness of my situation.

Sir David looked at me. I assumed he would refuse, not least because he was furious with his cousin. 'An excursion is a good idea, Nell. But what would you like to see?'

'The Queen,' I said, because I had been thinking about coloured inks, and because of course I had no desire to go anywhere.

Sir David laughed. 'The Queen! She may well be that yet. Caroline dines with Mr Brougham tonight,' said Sir David. 'He is one of her advocates in these putative divorce proceedings, so we will most emphatically *not* be welcome at his table. There will most likely be a throng on the streets to cheer her, which we could attempt to pass, if you like. It would involve a faintly circuitous route, but if we travel near Belgravia we may see her.'

'No, really,' I said, 'I am being foolish. We should go straight to Vauxhall, if we are going.'

But Sir David insisted, and so I caught my only glimpse of the Queen.

In truth I felt something like a Queen myself, for that night was my first and only ride in a carriage. Hetty and I faced forward, with the Gentlemen wedged together and a great tangle of legs in the middle. I had been living on top of my family and had shared a pallet with my sister all my life, and had spent five months pleasuring a man who paid for me, but I have to say that nothing struck me as more intimate than being thrown against each other in that confined space.

Hetty began by making bright conversation about some silks that she had seen in a shop on Regent-street. Noticing that Sir David was glowering at her, Sir Robin bade her be quiet. After that, nobody spoke.

We slowed from a trot when the cheering started. The crowds were sparse, for this was not a procession – most likely comprising of people who had heard the clopping of hooves, saw the plumes, heard the cheers and came to join in.

'Who has lent her his carriage?' said Sir Robin, practically blocking my view as he craned out to look.

Sir David pulled him in. 'Let Nell look. Which Whig has given Caroline transport is of no matter.'

So seldom did I see the cousins together that I was surprised by the submerged animosity between them. Sir David had always spoken of Sir Robin with an avuncular detachment; that evening I perceived that there was a connection between them, and it was under severe strain. Equally, the sound of London, once as familiar as the hum inside my own skull, had become jarring and noisy, and I felt that the world had been passing under my nose quite unnoticed since the day I entered St James's Square.

It turned out that I had a good look at Caroline, for she rode straight through my field of sight for half a minute or more. She was a grand matron in a crimson shawl and a small turban of a slightly darker hue, which she touched momentarily as she first came into view. I recalled accounts of her life in Italy which were dominated by her love of loose-fitting clothes and even of wearing no undergarments, and wondered if she felt constrained by her upholstery. Her cleavage was ample even from a few yards away, and her face the flat pinkish white which comes from sweating under a good deal of powder. Of course it was impossible for me to know this, but the overwhelming impression was of a lonely, disgruntled woman who knew that it would not be long before this huzza-ing crowd turned either away from her or else on her. If she had any sense, by that stage she would be abroad again, spending the shillings earned by the men who cheered her that evening on brocade for her Italian lover's breeches.

And then the Queen was gone, the shouts ended, and a strange flatness descended on the carriage.

Hetty sat morosely; Sir David seemed watchful, not least of me; and Sir Robin availed himself of a hipflask the size of a small bottle. I would have contemplated throwing myself from the moving carriage rather than spend my life with him, but I was not Hetty, and that evening the extent of our differences was all the more apparent for being aired in public.

Unlike Hetty, and seemingly in contrast to every other woman in London, I am not made for carousing. It was as if

Isaiah was by my side rather than Sir David, and in my head he sermonised his way through my *soirée* of vodka jellies and promenades.

Hetty made a study of fashions in shoes, since so many women were hitching their skirts over their ankles as they walked exaggeratedly or aped a dance to some tune as they passed a music tent. She decided that green suede was the most glorious material for slippers. Sir Robin, flushed with wine and groping – much of it, but by no means all, of Hetty – said that he would have her on a green suede sofa if it made her happy. Her expression suggested that it would not, but she laughed and thanked him, presumably because a suede sofa would cost a good deal of money.

My one pleasure was the Thames, for at Vauxhall it seemed cleaner and the air fresher than it ever did by Blackfriars, and I steered Sir David as far from the people and as close to the balustrade as I could.

The sun had vanished half an hour earlier, and the night was chilly. Sir David put his jacket around my shoulders. It was warm, and I fancied I was wearing a cross between a coronation robe and a pelt.

'You might perhaps be growing tired of me,' he said.

'You can see that I am not enjoying myself,' I replied. I wish I had mentioned the pleasure his jacket gave me. 'I do not want to appear ungrateful, really I don't. I think I have spent so much time bent over a press that I am not suited to so much light and air.'

'There is no light and air here, there is only noise,' Sir David cemented.

I did not understand why he had consented to come, beyond assuming that once I got here, I would enjoy it. 'There is the sea,' I said. 'Or at least, the promise of it.'

'You are a strange woman, Nell Wingfield. What does a press-bound creature like you know of the sea, besides waves parting in your Bible? Though you are right: in London the Thames loses the character of the river and takes on something of the greatness it is soon to join.' He held my chin. 'But are you honest? Or are you as murky as these waters and the ink that still stained your fingernails when we first kissed?'

I looked down at my hands, which were now as blank as an unprinted page, and as anonymous. I no longer knew myself, so how could I be honest?

He let go of me. 'Tell me, Nell: was it Hetty's idea? Be honest, please. I doubt Robin has the courage for it, not with me present.'

Of course he meant the engagement. 'I was instructed not to tell you,' I said. 'Please believe that I wanted to, but Hetty made me promise not to – she said it was what Sir Robin wanted, and he would tell you when he was ready.'

'Humph!' replied Sir David, sounding more satisfied. 'I wonder what he had in mind.'

'I do not know, beyond that it will be a very private affair –'

'It depends how you define private!'

'I repeat that I do not know. She said nothing of guests.'

Sir David stopped and looked at me.

'*Guests?*'

I waited, trying not to cry, wishing Hetty had never told me about her engagement.

'What are you talking about?'

I opened my mouth, but only a sigh came.

He shook his head, walked away for a few paces, and returned. 'They are *betrothed*?'

I rubbed my hand over my face hard, struggling to understand how the conversation had galloped off so.

'Your silence is chillingly eloquent.' Sir David pinched the bridge of his nose. He held the railing and laughed, a harsh bark. Paint crinkled under his grip and cascaded. 'It could be worse, I suppose. His mother hoped that he would marry an heiress, but I always knew he would not manage that. Tell me, does he intend to make Hetty the toast of the town? That will be expensive. I am curious to know how many thousands will be fluttering out of my pocket-book on constructing the flimsy edifice of her reputation.'

It had not occurred to me that Sir David would have to fund such a fancy, though I knew that Sir David was paying for Sir Robin's time with Hetty.

'What does your Bible say, Nell? The foolish builder constructs his foundations on sand.'

'Luke 6, 49: that the man who without a foundation built a house upon the earth; against which the stream did beat vehemently, and immediately it fell; and the ruin of that house was great.'

'The ruin of our house: that is what I am presiding over, Nell.' Sir David looked at me with such fondness that I began to cry.

'Don't blub or I shall think that is it I who am being played,' he said quietly.

'I know no more than that he has asked her,' I insisted. 'And that she has accepted. And that she is wearing his ring.'

'And so there are secrets between us. I had not realised that your loyalty to Hetty ran so deep. But I suppose you have your days together.'

I thought of how little time Hetty and I had spent talking of late, when compared to that first week when I'd thought our friendship would flourish. 'I hoped she would be the sister I never had. And I did not want to meddle in matters between Sir Robin and you. I thought it was for him to tell you, and not me. You are cousins, and that means more than friendship.'

He nodded, but he was still angry; he would not look at me.

Sir Robin and Hetty lurched towards us. 'Vodka jellies!' Hetty cried. 'You must try more of them!'

'You could perhaps have them at your wedding banquet,' said Sir David. Sir Robin and Hetty stopped, as if they were dancers on a music box whose key had ceased to turn. Then Hetty looked – what? Relieved, perhaps, that the deceit was over.

'Yes, we are to be married,' said Sir Robin. 'What of it? I know you think me a fool with the political wit of – of I know not what, but I will make my fortunes on the dungheap of this city's politics yet. There are rivers within rivers in this city, you know. Nell will attest to that.' He gestured at the Thames.

'I do not begrudge you any money,' Sir David said, 'for all the hasty words I spoke during our quarrel. Anything our family has, I hold in trust from our ancestors in order that I might steward it for our children. I do not own that wealth, any more than you do, Robin. And that, if anything, is the cause of my concern.'

And for this woman here, I willed him to add. But Sir David did not look at Hetty, and she, wise for once, stayed silent.

'You say that now,' scoffed Sir Robin, 'but who knows what you are plotting against me? For that is your way, is it not? All subtle intrigue.'

'You have never had anything to fear from me,' said Sir David. 'Your greatest enemy is yourself. There is no need to conjure me as your foe.'

The journey back was singularly awkward, and I was glad of the sparse lighting. Sir Robin suggested that he and Sir David sit with each other's ladies, and I was relieved that he refused, for I imagined that Sir Robin would not have been able to desist from a frotting festival, to judge by how he dishonoured Hetty's reputation while we waited for a carriage to take us back to St James's Square. Sir David was beyond disgusted, and thought twice about coming inside with us.

'The matter which you thought was Hetty's idea – what was that?' I asked, as soon as we were back in the comfort and safety of my room. In asking, I knew I might make matters worse, but whatever it was, it had made him angry with me, so better to clear it up than have something else festering between us.

He laughed. 'It seems all the more absurd now. And you must forgive me for assuming that you knew of it, for I can see that you do not. Your sojourn here has left you curiously immune to such depravities; your blackamoor stepfather has cast a long shadow over you, for all that you deny it, and you have tried to put your true calling behind you. It is trivial, really: Hetty and Robin proposed that we join them for the night.' He stood by the window, leaning his knee on the low seat. 'For a kind of tableau, shall we call it.'

'I promise you that I knew nothing of this,' I said. 'It is possible that Hetty herself has blanched from mentioning it, if she knew.' I could not imagine that she would want Sir Robin to come anywhere near me, and my fears for her deepened.

'If I know Robin, he will want to spectate. I doubt that he is driven by curiosity concerning your considerable charms and abilities, when after all, he had his chance on our first night here. So you should not be offended by that.'

'I am not,' I conceded. 'But what of you and Hetty? She is tiny, and blonde, and everything that I am not.'

'Yes, she is.'

My head bowed forward, as if my tears were millstones. Why had I ever come here? This humiliation was punishment enough, and it was nothing compared to what was in store for me for all eternity.

'Do not cry, Nell. You are being foolish, and I have seen more than enough of that tonight already. If you cannot see how fond of you I am then you are as foolish as all the other women in this house. Hetty is pretty, in an empty, doll-like way, but she is silly, and she has agreed to marry a degenerate half-wit for money that he does not have. All things that you will never be or would never do. In addition, Sir Robin is my cousin, and this makes me all the more alive to his faults.'

But I could not stop, and Sir David grew impatient, which was as unusual for him as my behaviour was for me.

'Damn it all, I cannot do or say more than I have. I will leave unless you calm yourself, which I trust you will soon do. I simply cannot abide *snivelling*. This is behaviour worthy of Hetty, and I do not warrant it.'

'Then go next door!' I shouted through my sobs. I had not raised my voice for years, and I did not recognise the horrible, raging creature I had become. 'She will find you there, if that is what you want!'

I surrendered myself to crying, knowing that it would be better to wash my face and run after him to propose a walk abroad or a glass of wine downstairs, but somehow I could not put one foot in front of the other, and I had only tried one vodka jelly. Now, I would say that months of grief had caught up with me, and this was the sort of crying that I should have done in my mother's final days, or at her sparse funeral. But all I felt that night was unloved, ugly and damned.

'I do not know you when you are like this,' he said, closing the door behind him. These were the last words he ever spoke to me.

13

THE NIGHT THAT TRANSFORMED our lives I was alone, trying and failing to sleep. I was used to lying awake, in part because Sir David was a fearsome snorer, but also because it comforted me to listen to the footsteps on the pavement below, and the drays clopping their deliveries – all the things I used to curse when I was living on Friday-street.

It was my third evening without Sir David, so my third night in a row of lying awake, trying to discern what was going on in Hetty's room, for she had been short with me the previous two mornings. Her severity had begun when I confided to her about my desire to depart from St James's Square. One consequence of our excursion to Vauxhall Gardens was my determination to return to my sister and to be ready for Isaiah's release from prison. I had entered into a form of indulgent despair, and it was time for me to jolt myself out of it.

It was not in Hetty's nature to perceive the complexity of my feelings, and I should have known that she would only interpret the news in terms of how it would affect her. 'So,' she said, giving a crooked little shrug and peering into her coffee cup, 'you will be scurrying back to Isaiah?'

'Yes,' I said.

'Sir David has not... given you any encouragement?'

Given our circumstances, this was such an odd phrase that I almost laughed. But I recalled our quarrel and my mirth collapsed.

Hetty must have seen my sadness, for she leaned forward and said, 'Tell me, Nell: why are you so sure that Isaiah will want you? Do not hurry from here, until you have made a plan of how best to ensure he will take you back.'

She had watched me avidly, and when she saw that this question had not occurred to me, she pressed on: 'After all, your mother is dead, so why would a man as impressive as you tell me he is wish to be saddled with two stepdaughters, one of whom should be making her own way in life instead of moping about after him, or else after some Gentleman who has been rimming her the past six months; and one of whom must be rather backward, if we are to be frank about it.'

I stared at the coffee pot, its gold spout shimmying through my tears. I wanted to tell her that we had always been a family, that Isaiah had pledged to return to us, that my brother might settle back to his apprenticeship as a cabinet-maker if I returned, but all these notions felt like pillow flock in a gale.

Close on a minute passed before I said, 'The time you are spending with Sir Robin is having its effect. You seem quite changed.'

She sniffed.

'You do not understand,' I went on. 'My feelings for Isaiah are – they are more – they are less...'

Hetty had smiled to herself then, with the look I imagined Sir Robin had when he and his hounds flushed out a rabbit.

'I am the only one who kept the wolf from his door,' I said falteringly.

'And you imagine that he will be grateful for that? There are plenty of women in this city who will work their fingers to the bone for him, if he is as fine as you say. If you want him, you had better win yourself a place in his heart. And you won't do that by fleeing here with debts to pay Mother Cooper, and a bailiff chasing hot on your heels.'

I abandoned my breakfast and went to draw myself a bath, where I sat for even longer than usual, watching the taps mist over and swiping them clear with my toes, dismissing the creeping fear that Hetty was right, and that it was naive to think I could leave 14 St James's Square without repaying my debt to Mother Cooper. And though I had wanted my mother to live more than anything, now she was gone, I did perhaps want Isaiah for myself as Hetty suggested, and some base part of me always had. As she had once pointed out, he was not of my blood, not even of my race. But for the accident of his having lived under the same roof as me for half my life, in the most profound ways he was a stranger to me. Perhaps she was right, and it was only a misplaced sense of propriety which prevented me from thinking of Isaiah as anything other than a father.

Though I could not imagine kissing Isaiah in a gaze-out-of-the-window-and-mope type of manner so favoured by many girls, he had appeared to me in my dreams, and once Sir David said I woke making strange moans. This pleased him, and he teased me that if I longed for him so in my sleep he would tell Mother Cooper, and insist that he get a discount, or even that he should be paid for his services. The prospect of incurring further debts put such a powerful terror in me that he begged my pardon and said he thought I would see the joke. If I ever dreamed aloud of Isaiah again, he did not tell me, and I have no memory of it.

❧

I had spent much of the previous two evenings in the parlour. Even the knowing looks from Mr Edwards – who appeared briefly on each evening – failed to confine me to my room, so disconsolate was I that Sir David had not returned. If he stayed away too long, I feared that I would have to depart without saying goodbye to him, and I did not know if I could face leaving him without an explanation. Equally, I hoped for his blessing. I did not expect anything else from him.

On the second evening, Mr Edwards poured me a glass of wine. 'There is no need to look so gloating,' I said, since I assumed that Sir David was away on business connected with him – or even on his advice, for Sir David's and Sir Robin's associates must surely be so appalled by the latter's matrimonial rush of blood to the head that they feared a similar one from Sir David, even though the characters of the men were so different.

Mr Edwards looked surprised, and for a moment I wondered if I had misjudged him. He shook his head. 'Go carefully here,' he said.

I failed to see how I was to do that, with no allies in the world and my departure imminent, so I merely nodded and sipped from my crystal glass.

<hr />

I must have been listing in and out of sleep without realising it, for I became aware of heavy, swift footsteps stopping under my window, and I sat up, convinced that it might be Tom, as often was the night I had kept myself half awake until he came home, once my mother had become too ill to listen out for him. I slipped into sleep again, and into a dream: my tears caused a second flood, and they washed away most of the city; carriages appeared like boats; portly old men bobbed along, clutching at their wigs as they floated away from them; and I was carried away with it in my blue silk dress, along with all the bedsteads of London, hundreds of thousands of them, some iron, some four-posters, most planks of wood with sodden rags clinging to them even more desperately than their occupants. Meg and Tom were swept past me without recognising me. There was only one figure who saw me, and he was standing on the prow of a solitary ship. It was Isaiah, and he watched me drown. I was too far away to see his expression as I struggled to stay afloat.

✦

The next time I awoke, the footsteps under my window became hammering on my door, and I leapt up, assuming that Sir David had lost his key. I pulled on my robe and lit a candle, which trailed wax like a train of tears as I hurried to help.

The noise came from the connecting door, and the key was not in my side of it. It was not on the shelf next to it, either. 'Someone has removed the key,' I said. 'You will have to open the door. Can you?'

'Oh no,' said Hetty, whimpering the words, as if this task was likely to take all her strength. After a moment and a good deal of fumbling, she stopped scraping the key against the door frame and engaged it with the lock. She flung the door wide, and behind her on the bed was Sir David, his neck and his crooked and spread-eagled body making him look as though he were a puppet which someone had had the notion of rearranging jauntily.

'What is he doing here?' I cried, in the face of the glaringly obvious.

Sir Robin was pacing up and down, up and down, as if his distress was a large dog in powerful need of exercise. He did not look at Sir David, while Hetty (who had by now turned round) and I could not take our eyes off him.

It was the sight of both of us transfixed so which brought an abrupt end to Sir Robin's walking. 'There has been a terrible mishap,' he muttered. It was the sort of thing he might have said if he had spilled a bottle of claret over one of Mother Cooper's white tablecloths.

'I can see that,' I said. I was about to comment on how Sir Robin's shirt was poking through his breeches, but I decided that I would speak only if it was absolutely necessary, and therefore kept silent. But he caught me staring, and tucked himself in.

'Nell,' whispered Hetty, in a small, distant voice, 'did Sir David ever suffer from pains in his chest when he was – when you were...'

I shook my head.

'Shortness of breath?' said Sir Robin.

'No,' I said.

'Well,' Sir Robin said, 'Hetty seems to have transported him to a level of bliss which has proved fatal to him, so unprepared was he for it.'

I did not tell them that most nights Sir David wanted to sit up and talk, or else sleep quietly, or else take me so gently that he would not need to pant and heave at the end of it: even in this terrible moment, I feared Sir Robin would see this as evidence of a shortcoming on my part, and report it to Mother Cooper, and I would be fined for it, and so would not be able to leave.

I looked over Sir Robin's shoulder at Hetty, who seemed to be ageing with fear; new lines had appeared round her mouth, and her cheeks were gaunt. I looked again at Sir David's twisted corpse and understood that Hetty must have rolled him off her, and this was how he had landed. I hurried to place his brocade dressing-gown over him, but this made him look like a rumpled eiderdown.

Hetty is worried that Sir Robin will no longer have her, I thought. He will not want to risk the scandal; and even if he does, perhaps he will not want to be reminded of the image of his dead cousin expiring on top of his future wife.

'I am sorry, Nell,' Hetty said, 'but he...'

But he what? But he insisted on having her? How many other nights had he spent with her? No wonder she did not want me to mention her engagement to Sir Robin to him. I shook my head; I would rather have remembered him in any way but this. And he had seemed so offended at my suspicions of him; how could I have been such a fool? I realised that I would be forced to remember my lovely David like this for ever.

'Shall we rearrange him?' Hetty asked.

'No,' Sir Robin practically roared; then he thought a little and said, 'I do not know. We should summon Dr Fielding. He is Sir David's most trusted physician. He would want him to be the man who saw him like this.' I wondered why so healthy a man as Sir David should have more than one physician, but I knew nothing of the ways of the rich beyond what they told me, so again I kept quiet.

'We will not get a doctor in here without Mother Cooper knowing of it,' I said.

'It is no matter. She will share the same concern as my family,' said Sir Robin.

'And that is, Sir?'

'That this is not viewed as a suicide.' He lowered his voice.

'How could it be?' I asked. 'You were both here to witness what happened.' And then I saw it: they would not want the doctor to know the true circumstances either, so they had to hope that Dr Fielding would conclude that Sir David had breathed his last tucked up alone in a whore's bed. No wonder Sir Robin was determined to call in a family doctor, for who else would put his signature to such a fiction?

'Here,' Sir Robin said to me, 'slip out, and get a message to the man.' He wrote a brief note, then folded the page, sealed it and addressed it to Dr Fielding, who lived only a few streets away. 'He is a gentleman's physician,' added Sir Robin when he saw me reading the grand address. I reflected that it might have been Hetty's own father we were calling for, had his fortunes been more favourable.

He took out a sovereign. 'Mind you get this message to him before rousing Mother Cooper.' He held the coin out to me. 'And you should wake her on your return.'

I shook my head. 'You do not need to pay me for this,' I said, noticing that Hetty looked fearful again in the face of my refusal. But I would not take a coin for fetching a doctor for any man, least of all for Sir David.

I cast one more look at Sir David before I left, part of me still hoping that he would show some sign of quickening, and that this would all turn out to be some terrible mistake. But Sir Robin's impatience buzzed like a hornet, and so I left.

There was no time for grief, so I concentrated on action and thought. It struck me as a tragedy that if one of the cousins was to die, it had to be Sir David, but the Lord often calls the more righteous back to Him sooner. And if it had been Sir Robin who had expired, then Hetty's hopes would have been ruined, and Mother Cooper would have ensured that she would be ruined too. As it was, if Sir Robin honoured his promise, she would survive. Wishing that I could stop trembling, I walked through the kitchen, waking Martha by drawing back the bolts with weak, clumsy fingers. I told her that help was needed upstairs, but departed before she could finish asking me what the devil was going on.

The grey cat slipped out with me and scurried towards the garden. Flight: that was a good name for him, I thought.

As I went to find Dr Fielding, I passed a poster. Something about it arrested my attention, and I paused to read it. It was a list of forthcoming executions. I had just taken in how crudely it was printed when a third of the way down, I saw my brother's name.

Part Two

14

As I sat on that bench in St Paul's churchyard, it was naturally on the final chapters of that sorry tale that I reflected. For there to be a murder as Mr Edwards had insisted, there had to be a murderer. I understood that Sir Robin Everley was capable of it, but I still could see no reason for the crime. For all Sir David's threats about cutting Sir Robin off, I did not believe that he would ever truly have the heart to do it. It was a threat to try and rein in his dangerous and increasingly erratic behaviour. In fact, Sir David had said when we were alone, the evening we had gone to Vauxhall, that it would be better if he set Sir Robin up to live respectably in his father's old house, than that he frequent places like 14 St James's Square for the rest of his life.

I returned to my first instinct: there had been no murder, and Mr Edwards was determined to secure my co-operation by any low means possible – Sir David's death was just the most convenient at his disposal.

As I was about to get up, a boy came to beg for an orange. Normally dirty children look eerily bright-eyed, but this one seemed to have grubby eyeballs and scarcely the will to ask. I gave him my last orange, holding my finger to my lips as I did so, for there were other children nearby, likely to descend like gulls. Too late: one saw, and scampered over.

'I have nothing left,' I said, my heart racing with all the sweetness I had just gobbled. He snatched the bag anyway, the torn paper spilling peel into the dust. He scooped up the peel and started stuffing it into his mouth. His face puckered at the bitterness but he stared at me defiantly as he chewed. I nodded, glad that he at least had some spirit in him, for he would need it, if he was to survive. He ran off, cramming peel in as he went. Some of the other children pointed, and one made to run after him, but they saw a baker's dray coming up New Change-street and charged towards that instead.

<hr />

The rest of the day passed in a humid fug of worry. Cheapside itself benefits a little from the Thames air, but Friday-street has a crook in it which traps heat and cold and allows no freshness through. Next door, the cow lowed and shuffled, and babies could be heard bawling and fretting above the church bells. Even their tolling seemed muffled by the heat, and it seemed to me that the bells of St Mary-Le-Grand could scarcely bring themselves to heave their weight to and fro to summon the sweaty citizens to their pews. At least the stone churches offered some sanctuary from the temperature.

I managed a few prints, though the work was slow because I had to keep my wrist off the paper so I did not crinkle it with sweat marks. Everything seemed to dry a little too crisply, and I worried that my eye had become less sure and my hand less confident in the time I had been away. I told myself that a little practice would not do any harm, and anything that distracted me from thoughts of Tom for even a few moments was a small miracle in itself. I gave Meg her usual job of pegging the prints to dry, though I am ashamed to say that I was so sharp with her when she dropped one and got black flecks in the Queen's vermillion cloak that she took to rocking herself by the door for a good hour before I could coax her back into the workshop with me. I felt all the worse because I was glad of her company, silent and reproachful though it was, as my thoughts swung between Tom and Mr Edwards' visit like some awful tocsin.

At six I could visit Tom. I spent the day worrying whether it would be the last time I would ever speak to him and wondering what on earth I would say. All I could do was escape the treadmill of my thoughts through work.

Leaving meant prising Meg away from the front door. I told her I was running a small errand to Mr Tagg's on Cheapside. That she did not believe me was evident; I soon realised that she was following me. She got as far as Wood-street, so I had to go back to the shop and threaten to lock her in before I could retrace my steps. I had told Meg that Tom had gone away looking for work, and would be back soon enough. If he had been transported, I wondered if we would have had to invent messages from some far-off place. We debated simply telling her that he might die, but we did not want to banish her further into the murky place within herself which she had inhabited all the more since our mother's death. It was perhaps worse to deceive her, but this seemed the least of my worries.

<hr>

As I entered Newgate, I was greeted by the sound of sawing. The platform was already erected, and the scaffold was almost finished, save for the crosspiece which would make it strong enough to carry the weight of all the men who would swing from it. This was being carried across the shoulders of a brawny carpenter. It put me in mind of a crucifixion, though here at least the condemned were not forced to construct the means of their own execution.

It is not for Tom, I told myself. *There are other men who might hang tomorrow, but not him.* There was no need to shudder, no need to hurry past; Tom would be saved. It was this ability, this desire of mine to believe that the best would come of the ominous, which had sustained me at St James's Square.

A sorry congregation of visitors was already waiting. Most were women, some with bread which they did their best to conceal under their shawls lest the gaolers should take a fancy to it. One carried a basket and wore a fine pelisse with an air of humiliated defiance that marked her husband out as a debtor. She stood apart from the other women, as if their poverty was a contagion. I had not brought food, for Tom would be given a meal on the King's shilling that night. He'd joked that it was worth being condemned to die if it meant getting fed a decent supper this side of Christmas, though he reckoned that once he was pardoned, the Crown would be after him with a bill for the beef he'd requested.

'Tom Wingfield,' I said to the gaoler. One of the women nudged her companion and pointed at me. To be the relative of a condemned man is to be a something of a personage in this city.

'He has been moved to a better cell in honour of his condemnation,' said his gaoler, ushering me in with a sweep of his greasy arm and a lopsided bow.

'I know,' I answered. The cell was above ground, though Tom said it was as dark as the one where he'd spent the fortnight before his trial. The worst thing about the visits was getting my eyes adjusted to the gloom: I couldn't see Tom at first; it was as if he had already been taken away.

I went over to him and sat on the bench. It was a plank fastened to the wall with two metal brackets, little more than a wide shelf.

'Did you find your spectacles?' I said.

He shook his head. 'They must have taken them. Still, there is not much to see in here.'

'We can find you some more tomorrow,' I said, searching his face for an echo of my hope. He wiped his nose on his sleeve, something I had never seen him do. He was as fastidious as our mother, and had always said that we were born to live in a more fragrant and ordered world than the one in which we muddied our feet each day.

Looking at the terrible transformation in him, it was impossible to believe that he had only been sentenced a fortnight previously.

'You are shaking,' I said.

'It is impossible to get warm,' he said.

I shook my head, feeling a damp chill beginning under my arms. It was like entering another world in there, where summer could not penetrate, and being above ground had little effect. The only difference, he said, was in the quality of the cold: in the cells below ground, it was stealthy and impossible to shake off; but in his last days, the cold came clothed with sun. The sunlight refused to cling to him, as if it knew that Tom was not with us for long and so it was not worth the trouble to warm him. Three days previously, he had developed a summer chill. Twice, fires had been made for him, and his gaolers, who were sometimes sober but mostly not, would linger over bringing his supper, wanting to know if he still believed in the cause for which he was about to die. If he had been Isaiah, he would have begun a sermon, and ignored the enquiries as to whether his cell gave him an adequate view of Heaven, and if he wouldn't like his scaffold constructed extra-high to help him on his way, and wasn't he grateful to have a brighter room so that he wouldn't squint quite so hard when he encountered the light of heaven? But he was not Isaiah, and so he simply thanked them and told them that anything he had to say, he would say to his family.

To me, he marvelled at the size of his quarters. He wished he could bequeath them to me for my private use after he was dead, so that I would no longer have to share with Meg, nor listen to Isaiah's nights with whatever woman he was likely to snare, now that our mother was gone. Mostly he made a comedy of things, just as our mother had tried to. So it was all the more surprising when he began to speak of our life before we came to London.

'I blame our father for her death,' he said.

We never mentioned our father, so at first I thought he meant Our Lord, or else Isaiah. I opened my mouth to argue with him.

He lifted his hand to silence me, but he could not raise it far for the weight of the chain. He had been strong, and it was shocking to see his thin shoulders strain with the effort. He stared at his manacle in surprise, as if he had forgotten it was there. 'No, I am convinced of it,' he went on. 'Seven years of living with him. Think of it, Nell. Seven years of watching him sleep, of breathing what came from his lungs. It must have been a kind of mal air, a disease which ate her from within.'

'But she left Preston more than ten years since,' I said, reminded of all the stories I had told Sir David.

'And all the marks he left on her,' he recalled, continuing as if he hadn't heard me. 'She said that death would be a welcome release from her scars. The ones on her back ached, you know. They seemed to get redder, the paler she got, as if they were festering.'

I did not know this, for she had never let me see her. Even when she had needed to be helped to stand over the privy pot, she insisted on having a sheet to cover her. I had assumed this was pure modesty, but now I saw that she had kept something from me which she had shared with Tom. Why, when I was her daughter? In an instant I was ashamed that I had been reduced to jealousy when my mother was dead and Tom condemned. I had always assumed he was her favourite because he was her first, and a boy, too: at that moment I understood how closely they were bound by what they had suffered while I had been too young to understand what I was seeing.

'I do not know,' I said. 'It is more likely that he was responsible for how Meg is. He beat mother often enough, when Meg was inside her.'

'Aye,' he agreed. 'He used to tell her that her womb was diseased, and Meg was the fruit of it; I always thought ill would have come from his seed, not from her. It was like him, to want to blame someone for his misfortune. Meg's simpleness was evidence of God's judgement on our mother – how could any father argue that? And so Meg was the reason Mother left, in the end.'

This was true – Mother said she knew there was something not quite right about Meg almost from the moment she was born, and she knew how much a withdrawn yet strangely wilful child would provoke her father.

'I hated him,' Tom said. 'And most of all, I hated that I was too weak to help Mother. When I was standing in front of a crowd and preaching, I used to imagine that Father was the Devil, and that gave me strength. I vowed that I would never be so weak as I was when I was in his house.' He shook his manacles. 'And now look at me!'

And may the Lord forgive me for this, but I could think of nothing to say. Even my tears were silent.

'We have never really talked. Forgive me, Nell.'

'We never stop talking, you especially. Talking is what brought you here.'

'I was becoming like Isaiah. I talked to God, I talked to strangers, I talked about God to strangers, but never to you, and less to Meg.'

You spoke to Mother, I thought.

'Promise me,' he pleaded, taking my hand in an icy grasp, 'promise me that you will do more with your life than set other people's stories, a letter at a time. You drove yourself away with too much work; you never looked up from the press long enough to find a good man, to go walking with him on Moorfields on Sundays.'

'Isaiah is at Moorfields,' I said.

'Isaiah! You might love him, Nell – no, there is no use protesting, not now – but Isaiah has his eyes too firmly fixed on heaven. I can see that it might be tempting to try to pull him to earth. Heaven knows, our Mother tried.' He held my eyes as he said this, and I was saved from replying by the return of the gaoler, who announced that Tom's last meal would be served presently.

'I don't know where you've been these past months, Nell, but I do know this: the Lord is full of forgiveness,' he said. 'Particularly for women.'

'Lot's wife did not find that.'

'But she was punished for looking back and that is what you must not do. Now leave me while I eat my beef.'

'Save your advice for tomorrow,' I said, wondering if I sounded as convincing as our mother had last December when she'd told us that she'd live to take us all to Moorfields at midsummer, for sure.

As I left, I handed the gaoler a shilling, for I doubted that Tom would be fed unless I did. It was the most expensive meal Tom had ever eaten.

15

WHEN MY TIME COMES, let it not be like this: Ketch the hangman stepping forward at an impatient signal from the Governor, the first condemned man blindfolded and led to the gallows, lifting his knees just a little too high in his desire not to stumble. An almighty clanking as the handle is drawn. Behind me, a man shouted '*Shame*!' and '*Liberty*!' but his voice was deadened by the rain. Ketch pulling on the thighs to finish the job he'd botched. Halfway down the left leg, the stocking stretched and went taut. A few hollow knocks, and a clatter like a rolling-pin as a wooden leg fell. The ripped stocking swung, already heavy with rain.

A gasp from the crowd: this was even more than they had bargained for.

'Ketch will not like that,' said a woman behind me with some satisfaction: dead men's stockings are a hangman's perk. 'And who would have predicted so much rain?'

'Aye, the weather has broken, all right,' said a man whose words seemed to be wrestling with his teeth. 'Just like that boy's neck.'

It was as Tom once said: these people no longer viewed the victim as a man – he was little more than a prop, a piece of wood or rope, something laid on for their entertainment. They should all have been on their knees praying for him, but instead they were joking and casting about for someone to fill their ale mug.

People often compare a hanging outside Newgate Gaol to a courtyard theatre, and I could almost see what it would be like if a yank on the ropes sent the men flying above the gatehouse, only to swoop down again in a blizzard of doves and silk scarves to delighted gasps and polite applause. The gents hanging out of the windows would be in red velvet boxes and they would not be swilling their ale so extravagantly. It was eight o'clock on a rainy June morning, but these men had the festivity of the night about them. One was dropping pistachio shells into the bodice of a girl about my age who was standing beneath them. She could not move for the press of the crowd, and the gents called down that she should have covered herself better or else grown a smaller cleavage if she did not want to attract their attentions.

Ketch had done a bad job, and there was shit blooming on the back of the hanging man's trousers to prove it. The body was still quivering as it died. The crowd was quiet for this, which meant that we heard the grinding of the rope. When it stopped, all that remained was the sobbing and the rain; the rain which was so heavy it was like a host of voices.

The crowd began to murmur, a susurrus of trouble: it did not approve of a poorly done hanging. The Magistrate took off his hat and tipped rainwater from its brim. The water slopped over his feet, and his shoe buckle glinted as he stepped backwards. This was the signal for the executioner to get on with it.

'Like as there'd have been a pardon, if there had not been a cloud in the sky,' someone behind me said. 'Guvnors would not have risked a hot-tempered riot.'

'Or if there'd been a coronation,' added another.

'Or if it had been yesterday.' There was general laughter at this.

'You must not listen to them,' Isaiah instructed, as much for my benefit as for theirs. 'It is pagan to see our destiny determined by the weather.'

'Is that so?' said a satisfied-sounding woman. 'Then why do we speak of the heavens opening?'

It would have made no difference if the sun had been shining; all those present would still have filled Tom's last minutes on this earth with their chatter about the weather.

Tom stepped forward. The ordeal was even worse for him on account of the waiting: he was given a few extra minutes on this earth in return for an intimate acquaintance with how his neck would loll and his shit might pour once old Ketch had dropped him. When I twisted my neck, I could see that he had drawn an *x* in the sawdust, then a line under the *x*, and some other glyphs which I could not make out and would not have understood if I could. My mother had always told him that he should do his sums to keep his mind occupied. As an apprentice cabinet-maker, Tom might have taken comfort from the familiarity of those rain-clotted shavings. He had not wanted to be a printer, though like his supposed apprentice-master Will Davidson, he could not settle to anything fully, beyond running to keep out of Isaiah's shadow.

A delay while they shortened the rope for him. Tom was tall, a full head above the hangman, and his arms were much thinner than the staves they used for the gallows. I'd spent all night awake, wondering if Tom had got his last meal, feeling the wind get up, listening to the rain start, shifting about and sniffing the air like next door's cow. Did Tom do the same? Had he spent the night praying, like Isaiah, who had come home late then paced the chapel until dawn?

Two giants with fine white-blond hair had moved in front

of us, and we had to crane our necks or else shuffle over if we were to see.

'We should be closer to him,' Isaiah said. 'It is like having two snow-capped mountains between us and Tom.'

'Tom asked that we stand a few rows back,' I replied. 'He thought he would be more likely to see us here.'

Isaiah nodded slowly and made a square line with his mouth, as if he was shutting in the thought that this was one more example of the poor judgement which had brought Tom there. I realised that Tom had wanted us to be here to spare us, so that we would see less, and not more.

'I did not imagine it would pour like this.' As I spoke, it was raining so heavily that I might have been looking at Tom through a window with streaky glass you couldn't clean, even if you could have reached it. I doubted he could see us, and the press of the crowd was so mighty that there was nothing I could do about it.

'There is a sound abundance of rain,' Isaiah agreed, as if the clouds were to be praised for their attendance. 'But this should not surprise you, Nell: the Lord bringeth water even out of fire.'

One of the giants turned round to see who was speaking, and I took the opportunity to move between them.

At last I could see him. Tom scraped his foot sideways, removing the marks he'd made in the sawdust. As he looked up, I glimpsed him as he might have looked if he had lived to Isaiah's age, which is forty: furrows carved around his mouth by twenty-one more years of the effort of suppressing a laugh. After what seemed a long silence, Tom called on the Lord to have mercy on his soul. His voice was loud, which was just as well, because the chaplain was not about to funnel Tom's words up to Heaven, on account of Tom being a Unitarian and not an Anglican. (The chaplain was of course happy to funnel into his purse his hefty fee from the

Magistrate for offering Final Offices to men who had as much use for them as a cat would.)

'And as for my so-called crimes' – Tom tried to raise his hands as he said this, forgetting that they were bound to his waist, and almost pitched forward – 'my only crime is to be the enemy of a borough-mongering faction! A faction who would deny the Queen!'

'A what?' One of the straw-headed giants shouted over the crowd's approval. He barged forward so that he was next to me, his face the very picture of anticipation: 'What'd he say?'

'It means that he has been defeated by a small group of men who control Parliament for their own ends,' Isaiah proclaimed to the crowd.

'That is like announcing that it is a summer's morning,' said the other straw-head, removing his cap. 'Huzza the Queen!'

'Stop, all of you!' I said. I couldn't bear any of it, Isaiah's preaching least of all; if he could have arranged the heavens, he would have ensured that the strongest rays of sunlight always fell on him.

'Step aside, Adam,' the giant who was still behind me said. 'The girl cannot see.'

'What? With legs as long as that?' laughed Adam, the giant in front of me. He received a thwack with his friend's cap for this, and Adam took a space behind me again. This movement increased the pressure of bodies, and for a moment I thought I might be pushed upwards or else trampled downwards, it was impossible to say which way the crowd would go. Isaiah shook his head and gave them his long *more in sorrow than in anger* stare.

I knew Tom was not going to say anything more – it would be too great a struggle for him to speak without waving his hands about. Isaiah straightened, his arm tensing next to me – was he about pull his red handkerchief from his pocket and wave it so that Tom could see him?

Tom gazed over the crowd again. He had no spectacles, and I could not lift my arms, so he would have to search for Isaiah's black face to find us, which he soon did: I knew he could see me because of how he smiled, and I jumped up, snatching Isaiah's red handkerchief and waving it high, calling 'God Bless you, Tom!' The people around me started jumping and shouting too, *God bless the Queen! Away with Old Corruption! Save this boy!* until the soldiers at the foot of the scaffold stopped shuffling and loaded their muskets, *God Bless the Queen* until the Under Sheriff called for Ord*ahh!* and pointed out hoarsely that there were men of the British Army *Down with the regime!* who were willing to fire on peaceful citizens, *Long live the Queen!* until a yeoman demonstrated this by firing into the air, and the press of humanity around me tightened like a noose. *Long live Queen Caroline! Hang the King!* The body of the crowd quietened a little while it decided if it would stampede.

'Let her lower her arms,' shouted the giant who was not Adam, pushing men aside so that I might put away my hand-kerchief. 'Do you want her to hang, too? If she keeps that red flag flying, the yeomen will know where to charge.'

The shouts died as suddenly as they had begun.

'Aye, if anyone moves, there will be a second Peterloo here,' said Isaiah. Last summer, hundreds of men had been trampled in a peaceful demonstration in St Peter's Fields, which is in Manchester, when the Hussars charged the crowd with their sabres. 'And Tom being executed for rousing a protest against it. There would be a sharp symmetry in that.'

The noose swayed in the wind, counting out what remained of Tom's life.

I braced myself against the forward press of the throng. To my left, a woman clawed at her own throat and fought for her breath, as though the crowd was savaging her. If they stampeded and men fell, dozens would be killed by working men's boots with no need for the soldiers' mares to lift a hoof. And what would become of Tom? Would they take him away, for fear of angering us? Would he be pardoned? *Perhaps we can save him after all*, I thought, pitching myself backwards into the throng; *if there is a disturbance, he might escape*. Isaiah caught my elbow. I pushed myself forward, only to be lifted at my waist by two large hands.

'Steady she goes,' said Straw-head. He set me down gently once I'd righted myself, but he did not let me go. I shook myself to be free of his grasp, but I could not move. He dropped his hands, saying he was sorry if he had hurt me.

Isaiah thanked him.

'Rightin' a knocked ale bottle in a tavern is easier,' he joked.

'And he is practised at that,' said another voice.

'You should come to one of my meetings,' Isaiah added. Imprisoned by the crowd, he listed from one foot to the other.

The yeomen fixed bayonets and pointed them at the scaffold.

Tom was led forward. The crowd stood calmed, quiet save for some hissing.

An agony of moments while the rope was checked. Old Ketch put one hand round it and tugged. He held his other palm up to the sky, as if it was the weight of the rain he was measuring.

At a sharp gesture from the Magistrate, the Chaplain stepped forward. Tom kept his eyes on the ground, but he punctuated the Chaplain's text with shakes of his head.

A black bag was placed over his head, then the noose. A

nod to Ketch. In a shriek of hinges Tom was gone. This time there was no scuffling below the platform, no yanking on his legs.

'The job's a good 'un,' a man said.

Isaiah watched Tom, his lips moving. Slowly he gained volume, and the people around us remained silent, listening. Isaiah has a voice like the ocean that brought him here: deep, rolling, full of the pitch of gentle waves one moment, able to threaten a storm the next. He recited verses from the Book of Revelation, his words falling in with the rhythm of Tom's swinging:

> And they cried when they saw the smoke of her burning, saying...
> Alas, alas, that great city, wherein were made rich all that has ships in the sea...
> For in one hour is she made desolate.
> Rejoice over her, thou heaven, and ye holy apostles and prophets; for God hath avenged you on her.

The rain made the buildings seem darker and more menacing than ever. Then Isaiah recited Psalm 120, which was my mother's favourite. Had Tom's head not been so angled, it might have been bowed in prayer.

My brother was dead. Isaiah said no more verses, but there was a liturgy in the falling rain.

16

THE COURTYARD WAS STILL thronging, but the press around us eased. Some men replenished their ale mugs from the seller to the left of the scaffold, and soon the chink of his coins was lost in conversation. Two women who looked a little like turkeys in their black Quaker bonnets discussed how to get from here to Drury-lane while avoiding the crowds. They concluded that it was impossible, and they were probably right. I still wished everyone would be silent, but there would have been even less use for it now that Tom was gone. All the while Tom swayed, as if his entire body was being transported by a tune that only he could hear.

'There is a wind getting up,' a man behind me said.

'Aye, that boy is like a weather vane up there,' said another.

'Hush,' said the first man, 'that's the fambly. Or the girl is, at least. I don't know about that blackamoor.'

A stocky man leaned a ladder against the scaffold, picked up a hacksaw and began to climb. He stopped on the second rung and bounced on it, testing. He put the saw between his teeth before he ascended again. He did not have far to go, since most of Tom's legs had disappeared through the trap door, and the care he took with his own body was in contrast to the ugly angle to my brother's neck. He leaned over and grasped the rope, wrapping his left arm round the ladder to brace himself against my brother's pendulous weight.

'Rain and rumbling bellies are proving more powerful than the urge to destroy a little of the wealth of this city,' said Isaiah, watching the queues for hot rolls and chestnuts grow. It was impossible to believe that a few minutes before, we had thought this crowd might stampede.

I raised my finger and shook my head so that Isaiah would not interrupt me: as long as I concentrated, I was convinced that they wouldn't let Tom fall like a piece of meat in my uncle's shop.

The rope slackened; Ketch or some other man below the scaffold must have been holding him. The man with the hacksaw could not rely on Tom's weight to keep the rope taut, but this presented no difficulty to him: in half a dozen cuts Tom was gone. His body was not given to us, because it was the property of the Crown. Isaiah became fond of saying that we could not have afforded a proper funeral even if it were not, for we had spent everything we had and quite a bit we didn't on burying our mother. The truth was, I had left 14 St James's Square with five sovereigns, half of the money Hetty had slipped me the morning after Sir David's death, and I would have found some way to give Tom a decent burial if I could. (I had given three sovereigns to Martha and two to Suky, though both had tried to refuse them. Martha had looked on them with sorrow, and said she would have made good use of them thirty years ago. Suky said 'I will only squander them, you know,' and had shaken her head with a strange blend of contempt and incomprehension when I said she should see them as her passage out of the house.)

'Ah, Nell,' Isaiah said. 'We must leave this place. We are like tigers, penned in by this mass of humanity. At moments like this it is hard to divine my mission.'

'Ah yes, your mission,' I replied, remembering how my mother would let Isaiah spend money on paper and printing ink instead of the medicine and firewood she needed. When I was a child, I had an unlimited appetite for Isaiah's sermonising. 'Tom followed you in it, and look at all the liberty he has.'

Isaiah wiped the rain from his nose while he thought. 'I tell you, what has happened here today is a sign: this world is ending.'

I shook my head. 'Last year, there were three prophecies of the Apocalypse in our chapel alone – three accounts of the end of the world being ushered in by some violent uprising. How many more prophecies are there in this vast city?' The crowd had thinned to the extent that there was room for me to spin around and hold out my hands as I said this.

'She catches raindrops like auguries,' said a woman in a tatty red satin bonnet who was clutching a grimy shawl that might have been white a generation before. She was one of a clutch of women standing nearby, peering upwards as if Isaiah was a mother-bird ready to feed them from his mouth. If Isaiah ran off to be a hermit, a respectful crowd would surely gather the first morning he came out of his cave.

'But there is mercy in the rain, sister, is there not?' said Isaiah. The woman turned her face up towards him like a poppy in a warm breeze, and in this moment she would have felt that they were the only two people on the face of the earth.

'Where is the mercy?' I asked. 'The only mercy is that my brother's body can no longer feel the cold.' The bonnet drooped, and its owner gave me a look wavering between pity for my loss and disappointment that her moment with Isaiah had been curtailed.

'Here is one blackbird who looks as though he might

fly,' smiled a girl with a gravel-pit of a voice, showing my stepfather teeth darker than his skin. 'The Black Prince!' He accepted the title with a benevolent smile. Everywhere he went, Isaiah Douglas absorbed admiration as his skin did the sun.

'Tom will have been glad that you were all here,' I said, partly to drag my stepfather's attention back to my brother, but mostly because it was true. Although Tom was never content to be a planet in Isaiah's orbit, he loved our stepfather as much as I did. But Tom had grown to admire him from a distance, while I could never be close enough to him. *There is no air for us to breathe once he enters a room, but you do not notice. First our mother, and now you,* Tom used to say. *Your eyes toddling about after him.*

'I am sorry about Tom,' another black-toothed woman with breath like the Fleet in summer offered. 'Your brother was nobbut a little lamb.' She was a Northerner, like my parents. I was seized by the desire to ask if she knew my mother, as if the country north of London were a small village. 'But Isaiah now, he is a wolf in sheep's clothing!' She laughed at her cleverness, a high hawking sound which was at odds with the depth of her voice. Two women whose pink and grey tear-stained faces I recognised from the very front of the crowd stared at her.

'Now is not the time to truckle with beasts of the field,' Isaiah said. 'Come to chapel this evening, and we will ponder further on this.' They would not need to wait that long, I realised: he was winching up to tell a story to anyone who would listen. 'Thank you, my friends,' he went on, his voice swelling. 'This man, my son Tom Wingfield, will be remembered for –'

'His *son*?' said the toothless woman next to us, her words accompanied by a spray of spittle, 'It is against Nature.'

'Stop!' I said, taking Isaiah's arm. The wool on his sleeve was wet, and the fine threads where it was wearing thin were like veins.

'They are silent, Nell,' he said, his voice all soothing. He thought I was shouting at the people around us.

'No!' I countered. 'If anyone was to speak today, it should have been Tom. As it is, they have cut the rope. Tom is gone, and you were too busy with these strangers to notice.'

Isaiah looked blankly at me, then shook his head, as if he had always known that I would turn on him in the end. He moved away from me and addressed the crowd. 'Jesus said, "Whenever three man gather in my name, then I am with them." I tell you, the Lord is with us today.'

'Aye, and some of his keenest pairs of ears are impaled on sticks twenty feet in the air,' said a voice near the front. There was laughter from men near the beer-seller.

I braced myself for Isaiah's response, for he liked to have the monopoly over all wit, but he continued as if he had not heard. 'He is on the scaffold, with these men; and He walks among us, if you will see Him.'

A slack-jawed girl with crusty pinkish lumps for a complexion looked round excitedly, then pushed through the crowd towards us. 'Is it you?' she asked, taking Isaiah's hand and lifting it to her face.

He watched his hand for a moment, then touched the flaking skin. 'You are suffering,' he said.

'Can you heal me?' she pleaded, the skin around her mouth and eyes puckering and breaking as she tried to smile at him.

'He is not the Messiah,' I snapped, pulling his hand down, aware that I was shouting, so angry suddenly that I was transported beyond myself. 'There will be no miracles here. Do you see my brother getting down from the scaffold and walking?'

Isaiah half led, half carried me away, steering me round a water-pump. People were huddled around the pillars, sheltering.

He stopped near a sleeping accordion player, the rise and fall of his chest making it appear as though his instrument was snoring. I did not know whether Isaiah was about to embrace me or strike me, so I closed my eyes. When nothing happened, I opened them again. He was watching me, the lines around his mouth tight. 'Do you think that my being mute today would save your brother, or bring your mother back?' he asked.

'No,' I answered. *But there ought to have been something you could have done. You could not even keep yourself out of prison, even though you'd vowed you would never be incarcerated.* I did not say this, for I was afraid: he owned the printing press which was my livelihood, as Hetty had pointed out. And there was my sister Meg to look after. Now that my mother was dead, only affection, habit and duty would keep us together. I did not think that Isaiah loved us. I was sure he loved my mother, for he told her so as often as she had doubted it, until she decided that his love was like a mountain: everyone could see it from a distance, then it all but disappeared once you got close to it.

And then he was gone. I scanned the crowd of stragglers for him – he was making his way towards two men who were standing, out of place among the shabby throng, in fine cloaks. I saw that there was a group of men behind them who from the dust on their coats must have been masons, and I assumed that Isaiah's business was with them.

The straw-headed giant called Adam lumbered over. 'What use has a girl like you for legs like that?' he said. 'You should be sharing them around, you should, not keeping them to yourself.'

'You've said that once already,' I said, shaking my head

and looking round for his friend.

A dwarfish girl of little more than four feet sidled up to us. She giggled, and had to tilt her head to gaze up at him. 'I could make better use of them than she ever will, I'm sure,' she said, waggling one of her short legs at him and showing a grey slip and a muddy ankle. –

I looked for Isaiah, who was talking to the men in the fine cloaks. I could not see who they were, so I turned back to the girl. 'There was an execution here today, and this is Newgate. You must be looking for Smithfield, where you will find meat of the quality you are looking for, or else Seven Dials, where you might be paid a farthing for what you are offering him for free.' I turned away with as much of a sweep as the meagre cut of my sodden skirt would allow.

One of the balcony boys waved his tankard as if he was beating time to some anthem. And I was almost glad of all this, because it distracted me from wondering whether Tom would have been alive now, if I hadn't run away after our mother died.

'I am sorry to my bones that you have witnessed this,' said Strawhead, touching my elbow again. 'I lost my father and uncle the same way, and Adam lost two of his brothers. I am guilty of making a festivity of this occasion to fend off my memory of that day.' He looked down at his empty ale mug and shrugged. 'And as for Adam? Well, as you might be able to tell, he was never so good at navigating the world, and he's only got worse since we came to London.'

'You did not need to come here,' I said, and regretted it the moment I'd said it. After all, he was trying to tell me that his presence was not a matter of sport or theatre as it had been for the men on the balcony, the men who could now be heard discussing the best place to buy steak for breakfast. Before I could say this, he let go of my elbow and was gone. Adam looked at me like a dog that was about to be beaten, so I smiled, mouthed *sorry* and pointed at his friend. He gave me a broad and trusting grin and trotted off.

Until that moment, I felt as though I had been seeing Tom's execution in a series of fragments, as if I had been trying to catch his reflection in a broken mirror. Most of what I saw was the ugliness of the world he was leaving and strangers getting their ugly fizzogs in my way. I berated myself silently: I would never see the two simpletons again, and I had not even had the grace to thank them for their kindness, just as the previous evening I had not been able to offer any words of comfort and love to Tom. But instead of giving in to crying, I looked over my shoulder at two men arguing and jostling. Isaiah saw them and left the man he was talking to with a nod. The man was tall, with an angular nose, and wore a black cloak so fine that the rainwater seemed to sit on it respectfully: Mr Edwards. Before I had much chance to wonder what business he could have with Isaiah, he came towards me. A chill ran through my sodden skin. I had put all thoughts of Mr Edwards' threats out of my head and now here he was, standing over me.

'Ah! Mistress Nell. I thought I might find you here. My condolences.' He wafted his hand towards the scaffold as if my brother's death were a minor inconvenience. Something white caught the light – at first I thought he was carrying silk gloves, but he was holding an envelope. 'Stow this about your person,' he said, his eyes passing over me as if my body were still for sale, 'though it is perhaps a little heavy for your hem?' I coloured, and he nodded with a knowing smile. Hetty's sovereigns were stowed there, but how could he have divined this?

'Make sure you deliver it. By noon on Wednesday at the latest.' He glanced behind him, but Isaiah was drinking from a fountain, the water joining the grey puddle at his feet.

'What if I cannot get away to deliver it?' I said, stuffing

the envelope into my shawl. 'What if I cannot find the place?'

'Oh, you are adept at escaping, are you not? Somehow I doubt your stepfather exercises that degree of restraint over you,' he said, 'because if he did, you would never have crossed my path. It is a dark species of fate which has brought us together, and things will go the worse for you if you allow it to cast us asunder.' He strode off, then called over his shoulder. 'And Nell, all women like you have coins sewn into their skirts. Be sure that no man removes them from you. Keep your feet on the ground for once.'

'A fight is a rock thrown into a pool,' Isaiah said, making me jump, 'and more violence is its ripples. We must leave. There will be a riot here, and perhaps that is good, for what else can men do to show their displeasure?'

Isaiah rallied a little with his talking, and this last sentence carried. 'Huzza!' said a man standing near us, gazing up at Isaiah's face as if Isaiah was the sun and he was St John the Baptist emerging dazzled from his cave. 'May Peterloo live for ever! Remember all the martyrs! Long live the Queen!' I recognised him, and the men standing by him: they were chapel men, Isaiah's congregation before he was arrested. Two Constables looked over, interested. One nudged the other and pointed at me.

Isaiah felt my anxiety. 'We will discuss this later. I do not want you caught up in this today.'

'You are right,' I replied, 'we must go.' I was relieved: with all his sermonising, Isaiah had not noticed how hard I had been staring at him as he had talked to Mr Edwards. I longed to know what they had been discussing, but I dared not betray any interest by asking.

The crowd parted for us, and Isaiah took my hand to lead me through. He rubbed my fingers, then lifted my hand to examine it. 'So smooth,' he said. There was no change in his countenance, so I assumed that Mr Edwards had not said the edge of a word about my time at St James's Square.

'I put butter on them, when I could. And fat,' I said, avoiding Isaiah's eye.

'Of course,' he said, smiting his forehead with his palm. 'You left your brother and sister and the profession you claim to love above all else to find work on a farm.'

'I could not stand living in a butcher's,' I said.

'Hmm. It is strange that your uncle and aunt are not here.'

'And I wanted to find the place where we rested when we first came to London,' I went on, knowing I was blathering. 'I wanted to find the farmer who saved my mother's life.' Of course this was not true, but it was an answer, and Isaiah did not question me further.

17

As I PICKED MY way over the cobbles of Friday-street, it struck me as odd that nothing about the place had changed in the wake of Tom's death. In my sorrow, I observed our shop as a stranger might: our window was filled with cheap engravings of London streets, larger versions of the cards Meg used to sell. Harmless pictures in themselves, though a careful observer would have seen the political message in them: Spa Fields, The Tower, Parliament and Carlton House, home of the new King's allies, were all there, along with a squib of the King when he was Prince Regent, spending money on grand building projects which had the bones of working men as their foundations. A discreet sign promised further *VIEWS* within – the views of course being opinions in pamphlet form, chiefly of Isaiah's. Tom had written one or two, but these had been removed by the authorities, along with much else of our stock. They had even taken his tools, as if a chisel and a bradawl were likely accomplices in bringing down the Government. They would have been returned if he had been acquitted, but now they belonged to the Crown. It was nothing more than legalised theft, Isaiah said; what would the King and his men want with a set of tools, they who had never done an honest day's work in their lives?

Meg was waiting for us behind the door. 'Where is Tom?' she said. Isaiah raised his eyebrow; I shook my head. I still thought it unwise to tell her what had happened. I'd hoped that she would have been incapable of understanding my mother's illness and death, but she did, and powerfully: it seemed to turn her more violently in on herself, and make her even more averse to everything in the world except Tom, whom she took to following about like a familiar. To make things even worse, she always seemed to take lying very badly. And now there was no Tom, and we had lied to her about him, but as far as I was concerned, now was not the time to set matters right with her.

'Tom is gone, Meg,' Isaiah said.

I widened my eyes at him, wondering why he had bothered to ask my opinion if he was so ready to ride roughshod over it. I busied myself by making coffee for us all – I couldn't bear Meg's silence.

'He'll come back,' she said finally, and sat with her back tight against the counter, nodding to herself. She seemed satisfied: Tom was coming back, and that was that, as far as she was concerned. I didn't have the heart to argue with her – in fact, I almost envied her, believing that he was still alive.

'You'll make yourself dizzy, moving your head up and down like that all day,' I said. 'Come and help me count some buttons.' She never tired of this, and I don't think she ever noticed that it achieved nothing but keeping her occupied. My mother always dreamed of having a haberdashery shop: we would have had to keep our hands clean to sell lace to ladies, and Meg would have had buttons to parcel to her heart's content.

I was hoping that Isaiah would stay and talk more with us, not because I believed that Tom was up there somewhere listening to us, but simply because I wanted to talk about him. With my mother gone, there was no one left alive who knew him as well as I did. But Isaiah said nothing, and was opening drawers to see where I had put the prints I had finished the previous day. He said nothing about my having worked on the Sabbath. It did not occur to him to reminisce with me about Tom, and he would have seen it as a weakness if I had asked him to; the church in my stepfather's soul had hard benches. Tom and I always said it was a pity that he was the preacher, and not my mother, for she would have converted far more people through the simple example of her kindness.

There was a silence, or what passed for one on Friday-street: all that could be heard was Meg's back rubbing up and down the counter, the cow or else a human snuffling about next door, coal rattling down to a cellar, and indistinct shouts from Cheapside.

'Perhaps it would have been better if I had stayed to see what they did to his body, for I doubt it could be worse than the imagining.' I said to Isaiah.

He looked at me over the rim of his mug. 'When I was in the navy, punishments were always carried out with all men present, for the sight of tattered flesh and bloodied skin on the deck was powerfully worse than the sound of the beating.'

'So it was better not to see... what they did?'

'Over such an abyss of a question, I think there is no "better or worse", Nell. But you are a wise girl, and you will have known what is best for you. The Lord sends us no more than we can bear, and therefore the strongest of us experience the most. Through that experience comes an acquaintance with truth.'

'And so from that strength comes wisdom,' I said, familiar with what Isaiah was saying, for it is at the heart of our belief.

'From strength, and from labour,' replied Isaiah. 'Talking

of which, we will have more work soon. There are portents in the air this morning.'

'I can't smell them for the coffee you are drinking,' said Meg, taking the cup from me and heading over to sit on the floor beside Isaiah. We looked at each other. It was rare enough for her to speak, but this was also the first time I had ever heard Meg make a joke. I shook my head. 'Today, of all days,' I said.

Isaiah nodded his disbelief, and held his hand out so that it skimmed over Meg's curls so lightly she wouldn't notice it. 'Meg has grown,' he said, looking at me. 'And you have put childish things behind you, I see,' he continued, watching me smooth my skirts like a lady, a conceit I had picked up in St James's Square and could not shake off. I wondered how many other habits betrayed who I had been while I had been absent.

'It is as if you have grown to fill the space your mother left behind. You are what – seventeen now? But any man passing would take you for the mistress of this shop.' He looked at me as if I was something he was seeing for the first time. 'Which I suppose you are.'

I was so proud in this instant that I wanted to run upstairs and tell my mother, but then I realised that I was an idiot and the only reason I would be taken for the mistress here was because she was dead. And so was Tom.

'I will do whatever needs to be done today,' I told him, 'so that you might consider your sermon.' If he went out, I thought, I might be able to go and deliver Mr Edwards' message undetected, and escape the memories the shop housed as I had done the past six months.

'Hmmm,' said Isaiah, who seemed full of his own thoughts. 'We will not open the shop, of course. Tonight's sermon has already been written in blood, but I do need to go out – I have some matters to attend to. A gentleman might call, and he will bring some plates with him.' The plates from which we took prints determined the quality of my work as much as the paper and ink we could afford; some we bought up second-hand from dealers, taking care not to find ones worn flat from years under the platen. Sometimes, but rarely, we were able to take a new artist's work. From Isaiah's tone, I judged this to be such an occasion. 'There will be much inking-in of skirts for you. If you like the look of the work, then take it.'

'I will,' I said, looking down to hide the pride I felt at the trust he was placing in me.

'It is perfectly respectable for a girl to serve a gentleman in a shop like ours, and you are always free to reject any printing which offends you,' he said. He often used this defence to any of the chapel men who challenged him about involving me so much in his work; many of them said they would not let their wives attend meetings upstairs because it would mean them sitting above a palace of pornographic imagery, though mostly I think they wanted a night away from their women and a chance to linger in the shop them-selves.

'I will probably have seen worse, I assure you.' For once, I did not mean my life at St James's Square: I was thinking of the prints Mr Tagg displayed in his quadruple-fronted shop window on Cheapside: women inspecting their private parts, a print popular with the passing coster-boys; or else scenes of harems inspired by the visit last summer of the Persian Ambassador and his beautiful ox-eyed wife, the women's eyes widened by the pleasure of being seen to by a man with a large turban while sundry eunuchs looked on.

'You said that yesterday,' remarked Isaiah, putting on his hat and striding to the door. Perhaps soon you will do me the honour of telling me what you happened across on your travels.'

'I will wait here,' I said. It was not an answer, but Isaiah accepted it. Like me, he was keen to quit the shop.

Once I was alone with Meg, I debated whether I could risk darting out to deliver Mr Edwards' envelope. Under the pretext of inspecting how much cleaning the chapel would need before tonight's sermon, I climbed the ladder and studied the address.

M Rosaria
St Vincent's Court
Westminster London W.

Rosaria. The name was familiar; Mr Edwards was sending messages to one of the Italians who had recently left St James's. Why he required me to do this, I had no idea, and why to Westminster? Westminster! A part of London as bad as the stews of St Giles and Covent Garden, frequented by disreputables of all kinds, and a favoured destination for immigrants and those who had been dismissed from domestic service from the grander houses to the north. When I was at St James's Square, I had overheard one gentleman saying that no one could produce an accurate map of the area, and he had paid an old woman and her son to escort him through, since the employment of her knowledge and his brawn was the only way to survive the place. Though he had sailed to the Indies, he insisted that the most dangerous journey he had ever undertaken had been not five miles from where he was sitting. The other gentlemen present had roared with laughter at his stories of women who could be had against a wall for a sixpence if one were willing to risk the swamp of their private parts. Better to find one who would suck him off for a shilling, another had observed. The women, some of whom reckoned that there but for the grace of God went they, had laughed hollowly and studied their pearly nails.

Given that I had as much knowledge of the area as I had brawn, how was I to satisfy Mr Edwards and come back in one piece?

It would also take me at least an hour to walk there, even if I took the shorter but more stinky and perilous route along the Thames. Missing our caller would mean explaining to Isaiah why I had gone out, and that I could not risk. So I hid the envelope along with my other most shameful possession: the dress in which I had left St James's Square. The week before, I had stuffed it at the back of a long, low cupboard which ran under the rough platform Isaiah had constructed for himself. No one ever went into the cupboard but me, for I was the only one who ever did any sweeping, and it was there I stowed my broom. (My scrubbing brush and bucket were downstairs, for although it was more difficult to carry water up the ladder than it was to hoist a broom, there was no way of getting water up other than from the pump near Cheapside.)

The dress was the one the colour of a perfect summer sky, and even in the murk of the cupboard it was eerily luminous. As I stroked the silk, I was caught between wanting to parade in it and see its fine colours again, and taking it away and watching it, and all my memories of what I did with it, turn to ashes. I imagined Isaiah sermonising about it, telling the congregation that, like the dress in the cupboard in that very chapel, sin was so luminous a stain on our hearts that it could light our road to hell. The idea of him preaching about Tom's death with only a plank of wood and some air between him and my whore's dress was grotesque enough to make me laugh. Sir David said its lace trim reminded him of light cloud; it had been a gift, but I had been careful to leave

Mother Cooper half of Hetty's money for it all the same. The dress had as much place in Isaiah's chapel as a harlot in heaven, but there it was anyway.

I stuffed the envelope in the dress's ample folds and closed the door swiftly, as if the cupboard's contents were likely to escape and come flying after me if I didn't get them shut in quickly enough. Then I went down to wait for our new work with thoughts of Tom as my only companion.

❧

Within the hour, a new set of engravings arrived, carried by the engraver himself. He set them on the counter carefully, with both hands, then removed his hat in so embarassed a manner that on any other day I would have laughed.

'Titus Soane at your service,' he said.

'Nell Wingfield,' I said. 'Mr Douglas has asked me to take delivery of these.' I wondered if he knew how much of the printing I did.

'Oh!' he said. 'I should show you these. I have been rec-ommended to Mr Douglas most highly.' He produced letters of introduction, taking a pair of wonky spectacles from his pocket at the same time. I nodded towards the letters. 'I – my stepfather – will not have need of those, I am sure,' I stam-mered, as though this were a mark of our trust in him, and not an admission that we had never taken on work grand enough to request references.

He looked confused.

'The letters are my business,' I said. 'What you do with your glasses is your business, Mr Soane.'

His smile was so much like Tom's that his face was like a chink of sun through the clouds. Tom, I thought, have you found some way of comforting me through this man? I shook my head, chiding myself: such crude ideas of a soul possessing the living are for heathens.

'Forgive me,' he said, mistaking my silence for consternation. 'Strange though it may sound, I find it easier to hear with these on.'

'No, it does not sound strange,' I said. 'My brother found the very same thing.'

He bowed slightly, shaking his head. 'What they did to him was a terrible business. And at one point it looked as though there would be a stampede.'

'You were at the – Newgate?' I could not say Tom's name, nor what they had done to him.

'Yes,' and with his reply, all the anxiety in his face melted away out of sympathy for me. *You are too gentle to be producing the kind of engravings we sell,* I thought. 'But I was not there to gawp. I met your brother and your stepfather last year, and we have a number of mutual acquaintances. I came as an act of witness.'

I nodded, acknowledging the depth of faith in his words. I realised that a similar faith no longer resonated in me, even though I had resumed a much more godly turn of phrase since I had come back to Friday-street. Perhaps Isaiah was right, and the wicked are exiled from their souls long before they die. So far gone was I that I reflected on this in the same way I might have noted that we were low on ink.

I saw Mr Soane looking at me and I tried to smile at him, but my face was all of a jelly and wouldn't do as I asked.

He shook his head again. 'You have been through a great deal,' he said. 'When my mother died, I continued working every day – I had an apprenticeship of sorts, and my place was far too valuable for me to risk missing a day, even for the funeral. I took a half-day for that.' He paused here, and I saw what this dedication had cost him. 'But even so,' he continued, suppressing a sigh and holding me with his clear greenish-grey eyes, 'When my mother died, I found that I could stare at the same plate for hours on end, and not cut a single line. My master was kind to me. He would place a hand on my shoulder once in a while and leave it there. It was enough, just about, to remind me that I was not alone in the world.'

'How old were you?' I said.

'I was fourteen, so this was eight years ago.'

'And do you feel less alone in the world now?'

He fiddled with his parcel of plates, plucking at the string which tied them. 'The grief fades in the way that a storm does,' he said. 'But as happens after a storm, you find that there are many unknown objects washing about, and they can be almost as treacherous as the storm itself.' He thought about this. 'I do not know how to explain this very well, for no one has asked me before. Which is, I suppose, in itself another answer to your question.'

I thought it a wonderful explanation. 'I understand you perfectly. Or at least, I think I do. Not all men have such a gift.'

He laughed and made a puzzled face. 'It is not one I intend to use,' he said, with a glance upwards to the chapel. 'Your stepfather would think it a weakness in me, but if I am called on to talk to more than one person, I clam up. I could never be a preacher.'

'I am glad to hear it.' My words came out with more force than I'd intended, so I tried for something lighter. 'Let's hope that St Peter is not accompanied by all his angels on your day of judgement or you'll struggle to make an account of yourself.'

He looked alarmed, most likely wondering if this was not blasphemous, but he managed to smile and placed a hand on the parcel. Fair skin stretched fine over long fingers.

I opened the engravings. The plates were separated by sheets of thick paper.

'I have printed them,' he said, pride and expectation in his voice.

You cannot tell the quality of a plate until it has been printed; some engravers do not understand how their craft will appear on the page, but I could see that these illustrations had just the right mixture of strong lines and lighter strokes. They were ambitious, too: one showed Queen Caroline in a procession through the streets of Hammersmith, her house etched gently in the background. 'You have not flinched from marking in the crowds, Mr Soane,' I said.

'Please, call me Titus. But you think the etching is too cluttered?'

'Not at all. You render the character of so many individual faces without detracting from the strength of the piece. And there is such a sense of movement; truly the Queen is carrying the crowd with her, or else they are carrying her. This reminds me of Mr Cruikshank's work, which I admire greatly – though you have your own style, of course,' I added hastily, in case he thought my praise damned him as a mere fair-handed copier.

'You are very kind. And your stepfather's terms are generous.'

'I'm glad, for we do not get much passing trade – you will need every farthing you can get from the prints we do manage to sell. You would be seen more if you were in Mr Tagg's window in Cheapside.' Mr Tagg: I had not laid eyes on him or his ferret of an assistant for months, and my spirits sank at the prospect.

'I do not seek fame,' he said. 'I will never live up to my name.'

'It is a grand one for a Welsh God-botherer, and no mistake.'

That smile again. 'I am full of admiration for you. I hope you will not have to labour too hard over these prints.'

He was gabbling a little now, and he pushed his letters of introduction forward, evidently having forgotten what I had said about them.

Curious, I read them. They were from two men who I am almost sure frequented 14 St James's Square: one a Lord from one of the Yorkshire Ridings, the other a Comptroller at the War Office who had little of the King's purse to spend and even less to do, now that our Foreign Secretary Lord Castlereagh was forever abroad settling disputes over a lavish dinner rather than going to war.

Had Hetty put in a kind word via her new husband or did this Titus Soane have some link with Mr Edwards? That would explain the conversation between Mr Edwards and Isaiah. I looked at him again, and now all trace of Tom had vanished. I was going soft in the head, I realised. Who but a well-connected man would have a name like Titus? He was here to spy on us, most likely. I looked again at the prints. There seemed to be nothing in them that would bring us to the gallows, but it was most likely a matter of time before someone was sent to search the premises; and then the constables would discover the dress I had stowed upstairs. We would have to take his work, or else we might well starve, but we had to be careful.

I recalled – as if I had been able to forget – what Mr Edwards said of the death of Sir David, that it was murder, and that we were in danger. Poor Tom hanged for far less, and I knew that in any court my word would have no more weight than a dot over an 'i' on my death warrant. My silks and sovereigns could well be a noose round my neck: they would not need to go to the trouble of trying me for murder; they could simply swing me for theft, whatever Mr Edwards said.

'I thank you for these engravings,' I said, my tone all starch by contrast with my friendliness of a moment before.

'I will be sure to pass them to my stepfather – who has just returned,' I added, smiling at Isaiah as he entered.

Mr Soane frowned at me curiously then turned to Isaiah. For once, he had little interest in talking, and attended to the engravings instead.

'The new times bring with them a different kind of work,' Mr Soane said, with a glance towards me. 'Safer for you, perhaps, too – if you can stomach it,' he continued, lowering his voice. He looked up. 'I would not wish to offend your, er –'

'Do not worry, she is discreet, and familiar with the in-offensive material we sell here. And I am happy to see that the worst excesses which often feature in cartoons of the Queen are absent from your depictions.'

'That is the beauty of the current climate,' Mr Soane said. 'No one can imprison a patriot who supports the new Queen.'

'Of course they can.' I said. 'My brother was *executed* for less than that!'

'That is true, Nell,' Isaiah said. 'But now we are being encouraged by supporters of the King's Government to do so.' And he shook his head, as if the ways of the world were surely lost on someone as soft-headed as I. 'Because,' he continued, 'the King's friends calculate that the more support there is for Caroline among us radicals, the bigger a stick they will have to wield against her in Parliament and beyond.'

This was all familiar to me from Sir Robin's outburst, of course. 'So they seek to frighten Caroline's friends into per-suading her to go away again, by suggesting that she will find herself at the crest of a wave of unrest, which the King's sup-porters will then destroy? And now she is here, all they need do is point to our work?'

'Precisely.' he said. 'Caroline knows that George will

never tolerate her by his side.'

'I can see that very well,' I agreed. 'But is there not a greater danger? For all her coarse features and crude manners, she is a member of a German royal family, and she feels it is her birthright. What did St Paul say? "They will seek a corruptible crown, while we are incorruptible." She has come back here to be crowned, and the Government has stoked the very fires it claims it wishes to dampen?'

'Yes,' said Titus. 'But they calculate that this would prove an opportunity to smite their enemies.'

'Exactly,' I responded. 'And we calculate that they will not be able to do this, and that they will unleash a plague of political unrest all the more powerful for having been encouraged by them.'

I said 'we', though even then I was no longer sure that I felt a part of their movement – if I ever really had. When Tom spoke of revolution, it was as though his eyes were lamps of fire. I was more like my mother, and found it hard to believe that with revolution suddenly everything would change and everyone's lives would be transformed overnight. As she used to say, all these men had succeeded in doing so far was bringing their own private apocalypses on their own heads.

'For once,' Isaiah said, 'we may win whatever happens, whether she seeks the crown or not. And we will ensure ourselves an income in the meantime.'

I nodded, resisting the urge to point out that surely if the odds of winning were doubled, then the odds of losing might be, too? For I knew better than to use a gambling analogy in Isaiah's house. But I could not help reflecting that Sir Robin Everley might be a fool, but he now had a lot more money, and this might buy him power and protection. Did Isaiah truly understand the forces he was up against? He was just a small pawn in Sir Robin's game and Isaiah's life would mean less to him than the cat's in St James's Square.

'Has Nell shown you our presses?' Isaiah asked Mr Soane. 'We have two here, of course: a fine one, practically new, for lithography such as your plates require, and a more simple press for the tracts we produce on occasion.'

The description amused me, for Isaiah implied that we made our living as purveyors of quality artwork, and omitted to mention that the lithograph had been procured at a bankruptcy auction and had almost ruined him in the process.

'She has not,' replied Mr Soane, 'but I do not doubt your expertise.'

The content of Mr Soane's letters convinced Isaiah that we must begin a run of a hundred prints right away. At just shy of a shilling's profit on each, the sale of these alone would see us through to the autumn.

After Mr Soane had left, I locked the shop door and rested my palm on the press lid, its struts like the bones of an old hand under mine. But even this could not comfort me when I remembered the main part of what Mr Edwards had said: if people were whispering that Sir David's death was murder, then Hetty might also be in danger. After all, a woman in her new position had even more to fear from wagging tongues and pointing political fingers than a nobody like me. Not only must I deliver Mr Edwards' message, with Mr Soane no doubt sent to check on me, but I must warn her. The question was – how?

I let my mind work on this while I inked the Queen's skirts. I chose a ripe plum colour which Hetty would have adored, and thanked the Lord for the good fortune which had brought us this work, even if it had not spared my brother.

18

THE FOLLOWING MORNING WAS if anything even worse than the day before had been. There was no anticipation, no longer any prospect that Tom might be saved, only the anxiety of the envelope upstairs that I had failed to deliver. I dragged myself to the press, and even Mr Soane's work looked lifeless. Mid-morning, the bell jangled as the door ushered in the sounds of Friday-street, and once again my heart raced. He will come, I thought: Mr Edwards will want to come here to see if I have delivered his message, and to show me that there will be no sanctuary for me, that he could lead the constables here at any time.

Instead, I was greeted by a red beard and a green silk waistcoat under a coat of wool so black that darkness itself would pale next to it. I would describe Mr Tagg as our greatest competitor, except we competed with him in the way that a tick on a vulture's back competes with its host, Mr Tagg being an even greater figure among booksellers than he is among printers. His dress had become even more extravagant in the months since I last saw him, so business was clearly good.

'Ah, Miss Nell,' he said. 'So your stepfather has reopened his premises. How valiant. You will not, I trust, be printing the trash which rained wrath on your heads last time?' He shook his head slowly. 'If you do, I fear it will be the noose for you all.'

I swallowed hard, wondering what was the quickest way to dispatch this man from the shop and back to minding his own sorry business. Tagg had a knack of swooping in on failing publishers, printers, even other booksellers; buying up cheaply vast amounts of unwanted or even damaged stock; gaudying it up with a flimsy cover here, a catchy title there, and piling his shop window like some Tower of Babel. These towers were soon demolished by the prosperous tradesmen's wives who were to be seen parading hereabouts in the afternoons looking like sheep in bonnets. Isaiah was a-simmer with moral outrage at these working men and their wives, who were growing too portly to keep up with the revolutionary throng and would rather see their neighbour starve than trim their spending on cheap lace. I must confess that my upturned nose had once been green at the tip with envy when watching them stroll the streets, for I would have liked to see my mother take a turn on Cheapside with a basket on her arm and wearing gloves buttoned for her by Meg.

'What can I do for you, Mr Tagg?' I said. I was confident that the answer would be 'nothing', and I hoped that drawing attention to the futility of this call might hasten him on his way.

He smiled, acknowledging my parry. 'On this occasion, it is more what I might do for you. Or rather, "we". I come at the behest of Mr Percival Smeek, my esteemed assistant.'

This was the first time I had heard him described thus: it was usually *Percival, you cretin, you have not done this*, or *Percival, you buffoon, come here while I box your ears*. The assistant's stoop was made worse by the habitual cringing and snivelling which his master's treatment of him inspired, but the most unattractive aspect of Percival's character was the contempt with which he treated anyone he could.

I said nothing. I had no desire to enquire after Percival's health, or any other aspect of his existence, and I could not imagine what Mr Tagg would ever want to do for us, apart from raise still further the price of the paper which we were forced to buy from him because we did not have enough capital to buy it in bulk from the wholesalers.

'Mr Smeek suggests that we might extend you some credit,' he declared. 'He points out – in a tone of considerable regret, I might add – that your lack of funds compels you to forever scratch about on the margins of this trade, and that your stepfather's inclinations propel you still further away from the prosperity which could so deservedly be yours.'

'Why should he regret that?' I said. 'It is obvious, and no concern of his.'

'Mr Smeek is superlatively aware of your talents as a printer, and indeed of your – how shall we put it – decorative qualities. Miss Wingfield, though your charms might be obvious, Mr Smeek is convinced that he has a peculiarly sharp appreciation of them.'

Mr Tagg, a-wooing for the oafish Percival Smeek: it beggared belief. Were there not the inevitable consequences of my refusal of this appalling offer, I would have been tempted to laugh him out of the shop. As it was, I wondered if Percival really had taken a fancy to me, or if there was some murkier agenda that I could not see.

'I thank you – and Mr Smeek – for your kind thoughts,' I said. In a monkey's chuff, I did, and this thought translated into a respectful pause. 'But I assure you, we have no need of your credit.' This was not true, but Isaiah would rather have spent a month in the Marshalsea than be in debt to this man, and I would rather marry Mr Edwards than allow Percival Smeek to be in the same dark store room as me. 'And in any case, let us imagine that we accepted your terms: how could

I trust that you would not change your mind, and have Isaiah thrown into prison? That would be a mighty responsibility for me to carry about.'

'Oh, I do not think our dark friend needs my assistance when it comes to finding himself a berth in gaol, do you?' And with that he tipped his hat, the brim too wide for a man of his shortness.

He was almost gone when he turned back, a look of exaggerated surprise animating his orange whiskers. 'But you may rest assured, Mistress Nell, that should you ever find yourself *sans* shop once again, which heaven forfend' – and with this he made to smite his brow, though all he succeeded in doing was to knock his hat backwards – 'you will always find an avid employer in yours truly. And Mr Smeek of course, on whose behalf I speak.' He adjusted his hat. 'Principally.'

'I thank you, Mr Tagg,' I said. 'And I am sure that we will not trouble you.'

I wandered back into the print room. The prospect of climbing stepladders at Tagg's pursued by the ardent ferret Smeek was a dismal one, but I knew that I would have to do it above seeing us all starve, or else asking for help from the parish, with all the horrors that might soon bring. Last year, Isaiah had read that the Benthamite reformers had a fantastical plan to bring about a revolution in the way England dealt with its poor. Men and women would be separated at the steps of new "Workhouses", institutions constructed on the principle that however dire the life had been that had driven people to ask for succour which would separate them from their loved ones, conditions inside these 'workhouses' would be a little worse. This, the administrators concluded, presumably over brandy and cigars at the end of a long lunch in Somerset House, was the way to eliminate poverty once and for all. Their scheme was so fantastic it defied belief, and would surely be consigned to oblivion, as had been all other initiatives concerning the indigent.

Yes, I thought, wandering into the back again and nodding at the press. *While such men as Mr Tagg and Mr Bentham exist, I will print Isaiah's pamphlets, even if it does land both of us in gaol.*

19

THAT AFTERNOON, I SENT Meg to Mr Tagg's for supplies. In common with many ignorant people, Mr Tagg was afraid of her, as if her condition was contagious or else she was able to curse him. She came back carrying a ream of rough pamphlet paper and some fine vellum. Isaiah had returned while she was absent, but he did not offer to assist me.

It was not only my work and Isaiah pacing about which kept me from delivering Mr Edwards' message. After her trip to Mr Tagg's, Meg did not leave my side, and for once she was talking. In part I was glad of this, but I wished to immerse myself in work, so being caught in an avalanche of Meg's questions was unfortunate.

In answering Meg, I had to take as much care as I did when inking plates. Too much, and what I said bled into Meg's mind and tainted her, making her more inward. Too little, and she mistrusted me and became outraged that I was being dishonest with her, which also made her withdraw into herself. There was no use telling Meg that I was not to know that Tom had got himself arrested, for that was the point: I did not know because I had not been there. When we were travelling to London from Lancashire, my mother used to say that if we all had to return to Noah's Ark in twos, Tom would be by her side and Meg and I would go in together. So my abandonment of her to the care of the Ingses – ha! as if life with my Uncle John could be described as care – lurked like a doom painting over my head.

I gave her another task which diverted her: pegging prints to lines all around the walls. She spent almost as long hanging them to dry as I did making them, ensuring that the print was perfectly taut and that the pegs were nicely balanced.

'Who is the fat lady in the round skirts?' she asked, after she had studied perhaps a dozen identical images.

I tried to banish the thought of Mother Cooper from my mind. 'She is Queen Caroline,' I replied. Surely she must know her face by now?

Meg thought about this. 'She looks pretty in these prints.'

The exiled Queen's appetite for eating, farting and sex had been staple items on the prints we made during the year before Isaiah had been sent to prison, and Meg was now suspicious because we had become supporters of a woman we had hitherto reproduced so unflatteringly. Meg's face was closing; if I did not explain this well, she would view the change in our attitudes as more evidence of my untrustworthiness.

'How our mother would have smiled to see these!' I said, trying to sound wistful, as though I was talking to myself and not for Meg's benefit at all; this sometimes satisfied her. 'And to think that another woman, a queen no less, would be the architect of our good fortune!'

'I only wanted to know who she is,' Meg said, becoming like an icicle with a voice, as if all sensibility had abandoned her. 'What has Mother got to do with her?' She studied the print all the more intently, as if our mother was about to appear from behind the Queen's skirts. My throat filled, and the smell of the ink overwhelmed me.

I knew the Queen's story almost as intimately as I had

known Sir David, and so I decided to tell it, hoping that the words would fill the space between Meg and me: 'In 1795, once Napoleon was busy turning France's Revolution into the Empire it soon became, and European monarchs started sleeping easily enough in their beds again to think about marriage, it was time for the Prince of Wales to find a wife.'

'Why couldn't they sleep?' Meg asked.

'Because they thought they might be killed.'

'Like Tom?'

I stared down, as if his name had landed heavily by my foot. *Yes*, I think, *just like Tom*. But unlike our brother, they would not have been hanged: they would have had their heads cut off.

'Yes, like Tom,' I said, being careful not to move on too quickly, for Meg was good at detecting evasion. 'And then the Prince of Wales stumbled (drunkenly, for this is the Prince of Wales we are talking about, after all) upon two problems: one was a shortage of suitable Protestant princesses; the other was that ten years before, he had married in secret. The lady, Mrs FitzHerbert, was a Roman Catholic, and so the marriage was invalid.' I anticipated Meg's puzzlement: 'No monarch is allowed to wed a papist for the same reason that there are no Catholics in Parliament: they are all supposed to be secret enemies of the Government.'

'Like Isaiah,' said Meg, while I reflected that it was practically Sir David's words I was using.

'Yes, though in a different way. Catholics are supposed to have loyalties to the Pope, so they will not obey the King, while Isaiah's kingdom is all in heaven.'

'So why can't he obey our King, until he gets to heaven? Why does he want to blow everyone up instead?'

'Some people want to blow everyone up, but Isaiah isn't one of them.' Perhaps she had heard some of the madder members of Isaiah's congregation. 'Also he can't obey him because this King is stopping people from getting to heaven, by preventing them from hearing the truth.'

'But Isaiah tells people the truth, so if they hear that, why doesn't God just let them into heaven, and not the King?'

I was unsure how to answer this, so I paused and opened a new batch of paper. This was for pamphlets, so I did not need to size it; I could not concentrate on making prints if Meg was going to ask such questions. Pamphlet paper is cheaper, and any mistakes I made on it would not matter so much.

'No, it is more than that. It does not matter which church you worship in, nor how you worship him: the King's Government watches people starve; it sends them off to war; it presides over slavery. So it must be overthrown.' I glanced over my shoulder as I said this, in case Mr Edwards or some other Government spy should hear me, a gesture that was a better illustration of what I was trying to describe to my sister than the words themselves.

'So people who do not worship the Lord in the way the King does are deemed enemies of the Establishment,' I said. I did not mention that presumably the heir to the throne did not take this view when he invited Mrs FitzHerbert into his bed, an absurdity which was not lost on the cartoonists, who produced such images as Mrs F's mouth over the King's Most Honourable Member, threatening to chop off its Head, &c &c. It always amazed me that the fine men who bought them could spend three hours with their tailors agonising about the cut of their sleeves, then drop into our premises and spend ten shillings or more on images of a carousing Caroline shitting on the head of the Prince Regent, who was crowned with a pair of cuckold's horns.

I was grateful that Meg did not ask what I was thinking, and I continued: 'In the eyes of the law at least (and the law must surely be as blind as she appears above the Old Bailey to think it), Prince – now King – George was Europe's most eligible bachelor. He was also six hundred thousand pounds in debt, which his father paid off on his wedding day.' Six hundred thousand pounds. It was an impossible sum for her to imagine, and I was glad Meg did not ask me how much it amounted to. At St James's Square, I never saw anyone paid more than fifty guineas to lie down. When Sir Robin proposed to her, Hetty joked that he and Sir David should have waited and spent the money on a fine chaise longue on which to have us gratis every afternoon. Six hundred thousand pounds! This meant that our new King had drunk and gambled the cost of twelve thousand nights of prime deflowering before he was even married. That was more nights than Tom had ever lived.

I resumed my story. 'And so he married Caroline of Brunswick, a woman of fine parentage who proved to be more coarse than Isaiah's prison blankets. They had one child, Princess Charlotte, born nine months to the day from their wedding night, which many wagered was the first and last night the couple spent as man and wife. Princess Charlotte died three years since, and this seemed to be the ultimate disaster in this ill-starred marriage.' Again, I was grateful that Meg did not interrupt me for an explanation of a wedding night. 'That is, until now, when Caroline plans to return to England and take her place beside her husband at his coronation, a decision that George is determined to thwart, with divorce if necessary. But a royal divorce means an Act of Parliament, and a great deal of fleur-de-lys-monogrammed dirty washing being aired all over Europe: George would have to prove that Caroline has not been faithful to him, which by accounts already circulating would not prove too difficult –'

'But you say that he already loved someone, before he married her, so why does it matter?' Meg asked. It was a good question, though an irrelevant one, in the circumstances. I was always as surprised by what Meg understood by what she did not.

'Infidelity on the part of the wife of the Prince of Wales is treason, and the macabre disgrace of trying a princess for a crime for which hundreds of ordinary men are executed each year' – and here I paused, for I almost mentioned Tom – 'is not lost even on a king who is reputedly as fat in the head as he is in the body.'

'But *Caroline*? What has she ever done for us? Why do ordinary men care for her?' Meg asked, as I finished a run of Mr Soane's prints, showing a kindly matron with a laurel wreath for a crown being embraced by a much more slender maiden, the blindfolded Justice. They were even better now I had printed them, I reflected. I perceived it would be a good use for my sky blue dress: I could cut up the skirts and etch these simple black images onto them. There would be no need to ink them in – the simplicity of black lines on blue silk would be infinitely more striking.

'Oh aye,' said Isaiah, who appeared from the passageway to the shop. 'They will. They already do. She is a victim of sorts, you see.'

'What is a victim?' Meg said.

Isaiah smiled, and though his figure at the door darkened the room, I felt warmed by his arrival, and glad that I was no longer facing Meg's questions alone. He was preparing to speechify: I could tell by his jutting chest, and the way he leaned on the edge of the press as if it were the back of a bench in the upstairs loft. 'Bless you in your innocence, Meg. A victim is one who suffers unwillingly. Now, I admit that our future Queen does not look as though she has ever been hungry, Meg – and whatever you think,' he said, looking at me, 'if we show her being dragged under the wheels of the royal chariot, she is a strong stick to beat this Government with. Caroline is living in London, so they will fear unrest, and in suppressing it will further reveal their enmity towards the people. And if proceedings against her indeed begin, a divorce will clog up Parliament so much that they will not be able to pass any more of their repressive laws.' He nodded his head. 'Aye, this summer the sewers of London will stink most keenly.'

Meg went back to staring at the prints, having lost interest now that Isaiah was there; she had never been able to follow conversations involving more than one person. I once asked her why this was so, and she said the noise was unbearable, like being in a sawmill when a trunk was being put through: sharp splinters of sound flying at her from all directions till all she could do was cover her ears and shut her eyes and wait for it to stop.

'These prints will sell well,' I said to Isaiah, 'But why do you think this man has come to us?' I regretted asking this the moment I'd uttered it, but the impulse came from the desire to know if Isaiah had any suspicions about me.

'Mr Soane, the gentleman's name is.' He looked at me while I took a discarded tract and folded it over and over, as tightly as I could.

'What is it, Nell?' Isaiah placed his hand on my head and said this so gently, in the way he used to speak to my mother when he solicited her opinion, that my throat filled and I had to swallow the urge to tell him my myriad worries about how exactly I thought we'd had the good fortune of meeting Mr Soane, so that he could decide whether he still wanted to sell these prints. I feared what he would say: that our prosperity was like the fool's house, built on sand, and we would better starve and repent than profit any further from my wickedness. And I could also imagine never hearing him speak to me so softly again, and that instead of seeing my mother in me, *Behold!* One of his Old Testament Jezebels would appear before his eyes every time he looked at me. And with this thought, my moment of honesty passed like a glimpse of winter sun. In time, I hoped this lie would not be such a burden; I would come to carry it like a limp I no longer noticed.

Meg stood next to us. She was not smiling, but there was something bright in her eyes I had not seen for years, practically since she was a baby, in fact. She pointed at the press, where she had painted a pink smiling face after the style of the Queen on the wood.

'Did you do that, Meg?' I said.

She nodded.

I looked at Isaiah. 'She seems more settled now than she has been since Mother –'

'Nell,' he said softly, 'not now. There is someone I want you to meet.'

20

'Who is it?' I said, wondering who next could come to try my already fraught nerves.

'Anne!' Isaiah called, and in trolled a woman whose hair was far redder even than mine. She hung back, though her eyes and her smile – an assortment of blacks, yellows and browns which suited her hair in a strange, rackety way – were all eagerness. She wore a bedraggled black crocheted shawl and an off-reddish skirt, and I couldn't help thinking that she looked like a carrot which needed the soil washing off it.

'This is Anne,' he exclaimed, in a voice that might have been announcing that he'd just found one of my mother's most treasured possessions for me. Except my mother had left no treasured possessions – what little she'd ever owned she'd sold over the years. And to judge by the way he rested his hand on her shoulder, this was the woman Isaiah had chosen to replace her.

'They call me Carroty Anne,' she said, in an accent I had heard before but could not place. I wondered who the "they" were.

'You were right, Isaiah, this is a fine place you have for yourself here,' she remarked.

'You are Irish,' I said.

'And you must be Nell,' she said, trying to make her voice sound like a possett warmed just for me. 'Isaiah has spoken of you a good deal.'

I nodded, eyebrows raised, aware of Isaiah watching us. 'And this is Meg,' I continued. Meg stopped staring at Carroty Anne's congregation of mottled teeth and returned to running her finger along a groove between the floor-boards.

'Hello there Meg,' she smiled, bending down in an effort to catch Meg's eye. Meg did not move. Isaiah's tightened lips told me that he was not pleased at this, but what else did he expect? Meg was a clam at the best of times, and this was not the best of times: our mother had been dead just six months, and now this woman was here. Of course I didn't know this for certain, but my worst fears soon turned out to be justi-fied.

'I am mightily sorry for the death of your brother,' she said.

I widened my eyes and rushed to Meg, but she darted out of the room more swiftly than a trout evades capture by a tickler.

'We had not told her that, Anne,' Isaiah said softly.

She looked at me. 'I am sorry. But perhaps it's best if she faces it. Honesty is always favourite, isn't it?' and her laugh jangled and jarred more than the shop bell. She stood up, knees cracking, and returned her attention to me. 'You will be wondering how we met. Me and Isaiah, I mean.'

I was wondering many things, but the nature of their first encounter had not been one of them. I did not reply: let her prattle on. There were shadowy stains on her skirt.

'It was in prison. We had cells next to each other. He would talk to me through the bars.'

'I was sermonising,' Isaiah interjected quickly. Sermonising was one of my mother's favourite words, and his glance at me said he hoped the use of it would please me. It did not.

'Aye, he sees me as a lost soul to be saved, right enough.'

'And you will be yet,' he said.

'Will you have some tea?' I offered, as it occurred to me in another of my absurd moments of optimism that I had made a mistake, and this woman was merely a visitor, another member of his congregation perhaps, and nothing more.

'You do not have any –?' she saw Isaiah's frown, and said she would have nothing.

'What were in you in prison for?' asked Meg, who reappeared in the doorway. It was not like her to talk to someone she had just met, and I feared she was about to form one of her attachments – now that Tom was gone, there was a vacancy. And, I realised with some despair, she would like Carroty Anne because she had been honest with her. I watched her for signs of distress, but she seemed to have stowed Tom's death in some locked place.

Carroty Anne glanced at Isaiah. He shook his head almost imperceptibly, and I knew that whatever she was about to say was not the truth. My mother never looked to Isaiah for permission to speak, and she was always honest.

'I got into an argument with a friend,' she said.

'You do not go to gaol for that,' I muttered.

'I hit him,' she went on.

'Hard?' Meg said, interested.

'Not particularly. But it wasn't the first time I'd done it.'

'Will you hit us?' Meg asked. I thought of my uncle, and worried about what he had done to her during my absence.

'Naw, naw, bless you,' she said brightly, beginning to swoop towards Meg again. Meg flattened herself against the counter. 'Those days are gone, and I never hit women or children.' She thought about this. 'Well, never children. Or never those as didn't deserve it.' She laughed, her throat crackling with phlegm and gin. She reminded me of Mother

Cooper. I hated the way the sound of her echoed through the place, touching everything as it went. If noise were like dust, I would have put a sheet over the press so at least she couldn't have been touched that.

'It was' – and here Carroty Anne glanced at Isaiah again – 'it was a dispute to do with business.'

I know your line of business, I thought, as I took in her rouged lips and careworn brightness. I wondered if Isaiah did, and if so, why it did not matter to him. There I was, living in dread of his discovering my time at St James's Square, while he brought home a Paddy Tart to fill my mother's shoes.

'And while we speak of business,' she said, 'how do you find yourself here, Isaiah?'

'It seems I am blessed with work of sorts,' he said.

His boots creaked as he shifted about. 'We have an engraver. Soane, a Welshman. I have not asked him yet, but he'll have fallen out with the Connexion somehow and made his way to us.' The Connexion is the central Methodist organisation, which many felt was too rigid in its authority. Chapels such as ours were a haven for such men.

'And now, this afternoon, our next blessing: your arrival, Anne.'

Carroty Anne smiled, her teeth making their presence felt once again. 'Well, if you could show me my quarters,' she said, making a crook of her arm.

Isaiah looked at her arm but did not take it. She glanced at me and let it fall.

'Why not instruct me to show her?' I said to Isaiah. 'It will be my Mother's room that you will be taking her to, after all.'

He shook his head at me, turned to Carroty Anne and made to touch her arm, which she had bundled under her shawl. 'You must excuse Nell,' he said. 'As Ezekiel put it, "the voice of her speech is like the noise of a host." But she knows whose house this is.'

I swallowed; this is the first time Isaiah had made reference to my residence there being dependent on his goodwill alone. *Aye, and who will do all your work for you if I go?* I thought to myself. *She does not look like much of a printer.*

'Are you a printer, Carroty Anne?' I said.

'The Lord love you, no,' she said. 'I can't read.' She anticipated my next question. 'I rely on others to tell me the Bible, and it strikes my heart, then the words fair pour out of me, as water poured from the rock when Moses struck it.' She looked to Isaiah again, and he nodded, all proprietorial approval, as if we were at Smithfield and she was a passing cow he was about to buy.

'Aye, and it is a purer spring for that,' he said, looking at me.

I could not believe I was hearing this. 'Yes, it will be a boon to our printing business to have another illiterate about the place,' I said.

'You must be careful not to play Martha to Anne's Mary,' Isaiah said, clearly enjoying the prospect of two women rivalling each other for his affection, one by working her fingers black with ink while the other rested from selling herself by sitting at his feet and listening to his sermonising. It was Mary the idle listener who had won praise from Our Lord. At such moments I almost understood the godless.

'You will not lose your way here, Anne,' he said. 'Top of the ladder then to your left – the two small rooms beyond the chapel.'

When she understood that he was not about to accompany her, she took herself off. I watched her taking the rungs on tiptoes, and this along with her cracked patent boots made her look grotesquely girlish. Isaiah made a parade of not looking at her, instead picking up a printing block and inspecting it.

'So your time in gaol was not such a wilderness after all,' I observed.

'That is just the sort of thing your mother would have said.'

'I do not know how you can say that to me. This print room, which is my favourite place on earth, will become a hell to me if –' I was about to say: *if I know that Carroty Anne is up there in my mother's place*, but I remembered his remark about whose house this was, so I didn't.

'You are a woman yourself now, Nell. And it is better if I have someone – for it would be a mortal sin if...'

I shook my head very gently, caught between wanting to ask him what he meant, and fearing that if he said the edge of one more thing I couldn't bear to hear, I would cry and cry and say things that would come between us for ever.

'Will she be here long?'

He rammed his hat over his eyes and left.

'So even she will not keep you at home, and out of trouble,' I said to the silence where he had just been.

Meg and I were alone in the house with her. My mother used to say that you should worry about as many things as possible, as it is the unexpected that will come up and catch you. I was glad she believed there was no heaven, and she would not be able to see the woman who was taking her place.

And with her to report my movements to Isaiah, there was of course no prospect of my delivering Mr Edwards' envelope that day. The knot in my stomach tightened – for each hour that passed must surely bring the threat of his retribution closer, and I could not see how worrying about it would save me from that.

21

ON WEDNESDAY MORNING, Carroty Anne struggled down the ladder as soon as she heard Isaiah leave. She stumbled with a 'JesusMaryandJoseph', before appearing at the threshold of the printing room. 'Where did he go?' she asked, round panic in her eyes.

'I don't know,' I said, smoothing a sheet of paper over the engraving. I could feel the outline of Queen Caroline's skirt. I inhaled deeply, taking in the aroma of ink as the room was invaded with the smell of Carroty Anne's sweat and musty clothes. Perhaps we all reek like this to strangers, perhaps Isaiah only smelled of onions, peppermint and cinnamon to me, and to the rest of the city he was just another stinking oik. And looking back on it, perhaps all Carroty Anne did was bring the city into my print room. To me, the smell of London is its waste: the sewers, the burnt and sieved-out remains of the tanneries, glue-makers and butchers – I shuddered at the thought of my Uncle and all that his fingers had touched – but its stink is as much the product of the living as it is of the dead. As we walk down Cheapside, we fester and we rot as much as a rat's corpse in the gutter does. Such was the turn of my mind that day.

'That cow next door makes a mighty racket in the night,' she said.

'She does.' I stifled the urge to say that it took one to know one.

'Do you ever get milk from it?'

'They do; we don't.'

Carroty Anne was waiting for me to rescue her from heaven only knew what. She would need Isaiah to care for her, that much was clear. *You might try to take my mother's place*, I thought, as I watched her rubbing her skirt *but you will never replace her.*

'When you do find him,' I said, 'tell him that he will need to mind Meg and the shop this afternoon, for I must go out. Alone.' I wiped excess ink from the edge of the platen.

'I can mind Meg,' she said. 'Can't I, child?' Meg stood at the doorway, clearly keen to accompany Carroty Anne.

'And are you going somewhere fit for the likes of Meg?' I said, sounding like a two-hundred-year-old spinster.

'She will not be a child much longer. I wasn't, at her age.'

'Precisely.'

Carroty Anne muttered something which sounded like 'lifting a jar', and she and Meg were gone.

'A jar of gin, more like,' I said to the stale air.

The smell of her skirt lingered. Isaiah had been with her the previous night; I had slept under the press. For all I was worried about Meg, I could not face spending the night upstairs and hearing them. Meg would come down to me if she needed me, I told myself. She didn't, of course.

Tawdry, my mother would have called Carroty Anne. But then, what would she have said of me?

Two tears splashed onto the print. I stepped back slightly and leaned against the wall. How could Isaiah inflict her on us? I had longed for the sanctuary of this print room, and now it felt as oppressive as a cell. My mother would never criticise Isaiah to me, but she did once say that living with him could be like embracing a wall. I pressed my fingers around the bricks and my head bowed with the weight of missing her.

⁂

I knew my way as far as Westminster, and spent most of the walk worrying about how I was going to find St Vincent's Court. As I passed the alehouses near the Commons, a loud clanging began: the division bell warning the MPs that in eight minutes they must vote. The crowds around me doubled as men appeared, rushing to Parliament, fighting through the match-sellers and the ranters, the laundry-women and the beggars.

Isaiah was fond of comparing London to Sodom, Gomorrah, Babylon and Babel; and the new lions in Trafalgar Square to the golden bull as worshipped by the Israelites, but I believe there is a providence to this place that would rival the most tranquil Edens of Isaiah's fancy. This contradiction is the essence of this city. It manages to be a village and a universe in a single smoky belch; it is a place to which people come never to be seen again, though it is equally likely that you will bump into a chance acquaintance twice in a week. And so it was that day: it took me a moment to place a familiar figure haring down the Strand towards Whitehall via Trafalgar Square. There was my straw-haired admirer from the day of the execution, all liveried up and heading for a job, to judge by the speed of him: he worked as a chairman. He stopped suddenly when he saw me, and this halted his mate who was carrying the poles behind, so that the carriage behind them had to draw up sharply and overtake. The coachman did this with at least twice as much cursing and whip-cracking as was necessary, but so it is in London.

'Mistress Nell,' he said, taking off his tricorn hat with a

205

flourish. 'I am honoured to make your acquaintance once again.'

'You know my name and this gives you an advantage, for I do not know you from Adam.'

'*I'm* Adam,' said his friend, appearing from behind the chair. 'And you are the God-botherer's wench that Gus has been on about each day since first he saw ye.'

I had not been called *wench* since my early days at St James's: there it was judged a fine fancy to speak of women as though we were all camp followers in some glorious military campaign, or else (and this among the men who had actually seen war, and had no desire for the whiff of dysentery, despair, death &c to be introduced into their drawing rooms) the sunny, buxom participants in some rural tableau, with the substitution naturally of French *parfum* for English manure and rank armpits.

'You must see a lot, in your line of work,' I said. It was a silly comment, but it did the job of ignoring Gus's question.

'Oh aye,' he said, 'if you are making a study of the soles of ladies' feet.'

I had heard of one gentleman whose pleasure was just such a study, and paid handsomely for it, but instead of announcing this I said, 'Nell. I am Nell Wingfield.'

'Isn't that short for somethin'?' said Adam.

'Come now, Nell ain't short for any man,' he said. 'Just look at her. She's the first woman I've scarcely had to stoop for. 'Tis a marriage made in heaven, for you will be the saviour of my back.'

'Aye, in the lookin' department at least,' said Adam.

I studied their chair with its velvet curtains and its poles all shiny from the effort of carrying. While I waited for a lull in their frivolities, it came to me: Gus and Adam might help me find St Vincent's Court, but they might also take me to Hetty, and I was almost as keen to talk to her and see if there was any truth in Mr Edwards' claims. Even if Gus had never been to Sir Robin's house before, it surely would not take him long to find out where it was. I looked at him, smiling with the realisation that suddenly I might not be alone in the world with Mr Edwards' envelope.

'Come on, Mistress Nell, out with it. What is it in particular you'd like me to look out for? Or should I say, who?'

I was so surprised at this that I looked behind me, as if expecting to see some imp signalling my thoughts to him. 'It is not what you think,' I said, fixing him with my I-am-as-honest-as-the-tides gaze.

Adam looked up from his polishing. 'Don't worry – he doesn't do much thinking.'

Gus and I smiled at each other in the way Tom and I used to over Meg.

'Come on, m'lady, tell me which lord it is you seek.'

'It is Sir Robin Everley,' I said. 'But I tell you again, it is not what you think: it is his wife I need to speak to.'

Gus did not say anything for a moment, watching me instead.

'You know Sir Robin?' I said.

'Only by reputation,' he shrugged, though his glance at his velvet curtains convinced me that Sir Robin had been a customer. 'There wasn't a gaming table he hadn't sat at, or a bed in a dolly house he hadn't bounced on, until one day he married –'

I nodded and raised my hand, as if the mere mention of the nunneries of St James's would send me into the gutter in a flat faint.

'I do apologise, Miss,' he said, and I could see him thinking that he might have to alter his opinion of me. 'He married a lady, I am sure. Anyway, this wedding fluttered quite a few skirts. But it need not have done, for he has not truckled with a honeymoon, and can still be seen most nights, passing by the coaching houses off Piccadilly on his way to –'

I shook my head again, propriety permitting me to hear no more, though in truth my head was bowed in sorrow at what a miserable, narrow life Hetty had sold herself into. And Sir Robin, back on the town already!

'But give me one guess as to the nature of your business in exchange for my services,' he said, 'for I do love a mystery.'

'Go on,' I said, worried again that he somehow knew what I had been.

'Sir Robin is your father, and you are now here to claim your inheritance, of which Adam and I will receive a goodly cut for our Christian charity in taking you to him.'

I clapped my hand to my forehead and made to fall backwards. 'Yes! That's it exactly,' I said. 'All my life I have lived in expectation of a fortune. How did you divine it? I must waft great whiffs of lucre behind me.'

'It's not money he's scenting,' said Adam, rolling a dried horse turd with his foot. We were in the shade of a grey stone building, one of a row of veritable palaces which housed political clubs and banks, so the sweat I'd built up walking was beginning to dry on me, and I could feel a mask of dust tightening on my face.

'And if I should happen to see Sir Robin, or better, to see his regular chairman, who hails by chance from a village not five miles from where we were born, what should I tell him?'

'Tell him – no, please get a message to his wife, Lady Hetty.' Lady Hetty! Would I ever get used to calling her this? When she heard of Hetty's marriage, Mother Cooper said she'd have thought it more likely that the scullery cat would be knighted than that Hetty would join the ranks of the

Quality, and even I who loved Hetty could see the wonder of it. 'Please tell her that I need to see her. No, there is no need. If you find me her address, I will go to her.'

Gus bowed to me. 'You still have not explained your connexion with this lady,' he said with mock-seriousness, and I knew that in his eyes I was no more a scented thing than the discarded handkerchief that was soaking up horse piss at our feet. Sir Robin Everley marrying a courtesan would have caused as many ripples in this town as a Cabinet minister marrying an actress. Gus would have recognised her name, and drawn the ineluctable conclusion as to how I might be acquainted with her.

'But now I have more urgent business,' I said. 'I do not suppose you know where St Vincent's Court is?'

Gus's face clouded. 'The area where the Italians live? I know it, but the question of what might take you there is even more mysterious than your acquaintance with Lady Hetty. It is such a lawless place, worse even than the dark places those who inhabit it mostly come from. Or so they say,' – the outrage left his voice – 'for I have never been further than Southwark, and I count that a lawless place, too.'

'It is an errand for my stepfather, whom you saw at Tom's – on Monday.'

He nodded. 'Well, I hope it is not business that will land him back in gaol, for the authorities will be looking for any excuse this summer on account of the excitement surrounding the Queen. They expect a rising. Can you imagine it? A revolution with a Queen as its mascot!'

'I can't,' I said, even though I'd explained the very same thing to Meg the previous day, albeit in much less clear terms, it struck me then. Like Titus Soane, Gus had a good head, and like me, was one of perhaps millions of people who were compelled to lift a chair or a press for a living rather than a pen. And our sense that we might do it a sight better than the pen- and sword-wielders of Westminster, where we now stood, was what had led to all the talk of revolution in the first place. Better to educate us than execute us, though they were even less likely to listen to me than they were to a blackamoor like Isaiah.

Gus agreed to take me to St Vincent's Court. I could have found my way to Smith-street, but beyond that I might as well have been in a foreign country. Dark-eyed girls stared from open doors, and a pungent smell of onions hung in the air, which made me powerfully hungry. Men shovelled flat bread out of stone ovens which they had constructed in the centre of the courtyard, and smeared cooked tomatoes over the bread while avid children watched.

'Isaiah would not have allowed me to venture into such an area.'

Gus heard the pride in my voice. 'It must be a fine thing, having a second father.'

I thought about this. 'There was only ever one family: my mother, us children and Isaiah. I never thought of Isaiah as anything: first, second or otherwise. We all just were.' Now I was not so sure, I realised: with my mother dead, were we still part of Isaiah, and he us? 'Where is your family?' I asked, in part to take my mind from such unwelcome thoughts.

'My father was a copper miner,' he said. 'He was killed in an accident in a mine just outside Tintagel. So we moved to Dorset, to live with my uncle, until he was transported. From the village of Tolpuddle.' He glanced sideways at me as he said this.

'He was one of the Tolpuddle Martyrs?' I said this with the awed tone Hetty had used when she first realised who Sir Robin was and how much he was worth, for the Tolpuddle Martyrs are the aristocracy of the downtrodden workers.

'Aye,' Gus replied, all modesty. He could see the effect this news had on me. 'He died on the way to Australia. His last words to me were: "Gus, you must leave this kingdom, but not in irons." He was a big man. When they arrested him, the chains looked like little more than women's finery, and I waited for him to snap them off and laugh at his captors.'

'Like Daniel.' This put me in mind of Tom, and how weak he had been as he ascended the scaffold. 'And by the time they transported him, the irons looked more than he could ever carry?'

'Yes. My uncle smashed the machine he'd tended for twenty years. He knew that machine; it was like a part of him. All the sounds it made before a shaft was about to break, how the damp affected it. When he came home the night he'd done it, he shivered and wept. He said he knew how the oak must feel when the ivy that chokes it is torn away. But enough of this, for we are here at St Vincent's Court.'

Children in rags stared at me in a way no one had done since I wore silks on the night we went to Vauxhall.

'Just as well you enlisted my help. Even if you could afford to bribe these children, I daresay you'd not find one of them who knew what you were talking about.' He winked at a girl who was hanging a wet sheet from a window. The sheet was so grey and so full of gaping holes it looked beyond washing; the window was just a narrow gap in the wall which she would have to stuff with paper once night fell, if not before; and the wall looked greenish-black with the slime that London rainwater trails in its wake.

I took out the envelope and looked at the front again. 'How will we know who Miss Rosaria is?'

'Are there any clues inside?'

Before I could prevent him, Gus broke the seal and peered in. He whistled. 'She'll come, all right,' he said, and shouted her name so loudly that it seemed to leap back out at us from the walls.

'Oo wans 'er?' a small man in loose breeches and a red shirt growled from a top window. Gus smiled at me, pleased to have been proved right. Soon we heard light footsteps taking creaky wooden stairs at speed, and a slight woman with a white-and-red floral scarf over her hair appeared.

'Miss Rosaria?' Gus said. She looked behind us.

'We're alone,' I added. She nodded again and smiled, but her eyes were narrowed, whether with calculation or fear, I couldn't tell. I had no idea if she recognised me, and with the scarf I could not be sure if she was one of the women I had glimpsed at St James's Square but I felt she was. Perhaps she too had hoped to escape the place for ever, only to discover that Mr Edwards had other ideas. She took the envelope Gus offered and darted back inside.

'We're safer now.' Gus blew out his cheeks as we headed back the way we came.

I didn't tell him that I felt safe anyway, with his hefty frame by my side. I'd always been about the same height as Tom, and had beaten him in too many childhood fights to feel that he offered me much protection, so the experience was a novel one and I enjoyed it. 'Why do you say that?' I asked instead.

'There was five pounds in that envelope,' he remarked. 'The last time I saw that kind of money was when they paid the man who shopped my uncle. Now what could a girl like that do that might be worth the handing-over of five pounds in broad daylight? And why would anyone trust you enough to do it? You are a woman of mystery indeed, Nell Wingfield.'

22

I HAD LEFT GUS where I had found him, on Whitehall. I refused his offers to carry me home, or leave Adam standing with his chair for another two hours while he walked me back. The city is a dangerous place for a young woman, he told me most earnestly, but I sent him away insisting that I had been making my way in it alone for years, and so was likely to survive another day without his protection. 'Mind you do,' he said, then told me that he and Adam usually stopped at that spot at around three in the afternoon, so I knew where to find him when next I had an envelope laden with someone's fortune to deliver.

The shop was empty when I got back. Isaiah had not done any print work, and this further reassured me that I was unlikely to be pushed out by Carotty Anne while mine were the only hands bringing in any money. I listed about, examining the prints, admiring again the gentle accuracy of Titus Soane's lines. There was no point in mixing coloured inks, as there would not be time for me to use them before the arrival of the congregation. Mindful of Mr Edwards' warning, I had broached with Isaiah the notion that he might not preach for a while, but I put no real effort into it, for I knew what he would say – I might as well ask him not to breathe as not to speak the Lord's words. The next day was the third after

Tom's execution, and I knew that the theme of Isaiah's sermon would be Tom's resurrection. As I stretched some more paper for the following day's work, I reflected that Isaiah had not preached since my mother's death, on account of his being in gaol. (Unless he counted his 'sermonising' in prison to Carroty Anne, which I certainly did not.) I hoped that he would not make reference to my mother's death that night; somehow I felt she would prefer to be left in peace. But I knew that he would talk about her, and of course he did.

Just after six, Isaiah came back with Meg behind him. She was practically invisible, she was carrying so many fir branches. I decided not to ask where and when Carroty Anne had palmed her off on to Isaiah, nor where she herself now was.

'You are a walking tree,' I told her. She rewarded me with one of her rare smiles.

'The windows are open to air the upper room, but I have been too busy to scrub the floors,' I said truthfully, but letting Isaiah think that it was printing work that had occupied me.

'Then let us do it together,' he said, clapping his hands before ascending the ladder.

Soon the place smelled of green wood, and you would never have guessed it had stood empty for six months. Tom had helped Isaiah build the benches, some from planks washed up on the banks of the Thames, but most from wood which my Uncle John had procured from the devil only knew where. The wood from the river was much darker, and the sheen it had acquired from my polishing and that of the backsides it had accommodated gave it an ancient look. There were two rows of benches on each side of the walls, the second slightly higher than the first, lending it the appearance of a small theatre. Isaiah and I tied all Meg's branches to the rafters, taking care not to place them directly above the worshippers, so they wouldn't get resin on their heads.

I asked him to carry up a tub of hot water, and suggested that he work on his sermon. He said he did not need the time to write it down, for he had already run the words through his mind, walking through the grounds of one of the Inns of Court – their peacefulness, combined with walking past self-important lawyers in their wigs, always helped him come up with some well-turned phrases. But before he left, he did as I bid, and I listened, smiling, to the familiar sound of Isaiah's dusty footsteps as he climbed the ladder, sloshing water as he came. He emerged, wearing his brown fustian jacket which made his skin shine bronze and his brown eyes glint almost hazel in the candlelight. How well the bower of firs behind his lectern suited him! He paced about again, sniffing the branches and humming tunes from his childhood; he was nervous, worrying that no one would come and his six months in gaol had killed his ministry.

His help amounted to little more than offering his instructions while I was on my knees scrubbing planks.

'That ladder was always a pestilence to poor John,' he said, meaning John Tibbs, the one-legged man we saw executed just before Tom. 'But Will used to say it was an advantage to be in a hayloft like this, for we could defend ourselves more easily, if it came to it.' He peered back down the ladder. 'When the slaves revolted, they poured hot oil on their masters' heads.'

For all the heat of the day, I shivered. Isaiah had made Mr L'Ouverture and his Santo Domingo rebellion a *cause célèbre* among the radicals of London. Meg, who had never shown any interest in God, King, or revolution, rolled *Loovertoor* around her mouth like a bulls-eye mint whenever the man's name was mentioned.

'Have you seen Will?' I asked. Will Davidson was Isaiah's oldest friend and Tom's apprentice-master, so it was strange that he had not been at the execution. Given that he was far more committed a rabble-rouser than Isaiah, I assumed that he was in some kind of trouble.

Isaiah shook his head and said quickly: 'Our news must not have reached him. He will appear soon enough.'

'I think pouring hot oil down would be too subtle for Will. He would want to smite men down as they appeared through the hatch. And the pouring of oil sounds like a woman's business to me.'

Isaiah smiled. 'Yes, that is Will. Not subtle, but not womanly, either. I hope we never have need for his talents. Nor your uncle's, either.'

'I doubt John Ings would take on a *man*,' I said, wishing at once I hadn't, because of the force in my tone.

'What did he do to you, Nell?' Isaiah asked, watching me rub my arms where my uncle grabbed hold of me the night I left his house and roamed the streets rather than be anywhere near him. 'Tom said that whatever had made you run off and leave him and Meg, he was sure John Ings lurked behind it somewhere.'

'I've seen worse.' It was an answer that was more likely to prompt more questions than end the discussion, so I made to descend the ladder. 'I should go back to the press if we are going to have anything to sell tomorrow.' Sometimes I think that we cannot afford for the revolution to come, for what would we sell afterwards? Unlike the men who came to hear Isaiah, I did not believe that even the most radical change of government would ensure bread and ale for all.

Meg was sitting in the corner, staring at the press. 'Will there be any cards?' she said. She meant for her to sell again.

'Isaiah has told you: we'll be not undertaking that kind of work any longer.' I was glad of this, for I knew what men had done to her while she stood on Trafalgar Square: how one tried to snatch her in broad daylight, how another slowed a carriage and craned out to take a good look at her. Meg had stared at him, and he ordered the driver to crack on. I couldn't see if the driver had noticed what had excited his passenger's interest, and I doubt he would have cared much if he had. I have no idea what Meg thought of these encounters, though they had clearly not upset her enough to discourage her from selling prints again.

Meg heard footsteps outside and darted into the back corner without replying: the first of the chapel-goers was arriving.

And this was the marvel of it: during the next fifteen minutes, no fewer than forty-seven men trooped in. I always counted, to see if the right number of ha'pennies had been collected at the end of the night. This used to be my mother's job, before her bones started to ache so much that it pained her even to sit in a chair. We asked Meg to do this once, but so many of the congregation spoke to her that she disappeared for three days afterwards.

Twenty men came most weeks, but a throng of sixty had been known on a Friday, which apart from a Sunday had been Isaiah's busiest night. This was, he said, to encourage temperance among the men, though the fumes that lingered long after they had climbed the ladder to the loft suggested that some got an advance start on the liquor in order to be full-throated in their worship.

I knew many of the faithful, by sight more often than by name, their collars hunched up, a nod to me as they come through, an irreligious wink from one or two. Furtive glances behind them marked out the newcomers, as if they expected the Government's spies to leap out from behind the door and clap them in irons the moment they crossed the threshold. For though this was ostensibly a religious gathering, it was clear to all that its intent was political – and such gatherings were, of course, illegal.

Mr Soane came in, just as I realised that I had done nothing to my hair that morning. To see how he stared, I must have looked like a horsehair mattress with its stuffing springing out everywhere. Again he turned his hat in his hands nervously.

'How are you, Mistress Nell?' he said.

'I am well,' I said. If I had trusted him, I would have told him that I had taken some pleasure in inking in the plum of Queen Caroline's skirts. It had been a fine choice of colour, for it looked almost as good towards the end of the printing, when the shade was more delicate. In my view, the more discerning customers would choose those prints ahead of the darker ones, even though they could see that they had a higher number. Usually people want the earliest print in a run, and will pay the most for it, but few artists or printers have their best eye for the first piece they do.

'Titus Soane!' Isaiah had appeared, to check that there were no more men to come up. 'Word of your talent is spreading. Or so our customers say,' he added.

How would he know? He was never in the shop to hear them.

'You are an instrument of the Lord, Titus,' Isaiah said. 'For our profits further our ministry.'

He ignored Isaiah's thinly disguised begging and fixed a time to collect his earnings. I wondered where and how Titus Soane lived, and whether or not he would spend all of the money. I could not help reflecting that he seemed a kind man for all that I had my suspicions. He would have to use most of it for materials, I decided, and what little he had left he would put by, until he found a wife. Sir David said that 'to cherish' was the most important marriage vow, and the one which received the least attention. My mother would have agreed with him; Isaiah would have lectured him on the importance of obedience and fear of the Lord.

'Come up,' said Isaiah. Mr Soane followed him, hesitating a moment before ramming his hat on his head so that he could use his hands to climb the ladder. I prayed that Mr Soane was not a spy, and that Isaiah had the sense to be wary of him.

My Uncle John was the last to arrive, looking almost as hunted as the new men. I expected to be afraid of him, but I felt only contempt. I saw him not as my Aunt Agnes's husband but as a man I might pass on the street. Truly I would cross over rather than get too close, for he is a barrage of trouble and no mistake. Even when he is at rest, his fingers curl as if in readiness to make a fist. He was talking to another man, and anyone would judge from his animated gestures and shuttered expression that a disagreement was about to start and a fight soon to follow. It was impossible to imagine him whispering, still less being tender.

'Your aunt would rather I was at the tavern,' he said. 'She thinks there is less trouble for me there.' This was startling, seeing that the phrase 'demon drink' might have been invented while observing John Ings over the rim of a tankard. I nodded and waited for my uncle to pay his ha'penny, which of course he did not.

The meetings lasted over an hour, and I had hidden myself up there enough in the past to picture the scene as I listened to the proceedings going on above me: first came a welcome to the men, especially to the newcomers, who would be caught between returning Isaiah's gaze and staring at the floor, and would spend the service glancing out of the corners of their eyes, watching for their cue to sit, lowering themselves down half a moment later than everyone else.

And now what they had come for: Isaiah's sermon. Most of them would have heard him preach before; though I did not recognise a good third of the men who had come, meaning that Tom's execution had helped spread the word. Or perhaps the newcomers would have learned of Isaiah from one of the regulars, pausing between swings of his pick while heaving out the foundations of the new houses out at Stoke Newington or Streatham to hear of this man who, though he be a blackamoor, preaches the Word like the whitest of the angels. I once overheard a pipe-maker say all this, an enormous man who held up palms black with lead to illustrate Isaiah's darkness. I'd wanted to interrupt, to point out that Isaiah's palms are pinker than Meg's, but I didn't.

I paused in my printing for the sermon, partly so I didn't disturb him, but mostly so I could listen properly myself.

'I came over London Bridge in my prison cart knowing that the Fourth King George would be the last, and that I would have a hand in the building of the New Jerusalem on the ashes of the Babylon I was entering...'

Carroty Anne blundered in. 'Am I late?' she said.

'Hush the gin in you,' I whispered. 'He is preaching.'

'Ah, he wooed me with that, you know. Through the bars.'

'You've been through the bars today, and no mistake. You reek. You can't go up there.'

'He said I could come up,' she whined, close to tears. 'He promised!'

'Did he?' I said, trying to remember if it was he or my mother who had decided that she and I would stay away from his meetings.

'Go up,' I said, wafting my hand at the ladder. At least that way I would not have to stare at her.

Isaiah continued, 'They imprisoned me in Dorchester; in order, they said, to make it the more difficult for my friends and family to visit me. Some of you overcame the difficulty, but my wife could not. And so Elizabeth died on my second day in Dorchester gaol...'

It pleased me that he was speaking of my mother just as Carroty Anne was heaving herself up. There was some shuffling of feet at the arrival of a woman but nobody made any objection.

I returned to the thread of Isaiah's sermon.

'...and on the evening of the third day, her son Tom arrived with a loaf of bread and the news that our friend and his apprentice-master Will Davidson would attend to the burial. I knew that the empty knapsack Tom carried away was full of the question of how he and his aunt and his sisters would live until I was released. I hardly need to remind you that last year's harvest was so poor and the people so distressed that we heard more sabres than scythes. And yet, and yet – the revolution did not come, and the people did not starve, either.

'But what of now? Have you all turned your swords into ploughshares before you have been given your rightful share of the harvest?'

There followed several exclamations of outrage at the very idea, accompanied by anguished creaks of the floorboards above my head as men stood up, or else shifted on their benches.

And so Isaiah went on, his voice at its full strength. He persuaded the men that there was not a rising last summer for a reason; that the time for the New Jerusalem was now. A revolution can only occur, he said, when the most acute hour of the crisis has passed, for who could ask a man to leave his wife and children with no means of sustenance and march off to storm Newgate? But Isaiah knew this: he was a man whose wife had died while he was in prison, and whose son had been sacrificed on the altar of this godless regime. Though he could not see me, of course, here Isaiah paused for the moment it took me to wipe a tear away before it dripped onto the paper I was leaning over. He was someone who knew that this suffering was almost as much as any man could bear. He said almost, because now that the crisis had passed, and now that this phalanx of strong men was sitting before him, it was as obvious to Isaiah as night follows day, as liberty follows captivity, as death leads to the eternal life of the spirit, that the hour was fast upon us.

Isaiah's words were met with many Amens – and almost as many Ahems and sundry coughs. I supposed that Isaiah was correct about the strength of the men before him, if he ignored the eternal sore throats and the odd touch of consumption.

One man rose to tell the group that the Kingdom was due to come on April 17th of the following year. There was excitement at this, and some positing of rival dates, a discussion conducted with an enthusiasm for numbers which rivalled Meg's.

'There are those among us who see the Bible as an abacus of the Apocalypse,' Isaiah said, 'and they look to John and the Book of Revelation for signs of the End Time, but –'

'Aye, Revelations,' said a voice I knew only too well: my Uncle John's. 'Chapter 18, verse 20 speaks of the destruction of cities, as you are fond of reminding us, Isaiah. The time is surely on us.'

'Perhaps they will destroy Manchester first, it is a pit of Satan far fouler than this one and no mistake,' said a man who to judge by his accent was clearly from those parts. There was some laughter, and more when another man said, 'Ay, but the Book of Proverbs said "let her breasts satisfy thee at all times", and how many of us want to read our future in that?'

My Uncle John, who has no sense of humour, sounded nettled. 'This is no time for titties, Walter. The Queen's coming is a sign. London is the Babylon the Bible talks of – or the great whore,' he said. I wondered how Carroty Anne was taking this.

'It is always time for titties,' the same voice said. 'Why, only downstairs –'

'Enough, Walter,' Isaiah said quickly, over Carroty Anne's laughter. 'Brothers, we are not here to destroy but to build. Let us return to firmer ground: the words of Our Lord Himself who seldom spoke in riddles and was not given to senseless acts of vengeance.'

'He cursed a fig tree,' said one man.

I wondered how Isaiah would explain this, for it is one of the passages I have never understood. I once saw the insides of a fig and couldn't believe that a tree could grow anything that beautiful, and why should beauty be cursed? Perhaps that was the point – my mother was beautiful, and so was Hetty, and look what happened to them.

'Let us look at the long night St Peter spent in Golgotha,' Isaiah said, ignoring the noise. 'For I was reminded of this powerfully when I was witnessing Tom's final agony. There next to me was his sister – and it was as if I could read her thoughts, so mighty was her distress. I could almost hear her saying: "I should have come with a sword, I should be storming the scaffold. After all, what if that yeoman who is leaning against the platform to guard my brother shoots me? The men around me might follow my example; at least I would not have to live with myself for standing quiet while my brother hangs. At least Tom would know that whatever world he was going to next, I would be there with him."'

As Isaiah drew breath, I wiped my tears with my sleeve. His words were better than my own thoughts, and I wanted to be the woman he described. This was Isaiah's gift: to summon that desire in anyone who would listen to him. I was glad that Carroty Anne was not there to see me cry.

Isaiah reminded the congregation that my brother and his

friends had done nothing more than seek the overthrow of a vile regime, and that these men had died in the hope that we all could be saved in this world and the next. Tom's only crime was this: he had convened a small meeting in a tavern to discuss the matter of four hundred dead at sword-point during a peaceful demonstration in Manchester, and what the working men of London might muster in response. The conspiracy went no further than the talking, but the idea of it alone was enough to condemn him.

'And now it is the time to act,' called out an unknown voice.

'We must be careful, brothers,' said Isaiah. 'They must not know the day or the hour.'

'Aye, but act we must,' insisted my Uncle John. 'And soon.'

I shook my head. If Titus Soane were indeed a spy, that would be the line which would hang my uncle, and Isaiah into the bargain. With remarks like that in the air, it would be impossible to pretend like this was anything other than a political meeting, and such gatherings were illegal.

'Surely, John,' Isaiah continued, 'we cannot make such a claim without Will Davidson among us? We could never settle on anything without him.'

The debate moved back to when the Second Coming would be. This was a popular topic, and Tom had never tired of it, since it combined his love of numbers and his thirst for something to happen. Even my uncle had an opinion on the matter, drawn from a night he spent in the tavern. ('Where else?' another man piped up. 'Hear hear', I said to the ceiling.) If all these men were right, there would be half a dozen Second Comings before the year was out. I resumed my printing.

'And from where did you receive this intelligence, brothers?' Isaiah asked.

Much of it had come from other preachers. This gave Isaiah the opportunity to remind the assembly that only false prophets reduce the will of God to a time sheet, and that we know not the day or hour; all we can do is be ready. And with this he bade the men goodnight.

As they filed past me, many were plotting no more than which tavern would have their custom that night. I checked that none of these thirsty men still owed us a penny. That is the truth of it, I thought: for all their talk, these men were no more likely to overthrow the Government than they were to become a horseman of the Apocalypse.

Titus Soane left with scarcely a nod. He would have heard plenty there to report back to Mr Edwards, if spying was indeed his true calling. My uncle lingered by the door. He and half a dozen others sat discussing what Jesus meant when he called on the apostles to arm themselves, and if he would say the same if he had been a dark-skinned carpenter in today's London. 'Your aunt wishes to see you' was all my uncle said to me.

I wanted to retort 'She knows where I am', but I did not. I simply wanted him to leave, and I knew we would have to go and visit her soon enough – Isaiah had not seen her since he had been released, which meant that they had yet to speak of my mother's death.

Once all the men had left, I went up to the loft. Isaiah and Carroty Anne were sitting on a bench, half a body apart. The peace resting between them made me want to shout.

'The air is so full of sweat and damp clothes that I feel we still have company,' I said. It was a reference to Carroty Anne, who smelled like an old divan left in the rain for the rag and bone men to collect, and we all knew it. She fled to their room like a whipped dog, and I felt the greater cur for my unkindness. I wanted to talk to Isaiah about Tom, and about Mr Edwards, and to tell him that Tom's conviction was not the only thing to have marked out our house, but I was too slow in finding the right words.

Before my mother died, this had been my favourite time with Isaiah; we would look in on my mother, and if she was sleeping, I would sit on one of the benches while he paced about and talked. Sometimes it was as if he had forgotten I was there, and he would talk about when he first met my mother, how he could not believe how luminous she was – everything about her put him in mind of light, he said once, and this had moved him to write sermons with illumination as their theme – that, and long passages from the Song of Solomon.

Isaiah shook his head at me and followed Carroty Anne to bed.

23

A WEEK OF SOLID printing followed. On the few occasions he spoke to me beyond perfunctory greetings and requests, Isaiah reported that all the talk was of the Bill which was to be put before Parliament so that the King could divorce Queen Caroline.

Carroty Anne and Isaiah were out much of the time, though they usually left and returned separately. There was a formality between them in their enquiries as to the course of each other's days which convinced me that they were not quite as close as two pages of a pocket bible. Although Meg grieved for Tom in her own inward way – I knew she was thinking of him when she took to scowling at me – she soon stopped trailing after Carroty Anne like a pup, so it was possible to forget about her for much of the time.

We ate because I was printing, some nights until my fingers were numb with the setting and I did not want to burn down another two of the candles which I had bought on credit from Mr Tagg. In addition to Mr Soane's engravings, we had acquired no less than fifty-six plates of a scandal involving the Duke of York. They were ten years old and worn, which was why we could afford so many of them. Isaiah picked them up at the end of a night-time auction of a printer near Liverpool-street, and it did not occur to him that they had not made the poor bankrupt's fortune and so were therefore unlikely to make ours. Most of the work we received was of the last-minute variety that the grander printers could not do so quickly: handbills for theatre troupes who arrive from out of town and find a room above a tavern to perform in; announcements of public meetings decided upon by wealthy patrons with the ear of a magistrate who will grant them licence to assemble; the rantings of any preacher who can persuade Isaiah to give him credit. And this city being what it is, around three-quarters of these tracts turned a profit. Printer: Isaiah Douglas, Bow Lane EC appeared at the foot of each one, so I was convinced it was a matter of time before one of these cranks attempted some insanity or other and brought the constables to our door.

❧

On the Tuesday night, Carroty Anne did not come back at all. This would have filled me with hope, had Isaiah not been so angry and fretful. On the Wednesday evening, he came into the back room and claimed he was now a calmed ship. I nodded and continued adding florid cheeks to one of the Queen's detractors, a figure who was attempting to pull up her petticoat only to reveal all the good people of London sheltering beneath.

'You have your mother's hair,' he said.

'You sound surprised,' I said, because he did – no doubt at my greyness, which was advancing almost by the day. (I had no mirror, so I had taken to running my hands across my face to ensure that I was not as wrinkled as I was silver.) I didn't look up because I hadn't quite forgiven him for I couldn't quite decide what.

He reached out and touched it gently. When my mother was alive, he would never use a pillow, but would bunch her hair in his fists and tuck it under his cheek instead.

'It will not burn you,' I said, but softly now.

Even so, he shook his head, and the lines around his mouth reappeared; I should not have said anything.

'Our only comfort must be in our enemies' hatred for us,' he said, stepping away from me a little, 'for it makes us stronger. In this way, as the Lord said, even those who are against us are for us.'

That night as I lay down to sleep, I was filled with hope: that Carroty Anne was gone, that Isaiah's calm would mean an end to his preaching, that I had discharged my responsibilities to Mr Edwards, and he would not appear again. Naturally, all this turned out to be nonsense.

~~~

On the Friday, so in the second week after Tom's execution, Carroty Anne insisted she spoke with me. (She had returned the previous Thursday, muttering some implausible story about visiting sick friends in Kilburn.)

'Come outside, where there's more air,' said Carroty Anne, wafting a be-shawled arm at me – she could not abide the aroma of ink. 'I might be in need of your help here.' The usual smell of smoke, sweat, tobacco and a distant echo of something perfumed came from her. The busiest maidservant in the land would look less flustered than Carroty Anne habitually did: she lived such a rag-tag-and-bobtail of an existence, always claiming that she was 'helping friends' or tracking down those who owed her money. I feared that we would turn out to have some mutual acquaintances who would send my tower of lies crashing around my ears, but none had emerged.

'My help?' I asked, so surprised that I followed her onto the street.

'Yes indeed. There are some lunatics in Isaiah's circle who

would make a Guy Fawkes of him.'

'There is always talk of revolution and the Second Coming'

'This is different,' she warned, looking behind her. A hod-man caught her eye and winked, telling her he'd be looking for her, come pay day. 'In a stables just off Marble Arch there is enough gunpowder to blow up the entire Cabinet while they dine,' she continued, seeming pleased at the man's attention. 'They could pick any one of those fancy houses they have for themselves.'

'Who? Who has this gunpowder? Who wants to do this?' I whispered this because I knew only too well that the whiff of such a conversation, never mind of gunpowder, would see all of us hang.

'Will Davidson has some wild friends,' she said.

I shook my head. 'Even if there is gunpowder where you say, I do not believe that Isaiah has anything to do with it.'

'You ask him, then.' And she took off up Friday-street with as much dignity as she could muster.

'I have work to do,' I replied to her dingy skirts, but she was already at Cheapside.

Gunpowder! As much as I tried to dismiss Carroty Anne as a lunatic, something about this worried me – not least Will Davidson's absence since Tom's death. Perhaps I had spent too much time listening to rumours of Sir Robin's schemes at St James's Square, I told myself. But then I remembered Mr Edwards' insistence that Isaiah cease his activities, and the fear crept in that I had been so blinkered by worry about my own actions that I had failed to pay sufficient attention to Isaiah's.

While Meg counted buttons with her back studiously turned to me, I printed a conjuror's handbill. He promised miracles:

birds would appear from hats, and large objects would disappear. I wondered if he could make whatever Carroty Anne thought was near Edgware-road vanish, and my silk dress along with it. I was so preoccupied with Carroty Anne's warning that I made a wealth of silly mistakes and soon had to stop.

The bell jangled, and I hoped it was Isaiah.

'Mr Tagg!' I said, my heart sinking like a sack thrown in the Thames.

'Miss Wingfield.' His face was devoid of its usual insinuating wolfishness, and I assumed that the man who entered the shop with him was of some importance in Mr Tagg's estimation.

'This is Mr Dunsworthy.'

He lived up to his name: everything about him was grey: suit, hair, skin – even the sheen on his top hat.

'He and I are associates. In particular, he looks after my financial affairs.'

Mr Dunsworthy bowed in acknowledgement of this honour.

'He reminds me that Mr Douglas is in arrears in his payments to me. How can you explain this, Miss Wingfield? For Mr Smeek reports that some of our customers have praised the work of your new artist. Soane, is it?'

I ignored the reference to Mr Soane, for Tagg would have made it his business to discover his identity. I doubted that Titus Soane would be interested in working with a scoundrel like Tagg. After all, a man of Titus' abilities could have sold his work on Cheapside straight off if it had suited him.

'Forgive me, Mr Tagg,' I said, 'but I was not aware that we paid you more frequently than once every twenty-eight days, and we have scarcely been back in business for three weeks.'

Here Mr Dunsworthy cleared his throat. 'Mr Tagg would,

I am sure, advaannce you credit for the quarter if you required it, but this is a debt outstaannding since before your, er, before Mr Douglas was saadly incarcerated,' he said in adenoidal tones.

'And it requires payment,' said Tagg by way of clarification.

'Or else, equally saadly,' Mr Dunsworthy said, 'we will have to return with a constable –'

'– and your rabble-rousing employer will find himself back in the clink,' interjected Mr Tagg.

Dunsworthy brushed something invisible from his shoulder – a speck of grey dust, perhaps? – and made to leave.

'I will communicate all of this to my stepfather,' I said.

'Make sure you do,' answered Mr Tagg. Mr Dunsworthy had already departed.

⁓⌇⁓

As I headed to one of the three coffee shops off Fleet-street where I was confident of finding Isaiah, I reflected that Mr Tagg's visit had been serendipitous: if Carroty Anne was right and Isaiah was placing himself in great danger, then a spell in prison for debt would keep him from more serious crimes. It was a testament to our predicament that my principal worry was not what on earth Isaiah had done with all the money I had earned at the press.

The first shop, the Turk's Head, was empty, save for some puny types who looked like the jobbing authors to whom I often advanced low-grade ink and rough paper. As I approached Braganza's, I knew I was in luck, for I could hear Isaiah through the window. *You are a fool*, I thought: *if I can hear you, so can any government spy or constable.* At the encouragement of a voice I did not recognise, Isaiah was rehearsing a sermon: 'As my namesake the Prophet tells us,

"The People who walked in darkness have seen a great light." The city, my friends, is the darkness, and the light is political maturity and wisdom.

I entered, noticing that I was the only woman in the establishment. By Isaiah's side was Will Davidson, looking impatient to speak.

'Nell!' called Isaiah. I approached the table. Five other men sat with them, none of whom I recognised.

'I am sorry,' Will said, standing up at the sight of me. 'Sorry for your loss, and sorry that I could not be here sooner to bear its burden with you.'

'You had business,' Isaiah pronounced, before I could enquire of Will as to its nature.

'I do not doubt it,' I agreed. Some said that Will had been in on the plot to kill the Prime Minister back in 1812; some that he was in the pay of Lord Liverpool's Government and could be relied on to kill a man if the price was right. There was even a rumour that he had been a highwayman, though this I found harder than the other tales to believe: his black skin and almost yellowish eyes would have made him far too easy to detect. I used to pick up those stories as Tom told them to Meg, and in consequence I always thought of Will in the exaggerated stage whisper of Tom's which Meg so loved. Seeing Will there with Isaiah made me all the more alarmed, and sorry that I had been so dismissive of Carroty Anne.

'Aye,' Will said, looking at me as if I were a parcel he was about to open. My cheeks flushed, and my irritation at myself made me colour all the more. If I were a cat, the hair would rise on my neck when he spoke to me. All I ever saw my mother give him were thin slices of politeness, so I think she felt the same way as I did.

Will's coat, once a dramatic midnight blue, had taken on a strange grey sheen. Some of the seams sagged where the stitches which had repaired them were stronger than the

cloth. 'The day will come when all our cares will be swept away, and we will know that Tom's sacrifice was a fanfare,' Will said to the men at the table, but for my benefit.

'I thought I would print a couple of your old sermons,' I said to Isaiah, feeling many eyes upon me.

'Have you come all this way to tell him that?' one of the other men sneered.

'I have some business which I must discuss with Isaiah outside.' I felt awkward, wishing I was behind the rampart of my press. If you had not gone to prison, I reflected as I watched Isaiah get up, I would never have had to abandon the shop and the work I love so much. Please do not force me from it again.

The coffee house bell jangled, and I was glad of the interruption – until I saw who it was. Heavy footsteps and nasal breathing marked the arrival of my Uncle John, and Carroty Anne with him.

'Not a month after her brother's execution, and she is gadding about,' John said.

'We were remembering Tom,' I said, glad that my voice was strong. However much Will Davidson made me uncomfortable, I would much rather be locked in a cell with him for twenty years than have to spend another night under my uncle's roof.

Here is all you need to know about my uncle. My mother had been dead three days, we had gone to live with him on account of the shop being closed, and he had insisted that Tom slaughter a pig. It was never too early to pick up a proper trade, he said, and learn what was expected of us, now that we were under his roof. This was just the beginning of it. I learned what was expected of me, soon enough, during the only night I spent there.

We could hear the pig, snuffling in the yard. Meg had been forbidden from making friends with it, and so had pressed herself flat against the back door, presumably in order to be as close to the animal as possible. The pig clearly felt the same, for we could hear its snout butting the wood behind Meg's back.

'Will you help me?' Tom said, and I widened my eyes and shook my head. 'We will all go,' said our Aunt Agnes, with a glance at Meg.

'It will be good for you to learn the business,' Agnes said. She also did not regard printing as a proper trade, and was often heard saying just within my mother's earshot that Isaiah's fixation with letters on the page would be the cause of our ruin.

'Shall I fetch the boys?' I said. I meant my three cousins, who at a stretch could muster one brain between them. 'And I will take Meg out, if you like.'

'The boys know the trade well enough,' Uncle John said. 'And you have spent long enough with ink on your fingers on Isaiah's account – it's about time you had some honest blood on your hands, like your aunt here. You look as though you've never eaten a pie in your life, let alone baked one.'

'I have a trade,' I said. 'And so will Tom, soon enough.'

'And we will not kill any of God's creatures,' said Tom.

Uncle John folded his arms. 'You call yourself a revolutionary, and you are not even able to shed an animal's blood.' To him, it was not religion which made us averse to eating red meat, but some desire to set ourselves apart and make ourselves superior to the world in general and him in particular. 'Isaiah has taught you nothing worth knowing.'

He herded us into the yard and handed Tom the knife. My memory of what happened next is at once very sharp and strangely distorted. We might have been there for hours, though it was probably only a matter of minutes. I remember the pig squealing as soon as it saw the blade, a hysterical keening which made Meg cover her ears as if the sound were a gale which had her flattened against the wall. I remember Tom refusing to take the knife, so that it clattered on the cobbles and hit a trotter, sending the poor animal into an even greater frenzy. My uncle wrestled the creature until he had its throat in a rough embrace, and I was looking into its eyes when he picked up the knife and slashed its throat. All this happened quickly, but then time slowed as we watched the life drain from it. There was something obscene about the leisurely meandering of the blood between the cobbles as it found its way to the drain in the centre of the yard.

Tom and I were spattered with blood. My uncle grinned at the sight of it. 'An initiation,' he said.

Tom snorted and shook his head. 'I do not belong to you,' he said. 'I am sorry, Aunt Agnes, but Isaiah is more my kin than he could ever be.'

'Why are you apologising to her?' I said, feeling most disgusted at her for choosing him as a husband; over many years he had proved himself such a vile creature that it was difficult to believe that he was remotely cast in God's image, but Agnes was my mother's kin and so must have known better at some time in her life.

The way Agnes stood a little closer to her husband said, 'I expected this from you, Nell, but you Tom: you were your mother's favourite, and this is all you are fit for?' And Tom truly was her favourite: all the rest of us came some way behind him, even Isaiah. If he ever noticed, he buried his head deeper in his bible until the special smile she gave only to Tom had folded away again like a fan. When she met Isaiah, I wondered if he would be able to interrupt the understanding between my mother and Tom. While Tom was alive, I would have said that he never did succeed, but now I think that Isaiah found another way: he made Tom earn his affection. And Tom, not used to having to raise so much as an eyebrow to be assured of his place at the centre of his mother's universe, swung between bending himself to winning Isaiah and pretending that he did not need to.

Strips of pork were roasted for our supper. It was the richest meal ever laid before us, but Tom and I refused anything but bread. Tom did so on principle, his eyes following the food to his cousins' greasy mouths, but I was sickened so much I did not want to eat.

I knew that Tom would not forgive our uncle the humiliation. I lay awake that night, expecting Tom to come with his plans for our escape, but he did not. My uncle came instead.

There was no mistaking him for Tom: Tom was silent and lean, while my uncle carried his heft as if it were some snuffling animal which he was forced to carry every time he mounted the stairs.

He held me against the bed by the neck while he pushed his hand between my thighs. He told me my mother had once resisted him, and assured me that he would not brook the same opposition from me. 'After all, as Tom said today, you are not my kin. There is no sin here. But I'll not touch your half-wit sister.'

'Should I be grateful for this?' I said, or at least tried to; for I was sure he was going to strangle me.

His breathing became more insistent, and it reminded me of the piglet when it saw the knife in Tom's hand. 'There are a lot of things you should be grateful for,' he said as he jabbed two fingers inside me. 'Plenty of room in there,' he said, flexing his fingers apart and together, apart and together. 'Sure you haven't been up to something already?' I shook my head, and some part of me thought I should bring my knee up to his chin, but my eyes were watering so much it was difficult to see and my legs felt a long way from me. My existence had become my uncle's two broad red fingers, his breath, and his voice. Looking back on it, I am most amazed at how the instinct to save myself was the one that kept me still.

'Meg has the best titties of any of you, mind,' he said, as if the topic of which of the four Wingfield women had the best bosom vexed him as much as any matter of Scripture would Isaiah. 'So perhaps I am starting in the wrong place after all.'

'You will not touch Meg,' I said, my voice no more than a shadow. Looking back on it, I do not think he would ever have gone near her: he always turned his face away from her, as if he viewed her strangeness as lime or mercury, something noxious he might inhale if he got too close to her. No, his threat of touching Meg was a threat for me: he knew that I had promised my mother to keep my sister safe, and he therefore reckoned on my remaining a pliant captive under his roof.

He rummaged in his trousers a little, and then grunted. 'Well, there will be more for you tomorrow, and no mistake,' he said, in a tone which betrayed that whatever he had found in his breeches was a disappointment. It might be a sin to sit in judgement on another man, but I do not think I could ever feel more contempt for anyone than I do for John Ings when I look back on that moment.

My aunt called his name sleepily from the next room, and as he lumbered away to her, I knew this: I would die, or else kill him, before I let him near me again. And if I told Tom or my aunt what he had done, what then? No, it would be better for everyone if I left. Tom would look after Meg. And Tom did – until he was arrested.

And now here was John Ings again, if anything even fatter and shorter of breath.

'What is that whore doing here again?' said Will, before Isaiah had the chance to say anything to Carroty Anne.

This was an interesting comment, but what was more surprising was the triumphant leer that momentarily inhabited my uncle's face; I was convinced that John Ings knew all too well where Carroty Anne had been.

Isaiah stared at him. Carroty Anne greeted the other men, ignoring Will.

'There is a comfort in working the press – will help the hours of grief pass,' said Will, watching me closely.

Will could never settle to anything, and so was hardly qualified to comment on the merits of work. He had been a catastrophic apprentice-master for Tom, all skill and no application. But there was an unexpected kindness in Will's voice, so I did not point all this out.

There then followed a conversation that I did not fully understand.

'Before you go, Isaiah – I had word from our benefactor today,' said Will. 'He was asking after your business.'

'I am not as convinced as you evidently are of his friendship.'

'He seemed sure that the chapel would close again for lack of funds. Perhaps he means to help us.'

'Having just been released from gaol, he will expect me to be most keen to avoid the Hulks. And of course,' Isaiah continued, putting on his jacket, 'he knows I was once a naval man, so the prospect of being on board ship again holds double the terror. But we must do things *our* way, Will. We do not want to be puppets, for puppets dangle on strings that soon become ropes. Look at what happened to Tom while I was in prison.' A shadow passed over his face.

'Tom was not alone –' but then Will saw me, and he fell silent.

'We are all in this together,' Isaiah said. 'I will never desert our men.'

I wished I knew who 'our benefactor' was, but I did not want to interrupt them by asking and thereby drawing Will's attention to my listening. It could not be Mr Edwards' because I knew he wished Isiaiah to halt his preaching.

'You mention your time at sea,' Will continued, 'as if you were a slave, but even as a child you were not indentured. And look at you now,' he wafted his hands at the crates of coffee in the corner as though they were flies that he would swat away, 'with your press and your inks. You are a shop-keeper, Isaiah, in a nation of shopkeepers, and no time on board ship or in a prison can alter that. But I warn you, this life will continue to alter you, as it has already done to so many in the north.'

'You say that our brothers in the north are losing their stomach for the struggle?' Isaiah said quietly.

'Losing their stomach? Their stomachs are the problem: once they can fill them, they lose all interest in toppling the regime which starved them in the first place.'

'Perhaps you are right, but you are mistaken about me. I will not lose sight of our cause.'

Will nodded, and I was convinced he suppressed a smirk. 'Then you will meet us at John Ings' shop in an hour?' he said.

'I will,' Isaiah replied. 'Though the chapel has been thronging and the shop is more salubrious than a butcher's, so I do not see why we cannot transact all our business there from now on.'

Isaiah and Will looked at my Uncle John. He scuffed the floor with a grimy boot, his face sourer than usual. While the shop had been closed, my uncle had provided a meeting place; now Isaiah was wasting no time in removing whatever status this had bestowed on him.

'Better to tell them to their faces that they are to traipse over to your shop again,' John Ings said. 'And I doubt Nell will be spending the afternoon baking pie for them, as Agnes did.'

'If what Will is saying is right, we had better not fill these men's stomachs so generously in future, or else we will lose them. And Nell has more than enough to do,' Isaiah said, smiling at me, so that he missed the fury which bulged briefly behind John Ings' eyes.

My uncle returned to his shop unaccompanied; he told Isaiah that he must 'attend to that business' and Isaiah gave him a little nod before ramming his cap low on his head. It was so greasy it caught the light, as if it carried a perpetual pool of rain.

'What business?' I said.

'Aye, what business?' said Carroty Anne indignantly, now that we had quit the coffee house. 'You have a turbulent nose for trouble, Isaiah Douglas, and no mistake. You will not rest until you swing like this poor girl's brother.'

Isaiah looked at her as if the printing press had spoken. It was something my mother would have said, but I was glad she had come out with it all the same. I wish I had been there to ask Tom the same question, the night he went to his final meeting. I would have been able to tell him that there is not a tavern in this city that does not have a government spy supping in one of its snugs. But Tom was hardworking and God-fearing, and he could not see that there are men who would happily spend their lives drinking their way through the thirty pieces of silver they would be paid for betraying honest men.

'We have... we are... a co-operative,' he said.

'A what?' I said. 'Are you all setting up a fund for each other's funerals? Is that it?'

Isaiah knew what I was aiming at.

Carroty Anne pulled her shawl around her and walked out ahead of us, but she was listening; I could tell by the stiffness of her back and the incline of her head.

'And now –' Isaiah swallowed hard, and I raised my hand, ready to tell him to stop, to say that I did not want to make him churn out his grief for me like some poor organ-grinder, but he shook his head. 'And now, business is better than it ever has been, and I find that I do not want us ever to be so vulnerable again. St Luke told us, "He who does not have a sword must sell his cloak and buy one." Well, it seems that we do not have cloaks to sell, but together we can buy swords. If the hour comes again, we will most likely be felled, but at least our remains will not be scattered like so much chaff.'

'If we are felled by the Government, our bodies will go straight to the sawbones for their experiments,' I said. 'But I do not agree that we are prosperous. This is what I came to tell you. Mr Tagg says we are already in arrears. How can that be, Isaiah? We have scarcely been open a week, but sales are steady, thanks to Mr Soane. Yet whenever I return to the takings drawer, I can never find more than a few pennies. How are we to pay our creditors? If you tell me you have been giving alms, I will cease worrying about your other activities. But I must tell you that soon our generosity will have expired, and we will be charity cases ourselves.'

Isaiah steered us across Blackfriars-road and up Ludgate-hill. 'Surely it would be quicker to cut along Carter-lane?' I said, making to dart across the road. Isaiah grabbed my arm and pulled me towards him, as the milk cart which would have snapped my leg or worse trotted past. Its driver, who sat so huddled he might have been a hunchback, shook his head.

'Where is your sense?' Isaiah said.

'I could ask you a similar question: who in their right mind would go into business with Will Davidson and John Ings?' Carroty Anne said, for she had stopped to allow us to catch up.

As we passed St Paul's, so intent was I on remembering the terrible meeting I had with Mr Edwards there that I almost ploughed into a chestnut-seller's brazier.

'You are bringing the trials of Job on your own head today,' Isaiah said, laughing. He bowed to the seller, and the man motioned to me to choose a parcel of nuts, but I shook my head. The seller selected the largest one and offered it to Isaiah, who pushed it into my hands. As I reflected on how the warmth made it feel eerily alive, Isaiah pulled a coin out of his pocket. It was not just any coin: it was a sovereign.

'There's gold,' said the seller, screwing up his eyes as if at the brightness of it.

Isaiah peered at the coin, and for a moment St Pauls' churchyard seemed to fall silent as he realised his mistake and stowed the coin back in his pocket.

'Where did you get that from?' I said, glancing round. The coin was as powerful as a sun, and I was convinced that everyone would have seen it.

'You'd best not be flashing that here,' the seller said.

Isaiah extracted tuppence and bid the seller keep all of it. The seller's look changed from conspiratorial to the slightly wheedling contempt with which the poor greet the rich in this city. If I were one of the novelists Hetty used to read, I would say that this exchange soured the taste of the chestnuts we scoffed, but we were too hungry for such a conceit. But whether empty or sated, my stomach felt full with worry for what Isaiah was involved in.

A number of men came to the chapel again that night. I listened to Isaiah's voice, how the floorboards resonated to the point of purring with it. Neither Will nor my uncle appeared, much to my relief. I collected only eleven ha'pennies and returned to my printing. I worked slowly, unable to discern what the conversation was about, for Isaiah was not holding forth, and the only exchanges I could work out concerned plans, routes and thoroughfares in the finer parts of the city. My worry felt like a ten-ton plate pressing on me. When all the other men had departed, Isaiah appeared at the doorway. 'Tell me, how did Will seem to you today?'

The question unsettled me, and I shook my head slowly while I wondered what on earth to say. 'He seemed to tolerate the company of my uncle quite well.'

Isaiah smiled, and I sensed that I had just passed a test. 'Yes, he did, didn't he? We must be careful with him.'

'Why? You have nothing to fear of Will Davidson,' I said. 'He is your oldest friend.'

Isaiah laughed. 'Aye, he is. But there was a long period when we did not see each other. Between the ages of fourteen and twenty-four, to be exact: the most important years of my life.' Isaiah had no truck with the papist idea that early childhood shapes the man; to him, childhood was a time of innocence and unreason, and the political education of the young adult was all.

He rubbed his face. 'Our friendship is like an old barrel that has become warped with age, though still held together by the iron rings which shaped it many years before. And iron rings truly shaped it: we both had slaves for mothers, and also Scots fathers keen for their sons to escape the life of a Jamaican mulatto. But all this I think you know.'

I did, but I never tired of hearing it, for it was a story more fantastic than any of the parlour antics Hetty read about.

'We were destined for Edinburgh: Will to read law, and I medicine. We'd pledged we would share a study at school, then go on to University together – we were good Protestants then, so all doors were open to us. Will's father was the island's Attorney General, which is to say that in matters of Law he was the last word between the Governor's hat in Kingston and the toe of King George's boot in Westminster. My father was a doctor, that much I have told you. He was also a despotic petty-slaver and a drunk, and though he regarded my mother's blood as a dark taint on my soul, I regarded his as the greater stain. He had given me to believe that I too was destined for Fettes – something I believed until I was taken on board the *Encounter*, relieved of my leather trunk and all its contents, and given a sailor's uniform. I thereby discovered that my education was to consist of seven years' naval indenture, while Will's was the very one I had been promised.

'As we grew into young men, I rose through the ranks – my willingness to work led my superiors to overlook my colour, for there was a harsh democracy of labour at sea – while Will was expelled from Fettes for reading Thomas Paine to younger boys in his dormitory and attending Methodist meetings.' Isaiah shook his head. 'And now, Will wishes he had done some legal training. He thinks that if he had, he could have defended working men against the Crown, and toppled the legal edifice from within. Will does not see that becoming a lawyer would have corrupted him. That is why I am content with who I am. Saving a soul is a way of saving a life, after all – and many of the doctors I have seen are licensed butchers and quacks.'

'So you and Will met again in a chapel in Walworth,' I said. 'The same chapel in which you met my mother.'

'Your mother thought Will and I spoke so much of the

future Republic as a way of forgetting our different passages over here. That while Will was a young gentleman with his own cabin and a cane to tap the decks during his evening promenade, I slept below decks, in a hammock, with ex-convicts and sundry madmen, my father having paid something less than steerage for me. My time in His Majesty's Service was worse than the slavery I grew up with. My father's slaves at least had their own huts, and their own women and children. But every inch of a ship is the property of the Captain, and men are driven wild by their proximity to each other and their fear of the sea. They develop superstitions about it – in fact, I was almost tossed overboard once because the bosun was convinced that a storm cloud which seemed to materialise from nowhere was the colour of my skin, and thus a warning to the Captain. It was on board ship that I realised that the end of slavery would not cure us. No: only the abolition of authority, and its attendants property and title, could do that.'

'Isaiah,' I said. 'Why are you preaching this to me now?'

'Did you see Will, while I was in prison?'

'You know I did not. Why do you ask?'

'I am trying to understand him. Your mother was right. Our friendship rests on the quicksand of forgetting the circumstances which brought us here. Will was educated to lead, and I to serve. But what do you think truly animates him, Nell?'

'Zeal? Fervour?' I struggled to see the danger of these in Isaiah's eyes, so I knew that this could not be the right answer.

'No Nell. We must always watch Will Davidson, because he is consumed with ambition – ambition that derives from shame.'

The ambition I could perceive, for Will had always struck

me as vain. 'Shame?' I said. 'Why?

Isaiah ran his hand over the edge of the press. 'Will had all the advantages: the social superiority, the fine education, and what has he done with these gifts from the Lord? He knows that he has squandered them, and you can never trust a man with such a shadow on his soul, however much he professes to love you.' He reflected on what he had just said, then added, 'But of course, Will has done much while I have been away.'

'Has he? Isaiah, I have been more worried by something Carroty Anne said.'

'You listen to her? I must confess that it is more than I have ever done.'

I laughed, and in that moment the whiff of gunpowder went away, and I said nothing of Carroty Anne's fears. At such moments, with the familiar prints all around us, such bizarre and terrible intrigues seemed almost unimaginable. S   o I merely bade him to take care, and reminded him of how easily Tom had condemned himself. He looked at me, astonished, and I took heart from this, too. It is ended, I thought: the terrible events which began with Isaiah's imprisonment culminated in Tom's death. Things cannot get any worse. You are like Meg, I told myself – always looking for disaster. Even this Government cannot execute every man who utters a word against it, or the streets will soon be sparse indeed.

Isaiah examined the prints I had almost botched that evening. 'This is good work. You will be able to finish these, Nell, will you not? I must go to your uncle tonight.' Isaiah said.

'Of course,' I replied. I never pointed out to him that the business ran perfectly well whether he was there or not. He was required to sign invoices – as a seventeen-year-old woman, I had no legal personality – but beyond that the shop was my kingdom, and I was content with it.

But the world being what it is, such contentment was destined to be fleeting. The more I thought I stitched our lives back together, the more they seemed to unravel.

24

THE FOLLOWING MONDAY, I sent Meg out to secure more paper from Mr Tagg. She thought about refusing, but went anyway. I did not know if Isaiah had paid Tagg, for he would not give me a straight answer to this most simple of questions. When Meg had been absent over half an hour, I began to fret that Smeek had transferred his affections and was holding Meg as surety in his storeroom. I was about to venture out when Meg ran in too fast for the door to open in front of her, with the result that she collapsed into the shop in a flurry of jangling, looking behind her in surprise at the invisible creature who could have been so clumsy as to collide with the door frame.

I was so glad that she'd come back safely that I did not chide her for dropping the paper; until a year ago, many was the time we would go out and find her in the gutter counting cobbles, or else in the alley at the back, opening and closing the privy door as if in a trance, paying no heed to the fact that half the flies of the metropolis were congregating over her head.

She was dirtier than usual, and her pinafore looked as though it had been yanked to one side. I raised an eyebrow at her, but she was already sitting on the floor, combing the dust into neat lines.

'Tom's execution,' she announced. 'What was it like?'

Isaiah and I looked at each other. Isaiah went into the back room, as he often did at any sign of difficulty.

'It was an execution, Meg,' I said quietly. 'Tom and two other men died. Other men came to watch. Then we all went home.'

'Apart from the dead men,' said Meg solemnly. 'They couldn't go home, Nell. Their heads are sticking on pikes, all shrivelled up like brown cabbages!'

It was no longer customary for this to happen after an execution, but the authorities had made a special example of my brother and his fellow traitors, so I knew that Meg had been outside Newgate.

'So, Meg, who took you to the prison, or did you make your way alone through the pedlars, the body snatchers, the gropers?' I would not have spoken so harshly to her, but it seemed that instilling the fear of God in her was the only way to prevent her from putting herself in the path of harm.

Meg's bottom lip and the two limp ringlets on her fore-head trembled. I had ragged her hair the previous night because she had asked me to, and I was so happy that she had let me touch her for once that I had spent half an hour teasing out her knots after my fifteen hours at the press.

'A friend of Isaiah's. He told me he can help me find work. And Isaiah too. And not in service, neither.'

I listened more closely, ready to pounce.

'Not in service,' I said, 'that's good.' I was careful to keep the curiosity out of my voice. The Wingfields have never been in service, and my time at St James's Square only strengthened my resolve that I would never see anyone I love disappear up some rich man's back stairs for an afternoon off a month and a few poxy shillings. That is, of course, minus deductions for: tiny singeings of damask tablecloths while ironing exhausted at dawn; shrinkage of lace through alleged over-washing when in fact it was m'lady's girth that had broadened, but who are you to argue?; or else profligate use of boot black in the business of rendering his Lordship's Oxfords so shiny he might see up some lady's skirts with them. All this I had time to think while Meg waited for me to say something, which I did not.

'He was a gentleman, Nell, of that I am sure.'

What honest work would a gentleman offer a girl like Meg that was not household drudgery, or Indenture to the Property-Owning Classes Without Prospect of Manumission, as Isaiah called it?

'We are not on the parish yet,' I said, rattling our takings drawer, which was light yet again. 'Any friend of Isaiah's would speak to him before he offered you work, or else to me. You should be careful.'

I did not know if she understood, but I said it anyway – all too snappishly I admit, but I felt foul of temper that morning. I had been brooding on my time at St James's Square, and worrying about Mr Edwards' next visit, my nerves jangling more than the shop's bell.

'You know when people die?' Meg said.

'Ye-es?' I replied. Meg might have been twelve, but she still had the habit of breaking her questions down into tiny morsels.

'And you know how Father says that their chattels are now as dust, for all the good they can do them?'

'Ye-es?'

'Well, what happens to them?'

'What, the chattels?'

'Yes,' she said. She looked at me with patient exasperation, as though I was the slow one.

'People take them away and sell them. There are no pockets in shrouds – if there were there'd be a sight more dodgers in cemeteries than there are now. But there are those who can fill their pockets legitimately with dead men's rags and bones.' Which wouldn't have been such a bad business for us, when I came to think of it: Meg would have loved all the sorting and counting. But Isaiah would never have stooped to it.

'Is this what the gentleman said you should do?' I continued.

'No.'

I waited for her to offer more, but she was busy drawing in the ridge of dust under the far counter in a way that reminded me of poor Tom in his final moments.

A customer entered, and Isaiah appeared, signalling for to us to go into the back, and Meg followed me to the press.

'I didn't like him,' she said, her tone accusing. 'But I listened to him because he said he was your friend.'

'Whoever he is, he is no friend of mine,' I wanted to comfort her but knowing that touching her would make her worse.

'But you don't know who he is!' she said, her voice rising. Simple she might seem, but she would always see any sleight of hand in my dealings with her, and they offended her to the core.

'Meg, did this gentleman have long thin lips in a bony face?'

'I didn't need to remember him,' she said, her voice rising. Isaiah's customer – if he had indeed been one – had departed, or else Isaiah would have been through to see what the commotion was. 'He said he would call on us. He specially mentioned you.'

'Did he give you any message? An envelope or a card? Did you put it with your tag?' Two years ago Isaiah fashioned a tin disc for Meg with her name and our address on it, and bade her wear it round her neck with a leather thong, so if she wandered off and had a fright which made her fold in on herself and take to moaning in the gutter, she might be brought home.

'What is all this?' asked Isaiah, coming in with two dusty hooves over his left shoulder and a carcass between him and Uncle John.

John Ings marched towards Meg, and she recoiled from him, her brown eyes wilder as she shrank away.

'Leave her, Uncle,' I said.

'I would not go near her, no fear, I wouldn't,' he muttered under his breath. 'Biting creature that she is. All she understands is the sole of my boot, and I'll happily see her bite on that!'

Meg darted into the back. Uncle John raised his foot a fraction as she passed; then saw Isaiah looking at his boot and lowered it.

'Why the fatted calf?' I asked my uncle. In fact, it was a rangy thing, though considerably fresher than the rest of the produce on sale at John Ings, Master Butcher.

'It's not for you,' John Ings, Master Butcher said. 'Isaiah is storing it for me, then we will bring it to the shop.'

'Aye, a print shop is the perfect place to store a bleeding carcass,' I said. 'I will be sure to let it go stale here, so it will not embarrass the rest of your wares. We will be transported soon enough for harbouring stolen goods,' I said, 'so it will have plenty of time to fester.'

'I told you she would be difficult,' Uncle John said to Isaiah. He hawked onto the floor, the spittle merging with some small drops of blood. 'And thank you for your assistance, Nell. Once again you prove yourself a pillar of the family. Oh, and your Aunt Agnes is still asking you to call on her. She has not seen you, she says, since you left our house. Not that you were ever much in it.' He said this with a keen glance at Isaiah.

'We will all visit you soon enough,' said Isaiah. 'You are

right: we have much to thank you for. I'm sure Agnes will forgive me for wanting to recover my standing in the world before I return to your fold.'

'Aye, she will take you to her, I have no doubt,' my uncle said. He hawked in preparation for spitting again on our floor, but he thought better of this and swallowed fulsomely instead. He drew himself up and wiped his hands on his apron, which would only serve to make them filthier. His fingers were broad and blunt, and so red you'd almost think they were covered in blood when they were clean. My mother could never understand why Agnes married him. On meeting Isaiah Douglas, Agnes and my mother had both found religion, but it was gentle, godly Elizabeth who had been chosen by Isaiah.

And so Agnes had gone and consoled herself with beer and sausages and John Ings with his filthy apron. As my mother said, it was one thing to feel grateful to a man, but quite another to marry him – particularly when the man was John Ings.

❦

He took his carcass away, and Isaiah with it. I worked until I could not tell if the handbills were blurred, my eyes were so tired, but even after eleven there was no sign of Isaiah. At length I crawled upstairs, wondering when Meg might tell me more about the mysterious gentleman, whom I felt sure was Mr Edwards.

Meg was curled up, her body too rigid for sleep. 'Will I have to go into service?' she said.

'Of course not,' I said.

'When you left us, Will said you had gone to a big house, and he is still saying it, because of how grand you carried yourself when you came back.'

I guessed this might be the answer, and for a moment I

was tempted to say *Yes! This is where I was, but our mother was right: I hated it so much that I ran away*. But I knew that there would be no end to Meg's questions, and details of a story like this would cling to me like burrs on a shawl: one week I would tell her the carpet in the parlour was green, then another week I would mention a crimson sofa, and she would want to know why the lady of the house could not see that these colours clashed more violently than the King and his estranged wife Caroline.

'When has Will been talking to you?' I said. I wished she were the kind of sister I could bundle up with and whisper secrets to – I felt as though the walls were listening to me more than she was.

She said nothing, of course. Will had been frightening her – of that I was sure. All he would have to do is remind her that I had left once, and wonder out loud about what would become of her if I did it again. I could just imagine him, winding his words around her like a hungry cat around its mistress. Why he would want to torment her like this, I could not guess.

'I will not leave you again,' I said. 'You do not need to find another protector.'

Again she said nothing. And why should she? I had promised our mother that I would take care of her, so she had already seen how little my word counted for.

Unable to sleep, I got up and went back to the print room. It was one of those draughty July nights that sends the first portents of Autumn, and I pulled my shawl tighter about me. I was so hasty I felt it give, and lighting the lamp in the press room revealed a rent in the back of it so wide that if I were to have pulled a little harder, it would have been torn in two. The wool had been thinning the previous winter, and when I put it on the day I left St James's Square, I fancied it was as thin as the cashmere I had given up. Pearl-coloured, the cashmere shawl was, and by rights it was mine, since it had been another gift from Sir David; but Mother Cooper was always keen to stress the communal nature of gifts: we should consider anything we had to be on loan in the way our bodies were to the men who visited, as if her house were some co-operative experiment in habitation.

The shawl was so thin that darning would not save it. I felt more naked because of the hole in it, so I shed it, only to miss the warmth on my arms. Somehow I would have to afford one before the winter came. My mother had always been so good at hunting out bargains, and at the thought of her I crumpled on the floor and cried, clutching the press leg. Even the press felt cold and hard, and I cried all the more: for my mother, for Meg, for our precariousness – but mostly, of course, for my shameful, lonely self.

Isaiah appeared quietly and hauled me up, with the damp air of the London night still about him. 'Don't cry, my precious,' he said, kissing my hair. I lifted my head, and flinched with the shock of his stubble against my jaw. He practically dropped me and stood up.

As I made a great business of smoothing my skirts and wiping my face, he studied my prints, running his finger lightly over them to judge the evenness of the application of the ink. He turned his hand over and rubbed his index finger, his mouth turning down at the corners. He was satisfied.

'Isaiah,' I said, speaking very carefully, as much to avoid crying again as with concern for the consequences of what I was about to say. 'I seldom make requests of you, beyond the unspoken one that we continue to live in your house in return for the work that I do, but tonight please hear this: do not allow your friends to endanger us.'

He thought about this, then answered in a characteristic way: by appearing to begin with something entirely unrelated to the question. My mother used on occasion to weep with impatience at this. 'You have never been on board ship,' he said, 'and you have never written a sermon. And you have never been incarcerated. While I was in Dorchester Gaol, I had time to reflect on the similarity of the forms my life has taken, and therefore to divine that there must be a plan to them. My seven years' indenture was a time in the wilderness, that I already knew: but I must confess that I had often asked, for what? Tell me, Nell: what was your purpose on that farm on which you worked through the winter and spring months? Were you alone?'

I knew what he was getting at – what farmer in his right mind would take in a girl during the shortest, slackest days of the year? 'Sometimes I was alone, yes,' I said. I considered saying that I was a dairy hand, but I have no more idea how to churn butter than how to cobble a shoe. 'Though of course there were the animals.' A sting of panic at this, as I tried to remember anything of a cow beyond its warm muzzling and the thwack of its tail on my infant arm.

He snorted with reproving indulgence, and then watched me for a while in silence.

'It has begun for you already,' he said eventually. 'As it had for me at your age.'

'What has?'

'The whittling. First your mother, then Tom. Add to that leaving your family in Lancashire...'

Again, he watched me, thinking. He was very good at fashioning arrows of the unexpected memories; I had heard enough of his sermons to know that there was something important he wished to plant in my soul. Since we left Preston, my only knowledge of distant relatives had been messages sent of their deaths, usually written in an idiosyncratic hand or else dictated to a stranger. Those messages came in an impenetrable copperplate which made the words look like the gates of heaven themselves.

'It is your lack of relatives that gives you your strength,' he said. 'When I was on board ship, I began to perceive that unthinking ties of affection were like motes in my eye, preventing me from seeing the injustices of the world.'

I did not see why this should be, and was about to say so when he continued. 'You are right to question this. The problem lay in the manner of my seeing. It is written that now we can only see through a glass darkly, and on the last day all will be made clear. And so I realised that we must recreate that sense of imminence in our daily lives, and so our ties should be with the dead and not the living. The living weight us, they pull on our petticoats, they compel us to look out for them.'

'They love us,' I said, thinking of how my mother had adored him with her fierce gentleness. And he had loved her. For all the eloquence of his preaching, he had never bestowed any fancy words on her, but his love was to be found in the fine detail. But they had never married, Isaiah being unable to bring himself to sign any contract, on account of his mother having been a freed slave. My mother had not minded: a strong union of many years is held together by thousands of tiny stitches, she said once; the kind that take hours of labour and which if done well nobody can see.

I looked down at my own hands and wondered if they had that quality of love in them.

'But the dead, Nell,' Isaiah persisted. 'The dead encourage us to look upwards.'

'To the heavens?' I said. 'My mother will not be there, of that she was sure.'

He ignored the flint in my voice. 'I watched you, Nell. At Tom's execution. For once, you were perfectly still. Your eyes were not trained on the ground, looking out for Meg, or looking for coins; you were not garnering the glances of men in the crowd; no, for once, you were looking upwards. It is out of that stark love, love which hurts the eye like a bright morning in winter, that the revolution will come.'

I remembered what Will had said, that men were forgetting the revolution now that their stomachs were being filled, and I imagined their eyes settling contentedly on their growing bellies. It did not seem such a bad thing to do, but Isaiah had that feverish look in his eyes, as if he was atop a mast and surveying the horizon for pirates, though he once said that the only pirates he had ever come across were the tax collectors of His Majesty's Government.

'Do you not think about Tom?' he said, his voice softer now. In this light, Queen Caroline's skirts glowed pinker and swayed a little in the draughts which came through the shutters. I shivered, missing my shawl.

'I do,' I said. 'I do, all the time. Even when he is not at the front of my mind, he is there, but my knowledge of the injustice done him feels like a dead weight. It is that, and not my love for Meg – nor for you –' I said, raising my gaze briefly and letting it fall, as if this dark man were too bright to look at, 'which keeps my eyes on the ground, as you put it. I can see that your grief is a glittering, hard thing, but mine is more like stones in my hem.'

'It is perhaps in your nature after all,' he said. He was close to me, as close as he had been during the execution. His breath was heavy in his lungs, and caught a little at his throat, as if his body was a mine shaft he was struggling to ventilate.

He took one of my greying curls between his fingers and thumb and pulled it straighter. 'But I can see something else in you, and I have yet to be wrong. I saw it in your mother, and it lives in you. And so, to answer your question, Nell: I cannot put us in danger, nor can I avert it. The Lord has His plan for us, and the worst has already happened. Yes, we must take care of Meg, but we are not doing that if we permit her and every other child in this city to be sold into the perpetual slavery of the current regime. Go to bed now, but I will make a revolutionary of you yet. You know not the day or hour, but your time will come.'

I went back upstairs, the rungs seeming even narrower than when I first came back to that house. I will never walk on carpet again, I thought to myself that day: never again feel as sleek and silent as the grey cat which not long ago had purred on my lap as though we both belonged in a salon in St James's. As if we both knew nothing of the world beyond the damask curtains and the sash windows which gave onto the square. If Isaiah is right about making a revolutionary of me, the time has not yet arrived, and he will never see it if it does.

I was uncertain how long I had been wrapped in my blanket, staring into the darkness, when Meg said, 'Now that mother is not here, he will want you to himself. He will hollow you out *drip-drip-drip*, and then he will wash you away, just as he did with Mother.'

'That is a wicked thing to say, and untrue!' I said, tucking my portion of the blanket under myself and not caring as much as I normally would about robbing Meg of her warmth. 'He has Carroty Anne!'

She continued in the same calm tone, as if I had not spoken; she must have been thinking about what she was saying while hearing our low voices downstairs. 'Nothing will stop him. He'll flood this place with his talking and talking until there is nothing left, until we are all in the ground.'

'And if he does lean on me, what of it?' I whispered fiercely, resisting the urge to shout in Meg's ear. 'While he is here talking to me, at least he is not in the company of the men who –'

I was about to repeat what Carroty Anne had said, but I did not, mostly because I knew that Meg was right: men can make plans together in rooms above taverns which render their love for their women as insignificant as the balls of cotton that I used to chase from under my mother's loom back in Lancashire.

'I would like to do as you did,' said Meg. 'I would like to go away from here.'

'No, you would not!' I said.

'I could live in a barn, and work all day in the fields, with only the clouds for company,' she said.

'After a week, you'd be crouching under a thicket, all balled up to stop the wind from tugging at you,' I said, 'and who would look after you then?'

She said nothing more. I lay awake, wondering why when the Lord had eventually given Meg a tongue, he had decided to give her such a sharp one.

At length she pushed something cold and flat into my hand: an envelope.

'Is this from the man you met?' I said.

She turned over, taking much of the blanket with her.

25

THE ARRIVAL OF MR EDWARDS' second envelope made it imperative that I went out the following morning, so I told Meg that I had a headache which required some fresh air. The idea of finding a cure in London's air was an absurd one, but she was too busy picking at her nails to look up, let alone argue with me. I stomped out, complaining of her madam-ishness, insisting that she would have turned my hair white by the time Caroline was crowned. I was sad that she seemed to be going inward again, and that we had quarrelled sharp on the heels of my conversation with Isaiah. Why did she have to spoil things? I wondered, and I was reminded of my pettishness with Sir David shortly before his death.

As I left, I reminded myself that I still had not warned Hetty – Mr Edwards' threat held to her as much as to me. I told myself that delivery of the envelope was more pressing – after all, she had a wealthy husband and I had nothing but my wits. Her wealthy husband might be a murderer, but I had no illusions about my powerlessness when compared to him. I could only hope that Mr Edwards had indeed turned against him, and that some machinations of his would bring Sir Robin to justice without sending me to the scaffold. My one source of hope was that Mr Edwards had warned Isaiah to stop preaching, which is the opposite of what a simple *agent provocateur* would want – and opposed to what Sir Robin had talked of that night he burst into my room at St James's Square.

That morning I was also crotchety with lack of sleep, having spent most of the night worrying that our growing business would have to be destroyed. The idea began with a memory of the first time Hetty had spoken of her father. I imagine that my anxiety to see Hetty had dredged it to the surface, but with the Lord's aid I turned my worries to good, for this recollection became the kernel of a plan. The only way I could hope to avert catastrophe was to remove Isaiah from whatever plot was being orchestrated around us. A return to gaol would be ideal, and the only way to secure his imprisonment and his safety was to create a crisis with our credit, rendering him a debtor as Hetty's father had been. Somebody needed to pursue Isaiah for his debts; this meant antagonising Mr Tagg.

As the Lord willed our fortunes, this was not to prove difficult for as I headed towards the Mansion House, who should snivel up behind me but Percival Smeek. 'Miss Wingfie*lll*d,' he wheedled, 'allow me to accompany you wherever you may wish to go.'

'No, Percival,' I said. 'I have a powerful wish for my own company, and even if I did not, I would not want to take a stroll with you.'

'Ahh, now that is a pity.' He offered me an envelope, much thinner than the one I was on my way to deliver. 'With the compliments of My Est*eeee*med Master.'

'This will be a bill for our materials, I presume?' I wondered if Smeek would have given me this bill if I had bent to his wishes, and hoped that my rudeness would hasten Mr Tagg to the recovery of his debt.

'Ind*eee*d it is,' Smeek said, bowing.

I hurried off, shoving the paper down my bodice as I did

so. Never had I been so happy to receive a bill from Tagg.

~~~❦~~~

The closer I got to Westminster, the more difficult it became
to negotiate the thoroughfares. In the House of Lords, the
Queen continued to sit in the gallery and listen to a parade
of witnesses who were called against her; Lord Brougham,
her legal advisor and, it was widely alleged, sometime para-
mour, had advised her to remain silent and allow his clever
friends to tear the Italian witnesses to shreds. It was rumoured
that she played cards during the proceedings. I thought again
of the Italians who had passed through 14 St James's Square,
and of the money Gus had seen in the first envelope we had
delivered. Now that Sir David was dead, were those witnesses being paid enough to keep silent? For if they were not,
and evidence was heard of all her scandals, there surely
would be sufficien grounds for a divorce. I was seized by a
strange wish that I had befriended them, and not spent quite
so much of my time apart from Sir David in the sole company of Hetty. If I had, I might have found myself able to
carry out Sir David's wishes, rather than being Mr Edwards'
pawn. But then I realised that it was as Isaiah said: whatever
occurred, whether the King was granted his divorce or not,
violence would have its day.

As I passed along the Strand, dozens of children offered
me postcards of the proceedings against the Queen, or else
broadsides offering a commentary, and exhortations to visit
shops around Albemarle-street where more substantial rep-
resentations might be purchased. I was struck by how most
of our wares were old news by comparison: with the exception of Mr Soane's work, they were worn, faded images
which would be of more interest years hence than they would
be to these people thronging the streets. These wares were
the equivalent of the Epistles of St Paul and the Revelation of

St John; ours were Ezra, Nehemiah and other lesser-known books of the Old Testament.

I reached Whitehall just before three, giddy with relief to see Gus and Adam leaning on a bridling-post next to their chair – I'd imagined that their work would keep them from their habitual rest. As I approached, a girl from the tavern across the road darted between the carriages to collect their jugs, and lingered to talk to Gus. I watched, all my joy at seeing him curdling, for he talked to this woman in the same way that he had talked to me! I had been guilty of pride and vanity, imagining that I had secured some special place in his affections. His was a public life, and he was easy with talking to people, that was all. As I had driven Sir David away with my pettishness, so I feared I was about to repeat that sorry performance with Gus.

He saw me first, though Adam nudged him soon afterwards. The girl was so captivated by the story Gus was telling she didn't seem to notice. I waited for perhaps half a minute – though I felt like such a bath bun standing there that it might as well have been a few hours – before Gus dismissed the girl and waved to me.

'Ah, Mistress Nell, you grace us with your presence at last.'

'It is good to see you, Gus,' I said, because it was. 'And you too, Adam.'

Gus bowed. 'This will not be a social call, Adam, I warrant – this lass only comes when she's got trouble she wants me to deliver.'

There was no point in arguing with this. Gus walked me a few paces away from the chair.

'Oh, I am used to being the gooseberry,' grinned Adam, blowing one which sent a spectacular spray of spittle onto the cobbles.

'He is half-witted,' smiled Gus, turning to look at Adam,

'but I cannot carry a chair without him.'

'At least Adam talks to you,' I said. 'My sister speaks more by the day, but she is as sour as prune juice.'

'Have you listened to Adam? You should be thankful your sister is inward.'

'I am sorry I have not come before. I am the only one who is earning for what is left of our family, and –'

'Hush,' Gus interrupted, 'I could just as easily have come to find you, but I did not know how that would sit with Isaiah Douglas, Esq. And I would rather you did not wander these streets alone, looking for me.' He took a step back, almost falling into a heap of manure as he did so. 'Don't laugh,' he said, reaching out his hand then drawing it back. 'It is so powerfully good to see you, Nell Wingfield.' And he smiled Tom's smile again, except this time it felt less unsettlingly like Tom's and more like his.

We watched eight mounted guards in their scarlet tunics trot past.

'I do have another message,' I said. 'But this must be a busy time, and I must not keep you from your work.'

'I have one more job to do,' Gus replied, 'but it is not until six, so we can go to St Vincent's Court once again.'

'We do not have to go there. There is a different address.'

'Well, that's a relief. For that was a rum neighbourhood, and no mistaking it.'

I showed him the envelope. He shook his head. 'It is no more than a turd's throw away from the last place. Other side of Strutton Ground, I'm almost sure. Why has she moved, I wonder? A new man, or the fear of being found with all that money in her petticoats?'

'I am none the wiser.' I did not want to mention Mr Edwards for fear that Gus would guess how I knew him.

'I have a theory,' said Gus, narrowing his eyes playfully at me, 'but I am gathering a little more evidence before I commit to it.' His blond eyebrows caught the sun as he made a serious face at me.

I supposed it was inevitable that he would find me out. Still, I told myself, he was willing enough to associate with me, his suspicions notwithstanding, and I was more than happy to accept his help.

He left Adam guarding the chair, for it cost money to stow it at an Inn. Gus explained that some hostelmen would house his chair for free during a slack half-hour, but this was not such a day: people were coming to London to share in the excitement of Queen Caroline's trial. Gus said the crowds had lined the streets from her house in Hammersmith to Westminster to catch a glimpse of her, and people who had secured seats in the spectators' gallery were mobbed upon exiting. We should print broadsides of the proceedings, Gus said – they were likely to sell more than the Good Book itself, if the throng on the streets was anything to go by.

'We have to go through St James's Park, and take the back routes,' he said. 'You cannot get close to Westminster this way.' I peered down Whitehall, and he was right: there was a mass of people outside Parliament.

We walked and talked as we passed the Hussars' barracks.

As soon as we left the main thoroughfare, Gus quietened. 'We are being followed,' he said. We had turned off Strutton Ground, into an area of tenements similar to St Vincent's Court. Some of the courtyards looked familiar, though they could not have been: we were approaching them from the opposite side to our last journey. No wonder people got lost around here, I thought – lost, and killed.

I saw a boy behind us pointing and whispering to his friend, and in that moment a man had Gus by the throat.

'Let him go,' I begged, 'I will give you my purse.'

'You have no purse, you stupid hoor,' jeered a Scottish accent.

I did not know that he had stuck a knife in Gus's side until he had pulled it out. In the moment that he leaned back to deliver a more deadly strike, Gus bent forward so that his head almost cracked against his own knees. This sent his attacker flying over him so violently that I had to step out of the way, or I would have been flung to the ground.

The knife landed at my feet. I threw it over a wall just opposite us. To judge by the stench and the *plip*, it landed in a cesspit. The attacker had staggered up and looked set to lunge for Gus again. But he was in no state to do so, and was soon to follow his knife, if Gus got a second charge at him.

Gus kicked him in the bollocks and was about to stamp on him when I grabbed his arm. 'He'll give us no more trouble. We should go,' I said.

'Who sent you?' Gus shouted at the writhing figure. His boots had good leather soles on them, recently stitched. He would not be pleased to see the brown stains covering them, but this was the least of his concerns – it would be a little while before he could get up.

Gus led me back onto Marsh-street, then we took the next right. 'We should be able to cut through here,' he said, reluctant to stop.

I forced him to halt and examined his wound. He was bleeding, but his attacker had done little more than tear a rent in his jerkin and leave a small cut across his left side. It was long, but it was not deep – the blood was only bubbling through the skin in places. 'You were lucky,' I said. 'On his second attempt I doubt he would have been so clumsy.'

'If it comes to it I will take us both drinking tonight, and have you pour gin on the wound before you burn it for me.' His voice was shaky, and I knew that he was making sport with me in order to calm himself.

'By the way,' he added. 'I have found your friend Hetty.' He told me the address and made me learn it. 'She has married well, the draymen who stock their cellar tell me, though she is little more than a caged nightingale. And her husband has little interest in her charms, to judge from the stories I heard. I do not know how to put this, but there is a traffic of young girls – and boys, some say – going in and out of that house, to provide entertainment for her husband and his friends. Be very careful if you go there, and do not get any foolish ideas into your head about rescuing her. Marriage to a rich man is a stronger prison than any other in this city.'

'I am shocked by this. I hope I did not put you to any trouble, asking you to go there.'

He insisted that I had not, and I was ashamed at his apologies for mentioning such unsavoury matters to me.

We walked on a little, and I patted my apron pocket to check the letter was still there. 'You know this area well,' I said. 'I doubt it is on your usual rounds.'

'You'd be surprised,' he said, reining himself back to a more steady tone. 'Gentlemen roam all over this city in the pursuit of their tastes.'

I was not all that surprised, but of course I said nothing of my expertise in this area. 'You have just saved my life,' I said, elated and tearful at the realisation. I wondered if I would feel like this on Judgement Day, but a thousand times more joyful.

'I was too intent on saving my own arse to have a care for yours,' he said. 'Though it is a fine one you have, now I come to think on it.' He slowed his pace and made a show of getting a better look.

The muscles at the top of my thighs tingled as I walked. 'You would shame a poet with your compliments,' I mumbled. 'Are we still going in the right direction?'

'We are, Ma'am.'

'We could turn back.' I did not mention that I was practically certain to hang, if I failed to deliver the envelope.

Gus wafted his hand and shook his head, and we continued through the grim tenements.

'He was well-dressed for a thief.'

'Perhaps he is a good one,' I said.

'A good one would have picked my pocket, or else he'd have stilettoed me better.'

'But who would attack you?' It occurred to me that Gus might not be all that he appeared. After all, I was not.

'It might have been you they were after.'

'You are teasing me again,' I said lightly, but as I said this I remembered the *'you hoor'*, and failed to sound convincing.

'Aye, I am. The man reeked of drink – I got a good whiff of him as he shoved my face into his neck. He was a desperate man, nothing more – and considerably less, until his bollocks recover from my ministrations. Cheer up, Nell. There's a danger in seeing a pattern in events, I find. It did for my uncle; everywhere he turned, he saw the world framed against him.'

'Have we far to go now?' I said. 'Because if there was no reason to that attack, there could soon be another.'

'We're here,' he announced, bowing and holding his arm out as if he was presenting me to the Queen herself.

A more dismal tenement it was impossible to imagine this side of Hell, though the only mercy was that it did not reek of the excrement that clogged the gutters, for women sold pots of sharp-smelling stew that filled the air. A boy huddled in a doorway, devouring the same thin bread that I had smelled on our previous excursion, while a girl with solemn brown eyes watched him. Mary Magdalene could not have gazed on Our Lord in the hour of His crucifixion with a more sorrowful look, and I wished I had a farthing to give her so that she could buy a sliver of something from the bread-seller, who was shamelessly rotund and using his spoon more to swat away the children than to stir his wares.

'Where is the message?'

'It is in my apron pocket,' I said, looking around me and wondering how on earth we were supposed to divine where anyone lived.

'I'm surprised you could spare the fabric for one.'

'Aye, I'm expensive,' I said, remembering a man in St James's Square who had run a bet with his friends as to the exact measure in inches of my inside leg. He'd offered to pay me a guinea just to conduct the measurement, and had said I could charge the winner thirty guineas for the right to part both of them. Of course, I did not have to subject myself to this; Sir David's anger at the wager had protected me. Again, I shuddered at what I might have become, had I not met him, and I regretted my remark to Gus.

'Give me the message and I will deliver it.' He took the envelope and opened it. 'No money this time but some instructions, including a summons to a tavern on Millbank at six in the evening on any day.' He refolded the letter. 'Wait here, and if someone comes, or you need me, give a whistle. Can you do that?'

My mother said whistling was for draymen. I made a sound *whah-who* like a doleful pigeon instead.

'That will do,' he said. 'There are no birds here, so I'll not mistake you.'

Odd that the recipient, with her newfound riches, should move to somewhere like this, I thought; she must be keen not to be found. No one would suspect that a dweller in one of these dank staircases would have more than a sixpence to her name.

'Miss Rosaria!' he called. He saw a twitch in the sacking

at a first-floor window and headed for the stairwell.

'Will you remember what she looks like?' I shouted after him.

'Oh aye,' he said, in a way which suggested she was beautiful. 'Be sure you wait for me,' he said. 'I do not like to work alone, and you are a sight finer than Adam.'

I laughed, imagining what it would be like to be carried through the finest parts of London in their chair, cushions shielding my backside from the worst of Adam and Gus's joggling, parting the curtains once in a while to glimpse the world outside.

'I will be here,' I reassured him, as his feet mounted the steps, *stip stip stip* on the damp stone as he went. Then a hand over my mouth as I turned, aware of a slight noise behind me. I was dragged out of the courtyard and into an alley, my bird call to Gus strangled in my throat.

26

THE PALM OVER MY mouth reeked of coal and something like excrement, and whenever I smell coal I am reminded of that moment. Gagging, I was dragged into a small room which was lit by a smouldering fire. The embers were so low that from the outside the building appeared unoccupied.

My captor pushed me forward, grabbing my wrist to pull me round. 'Give me your letter now,' he said, 'or I'll give you something to remember me by before I take it anyway.'

I considered telling him that I had no idea what he was talking before, but a minute ago, Gus and I had been joking about the contents of my pocket, our words echoing merrily about the walls. The difficulty was, I had just given it to Gus.

'Nell!' Gus called. 'Where *are* you?'

I willed Gus not to announce that he had delivered the envelope successfully. The man picked up a knife from the shelf behind him. With his free hand, he held his finger to his lips, while he made a slashing motion at his throat with the knife. What little light there was seemed drawn to the blade.

'*Nell?*' Gus paced a little, stopped, moved on. 'Nell, I have found her.'

My captor watched me, his eyebrows furrowed beneath his dark cap.

'Nell? You cannot have left me here?' He sounded worried, wounded, disbelieving.

'The message,' he said.

'There is no money with the message,' I said. His shoulders slumped, and this action told me enough. He was simply a thief who had seen his neighbour with too much coin for a poor Italian woman, and had worked out the source of her good fortune. He might not be interested in the instructions the envelope contained, but he was none the less dangerous to me for that. My life was worth no more to him than it was to Mr Edwards – perhaps less, for who would find me here, if my body went *splosh* into a cesspool in the way the knife of Gus's assailant had?

Gus's footsteps retreated. I pulled out Mr Tagg's bill and placed it on the table. Keeping my eyes on the man all the time, I edged towards the door.

'Not so fast,' he said, moving round the table. The knife glowed silver-orange where it caught the light from the embers. He picked up the message, turning it over and over as if attempting to conjure it into a bank-note, then he held it close to his face. The darkness presented a problem, so he had to move back, towards the fire.

I took advantage of his concentration on my bill to flee. Daylight stunned me for a moment, then I saw the entry to the courtyard and made for it.

I ran back through the lane where we were attacked, my feet slithering on the cobbles. I picked up my dress, but it was already heavy with whatever shit and other filth was beneath my feet. I did not slow until I was near Westminster Abbey. I considered taking sanctuary there, but I doubted that whoever had attacked us would respect the place. Gus's assailant must surely have been paid by someone to intercept our message. Whatever the instructions were, someone did not want to see them carried out.

I headed up Whitehall, looking for Adam and Gus, but there was no sign of them – most likely they had departed for their six o'clock job. I walked the rest of the way home, scanning the streets for Gus, but all I noticed were young men in the distance who had the look of Tom.

By the time I got back to the shop, it was past seven. Isaiah had returned and was upstairs with Carroty Anne. He was pacing up and down, having her listen to his latest sermon. This would not be her idea of a good evening, I was convinced; but I was too concerned about Gus and worried about what would happen to all of us if Mr Edwards' message had not reached its intended recipient to feel any narrow satisfaction at this.

Meg had not appeared either, something which Isaiah said he had been too busy to notice. I did not waste my breath asking Carroty Anne about her. With Meg out of the shop, I would have to the take the opportunity, however callous, to find Hetty. For it had struck me that Hetty might be able to shed some light on what was occurring all around us. So intent had I been on warning her that I had not reflected on this possibility, and it only intensified my anxiety to see my friend.

27

NEVER HAD THE CITY seemed bigger, as I struggled to the address in Belgravia, and never had I missed Gus's company more.

I had the time it took me to run there to think of some ruse to gain admittance to Sir Robin's house. I say 'run', but some of the streets were thronging, and it was all I could do to elbow my way through. The back alleys were worse: some were slick with excrement, slops from fancy kitchens and something which to judge by the unholy stench of it was liquid horse left over from glue-making. I had to take care not to fall, split my head on the cobbles and add my brains to the slew.

As I scurried through the new squares, with my wild eyes and quivering limbs I must have resembled one of the women of Shooter's Gardens when deprived of gin. When I finally stopped to recover my breath, I was overtaken by anger at Isaiah and Will: how could they be so foolish as to think that a few men in a loft could ever outwit the men who lived in these grand houses?

Once my chest no longer felt that it was turning itself inside out, I continued my journey. Each time I caught up with a sedan chair, I hoped to see two blond heads bobbing fore and aft, but no luck. It never ceased to astonish me how many people whom I did not know lived within five miles of me. Most Englishmen lived in villages where everyone greeted each other by name, and if they'd been asked to line our families up in order of godliness, or wealth, or looks, I'm sure that all would have been able to do it. But in London we were all grains of sand, and was it any wonder that our governors were content to let the tides of fortune wash over us?

I stayed north of Piccadilly for as long as I could, not wanting even to skirt the roads near to St James's Square. This meant passing through the southern parts of Soho; I had to cut down Wardour-street and through Leicester-square then past St Martin's and along the Strand. Thankfully, the roads were unusually quiet, because the crowds were all in Westminster. I waited for some bells to chime the hour, but I must have just missed them, for I heard nothing but the sounds of the city at night. There was the clopping of hooves as draymen delivered to the inns, and a costermonger wheeling his barrow with two children behind him, picking up any fruit which fell off and throwing it to the top of the pile. His children had their father's flat nose and identical widow's peaks of auburn hair. I touched my own hair, trying not to feel that my life was ebbing away along with its colour. The girl wore a pinafore, but it ended in pantaloons half way down the calf rather than in a skirt. I envied her the freedom of it, and the ease with which she could bend to her work, though I wondered if she would still be permitted to show her ankles to the world when she was older, and I worried that the thin strip of skin between pantaloon and boot would perish with the cold, come winter.

On Albemarle-street, a group of gentlemen tipped out from what was probably a club, for this was a part of London where drinking establishments did not advertise themselves with painted signs. Still, the puking looked the same to me, whatever gutter it landed in. I fought the urge to step into an alley until the men had gone on their way, but I knew that this is even more risky than passing on the other side of the road with my head down.

'Who tore your shawl?' one of them called. 'If you let me tear something else, I'll buy you a new one.'

I did not alter my step, and I did not even have the energy to think up a reply.

~※~

It took me half an hour to cover a journey which would have taken twice that time at walking pace, and I had to pause outside Sir Robin's house to catch my breath. It was a palace, really: five storeys including the servants' quarters, steps up to the double doors at the front, two sets of vast windows on each side of those doors. The stonework was stained black, so I judged this to be a house built perhaps fifty years before, in the time of the mad building speculation which ruined some and made others' fortunes, but left London with some fine houses as its legacy.

The kitchen door was at the side of the house: this I could tell by the retinue of delivery boys filing in and the fine smells coming out, wafting over my head as if the very aromas of Hetty's new life were too grand for the likes of me.

If I was caught trying to climb into the house, Sir Robin would see me hanged for housebreaking as easily as he downed half a pint of champagne for breakfast, and I doubted there would be much Hetty would be able to do to save me. I thought of how nonchalant I had been that afternoon, just before Gus had been attacked, and tried to tell myself that this visit was not as risky. But what if Hetty did not want to see me? After all, she had made no effort to find me, and why should she? Look at the grandness of her house, the success that was her wealth! Like me, she too would be trying to escape the life that had brought her to Sir Robin's door, and here was I to tell her that her husband's sometime associate was threatening it all with accusations of murder. Perhaps she already knew, and was working to thwart Mr Edwards in her own way. Perhaps she would rather not know; after all, she had never been interested in intrigue in all the time I knew her. I was not like most girls, because most girls had not spent their lives with their noses full of seditious ink.

To judge from the chinking of glasses and laughter coming from the elevated ground-floor window, Sir Robin and Hetty had company. My nerve faltered: but what if I had been wrong, and it was just Sir Robin there? If that was the case, I had no idea where on earth else I should look – I knew about as much of where Ladies of the Quality resided as I did about how to run a bank. My armpits were soaked, and there was little I could do to improve my appearance beyond retying my hair and stuffing it into my bonnet, which was so damp I was amazed the brim hadn't collapsed into my eyes. Making up in boldness what I lacked in presentation, I rapped the knocker hard.

The door-maid had a kindly, round face and an unguarded look which suggested she was not long from the countryside and had yet to discover what manner of gentleman her employer was.

'Forgive me,' I said, pulling my shawl tighter round me so she would not see that I was not wearing a maid's attire, 'but I have been sent from the house with a message for Sir George Combe.'

She thought about this. My reckoning was that she would not know the names of Sir Robin's guests, and would not want to risk a reprimand for pertness if she questioned me and I complained to my fictitious master.

'I don't know…' she said.

'I do not want to disturb the gentlemen,' I said. 'Perhaps if I could just wait in the scullery and give a message to one of the footmen?'

She laughed. 'There are no footmen here.' Sir David's money was not being spent on an army of servants, then. 'But give me your note and I'll make sure it gets to Mr – what did you say the name was?' She held out her right hand and began to close the door with her left.

'Oh! You are very kind. And if it doesn't trouble you, I must wait here to see if there is a reply.'

'Come into the kitchen a moment. I'll take in your note, and you can have a bite of bread while you wait on your master's reply.'

I was led down a long hallway. The parlour door was closed, and, I would have wagered a year's takings from the shop, locked. Music issued from within – the untutored ear would think he was passing a recital, being held perhaps to indulge a less talented member of the household: a pretty young girl or a governess desperate for any evening society, even if the men present placed their thoughts elsewhere through her playing and the ladies giggled into their lace-trimmed sleeves. As it was, I doubted there would be any ladies in the audience, though there would be female performers, that was for certain.

We passed down five wooden steps to the kitchen. I noticed a low door in the wall to my left, a place I imagined reserved for men who wished a private view of whatever entertainment was happening in the drawing room, so I could only hope that it was not already occupied.

My note informed Mr Combe that his wife requested his attendance at home. Should such a man be there, and had he summoned me to question me, I had no idea what I would have said, but this turned out to be the least of my difficulties.

'Master will be ringing for refreshment presently,' said the girl. 'I'll bring your note in then. Master said he wouldn't take kindly to interruptions.' She said this with some pride.

I looked at this girl, with her innocent upturned nose, and felt sorry for her: she evidently had no inkling of what sort of business her master was likely to be conducting. She was only fortunate she had not been recruited for it; she looked no more or less corruptible than the dozens of girls who rented their fannies on the Haymarket every afternoon.

'Yes,' I said, 'they do so hate to be disturbed. Is your mistress at home?'

'No, she is out visiting.'

I groaned inwardly: I had not bargained for this. I'd had some silly notion of a stealthy yet joyous reunion with Hetty on a back staircase. But for what? What could I possibly offer Hetty but trouble? She'd had a respectable life with her father, and could have settled his debts just as well by marrying some callow doctor, but she had chosen not to. There was little chance that she would now choose a life of even greater poverty. I had put away my silk dress with some relief, as if it was a costume for a part I was no longer required to play, but Hetty would not be so willing to do so. What was I to do? Persuade her that her husband was a murderer, because Mr Edwards had said so? I saw all too clearly how his threats could be empty, and that he had me delivering his envelopes because he could not show his face where anyone from St James's Square might recognise him for the scoundrel he was.

But for all this distress, I am ashamed to say that I was ravenous. I had just taken a hefty mouthful of bread when a ting-a-ling sent the maid off with a bowl of punch and a rattling tray of goblets, two of which served as a letter-rack for my note. I waited a moment, to see if a man emerged from the side door I had spied in search of some liquor, but there was no one. I climbed in.

The darkness was cut only by light from two small spy-holes just ahead of me. I took each step slowly, skating my feet along the boards, until I was level with the first of the spyholes. I discovered that there was a stool in front of each. For a moment all was black, but this was because a gentle-man in a velvet smoking jacket was leaning against the wall. When he moved, I could see a stage at the far end of the room, adorned with cheap pillars, paste lyres and urns – to secure items such as these, Sir Robin must have had an agree-ment with some theatre hand.

The chandelier was extinguished, leaving light only from numerous candelabras affixed to the walls just above the seated men's height. There was the sound of a match being struck, and a *whump* as flames leapt from the two largest urns at either extremity of the dais. The men on the front row flinched, and I squinted to see if I could make out any of their faces. A number seemed familiar, but as I often used to remark to Hetty as I watched them descend tipsily from their carriages at 14 St James's Square, a group of well-heeled gents in evening dress looked as alike as a flock of geese to me.

In truth, there was a portly man with ginger whiskers who I was sure was the youngest son of the Duke of Portrose, and a man who looked like Mr Edwards on the second row. The sound of the harp playing seemed quiet when measured next to my heart pounding in my ears – until the man turned, and it was someone with a doughy face and a vacant air who could never have been Mr Edwards.

The show was predictable enough. The harpist's cloak fell and settled prettily just below her waist, revealing smallish breasts with curiously large nipples, as if she had painted them up for the occasion. A woman appeared in a gold cos-tume which covered only her midriff and lower legs, and despite her carrying a bow and arrow, she was the one to be pursued – by a gaggle of girls who fell on her and pinioned her down.

A group of boys in animal pelts came on and salivated over the girls and the huntress. There was a commentary, given by a girl in a diaphanous pink dress. I call it a dress, but it left not a stitch of modesty. I could not hear what she was saying, because so many of the men were laughing and pointing at her.

Sir Robin was pacing at the back, forcing the man in the black velvet jacket to press himself up against my spyhole each time he passed. His perambulations prompted one gentleman with a white wig which ill-concealed a boil on his neck to keep glancing behind him in annoyance, as if his host were a fly he wished he could get up and swat. The man got up to speak to Sir Robin, and the interview was presumably not a happy one, since the boil-necked man strode to the door and was gone.

Onstage, the boys were allowing the girls to escape. The door to my left opened, letting in a shaft of light which felt as searching as Judgement Day surely will. Sir Robin was coming towards me. I shifted over silently, hoping with my usual senseless optimism that surely he was not expecting anyone to be there, so he would not look closely and therefore would not see me. I huddled against the far wall. I could no longer see what was happening outside and I dared not breathe.

Sir Robin settled himself in front of the second of the spyholes, no more than a foot or so away from me. He seemed intent on watching, but there was also a soft rustling: the narrow shaft of light from the spy-hole revealed that he was unbuttoning his breeches, and he took out his almost-erect member and fondled it with an indulgent smile. I was so afraid that I debated vaulting over him and running for the door, counting on the element of surprise and his flapping cock to give me the advantage.

When he grabbed my wrist I almost screamed.

'Maggie told me you were here,' he said. 'I have business with you which you will learn presently, but since you are watching, then let us watch.'

He pulled me by the waist so that I was level with the second eyehole, then pushed my face against it so that I could see the tableau. If he presses my face any harder, I thought, my nose will crack.

'What do you see?' he whispered in my ear. At least I now think it was a whisper: at that moment it was a blast of booze, snuff-breath and menace. At that moment I could see nothing: my eyes were streaming with tears, partly in terror, and partly at the pressure on my nose. 'You have seen much in your short life, have you not? And have you shared your visions with Edwards?'

I shook my head, for it was all I could manage.

'You cannot see?' he said. 'Let me demonstrate.' He pulled me back by my hair and clamped his hand around my mouth, before gagging me with a kerchief which smelled of stale men's parts and tobacco. I wanted to retch, but I knew that I risked choking if I did. With my head a little further back, I could see, but wished that I couldn't. A complicated mass of boys arrayed the stage. The tallest, a blond beauty who reminded me of Gus, was being fellated while a stocky hirsute youth thrusted at him from behind. The audience was more attentive than a congregation.

My mind removed itself from where I was, as it had at Tom's execution. As a result I was able to observe this scene as if from a great distance. Sir Robin kicked the stool away but kept my eyes level with the spyholes. With one hand he held both my wrists over my head and against the wall, and with the other he lifted my skirt and petticoats but did not part my legs. He licked his finger, making a small pop as he pulled it out of his mouth, then shoved it hard up my backside. 'Unclench and it will go easier for you,' he murmured in my ear. 'Though if you stay as tight as that it will pleasure me more.'

I was mortally afraid that I would shit onto him and he would kill me for it, but he hurt me less than I'd expected. Hetty told me he'd tried this with her once, and she'd been in such agony that even he had desisted.

One of the men in the front row had intervened to hold steady the head of the fellater, who was almost knocked off his feet by the force of one of the thrusts. I saw nothing more of the events on stage, for pain overtook me: Sir Robin was thrusting harder and at a higher angle, and I was convinced that he had stabbed me – except I knew this to be impossible, for both his hands were occupied. I tried to relax, but this only made the pain worse. I was moaning even through the gag, and Sir Robin let go of my waist and put his hand over my mouth again. This sent torrents of snot and tears over him, and he adjusted his hand a little when it started to slither. I seized my chance and bit down, but this only prompted him to wrench my head back hard as he came.

As the tendons in my neck fairly sang their protest, he withdrew himself and pushed me towards the door, pulling up my drawers and straightening my petticoats. All the same, I virtually fell down the five stairs before my skirts were properly back round my ankles.

At the sight of one of his guests, who was making conversation with the maid who let me in, Sir Robin held out his hand to help me up. 'Nell!' he said.

I pulled away from him and slipped on his marble floor, hitting my head on the banister as I fell. The last thing I could recall was the guest's alarmed cry and Sir Robin's insistence that he would attend to me personally. He came at me with a handkerchief, and I remember thinking that his hands were reddish, like my Uncle John's, and not a gentleman's hands at all.

'There, there,' he said, or some other coddling nonsense, but instead of mopping my brow with the handkerchief, he pushed it over my mouth. I gasped, and breathed in something camphorous. *Brimstone*, I thought, as Hell's own blackness engulfed me.

28

WHEN I WOKE, I thought I was on a golden ship, the mast glinting in the sunlight, and I was enjoying the experience until I saw blood all around me. I swam upwards to escape from it, and realised that I was not on a ship at all: I was waking on a crimson and brocade sofa with ornate arms. I was alone, but this was no help to me, for I could not move. Not since I'd had the fever the winter after we left Preston had my legs felt so weak. Whatever I had been drugged with, I could only hope it would dissipate soon.

Somewhere behind me, a door opened, but I could not tell if anyone had entered; for the first time since I had left St James's Square, I was in a room large enough for things to happen in it which I could not see. Back at Friday-street, if a cockroach scratched itself next door, we could hear it through the wall.

A bulky shadow moved across me.

'Ah, Nell. It was indeed a pleasure. My wife had always said that I should know you better.'

'Where is Hetty?' I said, my tongue sliding like paper on a plate with too much ink on it.

Sir Robin took a chair opposite me and watched me try to rouse myself. He was fatter than I remembered: his white waistcoat gave him a goosey look, and his jowls were as heavy as a caricaturist would draw them. But how else could they be, with his taste in oysters and plum duff for breakfast?

'Where is Hetty?' I said again. I looked down at my feet; I was not wearing my boots. I had been arching my back as a preliminary to moving, but I had no option but to sink back behind the golden prow of my sofa and watch Sir Robin.

He had now stood up and was heating a poker in the fire. *Perhaps it is only for mulled wine, a favourite of his*, I told myself, to quell my panic. The orange heat crawled slowly along its length. *Let it be too hot for him to pick up*, I prayed. I am not one for treating Our Lord like an extra pair of hands to be summoned as I would Meg when I needed help pegging prints, but I hope I will be forgiven for doing so at that moment, for I had never been so frightened – my abductor that afternoon seemed tame by comparison. How many more men would clamp their hands over my mouth that day? I felt laughter rising. Fortified by this hysteria, I felt well enough to get up. I staggered to a high-winged chair, from where I had a better command of the room.

'So Nell. To business. We never beat about the bush, do we? Do you want to hang?'

My stomach churned cold and fast, like the Fleet where it runs out into the Thames. 'Of course not, Sir,' I said, my eyes still on the poker.

'I thought not. But tell me, have you spent those five sovereigns my wife gave you?'

It was futile to deny their existence. 'As a matter of fact, no, I have not spent them, but if there is any misunderstanding about them, I will be glad to restore them to you. As you have just said yourself, Sir Robin, those coins were a gift.'

'If there is any misunderstanding about them.' He put on a high-pitched voice, as if he was crooning to a caged bird.

'Oh Nell, surely your months in St James's Square made you a better dissembler than that? You sound like a street urchin apprehended with heaving pockets. The constable might turn the boy upside down so that booty spills out like a conjuring trick, yet still he insists that his arrest is a mistake.'

'It will always be your word against mine, Sir, I can see that.' I had been a fool to accept that money from Hetty. She was now a married woman, and what little she had in the world was her husband's. I looked back on my time at St James's Square as one of incarceration, but it was clear to me then that Hetty had never been freer than when she was sharing a parlour with me. When I left, I had taken her money because I recognised that she and I were no longer to be equals; but as her husband took a dainty cake from a silver stand which would have cost more than our shop turned over in an entire year, I understood that it was Hetty and not me who had gone down in the world.

'Mother Cooper is still on the lookout for you, young Nell,' he continued. 'She could have you back, or else have you transported for theft. Your finery did not fall from the sky by divine providence, you know.'

'I sent back the gown she made for me,' I retorted. 'And left behind others besides. She was not light of purse on my account.' Of course I did not mention that I kept my finest dress, the one his cousin had paid for, in a cupboard in the unlicensed chapel above our shop.

'Ah, I do not doubt you,' he said. 'But Mother Cooper, who has seen more of the world than I, is not such a trusting soul.' It was a moot point as to which of the two of them had seen more of the nether regions of London, but I did not wish to debate this with Sir Robin.

'So, Nell, you see that I have rather a lot of information about your various – shall we say – misdemeanours.' And here his face darkened.

'You know that my late cousin and I always disagreed about the role of men such as your stepfather in the politics of this city. You might recall that I was always a supporter of their desire for political freedoms – in my own way.'

He had struck me as a supporter of anything which furthered his own ends, and rather relished the prospect of bloodshed and violence into the bargain, but of course I did not say this.

'And I still am,' he continued. 'While you, my dear Nell, in common with Mr Edwards, are not, as my informers tell me. So you must cease helping Edwards immediately or I shall draw your existence to the attention of Mother Cooper and indeed the constables. Turn your energies to aiding Isaiah in his endeavours instead. We are on the brink of ridding ourselves of this unspeakable Caroline, and it is rabble-rousing God-botherers like your stepfather that will get us our way. '

Even in my panic, as my mind flitted about like a caged bird, I saw that Mr Edwards and Sir Robin were no longer in cahoots after all.

Sir Robin opened the parlour door just in time for me to catch sight of the maid studying in the mirror next to the coat-stand a beacon of a spot on her chin. She collected herself, opening the door to show me out.

'One thing intrigues me, Sir Robin,' I said, as the clopping of hooves and the tang of London air rushed through the open front door. 'Is what Mr Edwards says about Sir David's death true?'

He smiled grimly. 'That man Edwards is a scoundrel, and he should know that any muck he throws will only land on his own doorstep. Do as I say, or you will reap the consequences.' And he turned on his heel.

'Does Hetty know what you did?' I asked to his retreating

back, noting how strained the black velvet was over his bulging form.

The maid propelled me out of the door, and I was left with my boots in my hands, and a congregation of questions. Did Hetty aid you? Did I plant the idea in her head, by warning her of Sir David's displeasure with his cousin and his threat of disinheritance?

I shivered, for there was a sharpness in the July evening air. If my mother had been here, she would have commented on a chill so early in the year. I thought of all that had happened since she had died, and for a farthing I could have sank down on the steps in tears. As it was, I hurried away in my stockinged feet. I could not imagine ever feeling secure in London again while Sir Robin lived. And worse, I could not help wondering if I had contributed in some way to Sir David's death.

29

I WAITED UNTIL I was a few houses away before I stopped, and had only just finished lacing my boots when an old woman appeared out of Sir Robin's, and hurried towards me. She had wild brown eyes and a crook in her back that I'd recognise anywhere. The mere shadow of her chin was unmistakeable.

'Martha!'

'I wondered when you would come,' she said.

'So you left Mother Cooper,' I remarked, a little too brightly, for I knew that my departure would not have boded well for her.

'As you see.' She clutched her red shawl tighter around herself, and something passed across her face which I took to be the memory of Mother Cooper's anger. 'You were lucky she didn't come after you. She knew where you were, you know. You weren't hard to find, trailing after your blackamoor stepfather with a gob on him the size of a Hulk.'

'Martha, forgive me: I had to leave. I should never have come to St James's Square in the first place.' I heard myself getting louder as I spoke. 'I had been caring for my mother, I saw her through her last days, and then I found myself on the streets, and Mother Cooper offered me work. I should have left that first afternoon, so I cannot be sorry for running away.'

'You do not need to justify yourself to me.' Martha rebuked, her voice less rasping now. *No, I thought, it is the Lord who will judge me, not least for my part in Sir David's death.*

'After you'd gone, I thought I was seeing my last days,' Martha continued. 'By the time Mother Cooper'd finished with me.'

'But like me you turned out to be wrong,' I said.

'Aye,' she nodded, not smiling herself. I didn't blame her; Martha had never been one for shows of kindness, and Mother Cooper in one of her gin furies would rival an Egyptian plague for the damage it could do. 'But you don't owe me that – as I say, if they were determined to go after you, they know where to look.'

'They could hang me for Sir David's death yet,' I added.

She drew her shawl tighter about her and retrieved a small flask from her apron pocket from which she took a liberal swig. The skin on her neck was wrinkly and her Adam's apple gobbled up and down as she supped. 'The Mistress was right. You don't know a monkey's chuff about what happened to Sir David, do you? I thought you had sniffed at something, but perhaps you had the sense to keep your nose out of such a stinking business.'

'I left so soon after the shock of it. It's only beginning to catch up with me now.'

'Aye, just as when you ran away from your poor dead mother. You weren't thinking straight, I reckon, and the Mistress gulled you good and proper.'

'Hetty did?' I smoothed my skirt and then began to back away from her. Two gentlemen tutted as they stepped into the gutter to pass us.

She grabbed my wrist. Though it quavered, her grip was

strong. 'You always rubbed your hands up and down like that at St James's Square, when you was distressed. You do not trust me, I can see that. But let me say what I came out to tell you, and then you can think on it. If you decide that I am a dishonest old vixen who was in cahoots with Mr Edwards, Sir Robin and even Old Nick himself, then there is nothing I can do about it. But I tell you this, what happened that night was one of the oldest stories in the world. Cain and Abel, in a manner of speaking. Sir Robin killed Sir David for money. I reckon he strangled him while the Mistress were in the privy. Makes you think about what can happen while you are fulfilling a call of nature, dunt'it?'

Given what I knew of Sir Robin, this did not shock me, but the memory of Sir David on the bed never failed to, and I blinked it back. 'So he bade Hetty not tell, on pain of death?' I said.

Martha shook her head, her mouth drooping even further in her sadness. 'The Mistress says she came out of the privy to find Sir Robin all hot under the collar and telling her that she had done for Sir David with her ministrations, and what were they to do? In a right panic he were – or at least he pretended to be.'

'Martha, was there anything between Hetty and Sir David, in the end?'

'Look at you, still worrying away at whether Sir David's prick were ever roused by any fanny but yours. Even if it mattered once, it doesn't now, for the worms are the only ones nibbling at it. And you are still not asking me the right question.'

'Which is?' I said, dreading what I would hear next.

'Which is: is Mistress telling the truth? Or did she know of the plan all along?' Martha waved her flask impatiently, making the stopper fly off into the gutter. I picked it up for her, and she smiled her thanks, and for that moment her face lost fifty years' worth of care, and I saw what a kindly grandmother she would have made to someone, if her life had turned out differently.

'And did she?'

Martha sighed. 'I don't rightly know. But what I do know is that Mistress resented the way Sir David was tom-catting it around after you each night. She was under no illusions that Sir Robin really cared for her, and there was Sir David, seeming to go all soft on you.'

'It had never occurred to me that Hetty might envy me.'

Martha looked at me quizzically, as if expecting me to signal that I was dissembling, but of course I was not, so she continued. 'Imagine how much easier her life would have been, if she'd turned Sir David's head that first evening – she could have had the money, and the love of a fine man into the bargain. As it was, she had Sir Robin, and you had the gentleman with the money seeming to eat out of your hand.'

Suddenly Hetty's questions about Sir David's feelings and whether he had hinted at offers of marriage flooded my mind. My blood ran cold. She had wanted to make sure I wasn't going to end up with the money *she* had her eye on.

'So what happened after Sir David's death?'

'They held a small private wedding almost immediately after; most say it was hasty, some say unseemly. Even Sir Robin wanted to wait, but Hetty was having none of that. She persuaded Sir Robin that he was an obvious suspect, and not her alone, if anyone was minded to see the death that way. She convinced him that a swift marriage might actually make them both seem more respectable, as if he was saying to the world that he believed her innocence, that he was res-cuing her.'

'What I don't understand is why they didn't simply accuse me.'

'They considered that but they worried that a sensation with murder involved would divert unwelcome attention to them in the way that some lord breathing his last in a house of ill repute would not. And they have been right about that. With the exception of Mr Edwards, of course.'

'But they could always change their minds.'

There was no answer to that. Martha took off her red shawl and put it round my shoulders. 'You are shivering.'

When I made to take it off, she shook her head. 'I have a sight more lard covering my bones that you ever will. But in all other respects, we are more alike than you think. We are both minnows in a murky river of pikes, and if we are not careful, we will get gobbled up and nary a soul will notice. I am not getting any younger, and I counted myself lucky that Mistress offered me a position, for all her sins.'

'So Mother Cooper did not want you any more, after you'd helped her lay out Sir David before the doctor came?'

'That is what she said. But I'd seen worse, so why dismiss me on account of that? I'm sure that Sir Robin paid Mother Cooper for me to come with them, because they couldn't be certain what I'd seen and what I hadn't, or what I might make of it: the Master coming over all gentlemanly – this were part of his act, of course – and scratching his 'ead, wondering aloud how in heaven's name he was to get Mistress out of this predicament.'

I shut my eyes against the memory of Hetty's whey-faced terror, the unnatural position of Sir David's neck.

Martha sighed. 'The rest you can guess, as I did: the crowner was bamboozled and signed off the papers. Sir Robin looked anxious enough about the prospect of suicide for that to be all the crowner looked for, and of course suicide it was not, so the coffin was nailed tight to save the female relatives any distress. And because there was no suicide, Sir Robin inherits the fortune. Anyone who raised a well-plucked eyebrow at his marrying the only other witness to his cousin's death was reminded that they were betrothed beforehand – and those who think this is fishier than Billingsgate can do nothing more than peg their upturned noses, for what's done is done.'

I shivered again; the evening was drawing in, and a lamplighter was whistling on the other side of the square as he hooked open an iron casing and lifted his taper. How easy he would have been for Mr Soane to sketch, with his arm and taper at a perfect angle.

Martha sniffed and shook her head. 'Mistress fancied that all this business would be swept under one of the expensive carpets upstairs, but there are no Persian carpets in our souls, are there? I know I lived in bawdy houses all my life, and there are those who would say I have the steadiness of a weather vane in a hurricane, but I allus replied that we never did anyone any harm. If men wish to pay for something they can get for free – or else if they couldn't, would only take by force – then it was a service I was performing, and not a sin or a crime I was committing. But this is different. I am sticking my neck out and telling you the truth now because I don't want to see you swinging from yours, and me along with you.'

'And Hetty?' I asked. 'What is her frame of mind?'

'She was all a-skitter herself at the sight of Sir David stiffening in her bed, and she's never rightly recovered from it. And Mr Edwards has been here, telling Sir Robin that all his schemes are about to rain down on his head. 'Appen the Master's questioning if she can keep her lip buttoned.'

'Surely she's the least of his worries?' I said, looking for reassurance that I knew I wouldn't find. 'Here we are, gossiping in the street like two Billingsgate women. He'll take a musket to the roof and be firing at us in a minute.' My voice was trembling as I tried to take in what Martha was saying. What else had Mr Edwards been trying to tell me that I might have misinterpreted or ignored? I knew there was more murk to this than even Martha imagined.

'You should leave, Martha,' I urged. 'What if they decide that you are more trouble than you are worth?'

She shrugged. 'They think I'm a failing old woman with warts for brains, and these days I do nothing to discourage them from that opinion. And more to the point, where would I go?'

'And what a fool they took me for.' *Hetty most of all*, I thought. My mind went racing back over all she had said and done in St James's Square, and I tried to work out what, if anything, was true in a friendship that was turning out to be as worthless as a credit note issued from the Marshalsea.

'I have no idea if they took you for a fool, though seeing how blind you've been so far, I doubt they would have had much trouble hoodwinking you, meself. From what I gather, they did not think you would be eager to get on in the world in the way that Hetty was. They had you down for a God-botherer, and it wasn't hard to verify those suspicions.'

Martha tipped her flask into her mouth, then peered into it, the disapproving downturn of her mouth suggesting that it was empty. 'No, I am being unkind. After a while even Sir Robin thought you might try to snare Sir David after all, for he were right keen on you.'

'Was he?' I said, trying not to cry.

'Aye, that were one of the reasons Sir Robin wanted to speed things up. Hetty had always told him you were soft on Isaiah, and likely to go back to him once he were out of the clink, unless Sir David persuaded you otherwise. And this was becoming more likely, the way you two were carrying on. Then Hetty tells Sir Robin that you were making noises about leaving St James's Square, and that got them in even more of a spin. For Sir David was sure to stop coming there if you weren't in his bed to keep him happy, and then all their plotting would come to nothing. So Sir Robin had to make his move fast: he murdered Sir David and then gave you some money to see you off.'

Had Hetty watched me growing to love Sir David more with every passing day, knowing that Sir Robin was going to kill him? Although the edifice of our friendship was crumbling, I held out hope that perhaps she hadn't known the full extent of Sir Robin's plan. But until I looked into her eyes again, I could not be sure of her innocence in his death.

'Was the murder always part of the plan?' I asked.

Martha sighed. 'What I know, I have gleaned from listening at doors, at St James's Square and here. Mr Edwards and Sir Robin tend to shout, so it has not been too difficult. Whether Sir Robin told Hetty or Mr Edwards in so many words what he planned to do, I don't know. And whether Mr Edwards had his suspicions before the deed was done, I don't know either. But he certainly knew from the moment of Sir David's death who was at the bottom of it, and he severed his business with Sir Robin from then on.'

'But I don't understand,' I said. 'Why does he wish to destroy me, if he knows I had no part in it?'

She shook her head. 'I don't think you've been listening proper. Mr Edwards is your friend, or the closest you have to one in this sorry business. In his way, he will have been helping you. It is help which benefits him, most likely, but help it will be all the same.'

I recalled Mr Edwards talking to Isaiah the day of Tom's death, and then the arrival of Titus Soane: was this Mr Edwards' way of helping us? If Martha was right, his discouragement of Isaiah's preaching and heaven knew what else would make more sense. But when I thought back over what he had said to me, I was not convinced that Martha was entirely correct. Mr Edwards might now be Sir Robin's enemy, but this did not necessarily make him my friend. And as Martha said, if he was helping us, it would be to serve some purpose of his own, and he would not blanch if that purpose destroyed us into the bargain.

'So Mr Edwards knew there was a plan afoot to gull Sir David out of some of his money – a pregnancy perhaps, some scandal of that ilk,' I observed. 'But he would never have imagined the business of Sir David's money would involve murder. To him, that would be another instance of Sir Robin's loss of reason and proportion.' I recalled Sir Robin's disputes with Sir David about fomenting revolution, how intemperate he had always been.

Martha inspected her empty flask again then glanced at my hip, perhaps hoping to see a flask there. 'Mr Edwards was angry, that's all I can tell you. As far as he was concerned, there had been no need to off Sir David, for he had already agreed to their marriage and all the cost it entailed.'

I knew that Sir Robin's own mother feared his violence, but even I could not have imagined this. Which was, I suppose, why Sir Robin was getting away with it. Reasonable men tended to assume that men of title such as Sir Robin would act reasonably.

'But surely Sir Robin could see that it was unwise to make an enemy of Mr Edwards?' I said.

'I doubt Sir Robin is that sharp,' Martha said. 'Though what is Mr Edwards to do now, without some of the muck spraying back on himself?'

I knew that Martha was right: Mr Edwards would have a mighty job convincing any decent person that he was willing to collude in extortion and sundry political murk but drew the line at murder. I thought about the ten pounds in Mr Edwards' envelope, the set of instructions, and what Sir David had said about changing fortunes at the new King's court.

'This isn't just about money, though,' I said. 'Mr Edwards is still being employed by someone to help prevent a royal divorce – and he is using me to help him. Now Parliament is hearing the case, and the city will riot. Some say there will be revolution, my stepfather among them. Those Italians we knew in the brothel are involved in all of this.'

'I don't know about any of that. I heard him tell Sir Robin that he thought it a bad business and wanted nothing more to do with it.'

'Thank you, Martha, for all of this.' For once I felt I knew what I had to do: find Mr Edwards. I clasped her hand, before heading off into the July night.

30

I COUNTED MYSELF LUCKY to get home without a third attack on my person, for it was long past the hour when any girl who did not wish to bring ruin upon herself would venture onto the streets. As I entered the shop, I was glad of the darkness, for I felt more shame and affliction settling on me than when I had returned there after my time at 14 St James's Square – and a great deal more pain, too.

I was sickened to think of Sir Robin and his wife, congratulating themselves with a chink of their crystal glasses that they could give me a few sovereigns and fool me into thinking that my freedom had been bought. Again, I prayed that Hetty had not known of the whole plan, and had had no hand in the actual murder, but it seemed unlikely, for all Martha's account of Hetty's state.

So my instincts told me that I should go to Mr Edwards, though I knew that I might be delivering myself to the lion's den as I did so. But as I also knew all too well, people lived with things that they knew to be wrong while they worked out how to put things right, and it was possible that Martha was correct in judging Mr Edwards to be one of them. And I might learn something of what he intended for Isaiah. Why should I judge Mr Edwards more harshly than I hoped to be judged myself? And perhaps Sir Robin might yet be brought to justice for what he had done.

On entering the shop, the smell of ink, paper and dust met me; I could have wept with happiness at its familiarity. A form was curled up under the counter.

'Meg,' I said softly, 'How are you?'

'The Black Prince met Guy Fawkes,' Meg whispered.

'Meg, it is not Guy Fawkes night for many a month,' I was alarmed that this was not the first time I had heard Fawkes' name mentioned in relation to Isaiah.

'Meg?' She did not answer, but there was a tautness in her silence. 'Meg!'

I touched her leg, and she shrivelled away from me. She had no idea what I had just suffered, and as far as she was concerned, we were still quarrelling.

'I saw our Uncle today,' she said, her voice now hard and flat. 'And Mr Tagg came. He wanted me to do some counting for him. He says that he will send some men, and I should tell them the numbers he showed me.'

Isaiah's debts. 'Can you remember how much?' I knew that this question would soothe her, since it involved counting.

'Fifty-four pounds, ten shillings and sixpence,' she announced loudly. I shushed her, not wanting Isaiah to hear. Even I was shocked at the amount – Tagg must have been adding interest at a usurious daily rate. Why, oh why did he have to call when I was absent?

Before I had a chance to forget, I ran downstairs and lit a candle with an ember. I wrote with a piece of charcoal the sum she had told me, then I folded the piece of paper into my hem. I held my hands over the fire, but it was so close to dying that it was scarcely warmer than a breath.

'Meg,' I said, when I had returned. 'This is important. Please don't turn to stone on me. Who is Guy Fawkes? Tell me what happened today.'

'Guy Fawkes has barrels,' Meg said. 'Will took me.'

'Don't talk so loud,' I whispered, though she was speaking normally. Her words felt like a foul gas whose reek would bring the authorities to our door.

'Was this before you met Uncle John?' I said. 'Who is this man with the barrels?'

She said nothing, no matter how much I pleaded with her. It would be futile to tackle Isaiah, so I would have to press on with my plan without confronting him. I doubted that my arguing with him would sway him; after all, my Mother had never succeeded in altering his course. I lay down, but my worries teemed. These barrels were no doubt filled with gunpowder, and a plot was in motion that would cause real distruction. Mr Edwards had perhaps caught wind of this, and I had not heeded him enough. The night had lifted from black to grey by the time Isaiah stopped pacing in the hayloft. Wherever he had been, it had not left him able to rest, either. I thought about going up to speak to him, and wish to this day that I had, though even I can see that it might well have made little difference.

31

I WOKE STIFF AND in violent need of the privy, where I was taken by such a pain in my behind that I cried out. I lingered before drying my tears, wishing that Tom had been there to chivvy me with reports of how close his bladder was to bursting while he waited for me to powder my arse, or whatever nonsense I was up to. He had always been such a devil in the mornings: crotchety when I was cheerful, full of song and good humour when all I had craved was some peace. And he had always claimed that he had no knowledge of women's doings, nor any time to go walking out with any of the girls who smiled at him. At least there will be no baby to worry about, I told myself, wiping my eyes on my skirt and going in to make sure that Meg ate her corner of bread.

The hours between six and eight unravelled and tightened like a tangled skein. Just when I would have welcomed a few stray hours to seek out Mr Edwards, we had never had so much work. Even Isaiah was forced to stay by my side, though he had eyes only for the door and clumsier fingers than a frostbitten accordionist.

'We must get a more sophisticated press,' said Isaiah.

It was all he could do to operate the ones we had. 'Why?' I asked.

'We would be able to do better engravings. We lost

Colonel Londone's pamphlet, you know, the one instructing the ordinary man in how to defend himself, on account of the quality of our images.'

I imagined the Home Secretary Lord Sidmouth's men coming upon me while I printed a roomful of instructions on how best to lance a Hussar while keeping your musket and your life in the way that Colonel Londone explained in his pamphlet.

'I am not sorry that we lost this work,' I said. 'Indeed, I was surprised that you had considered taking it. One of the Six Acts is a new law against drilling which the Magistrates will be keen to enforce. They would like to make an example of us. Let us not rain danger on our heads, Isaiah.'

'The Six Acts!' Isaiah cried, stopping work while he spoke. The press lid was down, and he had over-inked the plate in any case, so his print would be ruined. 'The Lord Himself had only four gospels. Wherein St Luke said, "whoever has no sword, let him sell his cloak and buy one." What good is that, if a man cannot use a sword?'

'You are fond of saying this, but I think swords are the least of our difficulties. Tell me, do you think the Lord would have used gunpowder, if he had known of it?'

He lifted the lid, inspected his work and dropped it. 'I must go out soon,' he said.

So must I, I thought; why did Isaiah never ask me if I had any business which might take me away from the shop? Without my mother and Tom, I was chained to this place and to Meg as surely as a factory worker was to a loom. I was determined to find Mr Edwards, though it was not clear quite what would happen when I did.

'And Nell, the answer is yes, I think he would. Sometimes a vengeful man is a just one.'

His tone alarmed me. I would try to save Isaiah, but without my mother, he seemed intent on steering a reckless course. Surely he could not think that she would want him to avenge Tom's death? She would have told him every day what Sir David knew: that violence only begat violence. Once a ploughshare became a sword, it could never be turned back into a ploughshare. Yet a part of me felt some sympathy with him. I had woken at five with some vengeful fire in my own belly, resolved to go to Mr Edwards and agree to anything he might suggest, if it meant that there would be justice for Sir David. I was still unsure if I could trust Mr Edwards and worried that I would be delivering my neck to him for some other purpose entirely, but this was a risk I had to run, or else I would have to live with my conscience. As the Lord says, and Isaiah would agree, what good is anything which profits a man, if he loses his soul into the bargain?

Normally I found solace in my work, but that day the prints all seemed to smudge, and the laughing faces of the gentlemen seemed to be winking at me, as if to imply that all the hours I had spent there were as hollow as the months I had spent in 14 St James's Square, for all the good they had done me and what was left of my family. And I could not drag my thoughts away from Hetty. Seeing Martha had reminded me of the gulf that now separated us and I did not think it any more likely that our eyes would meet again than that the King and Queen would be crowned together.

All these thoughts milled about, but still Isaiah did not leave. He leaned on the press, his skin lighter than the wood on account of all the ink in its grain. 'Nell, I am sharply mindful of all the time you have spent here alone, and while I have neglected our business here, I have by no means failed to notice that it is you who has secured any success that we are enjoying. What I mean to say is, thank you.' He said this so gently that my heart felt it had landed on a quilt.

So Isaiah worked with me for two hours, until he said that he was in powerful need of another mug of coffee if he was to do the Lord's work that day. He would not hear of having one at home and had been gone over an hour in search of one when the shop bell jangled. It made me jump so much I could have cried, and the consolation that work had provided evaporated. I prepared to face Mr Tagg, knowing that if I told him to set our creditors on Isaiah with a tear in my eye, Percival Smeek would have been at the shop quicker than I could say bailiff.

'Will!' I said, trying to keep the disappointment out of my voice.

He removed his hat, a black felt affair of which the Jews were mostly fond. He straightened its band. 'Good Morning, Miss Nell, I do hope that I find you well?'

'Indeed you do,' I said. (If I did not sit down, that was.) 'We have much work here, and I am glad to be on my feet to do it.'

Will looked round the room, taking in the rows of drying sheets. 'Isaiah is not at home?'

'He went to the coffee house. You might find him there, though it is a while since he left.'

Will's eyes widened, as if the pursuit of coffee was a cause for alarm. 'Did he say whom he was meeting?'

'He did not say he was meeting anyone, merely that a mug of brown liquid would aid him in the Lord's work. Meg is not with him, nor Carroty Anne.'

'Aye, that it might,' he said, lingering at the door. 'Might you walk with me one Sunday afternoon, Nell, if...'

He stopped himself. 'Isaiah has not mentioned me to you. I can see that this has come as a surprise. Think on it, and I will come at three in any case.'

But I only considered the unfinished part of his sentence. If what? If he is not in gaol by then? If he is still alive? If he has not blown up the Cabinet?

It is my lot to look back endlessly over what I might have

said to him then, but I said nothing, and let him depart.

Alone again in the shop, I rushed up to fetch Martha's red shawl, which smelled of her, of fusty upholstery and gin, and hurried to find Mr Edwards. It seemed that if I did not, events would overtake me, and Isaiah and God knows who else would find themselves victims of this madness.

32

To MY JOY, WHO should be standing at the top of Friday-street but Gus, reading the newspaper. I came up behind him, about to prod him, but I held back.

'The last time we met, I was abducted,' I said, 'and here you are, lounging about reading a broadsheet.'

'You are forward for scolding me this side of marriage, Miss Wingfield,' replied, his face sombre.

'Gus!' I said. 'I did not desert you, I promise you. Someone attacked me, and wanted the message.'

'Are you hurt?' He looked at me closely, as if examining me for signs of injury.

'No,' I answered. 'I ran away.'

'I imagine you are good at that. One day I hope to understand you and the extent of your business. You were easy enough to find though, for pamphlets printed by Isaiah Douglas are discarded in taverns across Westminster.'

We both watched the idle pie-boy across the road. He was letting his master's wares go cold while he chatted to a girl who was busy arranging fronds of blond hair from under her bonnet.

'Why did you not just come to the shop?' I asked.

'I would have done,' he said, 'in my own time.'

I did not understand whether his hesitation was born of

fear or nonchalance, but I was so glad to see him that I did not want to spoil it with too many questions, for once.

Gus kicked at the cobbles, then looked at me, his blue eyes almost grey with sorrow. 'But I had the message, so I assumed that you were safe, and had wandered off.'

'No, I would not have done that,' I said, recalling my abandonment of Meg. 'I was taken the moment you had left me, and I escaped by giving him one of Mr Tagg's bills.'

Gus laughed. 'You are a clever girl.'

I smiled, for I did not feel one, but my happiness faded as I imagined what he would say if he knew of what else had happened to me the previous night. There was no way of turning that into a bauble of a story for him to admire.

'Then I had to go and find Hetty and while I was about it, I met an old woman who works for her. Some of the intelligences she shared with me help explain why we have been delivering those envelopes, but some things still do not make sense to me.'

The excitement came back to his face. He waved his paper at me. 'Perhaps I can help you once again. It is a pity that you do not print the news.'

'Why?' I said.

He handed me a copy of the *Black Dwarf,* a newspaper devoted to the radical cause which the Government was attempting to tax out of existence on account of its huge popularity. NON MI RICORDO was the headline.

'Apparently it's Italian for "I don't remember",' said Gus. 'And this is a powerfully long article. More words on one subject than I've seen since the Good Lord wrote the Bible.'

If Isaiah had been there, he would not have been able to resist correcting him, but I am not Isaiah, so I did not point out that the Bible most likely had sixty-six authors at the very least.

The upshot of the article was this: some Italian servants had been brought to England to give evidence against the Queen. They had attended the bedchamber; they had sniffed the royal sheets. They alone could say with authority that Queen Caroline was an adulteress. Both sides of the case had been pressing them for over a week, but the proceedings against the Queen were collapsing because all the Italian women would say was '*Non mi ricordo.*'

'Look at where one of them lives,' Gus said, leaning over me to point to the relevant section. He smelled of sweat, wool and straw, as if a little of the Dorset countryside still clung to him.

I did not need to look, for I knew what the article would say. *You have prevailed, David,* I thought. *There will be no divorce, but no coronation for her either.* As to whether there would be no more violence, I could not say. But I took some comfort from knowing that I was working to the same end as he had.

The article explained that the woman had moved from address to address in the Italian quarter, making much of the irony that she had never been more than a mile away from the very court in the House of Lords where she had been called to give evidence. One of the addresses mentioned was St Vincent's Court.

'The instructions I read,' Gus said. 'The only part I can recall was that headline: SAY "NON MI RICORDO", written just like that, in capitals. That was what the servant was to say. And she has. And so the case against the Queen has collapsed: the House of Lords had a third vote on the Bill against her, and even in that Tory bastion of royalist privilege, the majority is down to ten. If even the Lords can only muster such weak support for the King, the Prime Minister will not risk a full airing of this matter before the House of Commons because the Bill against her is certain to fail. So there will be no divorce! And all because this Italian lady will not give evidence which incriminates her!'

'I think there is more to it than that,' I said, though I could see that Gus was enjoying the idea that his errand had been at the centre of the most exciting political development of our short lives. 'She won't incriminate the Queen, but she won't clear her name, either. All she'll say is that she doesn't remember.'

The radicals will step up their campaigns, I realised, *if they think that Caroline will not be crowned. Sir Robin might have his day yet.*

'I have no idea. But she has had a lot of money to say that,' Gus said, 'so it must be important.' He took the newspaper from me and continued reading.

'These men spend more than that hod-carrier over there will earn in a year on a new fireplace, so do not assume that profligacy and value go hand in hand,' I replied, blushing because I sounded like Isaiah. 'Presumably it is what Mr Edwards wanted. Or part of what he wanted, at least,' I added hastily.

'Who is Mr Edwards? Are you working for him?' said Gus. 'I think he is mentioned in this article of unholy length which I am failing to finish on account of your presence.'

'He is?' I exclaimed, almost snatching the sheets back in my haste to discover the reference.

And there he was, a figure of the shadows in black and white:

The reader might be interested to learn, how it was that such a fund of Italian information was seemingly so available and yet, once called upon, so remarkably elusive. In these Italians we see the rotten edifice of Government at work: the King wishes a divorce, and so the witnesses which might procure it are secured.

Yet who should be harbouring and, we must assume, financing these Italians? Here we must look to their first lodging, a grand house of ill-repute on St James's Square, where factions keen to support the King were often seen. And more often seen – though less often noticed – is the slight frame of Mr Edwards, who for decades has been the nemesis of many an opponent of the King. But the intelligent reader might ask himself why, having procured these Italians, they did not spout forth the evidence which they might have been expected to give? And though we can only speculate, we do know that Sir Robin Everley, no less, the foremost among Mr Edwards' cohorts, has recently signalled himself a FRIEND of the people, including those sympathetic to the cause of REFORM. It is our belief that Sir Robin refused to allow the Queen to be discredited so, and has thwarted Mr Edwards through the persuasion of cash. Now we cannot present Sir Robin Everley to you as a model reformer, but we can commend his defence of the Queen. Meanwhile, men like Mr Edwards remain the unprincipled OPPONENTS of all that might flower into progress for the working man of England. GOD SAVE THE QUEEN!

'I have been working for Mr Edwards,' I said. 'I thought he was my enemy, and he may yet prove to be, but as the Lord says, "my enemy's enemy is my friend", and he has proved to be that. My enemy is Sir Robin Everley, and the description you have just read of him is utter falsehood. Sir Robin poses as a friend of the people only that he may destroy them.'

Gus slapped his forehead. 'I do not understand you, Nell Wingfield. You are proving as well connected as Queen

Caroline. And let me guess: you wish me to help you find Mr Edwards.'

'No, I know where he is.'

'Ah, that is disappointing, and no mistaking it,' replied Gus.

'But I would welcome your company in getting there,' I added.

33

As if he knew that one day I would seek him out, Mr Edwards had given me his card the first time he had come to the shop. To my surprise, his address was north of Oxford-street. It was not far as the crow flies from Piccadilly, but further from his Tory friends in Carlton House Terrace than I would have expected Mr Edwards to venture. I did not know the streets well: they are handsome in a white, uniform way – and to me they signified the newly arrived respectability of their inhabitants. As we walked north, I understood that like me, Mr Edwards was perhaps attempting to turn away from his old life. How galled he would be, to see Sir Robin lauded in the Radical press as a friend of liberty!

As we walked down Ludgate-hill and Fleet-street, Gus and I went over what we understood of the summer's events and our slight role in them. I explained to him that Mr Edwards had been a supporter of the King, and that this had required the skills of a fairground contortionist in relation to the divorce proceedings.

'There are some supporters of King George who thought it a disaster whatever the verdict,' I said. 'And for that reason it was best if the Queen stayed abroad. For if the Queen were found guilty and the King were granted a divorce, it would cause a riot because she would have been trampled

316

underfoot in the way we all are, and all rioting ever does is lead to more rioting.'

'And if she was found innocent, it would be a humiliation for the regime, which would also lead to rioting, and possibly more,' Gus added, shaking his head. 'And now our fair Queen will go back to doing as she pleases as long as it is a thousand miles away from wherever the Prince – I beg his pardon, our King – continues to do as he pleases.'

I folded my arms over Martha's shawl. 'That article says that Caroline played backgammon while the evidence against her was read out. Part of me admires that, but another part of me rebels against it, for it shows her certainty that whatever happens, she will not be harmed.'

'Not in the way that your brother and my uncle were harmed.'

'What will she do for money, I wonder? Will he continue to pay her? I expect so.'

'Nell, it is you I am worried about,' he replied. 'Not some fat German princess.'

But I was busy reflecting on how my mother's death had made me too keen to trust Hetty. What a dupe I had been! Of course I could not tell Gus all that Martha had revealed, and I hoped that the sums of money involved in the divorce scandal and my connection with Isaiah would be enough to convince him of why I had become embroiled in it. For once it might work in my favour that London was such a morass of intrigue.

Once we got beyond Tottenham Court-road, we noticed smashed windows and rotten fruit in the streets. Charlotte-street was eerily quiet, its shops and chop-houses closed. Men swept up broken glass and children frolicked, enjoying the disorder.

We pressed on, noticing uneasily that the further west we went, the louder distant shouts and crashes became, until they did not sound distant at all. We wove our way past groups of drunken boys no older than Tom. They were singing new verses of the National Anthem, though they could not get much beyond God Save Our Gracious Queen. Soon the revellers had to flee into doorways as mounted troops rode by and constables charged past, and all attempts to sing the new anthem dissipated.

'It will be moving south,' Gus said. 'There have been many of these riots in Hammersmith and Kensington, for that is where the Queen has travelled from every day. It is odd that they have come up here, but there is a sense on the streets that something is afoot..'

As we rounded the corner of Thayer-street, I recognised the address on the card.

Gus whistled. 'They have gone over this place. There is not a window left whole.'

Two or three drays sat at the kerb, obscuring my view of Mr Edwards' front door. I assumed that on a normal day, these deliverymen would be replaced by carriages of wealthy visitors, though Thayer-street did not seem quite grand enough for that. It was the sort of place where a respectable lodging-house would be found.

Two men were carrying a roll of carpet out of Mr Edwards' front door, and I waited on the other side of the street for them to leave, not wanting my meeting with him to take place in front of strangers. Then I saw that the men were not carrying a rug, but a body, and the two men waiting with the dray were constables, one of whom was looking straight at me. A carriage passed, and the constable was surprised to see me still there. He crossed over.

'You knew this gentleman, did you, Miss?'

'What gentleman?' I said.

'Come now, to judge by the company he kept, this Mr Edwards had many friends like your young self.'

I felt myself whiten at the mention of his name. 'I don't know what you mean, Sir,' I replied, 'I am the daughter of a minister, on my way to buy fabric.' My skirts were mended, but not too much – I was not yet at the patched stage of poverty where this claim would have sounded ludicrous.

'Then hurry along, Miss,' he said, more gentle now, 'and no more hopping about here like a crow after carrion. There have been enough of them today already.'

'What has happened here?' said Gus.

'The crowd took him,' the constable said. 'Broke into his house and fair trampled him to death. Would have set fire to the entire row, if we'd not hot-footed it here. They were calling him a traitor, an enemy of the Queen.'

'Lunatics,' muttered Gus, shaking his head. 'I don't understand how people find it in them.' He was a fine actor, even in my shock I could appreciate that.

As we walked from the house, my mind teemed.

'I was not the only one to read that article, I'll wager,' Gus remarked, kicking a cudgel into the gutter.

'Someone will pick that up and use it soon enough,' I said. 'Sir David – and Mr Edwards – were right: violence will only lead to more violence.'

'Aye, but one man's violence is another man's justice, and this man was killed for being an enemy of the justice that puts bread on tables.'

This was the kind of reply Isaiah would have made, but I was no longer convinced by it.

Gus must have seen this on my face, for he added 'Aye, and don't forget that those in power favour violence when it favours them. Think of what they did to your brother.'

And I remembered Mr Edwards saying he had heard Tom speak once, and a terrible thought came bursting forth: what if my path crossing with Mr Edwards, at St James's Square had secured Tom's journey to the gallows? Certainly it had fastened his attention on Isaiah.

As we walked down Wigmore-street, I tried to calm my shaking at this realisation. I tried to go over everything that Mr Edwards had said, the first time he had visited the shop. He had told me that our cause was now the same, that I was in danger, that Isaiah must stop preaching. Martha had corroborated the first point, the second was obvious, and my instincts, along with what Meg had confirmed, told me that the third exhortation was also right. The only good remaining for us to do was to save Isaiah, but this meant diverting him from the course which he believed to be right.

'We are almost at Oxford-street,' Gus said, perhaps hoping that I would share my thoughts. But I did not know where to begin: why, oh why was it that just when I seemed to be getting close to unravelling this intrigue, it appeared to become more complicated? Mr Edwards seemed to be the key to all of it, and now he was dead. 'What now, Mistress?' Gus said, after perhaps another minute of walking punctuated only by the occasional crunch of broken glass underfoot. 'Where shall we go next?'

'I have to return to the shop,' I said. 'I must do all I can to keep Isaiah from harm.' I was resolved: only prison seemed safe enough to hold him.

'I will keep visiting you,' Gus responded, but I was half listening, so full was I of how I might save Isaiah. 'I will be your faithful friend, and then –'

But something he read in my face must have made him stop, for he walked towards Oxford-street without another word. I watched him scuffing his way through the debris, until he was obscured by a carriage clopping down a side road, and it was too late to follow him, however much part of me had wanted to.

34

I woke up the following morning with one thought: today is the day I must get Isaiah imprisoned. He might still hang as a conspirator, but my scheme seemed worth a try.

As I dressed, the madness of thinking that this scheme of mine would rescue Isaiah crept up on me: how could I really think that Mr Tagg would march down to the courts on the day I chose? And even if he did, what was the guarantee that the courts would issue a warrant there and then, and cart Isaiah off? It was far more likely that the bailiffs would come to plunder our stock while the courts deliberated, lost the documents relating to the case and came looking for Isaiah two years hence. But our stock was a species of property, and it might just give Isaiah some protection.

I looked at the ceiling and made the sign of the cross. If I did not try to put Isaiah out of harm's way, disaster was guaranteed. If I did, annihilation was likely, but not certain.

No Mr Edwards today, I thought as I descended the ladder. *No more errands, no more threats.* For a moment I was shrouded by a strange sense of loss. I had been half-mad since returning to Friday-street, and had almost welcomed my worries as a distraction from thoughts of all that had occurred since my mother died.

My first problem was Isaiah himself. I needed him to be

out when Mr Tagg should call, but easily found when the bailiffs arrived. They might impound the press, so Meg would need to follow them to find out where it would be taken. If we got it back at all, it would be on extortionate terms, but I could not bear it to be sold on or smashed up for firewood and scrap. I banished my worrying about this with the thought that if Isaiah were to hang, all his property would be forfeit to the Crown anyway. (If I were to hang, the Crown would gain nothing, for as a woman it did not recognise my right to own so much as a word which I myself had printed.)

Isaiah was reading the Bible over the press, his coat on. In the back, the fire was not lit. 'Ah, you are up, finally,' he said, though it could not have been much beyond six. I fought the urge to put my arm around his shoulders, to catch the scent of his neck. *You will not die like Mr Edwards*, I vowed: *you will not be killed by the forces you have spent your life trying to quell.*

'Will Davidson will be coming,' he said.

'I will attend to him if I am here. But there is also our business to run.'

'Of course,' he said, resting the tips of his fingers on the press. 'You must attend to the affairs of the world. But it is me he will be coming for.'

'Isaiah –' I began, deciding in that moment that I should speak to him, but he left. His steps slowed briefly as he passed through the shop, like those of a child who does not want to go to chapel. Perhaps he was considering speaking to me about the world of trouble he was bringing on his own account. I'll never know.

I doubt that I would have said very much to him if he had stayed, but all the same, I am now left wondering if that was the last moment in which it would have been possible to save his life.

I left immediately, for I knew that Mr Tagg would be out on Cheapside taking deliveries at this hour, and if I waited until the shop was open to talk to him, I risked his being generous to me and extending our credit in order to impress some wealthy customer.

Sure enough, Mr Tagg was standing with Percival, supervising the delivery of piles of claret-coloured volumes, signing for them with a perfect white quill. As he saw me approach, he stroked the bridge of his nose thoughtfully with the end of the feather. I tried to look haughty in the hope that this would provoke him.

'Ah!' he crowed. 'It is the new Governor of the Bank of England!' He bowed to me with a flourish of his arm, and this time his quill scraped the gutter. 'Yesterday not one, not two, but thr*eeee* impecunious scribes darkened my threshold with the request for credit. And most affronted was one of them, when he learned that Tagg's did not offer the same terms as Douglas's.'

It would have incensed Tagg to hear our shop mentioned in the same breath as his: this was all to the good.

'I have issued the odd bottle of ink to poor writers, Sir.' I said. 'What of it?'

'What of it? If you can issue credit, it stands to reason that you must have cash to buy in your materials, or at least be more confident of it than you claimed you were last week, Mistress Nell.'

Percival grinned and snivelled. My plan, which had seemed so foolish a few minutes before, now seemed possible after all.

'On the contrary, Mr Tagg, the drier our cash supply runs, the more Isaiah seems to grow full of the milk of human kindness. I do not understand it.' I could feel a summer cold coming on, and this thickened my voice a little. Mr Tagg was renowned for his godlessness, and regarded religion as at best an indulgence to be excused in women and children, akin to the belief in fairies. At worst, it was a pestilence gnawing away at the edifice of the City, built on the solid foundation of cash.

'You are old enough to leave his house now, are you not?' enquired Mr Tagg.

Percival practised a brooding gaze, except that he had to look upwards to do so.

'I am. Again, what of it?'

'You would do well to cleave from that stepfather of yours. There would always be a place for you here, you know.' His voice became almost kindly as he gestured to his shop. 'You are a fine printer, you have a way about you in the shop, you do not go silly over the riper material, and you are quite decorative.' He turned to his assistant, whose eyes were travelling along the curve of my bodice as if it were a hypnotist's watch-chain. 'Is she not, Percival?'

'Oh inded,' said Percival, who had assumed his master's liberality with vowels.

'Over my dead body,' I said. 'My backside would be a plum of bruises from all his pinching after a day behind your counter, Sir.'

'Indeed, I am *sorely* tempted to foreclose on you' – and with the sorely he made a swipe for my bottom, which I danced sideways to avoid – 'so that you will be forced to my door, but since Percival here is so fond of you, I will grant you a further seven days' grace. And who knows, in that time one of your writers' ships might just have come in – though I forget myself – this is a poor metaphor, for Isaiah will not take money from the Indies, will he?'

Seven days! There was nothing further I could do. 'Really, Sir,' I said, 'I do not know how we will repay you.'

'As I have said,' Mr Tagg said with a malevolent grin and a further expansive sweep of the arm, 'all in good time. I regard my benevolence as an investment. There is a whiff of worldliness about you which I wager is not pleased by Isaiah's feckless disregard for his liberty and your security.'

'No, Sir, you do not understand me,' I insisted. 'I really do not know how we will pay you, next week or any week.'

Tagg's brows furrowed, and the long hairs stood up like hackles. 'And you do not understand m*eee*,' he said, twirling his quill around the end of his nose until he smelt whatever gutter-dung he had dipped it in a few moments before. 'The uncertainty will be instructive to you. Think on what I have said.'

And with that, he entered the shop with his snivelling familiar at his side, sniffing fulsomely himself. As I wandered back to our small premises, I found myself facing certain ruin one way or another, and wondering if life back at St James's Square would not be preferable to working for that pair of gnomes. I had to remind myself – as if I could truly forget, but what we know and what our hearts truly understand can be different, at least for a time – that Sir David was dead, and my only friend had turned out to be as false as the scenery at her husband's evening entertainment when he had raped me.

35

As I ROUNDED THE corner, Will Davidson was rattling on our door. He disappeared inside, but not before I heard him calling to Isaiah that he had bad news.

By the time I got inside, Will was tending the fire: although it was still only late July, the air in the morning could be cool, and the heat required to boil water for coffee was often not enough to keep us warm. He performed all tasks with the same intensity, and the room was soon aglow with a neatly constructed blaze. He had used twice as much wood as I would normally dare to, but I doubted Isaiah would argue with him about it. Meg was sitting under the counter, but she was close to Will, and the adoring gaze she bestowed on him seemed all the warmer for the fire-light. I looked away when he caught me watching him.

The ceiling creaked: Isaiah was evidently back, pacing up and down in the chapel, which meant he was giving some matter serious thought and prayer.

'Your sister grows more beautiful by the day,' he remarked. 'Unlike you, she has been giving me some reason for hope.'

That was enough. 'A touching sentiment, if it were describing anything but the mute attentions of my sister. Can you really think that she responds to you as a young woman should? Have you spoken to Isaiah about this?' I said, raising my voice a little in the hope of summoning him down.

Will laughed and shook his head. 'Where were you those six months, Nell Wingfield? Carroty Anne thinks you were off learning something of the world. As for me, I did not think it a surprise that you left. What fills me with wonder is that you have returned. Did some man desert you, Nell? For why else would you come running back here, insisting that Isaiah gives you the place your mother left?'

'I do not –' I began, choked by the memory of the last afternoon I had spent with Sir David.

'Spare me,' interrupted Will. 'All I wanted to say to you was this: in the Jamaica we left behind, girls of Meg's age were women. My own mother was her age when she conceived me, so do not expect Isaiah to feed her for nothing for as long as you wish to pretend that she is an innocent and you are mistress of this house. You are nimble with your fingers' – he took hold of my left hand and gripped it tightly. I pulled away, but this only hurt me more. He continued, his voice cold and hard – 'but you are here because you are useful, and for no other reason. I told Isaiah that your mother was more trouble than she was worth, but at least he wanted her in his bed at night.'

He dropped my hand, but I raised it again. 'He might go off to bed without me, but this is the hand that feeds us!' Loud knocking on the door prevented me from saying more.

'Open up, Isaiah Douglas! We have men round the back, so there will be no eluding us!' We had no back entrance, so heaven knew where these men were.

'The constables,' said Will, shaking his head, as if their arrival was no more a surprise than the clod of shit that clung to your boots after a walk down Cheapside.

Four men came in, dwarfing the shop. They did not wipe their feet, and the first of them knocked to the floor a box of prints on which the third trampled. The fourth paused, as if considering picking up the ones which were not damaged, but he kicked them aside before following the others. The third man was carrying two sets of fetters, one short and one longer, for the hands and feet. As they jangled and clanked, they reminded me of the gypsy women's bracelets at the Moorfields fair.

'Four of you to arrest one man,' jeered Will. 'You must think Isaiah will put up a mighty struggle, or else you are even bigger cowards than the King you serve.'

'One of us would be enough for the blackie,' said the first. 'But we anticipated that he would have company.' He pulled a stout stick from his belt and raised it at Will. Meg, who was curled up in the corner, hissed at him, as if she were a cat in human form, and the constable stared at her and lowered his stick. The stick was shiny, though it had dents in it and was not entirely straight. I wondered if he polished it at night, and if it had been bent in the service of cracking someone over the head.

Will snorted. 'You will not provoke me, Sir. And you will find that Isaiah gives you no trouble. Since the day he was released, he has been waiting for you. What is it this time? Not blasphemy again, surely? Can you not find something other than that?'

'It is not for you to question the statutes of this land, you darkling dog,' he sneered.

'No, but I am astonished that your magistrates seem to know what will incur the Lord's wrath better than one of his own preachers.'

'Aye, but a self-appointed preacher,' said the man who had made to pick up one of my prints, a quieter fellow who clearly measured his speech. 'But let us get on with what we came here to do. You cannot reason with these men.'

I'd thought we had more to fear from the leader of this

sorry pack, but I saw I was wrong: it was quiet men like him, who took in all the evidence and anticipated all arguments, who would see us hanged.

Isaiah appeared in the doorway. He must have climbed down the ladder, but how he did so without making a sound was beyond me. Only Meg avoided making it creak as she scampered up it, but she is a feather compared to Isaiah.

'You did not need to come mob-handed,' he said. 'I am ready. You will not make a slave of me by taking me against my will.'

'What are the charges against this man?' I said. 'You cannot just take him.'

'They are not "just taking" me,' said Isaiah. 'It is the will of the Lord. As his only son said: "They know not what they do."'

The fourth man unfurled a piece of paper and shoved it in my face. 'Does this mean anything to you?' The hairs at the end of his moustache were crinkled, as if he had held his face too close to a candle.

'I can read well enough,' I said. The two men who had done little and said less made hoity-toity faces at each other, and for once I was glad that Will was there, since it would discourage these men from lingering once Isaiah was gone. It would not take four of them to escort him to Newgate – for I assumed this was what they intended. The writing was slanted and looped, but I could see that the charge was Sedition, and that there were witnesses who would attest to what they had heard when the matter came before the courts.

'Will he be in Newgate?' I asked, as two men put Isaiah's wrists and legs in irons. Never has a woman been more happy to see a man shackled. Will watched me, and I feared that he could divine something of my relief and would misinterpret my reasons for it.

Isaiah offered his hands to the men, and something about his stillness must have frightened one of them – the smallest, who had been the second to come in – more than the cursing and struggling to which they must have been accustomed, for he bunched his fist and examined it before punching Isaiah on the cheek. The fourth man opened his mouth, but said nothing.

Isaiah did not so much as flinch, though the pulse in his neck beat more strongly. Will and I looked at each other, calculating whether it was worth retaliating. It was clear we would achieve nothing but injury and arrest, so I stayed where I was.

I looked around me. 'Where is Meg?' I asked Will.

'Upstairs,' he said. 'I watched her go.'

Isaiah submitted to the leg-irons as meekly as a cart-horse does to its harness. What should have been a ten-minute walk would take at least three times as long in those shackles, and there would be no skin on his ankles and shins by the time he arrived. I resolved to go to him that night with something for his wounds, for men had been known to lose their legs and even their lives to the sores which could set in after such a journey.

Will and I listened to the chain beating the cobbles until the sound was replaced by someone whistling. In my usual way, I removed myself from the shock of the present, by reflecting that until that day, I had never seen so many people in our shop.

'So,' I said, 'is his arrest anything to do with the business you and my uncle have been cooking between you?' He opened his mouth in surprise, but I shook my head. 'I am only saying what I think my mother would have said, though I doubt she would have let things get to this sorry state.'

'It's best not to tell you anything,' he said.

'Someone has betrayed him. That much is obvious.'

Will snorted, and I understood what he meant by it.

'Surely you cannot think it is me?'

'I do not want to think it,' he said. 'But I saw your eyes when they chained him like a slave. You looked victorious, Nell. *Victorious.* There is no other word for it. And when Isaiah said to me, "Will, where was Nell all those months I was imprisoned? Did you see her? And what could take her from her sister for all that time?" When Isaiah voiced his thoughts to me, it reminded me of the nights I saw him on deck during our voyage here, when he would ask me how his father could have lied to him so powerfully about what he had in store for him: I did not know what to tell him then, Nell; and I did not know what to tell him now.'

'It is you,' I cried, remembering what Isaiah said about not being able to trust Will. 'It is you who has betrayed him, so that *you* might lead whatever it is that you have been planning.'

'You are wrong, Nell,' he said. 'Though I am not surprised that you think it. Your mistrust of me is the most poorly kept of your many threadbare secrets. If anyone has betrayed Isaiah Douglas, it is you. I have seen you, slipping out, visiting Tagg, encouraging that creep Smeek. What have they offered you? Have they said that you can keep the shop? You are an even greater fool than I thought, if you have sold Isaiah's soul for that.'

He put on his hat. 'Isaiah is my only true friend,' he said. 'And I will carry out his will today, with or without him, just as I carried out his wishes in looking out for Meg while he was in gaol. Do you not see that she came to love me during that time? It has taken me a while to see it, for I was blinded by the idea of you.'

'You scarcely saw her, and she does not understand about love!' I blurted. 'She is young and simple!'

'Does she not? I suppose that you have the patent on that, do you? And what evidence do we have of your fine sensibilities? You have a steady hand at the press, I'll give you that, but what else?'

'You will hang,' I said, 'if you continue with your plan. That is evidence of my fine sensibilities. And you will take Isaiah down with you.'

But he could listen no more, and with a slam of the door, he was gone.

36

I SPENT MUCH OF the afternoon pacing around the shop. I waited for Carroty Anne to appear – for once I would have been glad of her company – but she did not. In fact, I realised, she had been at Friday-street less and less recently, and Isaiah had not made much reference to her. I had been too preoccupied to notice, let alone feel glad about it.

One of the writers to whom I had been advancing paper and ink called in, hoping for more goods on credit, and I was generous with him. Now that Isaiah had been arrested, I was amazed at my foolishness in thinking that I could run up a debt and then hope for the bailiffs to arrive in the way that a rich man would summon his carriage. It was this kind of self-defeating optimism that had landed me in St James's Square, and it worried me how little I seemed to have learned from my time there. I tried to work at the press, for the profits from this were our only hope, but the question of our debts to Tagg gnawed at me. I had the five sovereigns in my hem, but even they would not cover all that Isaiah owed. I would need to spend money if I was to make Isaiah's life bearable in gaol, which meant going to a shop substantial enough to break such a coin yet not grand enough to send for the constables at the sight of me with so much money.

There was little point going to Isaiah before the evening,

for all that the prison was so close, since the business of arraigning him and assigning a cell would take hours. Visiting was erratic, but there was a better chance of being admitted at mealtimes, when the guards were hungry and so more likely to take whatever food people had brought for the prisoners in exchange for unlocking cell doors. So I arrived at five, having shopped on Cheapside at a grocer and an apothecary who knew me by sight. I told the grocer that we had just been paid for a bulk order of prints, and would he mind giving change for a sovereign? I fear he took me for a braggart, but I did not much care; I was just thankful that I had encountered neither Percival nor Tagg. The shop was so warm and bright that the evening felt chilly. I had to buy expensive jam and tea from him in order to have some pennies to use at the bakery.

On every corner there were posters announcing that tomorrow was the Coronation of King George IV. There was no mention of the Queen, and I hoped for her sake that she would not turn up, though most assumed that she would. There must have been thousands of these bills all over the city – good, easy work for the printers. Of course, no one would trust the likes of us with such a job: it would be too tempting to add the Queen to the odd batch, or to make the King a laughing stock by adding some setting error which the printer could claim was an honest mistake. I fell into imagining how much easier my life would have been, had I been born a country parson's daughter; someone who sewed and took tea and played 'God Save the King' on the pianoforte to divert the guests. Then an organ-grinder barrelled around the corner and almost knocked me off my feet, his monkey shrieking and chattering as he cursed me for failing to look where I was going, and I carried on towards Isaiah's gaol with my eyes fixed firmly on the streets of London in the Year of Our Lord 1820.

37

THE LAST TIME I had been at Newgate was for Tom's execution. As I walked into the courtyard, I was unprepared for how ordinary it seemed. It was just one more new building in a city of square stone constructions. With Mr Edwards dead, I reflected again with sorrow that the prospect of Sir Robin being brought to such a place as this to account for his part in Sir David's end was farther away than the Promised Land. I stood a moment, watching the more respectably dressed visitors trying to enter the gate at a distance from the more wretched.

A boy was selling buns to those who had not thought to bring food. The price was high, and the buns would be stale. If the inmate had no teeth, they would be about as nourishing as stones. 'Coronation buns!' he called out, though there was nothing regal about them that I could see.

As I expected, the gaoler – who had an undulating stomach and breath that would stun a rat – immediately identified Isaiah as 'the blackamoor', but then forgot where his cell was until I gave him sixpence and a quartern loaf. He studied the coin, as if weighing up whether or not to insist on more, then led me down a staircase not far from the gate.

He allowed me all the way into the cell without my asking, which made me wonder if sixpence wasn't too generous. He had assumed I was Isaiah's woman, and that we wished to be locked in alone.

He hovered at the door. 'You might be wanting this light. That's a further sixpence,' he said, hooking a foul-smelling rushlight on a weedy stick to a sconce.

Isaiah had been sitting in the darkness for hours. 'How much to keep the light burning?' I asked.

'How much can you afford?' he replied, with a look which I assumed was a leer, though it was difficult to tell in the gloom.

'I do not need light,' Isaiah said. 'The Lord sends it each morning. He knows how much we need.'

The gaoler snuffled. 'Just as well,' he smirked. 'For he is dark all the time, int'e? Well, int'e?' He laughed at his own joke and hawked onto the cell floor. When I did not respond beyond gazing at where his glob of spit had landed, he left.

Isaiah did not get up to greet me. As I moved closer to him, I saw that he had been stripped of his shirt. He grasped the bench to brace himself against his shivering. His skin was dull, as if a layer of dust had settled on him.

'Where is your shirt?' I said.

'There are more thieves on the Government's payroll than there are on the streets of Covent Garden,' he said.

I shook my head, wishing I had pushed the gaoler down the steps. 'But your shirt? It is worth nothing. Are they making a slave of you?'

'Perhaps,' he said. 'Certainly an exhibition, Nell.' He raised himself slowly and moved closer to the light. He turned slightly to show me his back. The light caught what looked like ridges. 'My wounds healed hard and proud. Scars are a mark of the strong, of those whom the Lord favours. My gaolers are fascinated by them.'

'Someone has carved a Jesse tree on you.' My left hand reached out, but I did not dare touch him. I imagined my mother running her fingers over his back. 'Was this on the ship?'

'I was never flogged at sea,' he said. 'Such punishments were for the ill-disciplined and weak. This was inscribed on my flesh by my father. My mother might have been a free woman, but she could not prevent this. No woman could.'

Footsteps passed overhead, and hooves. I noticed shiny jagged trails of wet on the walls. When it rained, the cell would be little more than a drain.

'Already the guards have brought two people in to look at me. They were disappointed, my slave disfigurements being less severe than the gaoler had described. They could see better at a fair, they said. One asked for a refund.'

'What tortures will they conjure next?' I said. 'It is cold enough in here with only a shirt, but without it? You will die. Here, take my shawl.'

Isaiah sat down again. 'No, you need that. And in any case it is not yours. Your old one was torn, I saw. You must buy a new one. If you die of cold, what will become of your sister? Ostentatious self-denial is a form of vanity, Nell. Think of the Sadducees.'

I did not understand this reference, but did not pursue it. 'Will you accept the food I have brought?' I handed him the basket. I waited for some comment about the ostentatious expenditure on jam, but none came.

'They have given me a blanket,' he said. It was folded on the edge of his pallet. 'The cold does not seem to have kept down the infestation.' He nodded to himself, in the way he did when he had made his mind up about something. 'If they hang me, Nell, I will ask that they turn my face away from the crowd, so that these wounds will bear witness.'

'They will not hang you,' I declared, with more conviction than I felt. 'Men do not hang for sedition, you know that.'

But now that he was in Newgate, so close to where they killed Tom, it was impossible to be confident of anything.

'Sedition! That is the least of my crimes. They will hang all of us, if Will has not word to this address.' He handed me a slip of paper. 'It is northeast of Tyburn, off the Edgware-road. You must take this message there.' He saw me opening my mouth to speak, and raised his hand, which made his shivering more violent. 'You do not need to tell me how fit-ting it is that these men are meeting near the old gallows, Nell. It is for you to ensure that they do not feed this Government's thirst for blood.'

'That was not what I was thinking,' I said. 'Our life is not a psalm, Isaiah. I am afraid for all of us. Even Queen Caroline has not won. Perhaps she will go to the coronation, but do you think she will be crowned? Of course she won't.'

'Will must know that I am here,' he said.

Then I realised that Isaiah was shivering so much not through lack of a shirt, but because he was feverish. 'Isaiah, Will was with you this morning. He saw them take you. They did not arrest him, and they have only charged you with sedition. Will has had time to issue whatever warnings are necessary.' I recalled Will's resolve, and knew that my reassurances were false. Too late it seemed, Isaiah wished to call a halt to whatever Will had conjured.

'Who betrayed you?' I asked. 'Do you think it was Titus Soane?'

'Soane?' he said, suddenly more lucid. 'Why do you say that?'

Now was not the time to confess to him about my involve-ment with Mr Edwards. 'Because he is a newcomer,' I replied.

'No,' said Isaiah, lingering on the word. 'This has the reek of an old friend about it. But whoever it is has not delivered them all the details, for they are questioning me too keenly about the whereabouts of the –' Here he stopped, and shook his head.

'They planned this while you were in gaol, didn't they? Will has been keen to take advantage of your absence to prove his power.'

'You must deliver this message, Nell,' Isaiah urged. 'And we will see what Will is made of.'

'And I will return tomorrow,' I promised. As I picked my way out past all the alcoholics, fraudsters and murderers, it occurred to me that he had not asked for Carroty Anne.

*

The gaoler emerged from a door near the top of the stairs and grinned at me.

'You can light his cell and heat it on the proceeds of your viewings of his flesh,' I said. 'That man is sick.'

'What viewings? Men from the Indies don't excite the ladies as much as they used to, now that there's so many of them here. But if it is heat you are looking for, it is warm in my room,' he said, holding his arm out like a butler to usher me in.

'Keep *him* warm,' I said.

'Not *my* job, pet,' he retorted. 'What's a dead blackamoor rabble-rouser to me? A vacancy, that's what.'

I left before I made matters worse by speaking my mind to this revolting man.

A wind had got up, and it tugged at me as soon as I left the courtyard. I picked up my step. For all that we only lived a few streets away, I wished I could have sent word to Gus to meet me. I was lonely and afraid and in need of a pie rather than my usual bread. If Gus had been there, I would have had the excuse of taking him to a pie shop, but without him I could not justify the expense. And I should not be so foolish, I told myself: I could not expect a man to chase about after me. At least it was not yet dark, so I did not need to keep to the main thoroughfares for fear of my life. I looked at the message Isaiah had given me. It said three words: We are discovered. I tucked it in the side of my boot. If I went there, all I would do is lead the constables to the plotters, and see myself hanged in addition to everyone else. It would not save Isaiah.

I thought of Mr Edwards being carried out of his house, and of Hetty's betrayal. How was I to know what to believe ever again? Or whom to trust? My judgement was so poor that perhaps the gaoler would turn out to be a decent man after all, and be feeding Isaiah porridge and broth when everyone's backs were turned.

I passed the Bank, glad to be so close to home. A man slept on the steps; it would not be long before he was moved on. It would also not be long, I reckoned, before I was compelled to share his lot, and Meg along with me. The Constables could take the presses and hold them in evidence, and then I would find myself as destitute as the orphan I was.

38

CORONATION MORNING WAS SUNNY, the sky as bright and clear a blue as any ink I'd used. I had assumed it would rain, perhaps because it had on the day my mother had died and on the day of Tom's execution. I was too afraid to work, and thought venturing to Tyburn would lead to disaster. It would be just my luck if some sharp-eyed constable had followed me from Newgate and was watching me. So I worked, then walked to Cheapside and bought bread, hoping to bump into Gus again.

Soon I was caught up in the crowds heading to St Paul's for the coronation. The rumour was that the Queen would turn up and demand her rights; speculation as to what would happen then knew no limits. One woman suggested that the Queen would be shot by the Hussars, and there would be a stampede, as there had been in Manchester the previous summer. A man who was almost as tall and blond as Gus suggested that the Archbishop had been bribed, so the Queen would be crowned before the King, who would be drunk as usual, had worked out what was happening. Listening to the conversation around me, it was clear that the King had already been upstaged – that was to be the Queen's only victory that day.

I skirted my way round the churchyard, remembering the

oranges I had eaten after meeting Mr Edwards, and how afraid I had been of him. And now Mr Edwards was in the ground; I wondered where he had been buried, and if he had kin who mourned him. In living a dishonest life, I had consented to giving him dominion over me. Whatever I did next, I knew I had to avoid such a fate. I wondered if such freedom could be possible in this city – I no longer believed that this mass of people provided a cloak of anonymity, nor that there was strength in their numbers.

Caroline arrived in an open-topped carriage, a tiara in her curled hair. Her purplish-crimson cloak was trimmed with thick fur – the effect was coronation combined with the finest Parisian fashion *bon ton*, as Hetty might have put it. She was helped from her carriage, something of her stiffness suggesting creaking knees, and made her way up the steps to ecstatic cheers.

The difficulty was that the doors were closed, and the guards were presenting arms: two silver axes which made an elegant cross. As she approached, silence descended, though no one would have been able to hear the exchange from where we were. The Queen spoke; the guards did not move. A gentleman in dark robes appeared, and the upshot of whatever he said was that the Queen began rapping on the door.

'She mustn't do that,' I said to the congregation in front of me.

There was not even a dramatic knocking sound – the door must have hurt her knuckles powerfully. She pushed and pulled a knocker the size of a noose, but the guards did not move. And neither did the doors. After all the summer's machinations and wranglings, all it took was two crossed swords to thwart her.

I am unsure how many minutes it took for Caroline to understand that the service was proceeding without her. She glanced back down the steps, the first signal that she was about to retreat. And here was the worst of it: as soon as she revealed this weakness, this capitulation in the face of the inevitable, a hiss went up from the crowd. Louder and louder it became, until wholesale booing accompanied her on the clop back down Ludgate-hill. I made for home, ashamed that the people who had championed her could turn on her with such ungenerous caprice.

My passage down Bow-lane was blocked by two men carting a heavy object into Cheapside. As I pressed myself against the wall, I saw a familiar pink painted face smiling benevolently on the side of it.

'Stop!' I shouted. 'Where are you taking my press?'

'Your press?' said one of the men. 'Why, it was the press belonging to Isaiah Douglas, Esquire until first thing this morning, whereupon the court awarded it to Josiah Atkins, Esquire, Ironmonger, in order to defray debts incurred by Isaiah Douglas.'

'To an *ironmonger*?' I said, hardly looking at the man, so reluctant I was to take my eyes off my beloved press, as if gazing at it would prevent it from being taken from us.

'Oh aye,' said he. 'If Isaiah is the blackamoor who is making a bonfire in his attic, you had better be getting home.'

Isaiah was in Newgate, so I took little heed of this. And I was not able to return yet, for who should appear but Mr Tagg, sniffing the air like a bear looking for bait. When he saw me, he rubbed his hands together and strode towards us.

'Perfect!' he said. 'Here you are, gentlemen. Now Nell, will you follow your press to my establishment? We will give you a space in the back room, and all the ingredients for pea and ham soup that you could want. If you cook, you will eat your fill, then you will be free to lick your fingers clean and return to your beloved rack here.' And with this he gave

Meg's pink Queen Caroline an affectionate pat before resting his sausagerial fist atop the press. It was all I could do not to slap his hand away, but I knew it would only give him an excuse to lay it on me.

A faint smoke wafted round us, and this effaced the smell of the bailiffs' armpits and Mr Tagg's objectionable cologne.

'You will no doubt entertain the fantasy that I will permit you to recover your presses,' said Mr Tagg, twirling his moustache. 'Which I have purchased at a knockdown rate from some illiterate spade-seller. Tusk, tusk, the company Isaiah keeps.'

I imagined twisting his moustache so tightly that first his face, then his head, then his entire body was caught in it, until he spun himself down into the storm-hole and did not stop turning until he bobbed out into the Thames along with all the other turds.

'No, I will not,' I said. 'You have made your position very clear.' I did not want to give him another opportunity to tell me how he and Percival looked forward to bending me over the press.

I gave Meg's painted Queen a farewell curtsey, and headed towards our shop. I had to make sure that Meg had not been too frightened by these men. I wanted to find Gus, and later I had to tell Isaiah what had happened. These three people, all I had in world, were more important than the press, even if it had secured our livelihood and been a companion to me. I did not know what we would do next, but Isaiah would ask the Lord for guidance, and I would ask my mother – and perhaps Gus too. Somehow, we would survive.

39

IT WAS AS IF a fog had descended on the shop, so at first I could not see Meg, who was curled up under the counter as she had been after our mother's death.

'Meg!' I cried. 'Meg! Get out! The room is filling with smoke, you foolish child!'

She said nothing, but this might have been because she did not hear me – her hands were clasped tight over her ears, and there was a strange dense quality to the air. The back room was less fuggy. It was strangely empty where the press should have been. I remembered what the bailiff said about Isaiah making a bonfire, and I looked upwards. Fronds of smoke seeped through the floorboards before spreading into the grey which was now so thick I could not see the door.

'I am sorry, Meg,' I said, as I grasped her round the waist and heaved. Or at least I tried to speak, for the smoke had intensified in a matter of moments and was tearing at my lungs. Her ribs were strong, and the soft concave of her stomach made her feel like a huge dry whelk. The gritty scraping sound under her told me that at least she was wearing her boots, so there was something that would be saved. I turfed her outside. 'On no account must you move,' I ordered, careful to let go of her before I spoke. 'Promise me.'

I was almost certain she nodded, but I did not have the time to wait for reassurance. Just as I turned to re-enter the shop, a canopy of flame landed next to us. My blue dress, like a piece of sky being hurled to the earth. This time Meg needed no dragging; we both leapt sideways.

We watched my dress burn. The flames raced each other to devour the fabric, leaving charred bones and fluttering ash, as if the dress had been a living thing and the silk was its skin. The flames shone a deeper blueish-green at their edges, just where they turned the silk black. I shuddered and rubbed my arms, as if a layer of my own skin was burning and the flames were ghostly tongues which would soon lick at me.

'It is *you*!' Isaiah shouted. 'Are you astonished at my release? I see you did not deliver my message. Will was right in his suspicions about you. *You* are the lion, Nell Wingfield. *You* are the plague. You are the curse on our fig tree. For how many pieces of silver did you betray me? And what use have you for this? Is this dress what you bought with your thirty pieces of silver?'

'Isaiah! Why are you here?'

'He will be back in gaol, soon enough.' It took me a moment to place the speaker: it was the quiet constable who had come to arrest Isaiah the day before. So they had used him to lead them to the other plotters, and now they had come to arrest him once more. But to say this aloud would be enough to hang me too.

My neighbour appeared with an armful of shoes. 'My stock is being ruined – smell these! My shoes are all smoked! And how am I to get Bessie from the attic? Tell me that?'

By Bessie, I assumed he meant the cow. I had no idea what to say.

A smell like singed hair competed with wood smoke. 'You are wrong about me, Isaiah!' I shouted. 'I would never betray you, not least because you have always concealed your intentions from me! I have not always been truthful, but I would never sell your body or your soul. I will come to you, but please make your way down before I have to climb the ladder.'

I did not wait for his reply before plunging indoors, but I was sure I heard laughter.

I knew that house better than I knew my own face, and I soon fumbled my way to where the ladder should have been. I walked back and forth, my hands disappearing in the smoke, until I understood that Isaiah had made a bonfire of it, and there was no way of climbing up to him. I blundered towards the door, crouching low, making myself a ball like Meg did, except it seemed to have moved and the shop was suddenly bigger than it had ever been before, and the smoke became grey silk wadded tight in my mouth, and I tried to call out, but now the smoke had arms – no, it trussed me with belts and straps, and I saw that there was a justice in this, that Isaiah had been right all along: we each create our own hell, and mine was a private place, where everything that Sir Robin Everley had ever wanted done to him would be done to me, again and again and again. Yes! The smoky arms became stronger, and I was being propelled towards the light. Death was as my mother always said it would be, and here was a blond angel to escort me.

'So *he* has saved you!' a voice shouted from on high. Isaiah, laughing again.

'Nell! Nell!'

Isaiah's voice, then two others, one male, one a girl's. I was warm, and there were footsteps around us, and I opened my eyes to a pair of boots with toes poking through it, one toe almost as grimy as the cobbles.

The smoke was gone, but it took me some time to understand this.

I was lifted up, and opened my eyes to find Gus pulling my hair back from my face.

'Are you all right?' he asked. 'You've enough sweat on you to put a fire out – your hair's like seaweed on a wreck.'

I tried to speak, but coughed instead.

Above us, like some dark angel hurling thunderbolts, was Isaiah. 'Was the dress for him, Nell?'

'Is this in your Bible?' said Gus, rubbing my back, 'for it is not in mine. He thinks that you are a harlot, and I your paymaster.'

'I am sorry,' I gasped, coughing violently, my throat feeling as though it had been dragged through a thicket by a pack of wild dogs. 'You are probably the most upright man I have ever met, and I have brought you nothing but trouble. Every notion I have turns out to be a disaster. Tell Isaiah that I have done nothing to harm him, and never would. Someone else has betrayed him.'

'Don't try to speak,' pleaded Gus, and I realised that nothing I was trying to say was audible, I had inhaled so much smoke.

I shook my head again. I no longer knew what to do, and if Isaiah did not come down from the chapel soon, it would be too late for him, and he would die convinced that I was a faithless betrayer.

Two men fetched a ladder, and some women brought two pails of water each. One gave me some handfuls of it before she attempted to throw the rest of it over the house. Friday-street was suddenly a-jostle with people craning their necks upwards for the next sighting of Isaiah; they might have been on their way to the coronation at St Paul's.

'I wonder that he did not think of using this window as a pulpit before now,' said one.

'Aye, and if we do not hoick him out of there sharpish, it'll be his own last rites he'll be saying, and no mistake.'

'Isaiah!' a woman with a huge chin jutting out from a black scarf shouted. It reminded me of the lone cry of *Shame!* on the morning of Tom's execution.

I knew that Isaiah meant to die in there, so powerful was his sense of betrayal. 'You should not have rescued me,' I chided Gus, wrenching myself from his grasp, for I realised that he had not let go of me all this time. 'I should be in there with him, for if he dies, I will not live with the shame!'

'You are a powerful strange woman and no mistake,' Gus said. 'I have meant you no harm, but each time our paths cross, I am sent off on wild goose chases to parts of town I would have blushed to imagine. I am attacked by strangers, and to crown it all, I am upbraided for saving your life for a second time. And you struck me as one with such a mighty faith in your own wisdom.'

I recalled a similar exchange with Will only the day before. 'I am sorry, Gus. Ever since my mother died, I have done one foolish and wicked thing after another. If Isaiah knew, I shouldn't wonder that he would throw himself from the window and dash his brains out on the pavement.'

'Better that than be taken to the gallows.' Gus rubbed my cheek. 'Soot,' he said. 'You are covered in it. Big flakes of it, like leaves.'

'Burnt silk,' I said.

Gus shook his head. 'I do not know what you did to send that preacher hollering in the flames. And whatever it is, I will never judge you for it. You have him up there for that,' he said, pointing at the upstairs window, or perhaps at the sky. 'What I do know is that after my uncle was hanged, I came to London, and if that isn't a mark of madness, then what is?'

'You came here to work. And there is a nobility in that. Why are you not working now, instead of wasting your time on me? It is coronation day, and people will have need of transport.' All this I think I said, but my lungs were so sore I doubt Gus heard much more than a series of croaks.

Mr Tagg appeared. 'So he has torched the premises, has he? Is that how he repays my kindness?' He made a trumpet of his pinkish hands. 'Isaiah!' he called. 'Come down! You have destroyed your livelihood in vain, for you will not go back to prison for the paltry sum you owe me! The magistrate knows you are a tradesman, so he does not want to see you under lock and key for less than a hundred pounds!'

'This has gone beyond money,' I said.

'Nothing is beyond money, Mistress Nell, if you scratch its surface.'

A great sadness came over me at the truth of this. I had not fallen into Mother Cooper's establishment out of greed and wantonness, but out of grief for my mother and fear of my uncle, but even so: if we had lived in a comfortable farmhouse of the kind we had begged from on our way to London, I would never have fallen on such desperate times.

Carroty Anne blustered up to us. 'I have come from the gaol. Will is there, and he is to be had as their ringleader. Where is Isaiah?'

I pointed towards the chapel. 'There is a constable here,' I said. But when I looked round, he had gone.

'Isaiah will die up there,' she said, with a matter-of-factness which astonished me. 'There is nothing I can do for him. He will join your mother and Tom, and no one ever stands in his way, least of all us.' She touched my arm in sisterly commiseration, and I wished that I had found the simple generosity in me to like her. Perhaps Will was right, and I had spent too much time trying to requisition my mother's life and lacked the courage to live my own.

'Why was he released?' she asked.

I swallowed down smoke. 'Because they knew that

he would go straight to Will and the rest of them, and lead them to their prize.'

She shook her head. 'And he did so at his own cost, like the sacrificial lamb.'

Like Esau, I thought: the dark, hairy son whom Isaac was willing to slay. 'Where is John Ings?' I asked, though I knew what her answer would be.

She shook her head. 'He has gone, Nell. And his shop is all shut up. They will have set him up with lodgings and a position somewhere in return for the information he gave. If I ever get hold of him...' she said, then she lowered her fist and looked away from me.

It all made sense to me then. Someone would have come into the butcher's shop and offered John money and he would have leapt at the bait, envy and greed getting the better of him. But the word of a man like John Ings would not have been enough to convict these men of a capital crime. And when the constables came to the shop, Isaiah was doing nothing for which he could be incriminated. By choosing to arrest only Isaiah and not Will, the constables must have thought that Will would then deliver them to the rest of the plotters, when he scurried off to tell them news of Isaiah's incarceration. But Will would have been too clever to do that. And that is where the difference between them was clear: Isaiah could not stand by and see his friends arrested when he had the power to save them, so when he was released he went to them. The note he had given me to deliver was intended to warn them off, but might have implicated me. My not delivering it made me his betrayer: my silk dress only confirming this belief. *Isaiah! You would have seen me hang along with you.*

'It is all right, Carroty Anne,' I said. 'John Ings is no kin of mine. All I have in the world now is Meg.'

Gus took a step closer, and Carroty Anne looked up.

'There is him,' she said. 'Someone whose eyes are all for the living and has no urge to take up arms with the dead. And if I were you, I'd take him up on whatever he offers.'

And with a sweep of her ragged jingling skirt, she was gone.

'You will not see her again,' Gus said.

'And just when I was starting to like her. But I think you are wrong: everyone I have ever known in this city reappears sooner or later. On occasion you can catch a glimpse of the dead.'

I did not have time to explain myself, for the top floor heaved in on itself. Isaiah leapt from where the window had been, and I had only the time to notice that a beam was following him before it struck me.

40

I WOKE COVERED BY a blanket in an unfamiliar room, and expected to find Sir Robin looming over me.

Gus rushed over with a cup of water. 'You have been out for hours,' he said. 'Meg! Make that sugary tea now, would you?'

I heaved myself up and began to cough, which alerted me to my cracking headache.

'This is my lodging,' he said. 'It is small, but it is above ground, and that is worth another decade of life in this city.' I marvelled that Gus's room was so clean, and that he had induced Meg to come with him *and* help him prepare tea.

'I have a way with simpletons,' he told me, in a tone which implied that I was one of them. I was in no position to argue.

I drank, and slept again, and it was not until the following day that I had the strength to talk much. Gus told me that after the falling beam had struck me, I had stood up, rubbing my head as if there was nothing wrong with me. I had covered Isaiah's body with Martha's shawl, then walked from Friday-street without a backward glance. I had walked as far as Whitehall as if on water, the crowds which had massed for the coronation parting for me as if they knew that I was being transported by a spirit beyond theirs. A carriage had clattered by, and everyone had craned their necks, and then who had stuck his head out of the carriage but the King himself, at which point I had cried 'Look out!', pressed myself flat against the wall of the Old Whitehall Palace – and fainted. Half a mile Gus had had to carry me.

I did not tell him about the first time I saw the King, that day when I'd been arrested by nothing graver than the smell of a cheese shop. But we did talk about much else in the following days, as we walked the streets of London and surveyed the devastation that a coronation leaves for the street-sweepers.

'I can't put out of my head that Isaiah died thinking I had betrayed him, for surely he will spend eternity enslaved to this sense of injustice.'

Gus picked up a discarded whisky bottle and shook it. 'My father told me that his heaven would be a perpetual bird's eye view of us, past, present and future. He told us we should think of that when he seemed far away.'

'A bit like Tom on the scaffold,' I said, relieved that Gus had tossed the bottle back into the gutter, for who knew what it contained. 'When he was a boy, he was forever climbing things and jumping up to get a better view, and there he was in his last moments, soaring above everyone. It cost him his neck to upstage Isaiah, but he managed it.'

When I thought about it like this, the question of whether or not Mr Edwards had led him to the scaffold receded, and I felt nothing but sadness for both of them – for all of them, counting Isaiah, too.

'So many people we have already left behind,' he said.

'It is they who have left us behind.'

'You cannot think like that,' he said, 'or you will go mad with it.'

'And dance in the flames until I die?' I touched his arm so he knew I was not angry with him. How could I be, after all he had done for me?

'Something like that,' he said. 'Look, Nell, what I am aiming at is this. I have been waiting for the right moment to say it, but I wouldn't know a right moment if it came with the Apocalypse, so I'll be out with it now, if you don't mind.'

No, I didn't mind.

'I want you to come away with me. I want you to come as my girl, of course – I mean as my wife, if ever you'll have me – but I want us to set that aside for now. Not because I don't want you, for I surely do, but because even if you could never look on me in that way, I think you should come away with me, and make a new life for yourself.' He pushed a handbill towards me, and took out a large handkerchief to wipe his face.

'You make it seem like a normal summer's day, doing that.'

'I think that is the longest I have ever spoken without stopping.'

The bill promised work in Cape Town, southern Africa, for respectable persons who were literate and numerate, and for craftsmen of all kinds.

'I have been interviewed already,' Gus said. 'And there is government work, but I thought you might not care for that, so I enquired about companies, and there are all sorts setting up there. It is a guinea each for our passage, though this is negotiable. There is Meg, of course. And Adam.'

'I have money,' I said. 'Do not ask me how I came by it. But Gus, is this not voluntary transportation? Would we not just be paying for what the Government would do to us for nothing, if we were convicted felons?'

Gus shook his head. 'You don't know how terrible the life is for transportees. This is different. There are opportunities out there, Nell. Think about Isaiah's father – he lived like a king in Jamaica, I'll wager.'

'He lived like a devil!' I cried. 'If he is the type of man whose society we would be compelled to endure, I will stay here and starve!' I was about to say that I had the press and would make my living that way. But I knew that this was a fantasy. A woman could own property without a father or a husband, but the press was with Mr Tagg. Which, I saw with a dreadful certainty, was where Meg and I would be by Christmas, if I stayed in London.

But leaving London? I could not imagine Cape Town, and I could not believe that we would survive the passage.

'Think on it,' Gus said, and he kissed me. He did not taste fragrantly spicy like Sir David, but like salt and fresh air, and as he pulled back to smile at me and brush the hair from my forehead, I wondered how it could be that men will pay so much for intercourse and not want kissing above all else.

I nodded. 'I must bury Isaiah. And find Hetty.'

'You will not let her make your mind up for you?'

'No,' I said. But when had I ever done anything so bold as make up my mind? I had lurched from one hasty, unwise reaction to the next. But then it occurred to me that Hetty had charted her course, and she had ended up with a corpse in her bed one night and a cruel man beside her for all time.

Gus shook his head. 'I am surprised you would seek her out, let alone cross the road to speak to her. You are worth ten of her.'

I was about to remind him that he had never met her, but I remembered the day I had divined that Sir Robin and Hetty had most likely travelled in his chair. And after all Martha had told me, I could not find it in me to argue with him.

'Once you are damned, you are damned,' I said, lightly. 'It does not matter how many times over. But there are some questions I would like to ask her.' In my heart of hearts I knew that there was never going to be such a meeting, and that even if I stayed in London until I was seventy, I would never know what of our friendship had been true, and what Hetty's involvement had been in the death of a man I had come to love.

'You make your God sound like a crotchety old dance master,' Gus said, 'always waiting for you to trip up. But perhaps he smiles on people who pick themselves up when they stumble.'

'I hope you're right,' I said, hearing from the edge in his voice how disappointed he was that I had not fallen into his arms immediately at his offer. But my affection for Sir David was not to be extinguished so swiftly, and how many cardinal mistakes had I made already?

'Hetty rescued me,' I continued, realising that nothing was going to make any sense unless I told him who I once was. And when I did that, he might be less keen to take me to Cape Town with him. At that moment I wanted to go with him more than anything else in the world.

'You were in that house with her,' he said, kicking gently at a cobble with his boot. 'Where she met her husband.'

'So why do you want me to go with you?'

'And you loved a man there,' he continued. 'There is no need to say anything about it – it has always been written all over your face. That makes it better, in my book. Not that it's for me to judge you – all I'm saying is that I don't mind.'

A horse pulling a squeaky Brougham clopped by, dropping plump turds as it went.

'Yes,' I recalled, almost laughing at how immediately he had said the thing I had most feared. 'I was in that house. But it was not for long. It was after my mother died, and Isaiah was in gaol, and I thought I had no-one – no, it was worse than that. I thought Meg would be better off without me.'

'And you think that if you had told me, I would want

nothing more to do with you.'

'When did you find me out?' I said.

'I wondered, the first time I met you. You have that polish that ladies' maids get. Not just how you speak, for that could have been the ink from the Bible rubbing off on you, but something else – a turn of the head, a self-possession. Then you mentioned Hetty, and I made some enquiries. Do not think I was spying on you, for it was not difficult to do. I did not judge you: your mother was dead, and you had Meg to care for. If there was enough bread and coal for all, there would be no need for women to sell themselves. It is a miracle that you escaped, and for that you feel a debt to Hetty, for I'll wager it was her husband's money that will pay for your passage.'

'For all that she lied to me, she need not have saved me,' I said.

'I wonder: was it your silence he thought he was buying?'

I ignored this, for I did not want to continue and therefore have to speak to him of Sir David. His was one coffin my heart would do well to keep closed.

'It is a pity we cannot take one of the presses,' I said. I thought of the pink face of Queen Caroline that Meg had painted on its side, and imagined her smiling at Tagg and Smeek as they churned out their inferior wares. Once again, you have gone down in the world, Your Majesty, I reflected.

'There is a need for printing in the southern colonies and we can educate those who cannot read.'

'We must start with Meg,' I said. 'She will always be a child while she cannot. I must try harder with her. But first I must walk the streets and think.'

41

WE PAID OUR PASSAGE from Tilbury the following Friday; once I had run out of objections, there seemed no reason to delay our departure. Tom, Isaiah, Mr Edwards: all devoured by this city and its politics. I seemed to have escaped, but how long would it be before another Sir Robin darkened my door? (And, the darkest recesses of my soul whispered, before I stumbled into the arms of another Sir David?)

My greatest regret was that there was not much to do before I went, and what little there was only brought more sadness. All of our printed stock was destroyed or damaged in the fire, though the ground floor of the shop survived in a charred state. I sent word to Mr Soane to collect his plates, for I would rather return them to him than sell them to Mr Tagg at some risible rate on his behalf.

As for Tagg himself, I cleared my debt with him: Mr Dunsworthy opined that it amounted to just over two sovereigns, once the press had been taken into account. Mr Tagg said that he would call it a round two, licking his lips with the certainty that I would not be able to pay and that I had delivered myself into his hands for sure. He was caught between avaricious delight at the sight of the gold I produced and disappointment that I had slipped from his grasp. Percival Smeek, who had been lurking all the while, disappeared into the storeroom and could be heard snivelling.

On the Tuesday before the ship was scheduled to sail, Mr Soane came to the shop. 'I am sorry to hear of your stepfather,' he said, turning his hat round and round in his hands.

'He never was made for this world,' I replied.

He did not pause to acknowledge this, so keen was he to get on to his next sentence: 'And I am sorrier still that you propose to quit these shores. We would have made a fine partnership. But now it is too late for me to mention it, and perhaps wrong of me to allude to it, so forgive me if it is.'

I was so astonished that I was as mute as Meg. As the smell of stale smoke and burnt wood filled my nostrils, I imagined the life I might have had as Mrs Soane, printing my husband's engravings on my beloved press, able to tend our children between working, with room for Meg aplenty. No need to sail thousands of miles, and no need to imagine anything beyond the streets of this city.

'I have shocked you,' he said.

'I am to sail on Friday,' I said, more quietly than I'd intended.

He nodded and placed an envelope on the table. 'Open this once you have left harbour, then let the wind take it away from you. As it will you from me.'

He was still turning his hat in his hands as he passed the sooty window and disappeared out of sight.

⁂

I broke into the last of the sovereigns to bury Isaiah.

None of his friends was present, since they had all been arrested. I discovered this from a handbill which one of our neighbours had thoughtfully posted on our blackened old front door, entitled 'Conspiracy Uncovered!' It listed Will

Davidson, blackamoor, as the ringleader, and speculated that Isaiah had killed himself in order to escape a worse fate. I was amazed that the constables had not returned to search what was left of our premises, but I assumed that even they could see that there was little left to ransack but ash.

So it was just me, Meg, Gus and Adam. I did not know where Carroty Anne had gone, and I did not have it in me to find her. I read from the Song of Solomon. Silently, I promised Isaiah that I would commend his spirit to the sea, and to the air, once I reached Africa. I consoled myself that he would have been more at home in the unknown places to which I was about to venture than in this rainy city. And as it did on the day of Tom's execution, it rained so hard that the gravediggers slithered and cursed their way through the clay as soon as our prayers had ended. I thought the rain an apt symmetry, for it was the final chapter in a rivalry between Isaiah and Tom which had only become clear when it had been too late to quell its destructive nature. Each had been much beloved. By my mother, and by me. Each had tried to prove to the other that he was the more effective insurrectionary, and each had died in the attempt. Neither of them had proved to be any use, and a change in government still seemed as far off as the Second Coming.

It was Adam who cried the most. 'He shoulders other people's feelings in the way he carries the chair,' Gus explained. 'He has always been like this. When we sail tomorrow he will be so excited that it will be all we can do to prevent him from jumping overboard.'

I paid for a small headstone in Whitechapel cemetery for Isaiah and for my mother, although there had not been time for the ground to settle properly around their graves. I wondered if buying the headstone might help atone for the sins I had committed and witnessed at 14 St James's Square, but I doubted it. After all, nothing was going to bring back Sir David, and I did not want to repent of the brief time we had spent together.

I had only a few shillings left from the five sovereigns Hetty had given me, but I was glad to be rid of the weight in my hem. After all, I would never know whether my time at St James's Square had hastened Tom and Isaiah's deaths, for they might never have been arrested, had Mr Edwards not taken an interest in them. Gus says that they might have been, and points to the thousands of men who are executed and transported every year for pettifogging crimes as well as hefty ones, the very men whom Tom and Isaiah wanted to make free. But the uncertainty feels as final as the space they left behind, and as difficult to bear.

'Until tomorrow,' Gus said, grasping my hand briefly. He had not asked me to spend the night with him, and I was glad of it. There was a closeness growing between us, but I was still content to enjoy it from a distance.

'What will you do tonight?' I asked.

'We have some haunts to say goodbye to. And we have sold our chair, so we will deliver that to its new owners.'

'Trusty chair,' sighed Adam, looking as though he was about to cry again.

'I do not need to ask what you will do,' Gus said. 'Though if I were you, I would not waste my boot-leather in going to her. But I know you will.'

42

I RETURNED TO BELGRAVIA that evening, though I did not expect Hetty to receive me. I was surprised to find the house all shuttered up. Rich men always have more than one house, so they could easily have gone away, but I did not expect the kitchen door to be locked, and for Martha and all the other servants to be absent. The house looked as though it too had died.

A nursemaid crossed the road and opened the square's garden gate. I walked behind her, wanting a rest on an iron bench while I had a think about what to do. A red-nosed freckly girl of no more than my age, the nurse hesitated for a moment about whether to admit me. I gave her my best smile – and before she could decide that she did not know me and should not let me in, I grinned at the baby too, saying, 'Hello again, baba.' The baby smiled and said 'Ba *baa*!' back. This satisfied the nursemaid, so she left the gate open for me to slip in behind her.

It was just after six, and the square was lovely. The bench was still damp from the morning's rain, but I did not mind. I watched a few blackbirds pecking about on the grass in the gentle sun. 'There is one blackbird who looks as though he might fly,' I said to myself, thinking of the woman who had admired Isaiah the day Tom died, and all that had happened since then. I knew that I did not yet truly understand that I would never see Isaiah again, nor Tom, nor my mother, though the idea of it kept swooping in like one of those birds, only for me to shoo it away again.

I did not know if I would enjoy such a moment of tranquil solitude again for many a month, so I read Mr Soane's letter.

My Dear Miss Wingfield,
News of Mr Douglas's death reached me before your message, so I have had a night in which to collect my paltry thoughts before committing them to some of the paper you most kindly procured for me.

Our lives (if you will permit me to yoke us in the same sentence), although blessed in many ways, have also seen losses which with the Lord's aid we have borne with fortitude. I do not dare to contemplate what the future holds, but my conscience tells me that there will be no further sentences which carry both of us in them if I do not explain how I came to your door. I hereby hope to purge any suspicion which might lodge in your mind concerning myself.

There is a gentleman, Mr Edwards – I believe you have met him? Isaiah Douglas certainly has, for Mr Edwards gave him my name. Mr Edwards is more or less a government man, but one who finds it irksome to be blown this way and that by the caprice of men with half of his intelligence. He talked a good deal of webs and nets and I took him to mean that his was as difficult a life to escape as the poorest man's in this city.

I like to think too that he saw his poverty as a spiritual one. Though he was hard and proud – 'I like to pride myself on not being animated by money' was a well-worn phrase of his – he came to see that in his world, politics and money were as one. He came to

London after a distinguished career in a Norfolk grammar School, keen to secure the wealth and preferment which so many men of his county had found in London. The longer he observed and served the men of Westminster and St James's, the more he understood that Principle existed elsewhere. But he was unswerving in his belief that the Radicals would be infinitely worse than the present Governors. He was not a good man, but he was not a weak one, either. The best of him was that he did what he thought was right; the worst that he enjoyed the power he had to carry out his judgement, and did not flinch from seeing men hang. It was for this that the radical press hated him. Indeed you may have seen how they described him and not Sir Robin as the enemy of their cause, and utterly misunderstood his motives – and the price he paid for this was his life. If he had had the temperament to seek more dull employment in a Bank, and if he had been animated by affection into marriage, his energies might have been better channelled. No one saw that more clearly than he did. It might be a vanity on my part, but I have the notion that he came to see my quiet workshop as a species of confessional.

You might be wondering with some consternation how I know so much of the man. In an earlier stage of his career he had procured evidence which had hastened my father to his death, and afterwards, as some sort of atonement, had ensured that I could complete my apprenticeship. Given his concern for you and his wish that we should work for each other's mutual benefit, I imagine that he wished to do the same for you. He hinted at this, the last time he visited my workshop. He said that he felt condemned to have Damascene conversions, only to find himself slave-driving others along the same road over and over again. I am sorry to report that he

*did not show any remorse for the fate of your brother,
though it was clear to me that his acquaintance with
you, the nature of which I never fully divined, had
brought Tom's activities to his attention.*

*The Lord had a purpose in sending this man to us,
and I cannot but be grateful to Mr Edwards as an
instrument of His will, for how else would I have ever
crossed your threshold, Miss Wingfield? In the light of
this intelligence, you may, however, see matters in a very
different manner from that which my most devout Hope
wishes to imprint on your Soul.*

I remain,
Your Humble and Obedient Servant,
Titus Soane.

I found that I did not blame Mr Edwards for whatever
part he had played in delivering Tom to the authorities. I
now understood enough of the motives of Sir Robin to know
that it was *he* who would have wished to encourage Tom,
only to secure his downfall. Indeed, if anyone was to blame,
it was me. Had I not been at 14 St James's Square, Tom
might have been alive today – and Isaiah too. Unlike Mr
Edwards, I was not able to see people as sole architects of
their fates; like all poor men and women, I knew how we
could be buffeted about by circumstances beyond our contol,
and how one misfortune could blight a life for ever.

I tucked the letter in my apron, reflecting that it was the
fourth envelope Mr Edwards had caused to be stowed there.
I resolved to throw it overboard, to let the winds which
Isaiah had so loved cast it where the Lord thought it ought
to rest.

If love were like Tom's sums, I thought, a mere set of
calculations, it was Titus Soane I would be marrying. But I
had always known it was not, for otherwise my mother

would not have given her heart to Isaiah Douglas.

I left the garden, shaking my head at the strangeness of it all, and at how after so much disorder, life in London seemed to be continuing as usual. The Queen had taken ill after being barred from the coronation, and most assumed that she would return abroad if and when she recovered. The Tories remained in office, and continued to promise reform. Few believed them, apart from the Ultras among their own ranks, who continued to fear any concessions as much as they did men like Tom and Isaiah. And of course, men would come forward to replace Tom and Isaiah for as long as they continued to harbour those fears, for it is right that men should vote if they pay their taxes, and be free to worship the Lord in their own way.

❧

I was distracted from these reflections by a man with a leather bag. He stood outside Hetty's house, gazing at the upper windows. Something in his face, a softness in his cheeks, held my gaze.

'Dr Faber?' I said.

He peered at me through thick glasses. 'Pray forgive me, I am sure I have made your acquaintance, but I am looking for Hetty – that is, Lady Everley, and –'

He was in such distress that my instinct was confirmed. 'You have not made my acquaintance,' I said. 'But I knew your daughter.'

He clasped my hands in both of his. His grip was shaky but strong, his hands cold. 'And I am too late!' he said. 'I have been searching for my daughter for what seems like an eternity, and I happened upon a reference to her and a marriage to one of the Everleys. The story was not a happy one, for there was a death and a disreputable one by all accounts.'

'But –' I said.

Hetty's father was in such a state of agitation that he would brook no interjection. 'But I did not think it could be Hetty, for she was such a good girl, and her half-sister assured me that she would bring her up well and find her a respectable husband.'

'But you –' I attempted, then I said no more, as I remembered that the tale Hetty had told me about her father encouraging her to take up the life of a harlot was another falsehood.

'But am I forgetting myself!' he said. 'You said you knew my daughter.'

He looked at me more closely. 'Did you work for her?'

'Yes,' I replied, without hesitating, 'I did. But I left her service in order to sail for a new life, in Africa. I leave tomorrow. I was coming to tell her this, but I fear we have both missed her.' I realised I had just told him an untruth: I thought I knew Hetty, but it had turned out that I did not. For even if I satisfied my desire to look into her wide blank eyes, I could never be sure that she had not been involved with Sir David's death. As to whether living with the memory of his last moments was sufficient punishment for her, I will leave that to the Lord to decide. I hope that Lucifer will take his time roasting Sir Robin.

'Tell me your name, and I will be sure to let her know,' he promised. 'For it is only a matter of time now before I find her, and she will introduce me to the source of her great good fortune.'

I told the old man my name, and hoped that he failed to find her, for it would bring him no happiness if he succeeded.

43

I HAD ALWAYS TOLD myself that my sojourn at St James's Square was a temporary one, and that I could not have survived there a day without Hetty. But without Sir David's death, would I have had the courage to break free? The feel of fine carpet between my toes; the taste of jellies or sherry; my hair being fussed over as I gazed into a looking-glass with a fire blazing behind me? A room with a bed, with feathered pillows, with windows? I like to think that all these things would have meant nothing to me, without the prospect of Sir David's approaching footsteps on the parquet outside my bedroom. But I cannot be sure – and as it was, I had done no more to avenge his death than Flight the cat had.

I have to confess too that my brief excursions into London politics had left me more than content to leave such matters to Our Lord, who is, I trust, much more accomplished at judgement and retribution than I could ever hope to be.

I am now like a pitcher which has been smashed and glued back together: I might appear the same, but look closely and you can see where the cracks are, the weaknesses. I am still four years off twenty-one; if I right the course of my mortal soul before I come of age, surely I will not be lost?

Soon London would not be my magnetic field, and nothing could have prepared me for the sight of our ship. Surely it would have dwarfed even the Ark.

'We cannot board that!' I cried, pulling Gus back as if the ship was about to tip over and crush all Tilbury. 'It will sink!' I could not see how anything so vast would ever stay afloat; it would surely not survive the weight of all the people and cargo on the quayside once we left the calm of the Thames. All of London seemed to be loading onto it, and I imagined that the shops would be bare and the thoroughfares empty by the time we had set sail.

I held on tight to Meg's hand. 'How is Meg to survive this?' I asked. 'I will have to keep her chained up for years, perhaps for ever, before I can allow her some freedom.'

'She will learn,' he said, nodding to Adam. 'We will keep her occupied, and we will be far safer living in groves of fruit trees than we ever were in this Babylon.'

<hr />

Perhaps the size of the ship truly confronted me with the enormity of leaving London. I had not imagined the vessel that would carry us, so it stood to reason that I had not even a teaspoon of an understanding of what was in store for me when we arrived in Africa. Gus's head was full of stories of oranges which could be picked off the trees by anyone who passed them, and infinite land on which to build a house and have many children. But I knew that Isaiah's mother had been plucked from that dark continent as easily as one of the fruits Gus was so keen to eat, and I feared for Meg in such a place. London might be a den of Satan, but there I had looked into the devil's face and got the measure of his ways. I had read enough of my Bible to know that Eden is in the first book because it was a long time ago and far away and not somewhere we were likely to pass through again. The

Lord is nothing if not honest with us.

Gus laughed at my fears, as he did at my sudden conviction as we stood on Tilbury dock that I could not in fact leave. He picked me up and spun me round, and I thought of Isaiah, whose feet were never truly on this earth; and of the manner of Tom's death; and of my mother, who became so light that she seemed to float away from us, and I shouted 'Do not drop me!' But I was smiling, because I knew that he wouldn't. And if I gave him half a chance, I knew that he never would.

Historical Note

Although this is a work of fiction, the story is constructed around the Queen Caroline Affair and the Cato Street Conspiracy. The conspiracy was a foiled plot to blow up the Cabinet; I have used little concrete detail from it. The account of the Queen's history which Nell tells Meg is based in fact, as is the importance of Italian witnesses in the collapse of the case against the Queen. For accounts of this I acknowledge E.A. Smith's *A Queen on Trial* (Sutton, 1993) and Jane Robins' *Rebel Queen* (Simon and Schuster, 2006). I have meddled with the timings in two key ways. Caroline did return to England in early June and did live in Hammersmith, but the case against her collapsed in November 1820, not in the July. Caroline was barred from the postponed coronation at St Paul's in July 1821 and not at the climax of my story the previous summer. All the scenes and the main characters are fictive, with the partial exception of three characters: Isaiah Douglas, who is loosely based on Robert Wedderburn, a radical active in London in 1820. For an account of his life, see Martin Hoyles' *The Axe Laid to the Root: The Story of Robert Wedderburn* (Hansib, 2004). Will Davidson was a man involved in the Cato Street Conspiracy, and Carroty Anne is mentioned as the flamboyant and unreliable Irish lady of ill repute with whom Robert Wedderburn associated; I have taken extensive liberties with these characters. I gave Isaiah Will's parentage and much else besides – it was Will who was pressed into the Navy after being sent to Glasgow to study law. Some figures who receive a mention, such as Lord Brougham, existed; while the Duke of Portrose, for example, did not. The brothel is situated on St James's Square as a playful homage to the key role the London Library has played in the writing of this book. It is a delightfully civilised place to work and its open shelves proved invaluable in researching this book – not least S.Capital and Labour and S.Sex.

I have been interested in the history of London for many years, and there is a vast literature on it. Peter Ackroyd's *London: the Biography* (Chatto and Windus, 2000) is an excellent starting point, as is Henry Mayhew's *London Labour and the London Poor* (Cass, 1861–2). For Nell's time in the brothel, Hogarth's series of images *The Harlot's Progress* was useful, as was Hallie Rubenhold's *The Covent Garden Ladies: Pimp General Jack and the Extraordinary Story of Harris's List* (Tempus, 2005). For a history of printing, Michael Tyman's *Printing 1770–1970: an Illustrated History of its Development and Uses in England* (British Library, 1998) was very helpful. Any technical errors and simplifications are of course mine.

Acknowledgements

Thanks to Heidi Amsinck, George Garnett, Suzanne Mackenzie, Barry Pike, Margaret Pike, Jeremy Thorp, Douglas Reith and William Weinstein, all of whom have read this book in manuscript in its various forms – Heidi, George and Suzanne much more than once. My agent Anna Webber has contributed so much to this book both on and beyond the page, and I cannot thank her enough for believing in it. Thanks also to Vanessa Webb for her astute editing, to Aurea Carpenter and Rebecca Nicolson at Short Books for giving *The Harlot's Press* life. Thank you to George, Elinor, Edmund and Gregory, who lived with me while I lived with the manuscript. Edmund, I am sorry to tell you that none of the characters was based on you, whatever you might say.

Helen Pike lives in Guildford and Oxfordshire. She is a History graduate of Oxford and holds an MA in Creative Writing from Birkbeck. This is her debut novel, and was in part inspired by her history teaching.

In case of difficulty in purchasing any Short Books
title through normal channels, please contact
BOOKPOST Tel: 01624 836000
Fax: 01624 837033
email: bookshop@enterprise.net
www.bookpost.co.uk
Please quote ref. 'Short Books'